Love is a path that is followed to the end,
Though there are those who should never
Have set out on it.

- Violetta Parra

Ghosts of The Altiplano

Eioloin Hand

Matador
5 Weir Road
Kibworth Beauchamp
Leicester LE8 0LQ, UK
Tel: (+44) 116 279 2299
Fax: (+44) 116 279 2277
Email: books@troubador.co.uk
Web: www.troubador.co.uk/matador

ISBN 978 1848762 046

British Library Cataloguing in Publication Data.
A catalogue record for this book is available from the British Library.

Typeset in 11pt Bembo by Troubador Publishing Ltd, Leicester, UK

Matador is an imprint of Troubador Publishing Ltd

Printed in Great Britain by the MPG Books Group, Bodmin and King's Lynn

In memory of the Captain, who once held Hannah in his arms.

CHAPTER ONE

The wind tugged at the edges of the car dragging him into the hungry city; the gear would not engage, it would not engage as the taxi driver's arm mechanically shifted and the car itself seemed to grate against the surface of the road. A multitude of other vehicles strained and whined as they whipped round the bend coming down off the fly-over, all of them racing, all of them late in the early-morning rush hour traffic. The locks of the briefcase were stuck, his nails struck the slick black plastic of its exterior and failed to feel the soft touch of paper that should be inside, so he clung to it like a baby instead. A lot of work was in that report; it was no time to be scrabbling around for its scattered contents now. His stomach rumbled and the bitter-tasting coffee he had gulped down in the half-dark of an urban morning came back to him. Through the tint of the windows the morning pressed against the flatness of the sky as a watery and far-off sun struggled to give birth to the day. Buenos Aires in early winter feeds itself on the indolence of the river which plays truant on the east side of the city, the one preventing the other from spilling over any further. Concrete washes into water and solid lumps of the river float into and around the countless buildings that seem to grow out of it. It is the widest river in the world but it is also one of the most polluted.

This morning, as every morning, José wore his sunglasses. They helped him concentrate and were a badge that all self-respecting taxi drivers wore. There were many cheap stunt drivers operating without a license or with a badly made imitation of one; they plied their trade like the tarts along the Rio de la Plata, picking up clients and attempting to overcharge them for their services. No, the genuine taxi drivers didn't need to stoop to the trick of wearing a shirt and tie;

though they invariably wore sunglasses and they kept their cars shiny with wax. Sometimes he even shaved in the morning and not at night when the stubble of his beard had blackened his face. José slicked out the ends of his moustache and pressed down even harder on the screaming pedal of the vehicle.

"I must look up Susana and see if she's there under her tree on the way back," he thought to himself, "It's been a long time since I last saw her, a little too long."

Pressed back into the sticky vinyl of the rear seat, the passenger glanced at his watch, from his watch to the plane taking off from the local airport that interposed itself between the speeding car and the river, and back to his watch. In one minute they would be passing the barriers of the toll road, in two minutes they should be on the overpass, in five staring the Avenida de Julio head on. Suddenly they swerved to miss a lorry which had been gaining ground on them and which seemed to have come out of nowhere. A flash silver saloon cut in on a diagonal from the right and three vehicles missed each other with the clinical precision of a tango trick like in the shows they put on in the big blousey theatres. David looked up to see the giant opening thighs of the brunette on the billboard rushing towards him.

"*Drive carefully,*" she was saying, "*Because you only have one life and you're beautiful.*"

At one hundred and twenty kilometres an hour he didn't feel beautiful, but there was nothing out of the ordinary about that. His mobile phone was playing the Pink Panther theme tune trapped inside his briefcase, like the buzzing of a fly being intoxicated inside a net curtain. The unpleasant sensation spread to the skin of his palms. What the colossal woman was supposed to be advertising he didn't know; all he knew was that she was beautiful and her dark penetrating eyes made him want to avert his glance from her and look at her at the same time. For a split second he wondered about asking the taxi driver to turn round and take him home but he realised that it was physically and morally impossible. He had his life in his lap but he had forgotten the combination to it.

In an office on the fourteenth floor of the steel and glass tower overlooking the Avenida de Julio, Eva Barona was stretched out in the Director's reclining easy chair. She was enfolded in its creamy leather contours and her eyes were closing. How she'd love to have him come walking through the doors to the office; she'd make that bastard work for his money. It hadn't occurred to her that the colour of her blouse almost perfectly matched the colour of the reclining chair, or that its silky texture was similar to that of the supple leather upholstery. She took a sip of her coffee and then settled back to close her eyes again. There was no other time when coffee tasted so delicious, or that the moment seemed to linger quite like this. It was worth getting up half an hour earlier than everyone else so that she could enjoy the moment. Each day for the last two years she had repeated the ritual and each day she had exactly the same thought. Fortunately, none of the other secretaries had the same desire to enjoy the chair as she did and the Directors always arrived late for work. It was an unwritten law that only the most senior or most daring of Directors - those that aspired to the chair itself- would arrive after the others. Somehow they always seemed to file into the office in exactly the same order, leaving the managing Director, (to whom she was personal- and most confidential- secretary) or his chosen upstart to arrive last with their coats waving, sweeping across the floor. She wondered if they did this in order to save on the cleaning bill and then claim over the odds on the dry-cleaning expenses incurred, but she'd never caught her boss looking as if he was consciously doing this.

The upstart was always fired at an appropriate time, of course, or posted to some forsaken outpost where such coats were really needed; but it was surprising how many joined the queue to fill the vacancy of the last one. It was always fun to see who jostled whom from within the ranks to emerge for one brief summer of glory before casting himself, voluntarily as it seemed, over the cliff of oblivion. The office girls always exclusively fell in love with the upstart, Eva noticed, lamenting his passing with a levity only matched by the gravity of their passion for the next one.

"Hello, yes, this is he speaking. I'm afraid I've had a little problem with the traffic. I'll be arriving about half an hour late. No, nothing serious, thank you," said David from the pay phone. As he paid the taxi-driver he began to recover some of his composure. He flicked open his brown calf-skin wallet and peeled back a note from the wad it held inside; one of these toy notes the locals used down in this part of the Americas. The taxi-driver stretched out his fingers and with the moistness of the morning on them it stuck to them and was instantly recoiled, folded away into some dark obscure place like a fly on the tongue of a frog. The driver looked smugly back at his passenger. This was all achieved with such an athletic yet indifferent motion that for an instant the passenger was left with nothing to say.

A woman's thigh brushed a little too close to his on the pavement and a waiter suddenly appeared, throwing off his lethargy as he sprang to attention outside the door of the street-side café. The woman was clad in a thigh-hugging black leather skirt and something about the noise of her stiletto heels on the pavement and the expectant manner in which she turned towards him caused the passenger to glance at his open wallet before closing it quickly with both hands.

"So, mister, do you think you can afford me?"

Her glance was penetrating, reminding him of the dark beauty on the billboard, and somehow he felt he'd committed a terrible faux pas. Her eyes slid past his before he found his coat and briefcase in the arms of the waiter and rather by insistence than by choice he was led towards a table inside the haven of the café. He was seated at a gleaming metal table, his coat neatly folded over the back of an adjacent chair with his briefcase at his feet. The reflection of the waiter on the cool surface of the table disappeared into the crowd at the bar.

Tall, leafy plants fringed the window at which he was sitting and he was able to recover some of his composure as he let his gaze wander out into the sunshine of the street. He watched the taxi-driver and the woman with the mini-skirt exchange a few cursory words before the woman tossed a glance back in his direction and the taxi pulled sleekly away from the kerb-side. In a few seconds the waiter had brought him a coffee and croissants he hadn't asked for. A copy of the New York Times was spread out like an ironed sheet in front of him.

He eagerly ate the first one and took a gulp of the rich coffee as news from the big city soothed him. He opened the large newspaper and embraced the world flowing around him. The mere reference to place names he knew and the names of one or two public figures made him feel more relaxed. He looked outside again but the woman had gone.

Then for one terrifying moment he experienced the sensation that he was looking at a map as he heard a scuffling sound underneath him, before realising that the man with the bowed head kneeling at his feet was polishing his shoes. The man's head was bald and very shiny, David noted, as a rare breeze caused a mirror image of the foliage of the pot plants to ripple on the surface of the table. Feeling that all was as it should be and that somehow the silent waiter had noticed this, he began at last to read the paper in earnest. It was most convenient that the waiter spoke to him in his own language, (all be it very broken and heavily-accented), as he enquired whether he'd like another coffee. The waiter asked him where he was staying and if it was comfortable enough, which the passenger took as sign of the man's good nature. As if by magnetism an extra note from his wallet was peeled off and he offered both the larger and smaller notes to the man for his inspection as he appeared with the bill. It was small and barely readable due to the faintness of the type, speared on a small metal object designed specifically for the purpose. Before he'd had time to look at it properly the man was already bearing the metal utensil and the bank notes to the till at the bar behind him.

In the reflection of the table he caught the image of the waiter and the shoe-shiner in what appeared, for one ugly instant, to be an over-heated discussion. But then the man with the bald head and blue overalls left the café and the waiter was once more at his side, waiting on him. The passenger received a friendly hand on his shoulder as the waiter deftly transferred his coat and briefcase to him at the edge of the doorway. There was the noise of metal being scraped on the polished floor behind them as three finely dressed men instantly took up their seats at the table he had just vacated. The passenger wasn't sure but he thought he heard a greeting extended to him in his own language as he exited the café and the sunlight bounced off his recently - purchased CK sunglasses. At last he was beginning to feel that he'd landed on his feet.

With newfound confidence he decided he'd make the trip to the meeting place on foot and in the process give himself time to think his words through beforehand. It had been a long, tiring flight and the chatter on the plane in the soft tones of Spanish they spoke in this part of South America had unnerved rather than soothed him. He felt like someone on the verge of being included in some whispered secret who'd been left somehow without understanding it. Back in the big city the Spanish they used in meetings or on the telephone was hard and cruel, but it was direct and he could get a handle on it.

As he stepped out to cross the road he felt the unexpected heat in his clothes so that he checked his stride and rearranged his raincoat. This he did with an ostentatious sweep of his arm in an act that cost him both time and energy. As his coat was rejoining his outstretched arm and his briefcase slipped in sweating fingers, the face of the driver who had borne him into the city flashed in front of him again, cursing him loudly for not watching where he was going. The passenger peered into the surface of the car's windscreen but the driver hadn't recognised him, and even if he had he was now indifferent to him as he ferried other passengers back and forth.

At the same moment the passenger caught a reflected glimpse of the waiter, standing behind him in some mirrored pose with a silver tray outstretched in his arm, and for some ridiculous reason he felt that he was looking right through him. The hush of a car sped past him and for a sickening moment its blackness rushed into him like a tunnel. He raced to the other side of the road like a matador, his cape unfolding and swirling about him as he angled himself in and out between the traffic. Feeling that he'd put enough distance between himself and the waiter's idly ironic gaze on the other side, he stopped to get his breath. He reached for his briefcase and found that it was gone.

He turned imploringly to the waiter but the man had already disappeared inside the interior of the shady café. He looked in desperation in the direction the taxi had just taken but it was already out of sight, or had merged into the many black or yellow cars that swarmed round him. He felt an impulse to go back into the café to ask if the waiter had seen anything but some impulse greater still caused him to reject the idea out of hand. The waiter had simply brought him coffee and would not be dispensing information. Turning smartly on his heels and greatly relieved to feel his passport and wallet in a pocket in the soft underbelly of the raincoat, he followed the people streaming down the pavement in the direction the taxi had taken. He had the address of the meeting place written on a piece of paper in the top pocket of his suit, so at least he knew where he had to get to. With one grinding, shuddering blast of fear like ice melting down him he realised that he could not present himself at the meeting without his briefcase. It was an absurd situation; it would be like the waiter making his way through the crowd of people in the café to present his clients with an empty tray. Now his relationship with the contacts waiting for him in the office took on another dimension and the passenger found himself wondering just who was whose client. Confused with the magnitude of this speculation, his immediate reaction was to find a payphone and call Head Office back home to find out what he should do, but then he came to his senses. He was paid to act on his own initiative. With this in mind he followed a group of three middle-aged men in suits in front of him who looked as if they knew where they were going. It seemed that they were discussing something to do with an article they had read in the newspaper one of them held tightly rolled up in his hand. This made him feel that they were men who dealt with facts; men who dealt with the business of the world, and he was certainly in need of information now. Careful not to walk too close to them, but anxious not to lose them in the tumultuous crowd, his legs quickened their pace and his hand increased its grip on his coat where his documents and currency were hidden.

The discussion ahead of him became heated at moments and the three men even stopped to unfurl the newspaper and argue about a detail of the text they were talking about. As they did so, the passenger checked himself in front of a large shop window and was pleased to see a smartly dressed man with a purposeful look staring back at him. He'd always been good at looking smart and he was sure it was one of the qualities that had led to him be in the position he was in now. It was he they sent on the difficult missions to the further reaches of the Americas, partly so because he understood the language and the manner of these people. After ten minutes or so walking he found himself, still apparently undetected, standing behind the three businessmen at a set of traffic lights, waiting to cross a major avenue where policemen stood blowing their whistles. They stopped the traffic with their white gloves and gesticulated in an agitated manner at the crowds of pedestrians to now stop, now walk as they deemed fit.

The pedestrians seemed undeterred by this and continued their conversations unhurriedly as they strolled across the avenue to the centre where a further set of traffic lights awaited. As they did so, the people coming and the people going met in the middle, spilling over onto the avenue itself so that one of the policemen came blowing his whistle and gesticulating even more wildly for them to climb back onto the kerb. All the while keeping his left hand raised, he turned on the traffic as if the noise and the roar of the engines would break free into the adjoining avenue which cut across the intersection, should he let his gloved hand drop for a fraction of a second.

Couples and businessmen, secretaries and cleaners all met in the middle, looked up for an instant, then threaded their way through as the browns and greys of suits, the blues, pinks and whites of shirts and the multi-coloured hems of dresses and skirts swirled towards each other and through each other. It was as if in some extraordinary, unrehearsed dance all the dancers knew where they were going. Noise and chatter fled in their wake, the odd glimpse and smile of a brief encounter remained in one or two eyes and colour streamed behind them like the glint of sun on water parted behind swimming fish.

He heard the whistle of the policeman directing traffic coming into the city, walking across the wide avenue where not two but four lanes of traffic were held in abeyance. The engines roared and revved, the policeman gesticulated furiously, but the people returning from or going to their mid-morning coffees were unwound and relaxed, slowing their pace down the further out into the road they got and taking their time to mount the opposite pavement. The policemen waved their hands at them, beckoning them on in ever more agitated manners while the people slowed their pace accordingly. Once given permission to cross the road, the road was theirs' for them to idle in. The policemen mopped the sweat from brows underneath their gleaming white helmets, exchanging consolatory glances as they cursed the pedestrians beneath their breaths and waited for more of them on either side of the huge artery into the city. Quite why there were traffic lights on either side, (and in the middle too) the passenger didn't know. It didn't seem to him that they were needed if the policemen were there.

He must have looked at the policeman directing the traffic opposite him a little too long or with too much intent, for in an instant he was upon him, blowing his whistle in short, sharp blasts; sweeping him onto the kerb with deft moves of his pristine gloves. The policeman seemed to be demanding something of him, blowing harder on his whistle as the sweat beaded on his forehead and trickled to a stain on the stiff collar of his pale blue shirt.

The loud tugs on the whistle became louder and although never once touching him, (or indeed speaking to him), the passenger felt that he was being manhandled onto the kerbside in a flurry of white gloves. The policeman's full attention was on him and David was feeling guilty. It wasn't his fault he'd lost his briefcase, (or had it stolen- which is what he tended to suspect). He'd only been following the three smart businessmen because he'd somehow felt they would lead him in the right direction. But it seemed to be to no avail; in any case, he couldn't expect a simple policeman to understand the complexities of his dilemma. David therefore reached for his only defence in such a situation; taking his wallet from the underbelly of the lining of his coat, he quickly extracted a note and pressed it into the policeman's gloved hand by way of explanation.

The sudden contact of the foreigner's hand in his made the policeman freeze as he began to emit distress calls. He was furious at this breach of convention and intimidated by it, although he took care not to show this in his gestures. The whistles became louder and longer in a progressive manner as the crumpled note was taken for examination by another officer and opened. With one hand clutching the whistle with the precision and tenacity of a surgeon, the officer burned with contempt at the unfolded, rippling note as he looked into the reddening face of the passenger; the other hand swishing and swiping in outrage. The pale blue and white flag of the Argentine republic wavered on the roof of one of the high buildings in front of him and it was only in that instant that the passenger realised he'd not only offended the policeman's personal sensibilities, but his patriotic ones as well.

The policeman was by now crying through his whistle from sheer exhaustion as a fellow officer rallied to his defence with a higher-pitched and more commanding series of toots. The carefree pedestrians of three minutes ago had by now formed a tightly rung circle round them. The colours of shirts and skirts and faces were swirling in angry condemnation at the man; the bemused, terrified look of the man who had lost his briefcase and been artfully ensnared grew and grew; the sounds of the whistles grew into the sounds of a siren.

He was pushed into the back of the patrol car and the dignity of the traffic officer was commended and restored by the officer riding alongside the driver. The traffic policeman bowed curtly but undeniably to the officers who had stepped out of the car they had slung in crazy fashion on the kerbside, breaking the order of the traffic laws but accomplishing it also. The crowds dispersed without a word and the passenger found himself handcuffed in the back of a dangerously speeding patrol car, being taken out of the city to the nearest police station on the very same road the taxi driver had borne him in on that morning. He was feeling sick to his stomach.

The faces on the pavements blurred, the lights purred through green to amber and red and on the billboards long-legged women lifted their legs at him. Coke bottles with neon froth projected into the sky; faces loomed large then became infinitely small again as the car dipped and sometimes seemed to float in the air down the tunnels that wove into and out of the city. As the vehicle swooned down another embankment there was a sudden release of pressure as the blurring faces retreated. The sun was obscured behind the solemn tall buildings of the residential area, grey and pointing inclining their faces down away from the sun. The front passenger window opened with its electric hush as a patrolman on a horse inclined his head to the accompanying officer's and words the passenger could neither hear nor understand were interchanged. The light was red. Suddenly the car took off with enormous acceleration and sirens blazing and they were speeding along the slick main artery out of town. The officers in front remained remarkably quiet, the noise of the taxis and other vehicles surrounding them seeming to fade away.

In the distance a plane was climbing into the vast pale blue of the sky. He remembered the last cup of coffee he'd had at the airport before embarking for Argentina; the curl of the smile on the waitress's lips as she laughed at some remark made by somebody else; the way her hair fell and reminded him of the woman he'd known who'd given him his only daughter. They'd been married for ten years but then they'd drifted apart and now hardly saw each other, especially as their daughter, Hannah was growing up at college and developing a life of her own. He wondered what she might be doing right now, out of which window she was gazing.

As he felt the force of gravity squeezing him further into the seat, the car accelerated out of the bend in the flyover and he caught a glimpse of small figures scurrying down near the deserted train tracks and rusting work sheds. There appeared to be some kind of argument going on between a dark-skinned woman in a tight pink dress and two or three men. As the figures came more sharply into focus he wondered why the woman was sitting on the bonnet of the black car with the taxi sign on it, and not the man in the sunglasses whose space was being reduced as shadows of the now-distant residential buildings obscured the figures of the two other men. The passenger strained out of the corner of his eye to see what might happen next but he was being taken away from the scene, pulled away from his power to stop and watch it unfold.

The flyover dipped down, the disused rail tracks rose up and houses made of boards, some with old sheets of corrugated iron on their roofs, straggled alongside the motorway with the undressed children who ran kicking in the dirt on the other side of the high perimeter fence. A girl with a ripped red T-shirt ingrained with dust was kicking a tin coke can away from the crowd of younger children chasing after her. A fire was licking at the midday heat from within a half-eaten, abandoned car tyre, belching filthy black reams of smoke into the air and into the windowless windows of the adjoining houses. Out of the corner of his eye he saw a completely naked infant stumble on his untrained legs, totter and fall face first into the dirt, his nose streaming. And then he could see no more.

Now the car was suspended in mid-air high above the surrounding fields and buildings, up above the training grounds of the River Plate football club with the immense steel of the river sliding past him. For one absurd moment he imagined that a stewardess might come to serve him a drink until he remembered where he was. Settling back in his seat and relieved that at least he didn't have to make a decision as to what to do next, he allowed himself to feel the contours of the upholstery. No ordinary patrol car, this. He didn't know why he felt safer in the back of the car with these silent policemen at the helm than he had earlier on that morning with the grinning taxi driver, but he did. He could see the far-off plane angling into its course now as it banked smoothly off on the right into the skies above Uruguay:...

"This is your captain speaking, we will be cruising at a height of ten thousand metres, please keep your safety belts on until the safety belt indicators are off..."

The car lurched down from the flyover in a jolt and was plunged into sudden darkness as it ran underneath it. The police sirens had been going all this time but he hadn't noticed them; only now did he do so as their pitch died and they were finally switched off. They had reached their destination. The car had climbed the pavement in front of a squat, ugly building with a heavy door, its engine still purring.

The police officers sidestepped neatly out of the still warm car and the passenger's door was opened for him. Without addressing him, the accompanying officer led him by the arm to the building while the driver of the car pushed the door open. A pungent smell of tobacco and coffee wafted down the corridor as he was pushed inside the building, the hard clash of heels on the surface broke his stupor and it dawned on him that he was being taken inside a police station. A surly thickset sergeant motioned to them from where he was sitting hunched at his desk behind a mechanical typewriter. He was holding a collection of papers in his hand with a clumsy torpor that suggested he was more used to holding a baton or a club there. If it weren't for the uniforms to distinguish them, the passenger thought that he might have been in the wrong place. Two officials at the end of the corridor were playing some kind of card game while they waited seated in front of imposing double doors. The two officers remained, flanking him on either side, motionless and without speaking.

The sergeant lifted his head again as if feigning to notice them, flexed his biceps making his three-striped badge ripple and punched at the typewriter five or six times before finally attending them. A brief conversation ensued in which he could pick out the words 'American' and 'insult'. He was by now straining all his resources in an attempt to stay in command of the situation. He thought he heard them mention his giving money to the on-duty traffic policeman. The gestures of the sunglass-shod driver perfectly imitated those of the man to whom the note had been given; the passenger felt a redness creeping into his cheeks as he became increasingly concerned about his involvement in the incident. Now all three officers were looking at him, for the first time there seemed to be unison among the three men who were looking at him without smiling. He felt guilt on his face and the more he did so the more the other officials in the hall seemed to look at him. The men playing cards had stopped playing. He had to concede that the man had taken it more personally than he could have possibly imagined. His two escorts deserted him and the passenger suddenly felt very afraid, like a child who is held tightly by the hand as he is led through an airport but then has to climb the steps to the plane on his own. He didn't know where the officers had gone to and he needed someone who would understand the situation.

Relief flooded through him as the doors in front opened and the two officers who had driven him from the scene reappeared. They flanked an older man who wore his white shirt neatly buttoned at the collar and his tie impeccably straight. David was escorted to this man's office and shown to a seat. Promptly the two men who had been present at the scene saluted this man, nodded courteously to each other without speaking and stepped smartly out of the office, the driver preceding the other officer. It then dawned on him that he was completely and utterly alone with nobody who would be able to argue his case for him. He had some trouble in handing over his passport to the commanding official when it was asked of him; it was one of the few things he had on him which gave him credibility. Of course, he fully understood by now that handing over even a large proportion of the contents of his wallet to the commander in front of him would not be acceptable.

The man looked at the picture in the passport and then at David. He put the document gruffly on the table. David shifted uneasily in his chair. He felt utterly at a loss without his briefcase; with it missing he was hard-put to explain in any satisfactory manner what it was he was doing in the country. It was more to himself that he was speaking in his broken Spanish, but the commander seemed to be taking a keen interest in what he was saying and this made him feel more at ease than he had done for some time. The commander took notes personally on the conversation and suddenly David found himself regaining the fluency he thought he'd lost.

"What is your purpose in Argentina?" the police commander was asking him.

"Well, it's kind of hard to say, I'm not sure I understand altogether myself now," he responded.

The police commander raised his eyes. He asked David to precisely recount the events of that morning.

"I see, so then you say you followed the three men across the road. Did you know these men personally?"

"Ah, well, of course not, I ..."

"So you didn't know these men but you decided to follow them anyway?" the police commander was saying, "Don't you think this is rather unusual behaviour?"

"Well, of course it is," said the passenger.

"So you agree that it is, good."

"No, well, ..." .

"Please do not contradict yourself," the commander said to him, "This will only cause you further inconvenience. I see here that it says that your name is David Salsa. Is that your real name?"

"Yes, of course it is, I've had that name ever since I went into business."

" 'Ever since you went into business...' And what exactly would you say your 'business' is?"

David instinctively stopped himself from telling the truth. How on earth would he explain to this proud wiry little man that his real business was to instigate rumours about the beef in the north of the country, support it with documented evidence fabricated in the Buenos Aires offices of a French-owned supermarket chain and enable them to sell their cheaper product, imported from Europe, at a profit? It was a simple law of economics that David wasn't sure the policeman would understand.

The official looked up at him, waiting for him with his fountain pen dripping ink. David felt himself sweating. He was a spin-doctor, a scandalmonger; he worked for a team of publicity consultants, but he was no butcher. There was a difference, for Christ's-sake. He debated trying to tell the police commander this, but for some reason he didn't feel confident enough. He decided on another, more strategic approach to the problem.

"Well, my business is rather complex and I'm not sure that a person such as yourself would understand; that is to say…"

"I think I do rather understand and rather well, too. You say you've had this name ever since entering your….*business*?"

"Yes, that's quite right. At college I was known by another name, you see there was already a David Selbourne in my business, that is–or was, my intended business, which is still my business now…"

"Are you sure you wish to continue?" interjected the commander looking him full in the eye.

"Yes," said David, "I didn't want to be competing against somebody who had already made a name for himself."

"So your colleague had already assumed another name and was operating under it?"

"No, he hadn't assumed another name, it was just that his name was already too well-known for me to use, if you see what I mean."

"Yes, thank-you, I think I see perfectly what you mean."

The commander stood abruptly to his feet and David felt two heavy pairs of hands on him. As if by magic two officers entered the room. The passenger was handcuffed once more and led down the corridor to an adjoining cell whilst the police commander, amazed at what he had just heard and the importance of the task now ahead of him, made a phone call to his superior at the central police station. He could believe neither his luck at being involved in such an operation, nor the brazen audacity of the foreigner who had calmly walked into his office and denounced himself as a spy. And what a name. Of course, the police commander wasn't stupid, he knew any real spies in the country would very certainly be here for a proper and intended purpose, but this man was definitely up to something illegal. That much was absolutely certain.

CHAPTER TWO

The prisoner's watch had been taken from him and he wasn't certain what time it was, nor how long he had been in the cell. With both his passport and his watch missing he felt more vulnerable than ever, but it was the watch that preyed on his mind most. It had been a gift to himself after he had been promoted, (this was just after he had successfully completed a deal with a leading representative from an important company in Venezuela) His superiors had been suitably impressed with the efficiency of his newly acquired language skills and he had acquired the watch. The strap was of sleek metal, narrow, and the watch face had just the compass points marked clearly, in the same platinum of which the casing was made. It was a work of art and an extremely expensive limited edition. When he wore the watch to important meetings one glance at its face was often enough to dispel any doubts he might have had prior to them. It reminded him exactly where he was and of the position he had obtained, not only within the company, but in life as well.

Without it now he was feeling alone. It was hard for him to feel his own worth without it, and the fact that his passport, (with so many entry and exit visas from so many different countries) was also missing made him feel somehow naked. But the cell was refreshingly cool and not unpleasant compared to the heat that had been building up in the city earlier. Now he had time to reflect on matters. The fact that he was in a cell on his own obviously spoke volumes for the seriousness with which the police were handling his case. The police commander had been kind, (secretly, he envied the man's calm efficiency, his air of being in charge) and he had assured David that his case would be given the utmost attention. Probably, they had realised who he was.

There was a window quite high up on one side of the cell, but not so high that it didn't allow him to see outside. Rays of sunshine played on the wall in front of him, they danced and flickered as the leaves of a still- laden tree moved into and out of its reach. He wasn't sure what time they would come for him, but the longer he was detained the more confident he felt that the situation was being resolved. The prisoner positioned himself on the bed so that he could see better what was outside his cell. Presently he was brought a cup of coffee and a bowl with which to wash himself at the tiny sink and this led him to confirm his assessment that they were treating his case properly. Unhurriedly he removed his tie, folded it carefully and laid it on the bed. For a moment he toyed with the idea of neatly rolling up his shirtsleeves, (as he was wont to do when the company director invited him and other section managers to his home for a drink after the completion of a successful operation). But this exposed the smooth tanned skin on his left wrist and showed up the white strap mark where his watch should have been. Slowly and deliberately he rolled his shirtsleeves down again and buttoned them. He hadn't quite yet made up his mind about the briefcase. He had cleverly told the police commander that he had 'lost' it, which would give him the possibility of adapting his account of the situation to his final assessment of things, as and when he decided he had made his mind up about them. Of course in Spanish the word had more of an ambivalence about it; had he been recounting details of the incident to his superiors back in the office it was doubtful that he would have used the same expression.

David decided that he would confirm whether he had lost the briefcase, (unlikely) or whether it had been stolen from him, (more probable). He was glad of the cool quiet shade of his cell in which to carry out this task and thankful that he no longer had to race around on foot in the smoggy heat of the city. There was of course one other alternative explanation open to him, but this was conceptually hard to grasp and it made his head spin with the effort of trying to comprehend it: that he had deliberately got rid of the briefcase in an act of self-survival. When he thought of his narration of events to the police commander there was a flicker of recognition as to the plausibility of this last explanation. But when he tried to justify this explanation to himself in the shade of his cell, alone, it was much harder to see how this could be true. A ray of light brushed past the shade of a leaf that had been magnified to outlandish proportions and the prisoner suddenly understood the true nature of the task ahead of him. Of course! It didn't matter that he didn't know which of the three explanations was the real one, (all three of them were plausible to some extent, he felt) but that the commander understood the plausibility of the one that suited him the best. It was a basic technique that had been expounded upon in countless company briefings and seminars and in countless shapes and guises before, and it was unquestionably the technique that had to be applied in this situation. Details and operators might have changed, (he realised, all be it dully, that his operational role had changed somehow in the course of this situation, though he wasn't sure why) but the market techniques were the same: they were universal. This made the prisoner understand that he didn't have to make the decision himself; that the decision was already made for him, it was just a question of his working out what that decision was. That there was an absolute answer to the question of how and in what circumstances the briefcase had disappeared was abundantly clear to him now. His task was limited to finding out what it was.

If he said that he had lost the briefcase, (it amused him how he thought of it as the briefcase and not 'his' briefcase now) he would seem incompetent; worse than incompetent, and this wouldn't do him any good. If he said that the briefcase had been stolen from him, there was a possibility that the locals would think he was suggesting they were thieves, and he didn't want to make them feel as if he were accusing them in any way. Certainly not in this situation- that much he understood. He had sensed the traffic policeman's offence and he certainly didn't want a repeat of that situation. The only viable explanation that was left- one that neither offended the sensibilities of the locals nor put him at a disadvantage in terms of having managed the situation- was that he had deliberately off-loaded the briefcase.

Somewhere deep inside him he knew that a successful outcome to the operation depended on his appearing to be in charge. If ever the people to whom an operation was being pitched suspected that an operator wasn't in charge, or that the operator himself was doubtful of this, then the game was lost. Not for nothing had he been to business school, and not for nothing was he in the position he was. He was fully aware of the dangers of not appearing to be in charge in front of the people he was trying to convince; whole operations had had to be abandoned and operators had been flown discreetly out of countries as a result of such inefficiency. But this had never happened to him, yet. The only alternative open to him was to say that he had deliberately got rid of the briefcase. This would show them that he wasn't incompetent; that he didn't mean to offend them and that he had been fully in charge of the situation. He congratulated himself on his thorough assessment of things, sat upright on the bed and, keeping his back as straight as possible, lent over to tie the laces on his shoes tighter. He was ready for them now.

Right on cue, two policemen came to lead him from his cell to where, the prisoner knew, he would be asked to clarify his view of events in front of the commander's superior or superiors. He felt more confident of his actions than at any time since he had landed in Argentina, and the fact that he was now to report to some high-ranking official or officials made him feel more confident still.

They were waiting for him in a quiet, dimly lit room full of cigarette smoke, without windows. A senior-ranking official beckoned to him and he took a seat as he had been invited to do. He was offered another cup of coffee and the prisoner looked in a deliberately nonchalant way at the cluster of officials around him who had been left to hear out the interview on foot. It reminded him of the secretaries who came into the meetings to take notes on what he and his colleagues were saying.

Nobody said anything. Presently a man appeared beside him who also took a seat, angled slightly towards him and also in front of the senior official. In heavily-accented but perfectly grammatical English the new arrival began:

"You understand why we are all here, do you not, Mr. Selbourne?"

"Mr. Salsa, like it says in the passport: Mr. David Salsa."

"May I suggest that you do not contradict me and that you answer only those questions that you are instructed to do so by the superintendent before you? It will be in your best interests. I will faithfully translate anything and everything that you have to say."

"My name is David Salsa and this has been my name ever since I finished my training."

The translator repeated everything that the prisoner said, taking care neither to add nor subtract anything and carefully imitating the tone that he used, as his address to his superior was in the first person. The superintendent straightened his shoulders and looked in silence at the prisoner for a moment. Then he said something.

"Are you aware that it is a criminal offence to carry a passport and use it as your own when indeed it is not your own?" he was asked. A pause, "You're not American, are you?"

"No," said David.

"Is this your adopted country?"

"It was, a long time ago," a chill went down his spine; he'd not been prepared for this. He'd got rid of the briefcase but he wasn't prepared to part company with his passport, "The document most certainly is my own and I have been in possession of it ever since it was issued," the prisoner stated, "This is what I use when I fly round the world and I have never had any problems with it beforehand."

The superintendent raised his eyebrows and turned his gaze almost imperceptibly to the next in command for a fleeting moment.

"The superintendent states that he is surprised that you have never been caught out before and asks which countries you are habitually used to visiting," said the translator.

David avoided commenting on the first part of what had been said to him and, remembering a common technique from his training, tried to provide the locals with as much irrelevant information as he could, (provided of course that the nature of that information was not classified).

"I regularly fly to Venezuela, Colombia, Ecuador and Bolivia. I have been to Peru once or twice, as well as the central American states of Guatemala, El Salvador and Nicaragua."

"I am sorry," said the superintendent via the translator, "I had not realised that the countries you have mentioned had become *states* pertaining to your country."

"Well they're not strictly speaking the property of the United States," said the prisoner, "But ..." and here just in time he stopped himself, having detected a tone of offence in the policeman's words but not in those of the translator. But the translator wasn't neutral, he surmised, he was working on behalf of the Argentine police force. As such he would be highly unlikely to compromise the position of his superior by appearing to lend to his speech anything that might make him seem not wholly just. It was a technique that he himself used whenever asked to translate his own superior's ideas to an outsider. The superintendent cut him short and seemed once again to have regained his composure,

"I see, yes," he was saying, (the prisoner's words had struck a chord too close to the his heart for comfort), "You say you have been to Peru and regularly fly to other South," he corrected himself, "Latin American countries?"

"That is correct," said the prisoner, "We have a special operative in Peru due to the nature of our work there and in Columbia there are many simultaneous but different operations. I'm merely there when they need help in sorting out minor disputes in operations that are already on-going."

"On-going operations…., Columbia, Peru" a voice from out of the shadows was dictating to another man also on the fringe of the room, who was taking notes with an expensive- looking pen.

"How long have you worked for your…*company?*" the translator asked him.

"I started working for them almost immediately after finishing training at college and have worked for them ever since," David responded, "Once you start in a company like mine, it's hard to leave or get a job with another company in a similar line of business. We're one of the best at what we do and …"

In that moment the prisoner doubted whether what he was saying was advantageous to him; and in any case, if he was a good judge of people, the superintendent was becoming increasingly ruffled by his responses. All the while the translator was working increasingly hard in his attempts to make the superintendent seem less so. David decided there and then to move into another gear and, swiftly changing strategies, provide as little information as was necessary to sufficiently answer the superintendent's questions.

"Let us return to the issue of your name in an attempt to get to the root of the problem here," the translator was saying. A general chorus of agreement greeted the words.

"Which is your real name, David Salsa, or David Selbourne?"

"Both," the prisoner answered curtly.

"They are both your real names?" the superintendent echoed via the translator, "How many other names do you have, either real or unreal?"

The translator had trouble expressing his superior's line of thinking. "None," answered David.

"And it is permitted in your country and encouraged by your *company* to have two names?"

"It is actively encouraged by my company when the need arises," the prisoner responded with a slight flourish.

"...When the need arises. You have operations in many Latin American countries and sometimes even in Columbia and Peru,"

"Yes, we're in many Latin American countries including Columbia and Peru."

"You have received extensive training and know exactly the methods needed to accomplish your operations."

"It's more a case of training on the job," David said. He paused; perhaps it was better to let the superintendent know he was dealing with someone important, "I have been involved in the extensive training of many others in the field."

"...Many others in the field. You have been working for the same organisation since completing your training and are paid well for your services."

"My remuneration is appropriate," David affirmed, trying to conceal a slightly wry smile. Now David felt the superintendent was beginning to understand the situation. He felt a glow of satisfaction. "It's quite a skilled job," he added.

"You will not attempt to answer before the official translator, (that is me)," the translator added in self-congratulatory tone, "has spoken to you in your own language."

"It's okay, I won't answer."

"...He will not answer."

The superintendent thumped the table. He leant menacingly towards the prisoner. The coffee from the cup was running, ruining the papers on the desk and the translator was trying to mop them up using his bundle of notes. David was trying to help him.

"Thank-you."

"Not a problem."

"You idiot!! Leave that for someone else!"

"You idiot, ..." echoed the translator for David's benefit. The officials taking notes in the room stopped what they were doing and glowered, showing their disapproval at the conspiratorial manner of the translator.

"*Imbecíle!* I can erase every word from your stupid mouths."

A firm hand reached out of the shade and clutched David's wrist, politely encouraging him to leave the translator to his own devices. David Salsa felt emptiness where his expensive timepiece should have been.

"You deliberately got rid of your briefcase containing important documents in an attempt to cover up for yourself."

"No, no, it wasn't exactly like that. I lost my briefcase because I knew that if it were stolen you might take offence and think I was accusing your... Look, I was in charge."

"He was in charge," beamed the translator.

"You are being charged!"

"Okay, look, I'll be honest. The waiter confused me and the taxi-driver definitely over-charged me, I think there was some plot with a hooker who was planning to rob me. Then there was a baby with its face down in the dust...."

"A baby! Whose baby?"

"In the dust," added the translator for good measure.

"Some idiot was burning a house, or attempting to do so, but they drove me off before I could see properly..."

"Monster! Are you responsible for the suffering of this child?! What other horrendous crimes have you committed?"

"I don't have to answer that question. I'm not responsible. "

"He says he's not responsible."

"YOU SADISTIC SON OF A ... AND YOU WERE TRYING TO GET A VIEW!"

He had pressed himself close to David and was screaming at him in the face. It was going horribly wrong.

"You're trying to frame me! I had nothing do with the baby...it wasn't me who set fire to it, or the hooker, it was just something I saw from the car while I sat in the back. Those two goons with their dark glasses who said nothing kept running through the lights all because I'd given that dumb policeman some useless currency and the stupid …"

The prisoner heard a cold hard whack on the back of his head, an instant before he felt it, and then he slumped into his chair and the coffee and the papers and his expensive watch which wasn't there fell from him in a heavy, sick darkness.

"David Salsa, you are a *shit!*"

He was drifting into and out of consciousness. There was a cold wind on the back of his neck and moonlight also. He reached up to touch his neck which was feeling stiff and found the hand of his daughter there. She was about a year old and he was carrying her in the special child carrier on his back. The moon shone hard and cold on the ground and here and there it cascaded off the leaves swaying in the large tree above them. It was night and it was winter but in this part of Mexico winters were dry. The day had caressed them with its sunshine and Hannah had been content to travel on his back. They stopped when they came across a stream or to change her and she seemed as alive to the wonders of the place as they did. They had stumbled across an orchard as they reached the outskirts of the village, tasted forbidden fruit under the shade of a dry dusty tree that took the rays of the sun and made its fruit plump with them. Hannah had laughed. Her eyes were wide open and she seemed to be drinking in everything around them.

They hadn't had much chance to travel as a family, and still less chance to take off on some adventure like this, packing rucksacks, (although his wife had brought a small suitcase with her also) and boarding a plane to land hours away in some remote country. They had found a small posada, or inn run by a firm but kindly old woman. She kept her dogs and her chickens at the back and her hotel staff there too. David wasn't quite sure whether the benign, old gentleman who did the cooking was the woman's husband; few words were spoken between them and when they were they were usually instructions, given to the old man by the woman and accepted by him in what seemed an air of quietly defiant resignation. He spoke little but he cooked extremely well, even with some extravagance, David's wife had commented. They were both glad that there were no other foreign tourists there, and when David's wife looked at him at dinner, when the moon was high in the trees and the little one was gently snoring in the high chair beside them, she did so in a way which made him feel special too. His wife's suitcase remained on a chair the whole time they stayed there, only partially opened one evening when she had decided that she'd wanted to wear something special, but then she'd changed her mind and decided that she didn't want to stand out too much. So she'd combined a skirt and a blouse whose colours she'd never normally wear together, combed her hair and put something in it that made it look smooth and shiny and they'd ordered exactly the same meal as they'd had the night before. David was happy. His wife was happy too.

Here now, underneath the trees Hannah was still partially awake, she gurgled and mumbled to herself in contentment and once they'd changed her for the last time, given her her milk and clothed her in an extra layer to keep out the chill that was creeping in, they set off in what they knew to be the direction of the hotel. David didn't know how he knew that their warm hotel room was down there, there where they were going, waiting for them, or that the old woman would have kept the lights on in the dining room to accommodate them; but he did. They walked in silence and sure of their steps, even though they said many things to one another and had never been in this forest on these slopes at the foot of this mountain before.

David had a premonition, it wasn't that he felt he'd been here before, but that he was on his guard, alert but not frightened as they made their way under the canopy of the tree where the moon shone on the leaves and on the ground before them. That was it. The tree had leaves on even though it was winter. There were many varieties of exotic trees and shrubs that grew here that didn't grow in the States. The tree had a huge trunk and seemed to pull all the light of the night sky about it, as if wrapping itself in it. David felt the cold hand of his daughter resting on his neck behind him, he squeezed her tiny fingers gently to put some warmth into them and as he did so her weight seemed to become part of his own. It was comforting. When they last stopped to change and feed her he had felt less purposeful without the weight of her in the carrier. Now, though, he knew where he was going. David's wife was content to let him take the lead and guide them back to the hotel somewhere down in the valley below them. They stopped to consult each other on occasions and were in agreement as to which way they should go. David was happy. His wife was happy too.

A night owl swooped down gently to take up its perch again in the tree under which they had just passed, and as they came out from underneath its foliage they could both see the tiny fires of the village lights down in front of them, burning gently into the night. David estimated that they must be about three or four kilometres away from its outskirts where their hotel nestled amongst the trees at the end of the dusty track. It was perched on the hillside on which they were now walking, though the hills they had clambered up in the morning, idly letting their imagination dictate their route, had become steeper and risen into the stiff fingers of mountain slopes.

David felt as if the hill on which they were walking and which surely led down to the hotel contained the tangled rope of a root that led off from the great tree they had passed under and travelled all the way down into the valley below. He could feel that Hannah was asleep now and that she had allowed herself at last to succumb to the magic of the night that was about them and that she had trusted him with that magic. David felt strangely lethargic too, as if someone else's legs were carrying him back down to their sleeping place, though his body was light as air. The going was easy and here and there they stopped to admire the silver of the moon, behind them now, floating on the back of the stream which ran alongside them and showed itself at intervals.

Sometimes where the water gathered itself in pools it seemed to have taken on the qualities of the light that flowed into it; the moonlight seemed a part of that of which it was made. In these places where the track led them close to the water's edge they didn't stop to refresh themselves with it or scoop a handful over their faces as they had done previously in the day, they kept their distance and admired the way the moon swam in it. The tree stretched on and on down into the valley and David and his wife were sure of their way.

As they neared the lights of the hotel David could see that the owner had left the light in the dining room on for them. He didn't know what time it was but he estimated that it must be late; the weariness of the journey had accumulated in them and the night was quiet. Now they knew what lay off above in the hills they saw out of their bedroom window. They wondered at them as they glowed orange and then purple in the fading evening sun every day.

"Doesn't it rain here?" David had asked the old woman in his rudimentary Spanish. She answered back that there was always rain; it was just a question of knowing where to look for it.

"You two! You must be dog-tired," she said to them, "Come in and get that poor sleeping child off your back while I tell Patricio to get your supper ready. There's a thunderstorm forecast for tonight and I was wondering if I'd have to go scampering about up there looking for you two gringos!" she said good-naturedly, but not without a hint of sarcasm in her voice. David and his wife had come to understand her, even though she said relatively little to them and didn't intrude on them at meal times when they, too, were locked in deep and silent communication. David's wife spoke practically no Spanish and he'd only just completed an elementary course in it, but he managed to convince her that this trip would be a good means of testing it out; in any case, he needed it for work.

David could see the pool of light on the floor where it came in through his cell window. He wasn't sure how long he'd been out but his neck and his shoulders were stiff. There was a breeze blowing in through the bars. He put his hand up to feel the back of his neck and for a fleeting moment half expected to find the tiny hand of his daughter there, and then he remembered. He remembered being dragged from the room with his feet scuffling along the floor behind him, he'd tried to pick them up to walk but he was being pulled backwards and they didn't respond.

He remembered people shouting at him in that strangely formal way of theirs', how the meeting with the superintendent had suddenly changed course for no apparent reason. He'd suddenly felt that they were accusing him of something when it was he that had gone into the meeting acutely aware that he mustn't be seen to be accusing them. He couldn't fathom these people out. They seemed to want something from him and he had nothing to give them; in any case he no longer had the briefcase and somewhere in the back of his mind swelling and closing like a fist was the realisation that it was probably better that he didn't. His office seemed a million miles away now and he was struggling with the effort of remembering exactly what it was that he was there for in the first place. He was dimly aware that he should have made it to an office in the centre of town that morning, (or was it yesterday morning)? He was also aware that he'd had to hand over the briefcase, or rather its contents, to some people in that office. Yet still the rumour persisted in him that somehow he was to have been more involved than simply handing over the briefcase; in any case, he'd already done that, hadn't he? Certainly, the police had to know what was inside the briefcase by now.

Then it dawned on him, he couldn't possibly let the police get their hands on the dossier he'd compiled; if he did, it would be the end for him. This was the first time it had occurred to him and now he was frightened. Immediately he felt the swelling on the back of his head grow tighter. The pain in his neck was indescribable. For the first time he felt like a prisoner in this tiny room and he didn't feel comfortable here any longer.

They'd got it all wrong; they were trying to implicate him in something that had nothing to do with him. The beef issue was one thing; the other stuff was something else. And why hadn't they warned him that this was such a dangerous country? Goddamnit, you came here just trying to do your job and give these locals a chance to earn some money and keep people in their jobs and all you got was a stinging headache for your trouble! Couldn't these policemen see that all he was doing was trying to maintain the local economy and make sure ordinary decent people could afford to eat meat? Prices for their own beef had gone up; he was well aware that their standard of living and their salaries were nowhere near those of the States, and this would give people the opportunity to put beefsteaks back on their tables. It was ridiculous, in a country where the best beef in the world was produced, the locals couldn't even afford to eat it!

He felt up and reached round the back of his head to where it glowed and throbbed raw; the analogy made him so dizzy that he immediately threw up and collapsed unconscious onto the bed again. A fly was buzzing in the room. It had been waiting for its chance. The police officer on duty who had observed all this through the hidden video camera slowly and unhurriedly unlocked the door to the cell. He lifted the feet of the prisoner onto the bed in one deft swing and called to the cleaner to come in and mop up the mess. This was their VIP suite after all; he wasn't going to have some filthy foreigner mess it up while he was on duty. In an after-thought he untied the prisoner's shoes, removed them and placed them neatly at the foot of the bed, toes pointing towards the door and side by side, touching one another. He took some time in this act and even rearranged the blanket underneath the prisoner, smoothing out its creases quickly with his hand, as if he were afraid someone might be watching him. It always made him feel like this when he stepped inside the cell he was observing; he didn't want to be seen to be guilty of anything himself. The chief had said to watch him closely, and watch him closely he would.

The prisoner had been muttering gibberish in clumsy Spanish about a young child. Something that the policeman had overheard one of the officers present at the interview say to a colleague suggested that this man was caught up in something really sinister, something really ugly, he thought he'd heard the detective say. Countless hoodlums and ruffians were brought in from the ghettos beside the motorway, often involved in all sorts of dirt, but this guy was a foreigner and it was different. If this foreigner was messing up the lives of innocent Argentine children then he was going to have to pay for it. Who the hell did they think they were, always so arrogant, thinking they were above the law? It was as if they thought that money could change the laws of the country for them. You wouldn't catch him accepting a cheap ten-peso note from some taxi-driver who'd been caught in some violation or some cheap tart that'd just got it from a client, what filth! With that, he spat on the floor and then had the cleaner come and clean it up for him. They treated people like dirt, these people.

Back in his dreams as he slipped into and out of consciousness David Salsa was confused about his part in all this, but what else could he have done in the situation? It hadn't been his fault but somehow he felt a growing sense of guilt about it. He needed to distance himself from the people that had got him into this situation. How on earth had he allowed himself to get into such a mess in the first place? He should have known that the trip to Mexico would have ended in tragedy, his wife needed a cute package tour like the ones in the brochures, but he'd thought that he was doing the right thing at the time and that things would work out between them. How wrong he'd been – now she was in possession of their daughter and his life was meaningless. He reached up to feel Hannah's hand again but it wasn't there.

In the morning he found himself sitting up on the bed with a doctor attending him. The man asked him a few simple questions in his own language and explained to him that he'd had a nasty accident and had slipped and hit his head getting out of the patrol car whilst he'd been kindly escorted to the police station. It seems he'd lost some of his possessions while he'd been in the city the previous day, among them his briefcase and his watch and he'd obviously been the victim of some unprovoked attack by some unscrupulous villain or villains. One couldn't be too careful, the doctor advised him; that sort of low-life scum would stop at nothing if they, forgiving the expression, saw easy pickings. Not that it was his fault, of course, one simply had to be careful in a city like Buenos Aires.

David asked the doctor if he were Argentine and the man replied that yes he was, but that his family were originally partially of English descent and that he rather wished that he wasn't living in Argentina. The man said this as a joke but there was more than a hint of irony in his voice. David was surprised at the man's words but said nothing. He was learning that the best form of self-defence was inaction and that not speaking or speaking as little as necessary was part of the strategy. It was used in extreme situations in his line of business and David had already surmised that this was one such situation. He was told that the people at the office had got worried when he'd failed to show up and had eventually sent out an alert to the local police force. They'd been worried, you see, an American on his own who obviously knew enough Spanish to get his way around; it was likely to mean that foul play had been involved. David explained to the doctor that he hadn't been able to phone them again because his telephone was inside the briefcase that had been stolen from him. The police had seemed particularly concerned about the briefcase, he explained, but the doctor assured him that he need no longer worry as they, (the people at the office) now had it in their possession and that everything was okay.

David wondered how on earth it was that his contacts could have ended up with the briefcase he'd been so terrified of having lost, but decided to say nothing to the doctor. The director of the company had personally been to see the superintendent and had cleared the matter up, the doctor explained. He was to understand that everything was all right now. The man repeated this phrase to him carefully and deliberately a couple of times so that David understood him properly. Then he informed him that a car would be coming for him in a couple of hours after he'd had something to eat and had chance to have a wash-up.

"Do you feel like eating?" the doctor asked him.

"I'm not so sure," said David.

"Ah, Mr. Salsa, you are in Argentina and have not yet tried one of our famous beef steaks. I presume, when in Rome..."

David wondered how it was that his briefcase had ended up in the hands of the very people for whom it had been intended.

"It must have been the taxi-driver. Cunning dog," he said to himself, and then he remembered the dark shadows of the buildings looming in on that small figure he'd seen from the police car; how he'd seemed to be swallowed up by them.

"I must get to the office," he said to the doctor and then wondered whether he really would go there after all and whether or not it was wise for him to do so.

CHAPTER THREE

By now, David was getting used to the way they drove in Buenos Aires. He understood that if the driver of a vehicle went slowly on the freeway he, (most of the drivers were men in this part of the world) was likely to cause an accident; especially as the truck drivers dictated the pace and it must be hard for them to accommodate much smaller vehicles on the road. They had such long distances to travel in this enormous country of theirs, no wonder they had to travel so fast. It wasn't uncommon, though, to see a truck speeding along with just a few planks or lengths of overhanging pipe on its deck. The car in which he was travelling suddenly swerved violently to avoid one such six-wheeled monster that had come crashing in at them from the right-hand side and the driver of the car exchanged the usual customary greetings with the driver of the lorry.

"Son of a thousand bitches," he cursed with one hand on the steering wheel whilst the other was engaged in dialogue with the lorry driver, "He tried to ram us. Did you see that?! He could have killed us, man, and then we'd be spread out like raspberry jam all over the tarmac – just like those poor suckers that were on that plane at the airport over there."

It was true, but only now did the passenger connect the driver's words to the horrendous crash that had been in the papers at the time. It had even scraped into the news in his hometown, all be it as a small column in the international section of the newspaper. The writer had paid particular attention to the fact that the plane had ripped through a nearby petrol station and that the station had been owned by a big English refinery. David wasn't sure whether the writer was sympathising with the owners and workers of the petrol station or with the people on board the plane, but the story had stuck in his mind.

"That idiot should have his license revoked, who the hell does he think he is?" the driver continued, still with one hand on the wheel, "Who ever saw such disregard for human life? Just wait till I get my hands on that son of a bitch!"

David reflected with some irony that the expression used in this part of the world was identical to the one used in his.

"*Drive carefully,*" she was saying, "*because you only have one life and you're beautiful.*"

The expression seemed to make more sense than ever and he thought for a moment whether things were always like this; whether one only saw the true meaning of things if one was prepared to look at them closely enough. David thought again of the briefcase. It should have been in the car with him but now he was glad it wasn't. How the hell they'd got their hands on it he really didn't know, but he was glad they had and that he didn't have to worry about it any more.

And then it struck him; maybe they didn't have it at all. The image of those svelte long legs embraced him again as the car suddenly dipped to go into the underpass beneath the pulsating freeway. What was it she'd said to him? -

Without a second's hesitation David instructed the driver to take a right turn rather than the left which would have taken them closer to the river and eventually straight into the mouth of that enormous, wide road he'd got caught on the day before.

"What, are you crazy, man, we'll never get to the address I've got written down here if we take this route," said the taxi-driver, "Those people, they told me good and proper to make sure that I take you right to the door of their offices and I'm not about to turn down my bonus just like that. They said they'd pay me twice the usual fare if I got you to their front door and hell, we poor locals don't get much of a chance with you foreigners too often…" with this he stopped and did what he was told. In any case, David had ceased to listen to him.

A white statue was pissing into a pool and some of the spray was being blown by the wind onto the surrounding grass. Here and there it grew in denser tufts around the ornamental pool and David conjectured that it must be possible to work out which way the wind blew and in what seasons of the year if one were to study the grass closely enough. For some inexplicable reason the thought seemed wholly appropriate to him. The driver was still mumbling, cursing the lorry driver under his breath and David wondered whether he'd live very long. What a stressful and dangerous job he had, David thought, but then it occurred to him that his own line of work was equally dangerous.

"Where on earth am I going?" he said out loud and with that the car came to a screeching halt.

"You told me to come this way," said the taxi-driver, "You said you knew where you were going and now you ask me where the hell we are! What the hell do you think I am, some kind of criminal? Listen, mister, I drive the car and you get to where you need to go, okay? Nobody's going to overcharge you and in any case your damn company is going to pay the bill and at exactly the same rate I would have charged you, anyway. What do you think; you think I'm not honest? I have a wife and children to feed and here I am just trying to make a decent, honest living. You foreigners, you're the curse of my life!"

"Shut up," said David, calmly and efficiently.

"What?!" said the taxi-driver.

"I said shut up and drive where I tell you to. I'll pay your bill and I'll tell you where to go."

"Okay, mister, I'm just trying to do my job, you understand, it isn't easy for me and…" said the taxi-driver.

"Okay," said David.

He needed time to concentrate his thoughts before he worked out his next move. He reached inside his coat pocket and was relieved to find his wallet and to find it full, too. At least they hadn't taken that from him, nor his passport. They'd stolen his briefcase and his watch from him so that he couldn't orientate himself and had left him without a reason to stay; but at least they'd had the dignity to leave him with sufficient means to get out of their awful country.

"Those bastards, that was a present," he said.

"A present?" asked the taxi-driver, but David was too engrossed in his thoughts to answer him. Somehow, though, David didn't feel that he'd be getting on a plane just yet. He had some unfinished business to resolve, though he didn't know exactly what it entailed. "It'll come to me in time," he said.

"Yes, of course it will," said the taxi-driver, "Those criminals will probably realise it was a present and hand it in to the nearest police station. Was it a present from your wife?" he asked.

"Yes, you could say that," said David and in a funny sort of way it was true. He'd bought it not only for his own gratification but to impress her as well, he realised. He was sure she'd thought he'd never come to anything and that their hippy excursion, (as she'd called it) to the hills of Mexico had been a waste of time. The trip had been a disaster. He should have known better.

'Who was he trying to please now?' he wondered. How the hell was he going to explain all this back at the office and what the hell were they going to say?

"Listen, mister, you don't worry about the office. I'll explain to them that you needed a drink, a cup of coffee and that that's why we turned up there late. Hell! Can't a man even take a little time to enjoy a place when he's flown thousands of kilometres to get here? What's this damn world coming to? I'll show you some of the sights of this city, best city in the world this is, I'm not surprised you came all this way to see it," said the taxi-driver.

The driver was beginning to like the foreigner. Of course he was right, the man just wanted a little time to enjoy the place before he had to get on the plane again to fly who knows where. What a life, he thought to himself, always running from one place to the next without having time to pause; he certainly wouldn't like a job like that. And with this thought in his mind, the driver decided that he'd stop and take a coffee with this poor, tired man.

"We'll pull up here, mister," he said, "Here you'll get a taste of the real Argentina, not some of that crap they dream up for the tourists. I'm going to take you for a meal in my own front room, this is where I always eat," he said to David.

"Fine," responded his passenger, "That sounds good to me."
And it was true, it was where the man usually ate when he could afford it, (although that seemed to be less and less these days) and it was fine by David.

"Hey, mister, what's your name anyway?" he asked.

"David," said David, "David Salsa."

"Mine's José," said the man, "And I'm really pleased to meet you." And it was true, he was.

"José, you son of a thousand bitches! I thought you'd run off without paying your bill or without dropping in to pay your respects. What's the matter, we're not good enough for you anymore?" the cheery greeting met them.

It was a long time since José had last sat down to eat here, longer than he could remember.

"No, man, you know how business is these days, what with the price of petrol and those crooks siphoning off all the extra. Anybody would think it was gold we were putting in our cars, though they always seem to be dripping in the stuff like they'd just picked the honey off the trees," he said.

The division had been made; things were as they should be. This brought a chorus of approval and José was back in business, doing what he did best.

"Why only this morning my good friend and me were almost squashed into the road by one of those villains, I think he was trying to crush our car like an olive for its oil!" he shouted out to anybody that would hear him as the whole place erupted.

"So who's your friend?" the restaurant owner asked José.

"David," said David, "David Salsa."

"You speak good Spanish for a foreigner," the man responded and David and José sat down. Their table was facing the window and from where they were sitting they could see the nightmare road they had just left behind, rising up seemingly suspended in the air like the trail left by a mad buzzing wasp, or a whole nest of them.

"Gets worse every day," José said, "One of these days it's going to kill me."

"I know exactly what you mean," said David, "It makes you wonder why you're doing it, doesn't it?"

"It must be four months since I last sat down here to eat," said José, "What's the world coming to when a man can't find the time to call in on his friends and enjoy a bite to eat with them?" he asked.

"Two beers," the driver said to the restaurant owner, "And bring us the menu too, please; me and my good friend here are going to have ourselves a meal."

"Right away," said the owner sensing the mood of the taxi-driver. At one time they all used to come in here, especially in the summer months when the tourists were rich for the picking and a few journeys a day would suffice. Now though things were different and the restaurant owner knew it; his business had been hit hard as well. Mostly it was the banter and the camaraderie he missed, but somebody had to pay the bills. He'd become quite an expert at reading people's moods, and was astute enough to realise that sometimes the louder someone talked the quieter it meant they were on the inside. José had aged even since the last time he'd seen him, he thought.

'I wonder who the foreigner is?' he thought to himself and went to fetch them two of the best beers he could find.

"Well, Mr. Salsa, here we are," said the driver as he raised his bottle to David. No glasses had been provided for them as was the custom with the drivers, but the owner had discreetly wiped the tops of the bottles with his dishcloth as he opened them. It was a practised movement and one that he'd been perfecting for years; the swish and click of the bottle top opening at almost exactly the same time as the cloth passed over the neck with its own swishing movement. It took greater skill than opening a bottle of champagne. His customers knew who was serving them.

"Please, call me David," said David.

The driver knew he'd picked exactly the right person to go for a meal with.

"I'll salute to that," said José and the two men both took a drink from their bottles. The beer tasted good.

José had been divorced. That was before he'd remarried and had two children, one after another in quick succession. David couldn't help but feel that this was appropriate for a man who plied his trade on the busy artery of the city; two quick steps on the pedals and your life was changed in an instant. David and his wife had only had one child, he told José. He'd felt that she was beyond his reach and had been surprised when she'd accepted his proposal of marriage; then surprised again when the union bore them a child. She was beautiful; his wife.

He explained to José that she'd been everything he'd ever wanted. David unbuttoned his shirt cuffs but there was an uneasy silence as both the man and he looked at the place where his watch should have been. They both understood what it was that had been taken from him.

"The journey's what counts," said José, quoting a line from a book he'd read, even if he'd made the line his own, "If you can't take any time to pause and enjoy it for a while, then it becomes meaningless," he said. David knew what he meant.

"Take me, for example," said the driver, "I get more satisfaction from watching the cars go by than I do from actually driving one. Out there it's chaos, but in here," he gestured to the crowd in the room with a sweeping movement of his arm, "People understand each other. The very person that's just cut in on your lane could be your best friend," he said, "It's like I've got so many things I want to say to somebody when I'm in that damn furnace of a car, but nobody to say them to except myself," he continued. "Most passengers just get in, give you orders and toss the money at you when you're done like they've just done you a favour. You're different, I could see that the moment you got into the car."

David flushed red and wondered whether he really was any different from the majority of the passengers, but then he satisfied himself with the thought that he would be paying for their meal and immediately felt better.

"So, what are we going to have to eat?" José asked him.

"I'm going to have the biggest beef steak that money can buy and another bottle of beer," said David, "I want to see what all the fuss is about," he said with a smile.

"A man after my own heart," said José, "None of that hamburger crap they try to push on us these days. Do you know that there are farms on the outskirts of this city where they cultivate earth worms and then they get chopped into little pieces and sold as hamburgers?"

"What, here in Buenos Aires?" He flicked a glance at the menu again, just in case.

"Right here."

The man was perfectly serious. David was only just beginning to realise how complicated the beef situation in this country was; the very thought of it was disgusting.

"Who the hell do they think they are?" David said solemnly.

They ordered the same, together with another bottle of beer each and raised what remained of their first bottles to each other. This taxi-driver was the first person he'd really understood since he'd arrived in Argentina, but then David was beginning to understand himself better.

"That woman, she took the only gift life has ever really given me," he said, but even as he said it he knew that it wasn't true: he was also somehow implicated in the circumstances of their separation. Sometimes a person just holds onto the dream even when that dream has never been true, but humans are weak creatures and need devices to prop them up; there'd be too much real thinking going on that way and life would be dangerous. The governments knew it, though not as individuals. They simply couldn't allow themselves to.

"So how'd you come to be separated from her in the first place?" José was asking him. The conversation had taken on a more intimate tone with the arrival of the fresh beer. José felt that the foreigner had a need to talk.

"I don't know," said David, "I just walked across a city street one day and she was gone," he said.

'Goddamnit this man's had it tough,' José thought to himself, 'He said she was beautiful but what kind of a sneaky low-life would pull such a trick?'

Maybe the cities they came from weren't so different after all. While one spoke the other one ate, and when the other one ate, the other one spoke. David and José weren't aware that they were doing this and if anyone had pointed it out to them they'd have been shocked. Neither man realised that the most important dialogue was with himself. The man at the bar polishing his glasses for the directors of the two big bilingual schools close by realised it though but kept quiet about it.

"So, tell me about your line of business," José was saying to him.

"Beef," said David, "I'm here to do with beef," he said, which was true.

"Ah, now there's a coincidence, you don't say. It must be a pretty important job," said José, wolfing down another lump of steak.

"It is," said David, "And there's a hell of a lot of work to do, more than I had imagined at first. The more you look at it," he was saying, "The more complicated it gets. Why the hell they couldn't have told me that things were so mixed up here, I don't know," he said eyeing the steak, "But I think there's more to it than meets the eye and I'm determined to get to the bottom of things before I leave this country."

"Good for you," said José examining the quality of the rump steak, "One of my friends was telling me only the other day that some unscrupulous supermarket was importing beef from France, of all places. Importing beef from France! Can you imagine it? It just doesn't make sense, I'm telling you."

"You're right," said David, "They are and it doesn't."

José was pleased to have found a man who felt as strongly about these things as he did himself; why, the way the man spoke he could almost be Argentine. He knew he'd been right about him; always trust your gut instincts. - That much he'd learnt by now, especially out there on those treacherous roads.

For his part David knew that he was going to go to those offices in the city after they'd finished their meal and that this man was going to take him. He knew that the people there were waiting for him and that he had an explanation to give them; perhaps they had an explanation to give him too.

However much a sense of foreboding he had, there were a lot of things that needed resolving and he was going to have to use this trip to try and sort them out. He had to find out what it was all about even though there was a knot tightening in his stomach.

"I'm paying for the meal," said José, thumbing the notes in the wallet he'd removed from the back pocket of his jeans.

"What, are you crazy, it's out of the question," said David, "Of course you're not paying for the meal, I am," he said.

"Look, man, I'm the one who invited you here," José was saying, "And there's no way I'm letting you pay. What, do you think I don't make enough money to pay for this?" he was asking.

The whole bar was listening.

"There ain't nobody paying for José Afortunado's meal but me."
The bar roared its approval.

"These foreigners, they think that they can buy anything with money," José said to them in a jokey tone of voice as he held up his wallet and flicked it. However, David had understood the man enough to know that there was a hint of sarcasm in his voice. He decided to let him pay for the meal and not to offend him, even if he was only joking.

"Hey you, where are you going!?" said the restaurant owner as David followed José out of the restaurant into the late sunshine of the morning, "There's not enough here to cover everything."

But José was already approaching the car and David had to hurriedly thumb through his wallet and fling the notes at the owner; it was just possible José might take off without him and David didn't fancy getting left on his own in the city again. Once had been quite enough.

"These bloody foreigners, they're all the same," said the restaurant owner as he raised his hands to the departing car with the excess notes falling from his grasp.

They travelled the rest of the journey in silence, retracing the route they had taken, entering the city by the huge avenue where the police had picked up David. David tried not to think of what lie ahead of him. He had a vague memory of the creeping tower blocks reaching out to the ghettos he'd seen the previous day. He was confused as to what was expected of him. As he stepped out of the car José escorted him to the front door of the offices.

"Here's my card," he said to him, waving away the money he had been offered by his passenger, "If ever you want to see the real Buenos Aires, give me a ring."

With that he left, but not before he had seen his passenger step safely inside the imposing revolving doors of the tall building. A man was waiting for him on the other side.

"I expect you must be Mr. Selbourne," the man said to him in very good English.

"I expect so," said David and allowed himself to be escorted into a lift down the cool grey marble corridor. David glanced back at the street for an instant but the contrast of the glaring light outside and the cool darkness inside prevented him from seeing much. It was only on his way up in the lift that he thought to take his tie out of his pocket and put it on again. It felt tight round his throat. The guard eyed him with a cool detachedness and privately thought to himself that the man didn't look like much. Classical music was playing on the piped music system inside the lift but it wasn't at all relaxing. As the doors of the lift swished open on the fourteenth floor a woman came to greet them; the guard retired into the shade of the lift and with a swish he was gone.

"Welcome, Mr. Selbourne," she said, "We have been waiting for you."

Eva Barona escorted the man across the sweeping office floor towards the cream-coloured doors of the Director's offices at the back. At open workstations smart young men and women sat typing at computer screens. None of them looked up as they passed.

"Let me take your coat," she said to him.

"No, thank-you," said David, politely but firmly.

He'd let go of far too much already on this trip. If Mrs Barona thought the man a little odd, she also thought that she could smell beer on his breath.

"What an idiot," she thought to herself, "The Director's been tearing his hair out, he's hardly eaten anything at all and this clown's been boozing it up for the last twenty-four hours."

She smiled at David graciously and ushered him into the meeting room.

"The Director will be with you in a moment," she said, "Just take a seat and make yourself comfortable."

David looked round as the heavy doors closed behind her, but she had already gone. It was a while since he'd been to the bathroom and the piped music was doing him no favours. After what seemed like an eternity, the Director finally emerged from his rooms.

"Ah, Mr. Selbourne, what a pleasant surprise, we have been expecting you."

The man extended his hand towards David and he made to stand up, but the man waved him back into his seat. As David reached up to shake the man's hand the man allowed the tips of his fingers to make contact and then retracted his hand. The Director's English was precise but affected, rather like a book which had been left out to dry in the sun and whose words were being read out by someone who didn't know the language, but who could imitate its sounds perfectly. The

Director pressed a buzzer with his left hand on the enormous table and Eva Barona retrieved David's coat from him. Fortunately he'd kept his wallet in his jacket pocket this time.

The Director had sleeked-back platinum-coloured hair which almost perfectly matched the décor of the room. Everything was light and luminous, but it was impossible to see anything outside due to the glare of the sun through the closed window blinds.

"I do hope you have had a pleasant journey," the Director said to David.

"Ah, yes, of course," responded David in the manner he was expected to. There was no hint of insincerity in either of their voices. David found himself with a cup of hot black coffee in his lap.

"I understand you had some trouble with your briefcase," enquired the Director. As he said this he clicked open a briefcase that looked remarkably like the one David had lost and took out the solitary piece of paper it contained. It was a letter from David's superior in New York outlining the details of David's visit and signed in ink at the bottom. The Director was standing and David could see through the piece of paper as the Director held it up before him.

"Yes," said David by way of an apology, "I lost it," he answered truthfully.

"Most, most unfortunate," the Director was saying as he continued to peruse the letter, "It mentions here that you will be bringing your report with you."

"Yes, in fact I have brought the report with me," said David as he reached inside his jacket for a handkerchief with which to wipe his brow. The Director looked inquisitively at him as David pulled out his handkerchief and then he turned back to the letter.

"And where exactly is this report?" asked the Director, interposing the letter between himself and David.

"Well, I suppose the report is still inside the briefcase," answered David, though he wasn't at all sure that it was.

"Most unfortunate," the Director was saying, "Well, we will just have to see what we can do, will we not?"

David felt relieved.

"And what exactly do you propose to do?" asked the Director.

"Well, I rather thought that you might have one or two

suggestions..." David's words trailed off into the hazy air inside the room.

"Yes, yes, of course," said the Director, "Let us examine the facts." The coffee cup was growing cold in David's lap.

"You came here with the report, which was inside your briefcase. Does it have your name on it?"

The man's tone of voice had changed.

"Er, yes, I suppose it must do," said David.

"You suppose it must do. Good," said the Director, "And this report was drawn up prior to your knowing that we would be your contacts here in Argentina?" enquired the man.

"Oh yes," replied David, "I had no idea who I would be working with down here when I was originally compiling the report. Usually it doesn't matter, you see; most operations are worked out that way. Then it's just a question of finding the right people to do the job."

"Excellent," said the Director with barely-disguised light-heartedness.

"Excellent," repeated David with a growing sense of relief. Somehow he'd felt that more would have been demanded of him.

"In that case I think we can say that our business is concluded," stated the Director. That was it, it was as easy as that. David couldn't believe his luck. The man proceeded to take out an expensive-looking cigarette lighter from his jacket pocket and lit up a cigarette taken from a slim silver case. With the lighter still in flame, he singed the bottom right hand corner of the letter with it. David could see his boss's signature curling into smoke as the Director held the document at arm's length like a venomous reptile. He pressed the buzzer with his other hand and his personal secretary came in, quickly assessed the situation and immediately returned with a large heavy ashtray of dark wood that was obviously not of the Director's collection. She moved effortlessly out of the door and soon returned with a perfume vaporiser that she pressed into the air above the table. David was impressed by the efficiency of it all. A smile had returned to the Director's face.

"So," he was saying, "I think we can say that our business is concluded. Thank-you so much for your trouble, Mr. Selbourne, it has been a pleasure."

He pressed the buzzer again.

"No, it's I that have to thank you," replied David, "I don't know how I could have got through this without you," he said.

"It is most generous of you to say so," said the Director, "But completely unnecessary. Now, if you have nothing else…"

"Nothing else," echoed David.

"I have some matters to attend to," continued the Director.

"Yes, of course," said David apologetically, removing the cold cup of coffee from his lap as he got up from the creamy sofa. "What about the briefcase?" asked David as he was being reunited with his coat.

"Briefcase? Now what briefcase would that be?" asked the Director as David was being shown from the room.

"Ah, yes," said David, "I quite see what you mean."

And with that he was escorted from the room.

"Good afternoon to you, Mr. Selbourne," said Mrs Barona as she escorted him to the lift, "I hope you will enjoy what remains of your stay in Argentina," she said to him in Spanish, "Are you planning to travel anywhere in the country before you leave?"

"Yes, yes, I think I must," replied David.

Eva Barona again thought the man a little strange, but said nothing. The impassive face of the guard greeted them as the doors of the lift opened.

"Goodbye," she said as the lift doors were almost fully closed and with a whoosh he and the guard descended towards the ground floor.

"Ramirez, make sure the American gets into one of our cars," said the Director to the guard via his ear-piece as the lift was still descending, "Tell the driver to take him to the Hotel Espléndida on Avellanada street. Please inform him that arrangements have already been made for his stay here in the country."

"Very many thanks," said David in an attempt to counter the guard's excellent English with his own Spanish after he'd been informed of his agenda, "Thank-you."

David hadn't been sure of the arrangements following the meeting and was pleased to see that everything had been taken care of. He was still trying to work out what significance the burning of the letter had as the doors of the plush saloon were locked electronically and the tinted windows slid up. Why the briefcase had become so unimportant now he really didn't know. The driver nodded to him in the mirror as David raised his gaze to his and quietly and effortlessly the city slid away on either side of them. The driver's movements were careful and precise; he changed gears as if he were slicing an elegant wedding cake with a silver skewer. David felt like something of a celebrity and if it weren't for the fact that his watch was missing to remind him that something had gone wrong, he would have felt perfectly at ease.

He affected nonchalance as he attempted to see out of the tinted passenger window but secretly the matter of the briefcase was troubling him. Yes, the report bore his signature; no, it didn't make reference to his contacts here in Argentina; no, it wasn't in his possession any more. The Director seemed confident in his affirmation that their business was concluded, as he had put it, but deep down David didn't really feel that their meeting had resolved all the issues. Certainly, his superiors back in the States would expect a more successful outcome, he thought to himself. He stretched out in the back seat of the saloon and allowed himself to reach his arms along the top of it, where he could still feel the sun a little. His baggage had been sent on ahead of him directly from the airport. In any case it was only one small case, just the bare minimum and David had been instructed to buy any garments necessary on his company credit card, "If the going gets hot!" his boss had joked with him.

He was missing his bathroom stuff though, that would have come in handy now. There was a schedule for the operation but David was to leave the logistical aspects of it to their contact in the local country; that meant the Director. But the Director hadn't read the report. He couldn't know the procedure. He was to handle it through his people and David was to have given him the game plan, so to speak. It wasn't unusual that David didn't know the name of his contact, things were often like that. The Director had seemed very confident about things, though, and the fact that David was finally travelling in a car which moved quietly, without violent movements, and which was driven by someone who treated it like a precious object made David feel assured that things were finally taking their correct course. The driver knew where he was going even if David didn't.

'Let somebody else take the strain,' he thought to himself, 'Things have been stressful enough as it is. It'll be nice to take a bath and relax before I'm told what's going to happen next. In any case, the guy down here seems to have got things under control; it wasn't my fault that my briefcase was stolen and he, at least, seems to be aware of that. Why, he even asked me what briefcase I was talking about. He even asked what briefcase I was talking about…!' he repeated to himself and laughed inwardly.

As he was doing so, the car glided up to the small forecourt of an old but elegant-looking hotel and came to a gentle stop. As he had no luggage with him, the driver simply handed him a card which had the name of the company on it and which he understood he was to present at the hotel check-in. The hotel porter had no bags to carry but charged David for accompanying him to the check-in anyway, waiting with him whilst he picked up his key from the hotel receptionist and escorting him upstairs in the lift whilst they both looked for David's room. David found the door that matched the number on his key before the porter did, but nonetheless paid him for his efforts. He was dying for the bathroom and dispensed with the man as quickly as he could. The receptionist downstairs had told him not to worry about the paper work and that it could be filled in later on in his stay. David didn't really know how long he'd be staying at the hotel, but anyway, it was good of the man not to even ask to see any documentation. Things certainly had been taken care of. Just as efficiently, he found his small but expensive suitcase waiting for him on the made-up bed. He unlocked it and opened it, peeling back a corner of a shirt as he looked for his watch, but of course it wasn't there.

He rubbed his left wrist with the fingers of his right hand in a circular motion. Something wasn't quite right, he decided. Some tall blue flowers needed rearranging in a vase on a side-table where the sun cut in through the window and the half-drawn curtains reached down to the floor.

'Irises,' he thought to himself as he straightened them. There wasn't much of a view through the window as he peeled back the curtain further to take it in. He looked out onto the interior yard of the hotel and down below at an angle he could see the distinctive black saloon that had brought him to the hotel. The driver was leaning against the car smoking a cigarette. There were discreet ornate bars outside the window so that nobody could get in, but David opened the window on its in-swinging hinges to let some fresh air in. He went to the bathroom and opened the taps to the tiny sink wide open; as he did so, he remembered that he needed to go to the bathroom.

'It's nice to be where you're supposed to be when you're supposed to be there,' thought David. The water in the basin was fresh and cool and snapped him out of his trance as he splashed it over him. "It isn't so much what's going to happen as when it's going to happen," he said out loud; for David was smart enough to know that his contacts here in Argentina hadn't finished with him yet. Something else was bound to happen, of that much he was absolutely certain.

'No, I'm not here for no reason. There's a reason these people need to keep me here. They know whom they're dealing with. And in any case,' he continued, sitting down on the bed in front of the mirror which was to one side of the flowers, 'They need the details in that report from me, otherwise they haven't got anything.' What he was beginning to realise, however, was that the Director, whilst giving off an air of supreme confidence, was pretty inept. If the man had really known what he was up to, then he'd have simply asked him for the details of the report verbally. He was the one who had the answers, not the Director. How stupid he'd been. Hadn't he realised that the solution was right there in front of them?

David saw that he'd been observing himself in the mirror without having been conscious of it. He saw the pale blue of his shirt against the dark blue of the irises; he discerned the mid-shade of blue of his own eyes looking into his eyes from the other two shades. Sometimes you can do that, it just takes a little longer to look at things than you're normally accustomed to, but sooner or later it's possible to see how things really are.

CHAPTER FOUR

"They come up through the water. When the moon is on it they swim up to the surface to catch the flies and then retreat to secret places deep inside. Sometimes those that are skilled and understand their moods can slip their hands underneath, tempting them into a trance from which they never recover. They breathe in our air but it is poison to them and they suffocate," said the old man, "But those that are caught under a full moon often have its death on them, you can see it along their backs, and they are thrown back into the pool. It is not good to eat such fish," he said.

David sat in silence, listening to the murmur of the fisherman's words like the ripples in the surface of the dark pool. They had brought a flask of coffee with them and told the old woman and David's wife they would be back with something to put on the table. Patricio had insisted that the coffee should be black and strong; no milk, he said, on a night like this. David admired the skill with which he wrapped and wove his snares around the hook and then cast them silently into the sleeping pool. His arm traced a motion like that of the willow tree blown back in the wind, elastic and unhurried and never seeming to overreach himself. The bait hit the water exactly where the old man seemed to want it to, but you could never tell when a fish would be lured to the spot. At least, David couldn't. Even after the fly had been cast and the silver hook had sunk into some far-flung corner of the motionless pool, Patricio seemed to be exerting his will upon the line. The pool was quiet; it was the action of forces upon it that temporarily disturbed its equilibrium, but the pool always absorbed them and returned to its trance.

The fisherman's movements had a beauty all their own. When the deep water swelled with the breath of the mountains upon it, he would breathe in and arch his arm into the air. As its cold sides slapped into the grassy banks the line would be flying like a silver thread through the air, before the pool sucked in and in doing so unwittingly swallowed the hook and the line that went spinning dizzily after it. "Plop," the lake would echo and the line would have been cast. David turned to the man.

"You must have been doing this for years," said David.

"As long as I can remember," he replied with his gaze still fixed on the spot where the line had entered the water, "I can't tell you how deep it is, but it's deeper than it looks," he said.

The man snapped the line out of the water to recast it just a metre or two from its original spot and "plop," the water echoed again. He seemed to do this almost without thinking.

"It's to do with the vibrations," he said to David at length. And then, silence.

"You have to feel where the right place is," he added.

The man went quiet again and David understood that he was not supposed to speak but to watch. That was what he was here for, to watch. And then the man said to him in a manner which caught him unawares,

"You have to do it without thinking."

The words echoed in David's mind; at least the sound of them did even if the sense of them didn't. David flicked his glance skywards and saw that the clouds had parted briefly behind the looming mountains. They looked much bigger at night, when there was only the starlight to frame them in silhouette or the moon to bathe their shoulders. The moon was out but it wasn't quite yet full. David thought of the white of his wife's shoulders when she wore a dress that revealed them, but it was like thinking of something that didn't belong to him; like something he could look at but not touch.

He was snapped out of his reverie by the sound of a fish leaving the water. David hadn't even noticed that Patricio had caught one and was reeling it in.

"Pass me the net," said the old man and David did so.

It flopped around wrapping itself more and more into the strings of the net, its body shuddering as it strained to breathe in more and more of the air that was killing it. David thought the process a little

51

cruel but Patricio was already knotting a fly on the hook again and had turned away from his catch. The clouds parted fully and the nearly full moon shone onto the bank where they sat. The fish had stopped trying to breathe but David sensed that it wasn't completely dead yet; after a couple of loud smacks on the bank it now seemed to be waiting calmly for its death. Patricio hadn't seemed in the least bit perturbed about its struggle, or that it might suddenly leap free of its net with one lucky movement as David had thought it might do at one stage. He half wanted the fish to do this, but would have been greatly disillusioned had it done so; much more so than Patricio would have been. David reflected on its muscular stillness and looked back out at the water. "It was just something you said," he said to the old man.

His companion didn't answer.

"I suppose it is possible to feel when things are right, isn't it?" David continued. He wondered what his wife and the old woman would be saying; what she would be saying about him. He suddenly wanted to be closer to her, not because he wanted to be near her but because he was frightened of her. He was frightened of her words. The old woman had said not to worry and that they could take as long as they like and damn the supper, but David's wife had asked him what time they would be back and not to take too long. The hotel owner had reached for a bottle of something on the shelf as he and Patricio had been leaving. Patricio had looked at his wife but had seemed to look right through her at the same time. David could feel the gaze of the old woman burning into them as they walked through the door.

"There's another one coming," said the man as his wrist flexed to tug the hook deeper into the fish and then spun to reel it in in spurts, stopping on occasion to tease the fish out of the water.

"If you struggle to keep them too much they escape," explained the old man. The man made a show of offering David the net to land the fish but he knew that the old man was quite capable of landing it on his own. David reached out and took the net. Patricio placed the fish inside it. Dinner is served, David thought.

"We'll stop when they have," Patricio said, "You are surprised that I just leave them to get on with it," he was saying to him, "But it is better this way."

It was strange to hear him speak so much, normally the old man just seemed to listen. His arm was already casting out into the pool again. David watched to see where the silver thread was trailing. He wondered how long the process would go on; when the spell would be broken. He hadn't asked to accompany the man on his fishing trip; it had simply been assumed that he would do so.

"My husband's going out fishing tonight," Maria had stated to David earlier on in the evening. David understood that she had told him this for a reason and wondered whether she and his wife had planned it in his absence whilst he was shaving for dinner upstairs. Without further discussion David had invited himself along with the woman's husband and after briefly mentioning to his wife where they were going, the two men had set off together. Patricio didn't seem to mind David's presence but neither had he looked for it. He simply accepted it. With his coat under his arm and a flask of coffee that the old woman had prepared in his hand, David had followed the owner's husband out of the building.

"Not all the fish are good to eat," Patricio said.

He was wearing the same sweater he wore during the day when the sun was shining hot in the sky. In the evenings when he served them their meals he simply put his white apron on over it. The jumper was in threads but the white apron was always immaculate. The fisherman prised the hook out of another fish that had been landed and tossed it back into the pool. He unscrewed the top off the flask, placed it in David's hands and poured some of the hot black coffee into it. He turned to David, temporarily,

"Take this," he said, "It'll help to keep you focused."

With that David lifted the cup to his mouth.

"Thank you," he said. When he'd finished it he poured his friend a cupful and handed it to him. For a moment Patricio let his rod rest on its perch in the water and took the cup that had been offered to him with both hands.

"It's going to be a cold night," he said to David, " Look how the clouds are parting. All the fish will come to the surface now."

He screwed the cup back on to the top of the flask, reeled in the line and then soon had it back in the water again, at a place a little bit farther out than the last, towards the centre of the dark pool. A smooth 'plop' was heard and ripples emerged from near the far bank where the rushes grew.

"You see? Now they'll be dancing."

David thought for a brief moment of his wife with Maria back at the hotel. He wondered what she'd be doing now. His companion stirred at his side.

"This one's a beauty, here she goes," and with that Patricio fought to reel it in. The man had become positively transformed now and was animated in his movements and in his speech. Maybe it was the coffee, David thought to himself. As the fish thrust itself flapping out of the water and was lured closer to their side of the pool, Patricio's smile began to grow.

"Wait until we show them this one," he said as much to himself as to David, "They'll have their dinner. She's a beauty."

David watched as the huge trout was pulled and tugged out of its pool, it gleamed silver out of the darkness of the water and thrashed as if it was never going to give in.

"You look as if you're afraid of losing her," said his friend, "Here, quick; pass me the net."

David helped Patricio slide the net under the writhing fish and between them they managed to raise it over and around their catch. It was a magnificent specimen. Patricio's face shone with the effort of it; there was something child-like about his features, David thought to himself. He couldn't help smiling to himself.

"This calls for a celebration," said the old man producing a large hip flask from his pack. He offered the strong tasting liquor to David to drink first; it was sweet but very potent. Patricio wiped his mouth on the back of his hand when he'd had his turn, the flask still clutched there and his gaze still fixed on the fish.

"It's been a while since I've caught one like that," he was saying.

"Yes, me too," replied David.

Back at the hotel, Maria and David's wife were laying the dinner table in preparation for their supper. The last remaining guests apart from her and David had left the day before but Maria hadn't seemed unduly preoccupied. She seemed to know in advance when people would be turning up. Patricio busied himself with his own affairs at the back of the hotel and in the kitchen. He never seemed greatly concerned about anything, but if he smiled much he did so largely out of view of the guests and out of the view of Maria. After Hannah had been fed for the last time the two women had raised a small glass to each others' health. David's wife had picked up enough Spanish by now on this trip to recognise the greeting and even to imitate it.

"*A su salud*," the old woman said to her as they were waiting for the men to return. They'd not said much to one another all evening, but what had been said they'd been able to understand perfectly. Of course, David's wife's Spanish was very limited and the old woman was far too fond of her own language to venture into the realms of another one. Yet they'd managed to communicate by smiling appropriately when one made a comment, or nodding their heads to one another. Much of the conversation had centred on the sleeping child. The old woman thought the little girl beautiful and a delight and this had touched David's wife; she knew the old woman was being sincere. Not once had Maria asked to hold the baby, so when the little girl had been offered to her she understood that it was because the mother of the child trusted her with the infant. Both women felt a deep glow of satisfaction and whatever obstacles there were that might have prevented the woman from attempting to learn the foreigner's language, had simply and effectively been removed during the course of the evening. Small children have a habit of doing this; they can secretly make adults speak their language.

Besides, Maria secretly thought David quite agreeable, always polite and never demanding in the way that some of these gringos with their wallets stuffed full of cash were. As for the woman, she'd thought her simple and uncomplicated. It wasn't her fault that she was married to an American.

They let the evening drift into itself, the pale orange on the underside of the clouds drifted into pink and then into a deep-hewn purple as the shapes and forms of the mountains behind the hotel became more prominent. The older of the two women leant forward,

"Sometimes you've got to stop seeing in order to be able to see more clearly," she said, but Maria knew that the woman wouldn't understand her words even though she'd decided to say them anyway. She gestured to the tumultuous peaks that looked so soft and gently-sloping during the day,

"They seem to be more dangerous at night, but really it's just that we tend to see them more for what they are at this time. Their dangerous side is always there," she swept her arm up to where the crimson-purple peak of the highest mountain began to show its treacherously steep rock face. During the day guests wouldn't think twice about setting off on a jaunt to see what lie 'beyond those hills'. David's wife wondered how long it would be before they returned. It was not that she was massively hungry; the dull fire of the old woman's liquor was still warm in her belly. It was just that she wondered what her husband was up to.

A little below the hotel, at a place in the river where it seemed to lose momentum as it flowed through the field and oozed into the pool made by the declivity in the land, David and Patricio were packing up their gear. Patricio had insisted on catching one more trout to take their tally for the evening to five, even though their real catch of the evening would have fed two people and some more. It had taken them some time to land the fifth after the giddy exhilaration of landing the big fish. They'd put the coffee to one side and drank the contents of the hip flask, sip by sip, as if in a race to finish and rush home with their trophies. The old man seemed particularly content that he would have something to show 'the women' as he put it, but really David understood that he was referring to his wife, Maria. He began to understand the equilibrium with which they balanced their marriage and saw that Patricio could do what he wanted to within the context of a grudging respect he and his wife had for each other, but which remained unspoken. David envied the man – he seemed to understand his wife. The old man's silence had been shaken off for good, at least for that evening. It wasn't that he was speaking more now that they retraced their steps up the gently-sloping track back to the hotel, it was that his humour seemed to have changed.

David thought of his daughter for an instant and imagined her sleeping. As he remembered her he was surprised at the recognition that she was his daughter and filled with love for her. When he thought of her sleeping he was reminded of his own age by her vulnerability; he wondered whether his wife would have put enough blankets on her and whether she'd hear her upstairs in her cot. But then he comforted himself with the thought that his wife was a good mother and that in any case Hannah usually slept soundly after she'd had her last feed. He didn't know that the two women had in fact passed the entire evening holding the baby alternatively in their arms.

When David's wife said "Café?" she got up herself to make it and left the old woman pleasantly ensconced with the child in her arms as the evening dipped into purple by the partly open window. They'd shut it properly when the night air had become too chill for them and when it was finally too dark to see the mountains clearly any more. Both women had enjoyed an evening without anything to do, just as the men had.

"Let her breathe it in, it's good for her," Maria gestured after she'd wrapped the sleeping infant deeper in the blanket, but the child's mother was perfectly content to let her do so; she was of the same opinion without having to say it.

"They'll be back soon," Maria said, pointing to the heavy clock on the wall.

"We'll lay the table for dinner, then," said David's wife, circling her stomach and gesturing towards the table. She was smiling. The old woman was smiling too. At the corners of her mouth the creases ran upwards in not quite complete circles, just like the moon that now shone on them and bathed the walnut coffee table between them in its light.

"It's nearly time for the full moon," gestured the old woman, "The wolves will be returning soon!" she made a gentle growling noise, not too ferocious so as not to disturb the baby, and both women laughed.

The fisherman was singing gently to himself as he and David made their way towards the lights of the hotel dining room. It was something about a young lover who lived high up and far off in the mountains and told of the difficulties the singer had in making his way up the mountainside to meet with her. David thought how Patricio must have been a young man once himself. The old woman hummed to herself quietly as she dressed the table for dinner. She produced two candlesticks with wax candles that had spilled down the sides and then lit them, one at either end. The women had already peeled and cooked a pot full of potatoes whilst the baby lay asleep on one of the sofas. Now they served some green beans with garlic onto the four plates and steam came off the butter that Maria had put on them in the night air.

"I'd better put a log on the fire," Maria gestured towards the open grate that was still smouldering but had been allowed to burn down. The two women had hardly noticed that it had done so.

"The old man's going to want to warm up his tired bones," she said, but as she did so she gestured towards the baby. Her relationship with her husband was private, however close enough she felt to another person to talk.

"Si," said the child's mother starting to feel the cold herself. The old woman smiled to herself that the foreign woman had spoken to her in her own language.

'What a pity that they're not staying longer,' she thought to herself, 'If you ask me, they still need to spend some time together.'

In his hotel room David's eyes were misted. He didn't know why he'd been remembering his trip with his daughter and his wife that time in Mexico, or maybe it was because he did that he felt uneasy.

They'd be coming for him soon, he was sure. He'd only got to wait for them and matters would be brought to a conclusion. He got up to look out of the window again and saw that the driver of the car was still waiting there down below, propped against it reading a newspaper. He couldn't see the man's face clearly because his cap was angled down obscuring it. David ran his finger against the irises in the vase. Then he lay down on the bed.

There was a small picture above the bed, encased in a dark frame. It depicted Christ on the cross, suffering for the sins of the living high up out of reach on the wall. It took him a long time to rise from the bed this time. Slowly he unpacked his small suitcase and hung his shirts and ties in the slim wardrobe. Out of habit he removed his shaving gear from the suitcase and placed the rest of his bathroom toiletries in the bathroom cabinet. He didn't know what to do next so he sat back down on the single bed. He must have drifted to sleep because when next he became aware of the room it was to wake to the sound of knocking on his door.

"Mr. Selbourne?"

He recognised the voice of the hotel receptionist from downstairs who must be on some errand or other.

"Yes, what is it?"

"I've just received a call from the centre. They say that they'll be coming to pick you up in an hour or so for a meeting with the Director. Would you like me to bring you something to eat meanwhile?" asked the receptionist from behind the door.

"No, thanks."

The sound of the man's footsteps could be heard receding down the corridor. David got up and went to the door. It was locked.

He walked over to the window and peeled back the curtain, but the driver was no longer there resting against his car. David entered the bathroom and turned the shower full on. He undressed briskly and stepped in. He needed to cool down.

He was breathing hard. The water was drumming on his head, running down into his eyes and off his shoulders. It ran down his legs and disappeared down the plughole, spiralling anti-clockwise as it did so. Many things about the events of the last two days struck him as curious and he reasoned there must be some answer as to why the water went the wrong way down the plughole. He looked at his watch, half-expecting the hands on its elegant face to be turning backwards, but then he noticed the white strap-mark on his skin where it should have been and was reminded that he'd lost it. Or they'd taken it.

He rubbed his eyes to see more clearly through the rivulets of water running through them. She was standing on the other side of the curtain of water pointing at something but he couldn't hear what she was saying. She was pointing up at the mountainside at something and then she was suddenly covering her face. He couldn't understand. The volume of water passing over him suddenly seemed to swell and in an instant he was knocked off his feet.

David saw the small white bar of soap at his feet slip towards the plughole. He saw how it lodged against the mouth of the aperture and then got jammed inside it. It was being smoothed and flattened by the hot water and at any minute might be pulled down with it. He turned off the water abruptly, stepped out of the shower and threw his clothes on without drying himself fully. He grabbed his wallet and his passport and stuffed them into his pockets.

They'd left a painted wooden stool inside the bathroom and he placed it underneath the skylight. He touched his shirt pocket and felt José's card through its material. With a punch from the wooden shaft of the bathroom mop the skylight was cracked and soon he was clearing the glass out of the frame. David gripped the iron rim and pulled his chin up level with it. The ripped towel he had wrapped over his fingers turned red and dripped onto his shoe before spilling onto the bathroom tiles.

For a moment he hung suspended in the air; neither able to go up nor down. There was a loud knock at the door and two voices could be heard demanding to let them in. Soon somebody could be heard running up the stairs and down the silent corridor with a bunch of keys jangling. With an effort he pulled himself up, scraped through the skylight and started running along the flat roof. He didn't understand what was happening but he knew that he had to run. He had no time to think about the leap from the second-storey roof onto the flat-roofed garage that was separated by a narrow passageway, he only thought about it as his feet made contact with its surface, jolting his knees, and his hands burned.

The car was still there but the driver wasn't. He tore the remaining rag from his left hand and dropped down over the side of the garage. His feet skidded on loose gravel chippings next to the drainpipe but he made it to the car. The door was open and the key was still in the ignition. He slammed the door shut and in an instant was tearing out of the forecourt of the hotel, his hands glued to the steering wheel. As he sped off down the road opposite to the way they'd brought him he felt for the card in the breast pocket of his shirt; it was still there. His heart was pounding. He looked up into the driver's mirror to see if he was being followed but could distinguish nothing in the traffic flowing behind him. He didn't know where he was going but that was unimportant now. Then he remembered he should still be carrying a business card from his own home office in one of the credit card compartments of his wallet.

He'd sensed the danger before he'd become fully conscious of it and now dark thoughts were creeping up on him. The blood from the cuts on his hands was beginning to congeal and it was painful when he had to remove his right hand from the steering wheel to change gears. David made a conscious effort to slow down and drive more normally and as he did so he found himself slipping through the stream of cars more easily. He raised his hand to straighten the fringe of his hair in the mirror as he checked it but as he did so he left a stripe of blood on his forehead. He spat into his hand and erased it as best he could.

He only knew he had to get onto the open road, get some air, so he followed the signs that said 'La Plata' and eventually ran past the shipyards where the lorries seemed to be heading, trailing one with a particularly heavy cargo. What he didn't know was that he had also passed the ferries that would have taken him across the other side of the river to Uruguay. But he had no time to think of that now. He followed the truck round a large roundabout and as the truck gathered momentum coming out of it, so did David. After the building sites and warehouses faded away he found himself on the open road where a dense forest of pine trees ran down either side. He allowed the truck to get a little farther away from him and determined to keep a steady distance behind it.

They reached the outskirts of the city of La Plata after little over an hour and the truck took the ring road which by-passed its centre, picking up speed again after they had passed the patrol cars that lay in ambush; only their white noses visible in the darkening skies. Some fool had been caught and an officer was writing out a ticket, too preoccupied with his capture to notice David and the lorry leaving his territory. David wound down the window a little and breathed the air that rushed in, panting as he did so. His shirt and trousers were stained, probably his shoes too and he would have to find some way of changing them at some point. He looked into the mirror to see if anyone was following him. They'd be after him at some stage, he realised, but for now he'd gained valuable time. As he was thinking this, he heard a patrol car speeding up behind him, its lunatic siren screaming at him in the darkness. David took his foot off the accelerator slightly in an instinctive move as the white car lunged at him from behind. Then it was alongside him out of his side window as it roared on past, clearing other drivers out of the way with its moaning cry trailing blue in the night air. He was breathing hard and in deep gulps, but he'd kept on staring straight in front of him all the time.

Two minutes later he passed the lorry he'd been trailing. It was pulled over at the roadside with the police car nudging it from behind.

There was a strange moment of recognition between the lorry driver and David as the driver looked up momentarily as David passed. David neither slowed nor accelerated as he pulled close but one of his eyes was fixed on the speedometer as the scene blurred alongside; the other resolutely held out faith in the road ahead of him as it disappeared under his head lights. One of the policemen had been in the process of uncovering the tarpaulin on their bounty, the other was carving strokes into his clipboard, his head bowed to the glare of their car's head lights, making the process legitimate.

They hadn't noticed him and David wasn't about to do anything that would make them do so. He slunk into the right hand-side lane near the verge and tucked himself close to it. He was still breathing hard and he needed the air, but it hurt his lungs as he strained at its cold grip on the back of his throat. With his eye still on the speedometer he waited until he thought he was out of the patrol car's glare, then he lessened the pressure ever-so-slightly on the accelerator; making sure that the car did not lose speed in an abrupt manner and also that it was more than safely within the required speed limit.

'That was close,' he thought to himself and bit in to the cold night air again. For some reason he let out a laugh, but it was a nervous laugh that didn't fool him in the least; he had one eye still fixed resolutely on the road that was being devoured under him and one eye on himself in the mirror. There was no way he was going to let himself get caught. If he'd had a cigarette he would have smoked one, but David seldom smoked and he wasn't carrying any cigarettes with him now.

Three hours later, after quite a few more miles and when he was absolutely sure that the police were satisfied with their capture, or that they had abandoned it, satiated, he allowed himself to be lured into a side-road by the lights that were shining part way down its length. He reduced speed and crept down the dark lane with its bushes showing dusty under the glare of his headlights. So soon the hunted becomes the hunter. David was thirsty now and could feel his throat dry and tight. As he rolled up to the van with its open porch bedecked with the fairy lights that had attracted him to it in the first place, he caught sight of a public telephone at the corner of the lay-by. He needed to speak. After changing a note at the burger-van in exchange for an undercooked hamburger encased in a dry bread roll spitting tomato and mustard at him, David dropped the coins into the slot and prayed with all his will that José was home.

"It's me, it's David Salsa," he said.

"Man, where are you phoning from at this time of night?" said the taxi-driver recognising his client's voice. "You're at a hamburger stand on the junction turning off to Valeria del Mar?"

The taxi-driver had been astute enough to realise that David was a generous man, otherwise why else would he have offered to pay for the fare earlier on in the day when José had explicitly told him that David's company were taking care of it?

"Of course I'll come out and pick you up. No, I've got nothing else to do at the moment. You say you're at the two hundred and fifty-kilometre marker? You must have been driving for quite a few hours. Whose car is it anyway?"

"It's the company's," replied David truthfully.

"I see," said José, "So anyway, man, what are you doing eating some crummy hamburger stuffed with worms when you're only an hour and forty minutes' drive away from the best sea-food restaurant in Buenos Aires province?"

He laughed, although he was asking David the question seriously.

"I'll give them a ring and tell them we're on our way, I know the people. But it's going to be breakfast now, you realise that, don't you, Mr. Salsa? It's going to take me an hour or two to get to where you are. No, don't you worry at all, I'll find you easily enough. You say you're at a hamburger stand on the side-road just after the two hundred and fifty-kilometre marker for Valeria del Mar? Easy. I'll tell them to catch something special for us for breakfast!"

With that the line went dead and David hung up the telephone. He took his disgusting hamburger back to finish it off in the privacy of his own car where it was warm, out of the chill of the wind whistling across the wide-open plains. He mauled it a while then took a snatch at his bottle of beer; instantly its cold liquid contents felt like they were drawing blood from the back of his throat. Or maybe that was just his hamburger, its tomato ketchup slopped over the meat in uneasy fashion. David tossed what remained of the dry bread roll and its contents out of the side window towards the dusty shrubs as he reversed back down the road a little to wait out of sight for José. The rodents would have something to nibble on while he waited, he thought to himself, or perhaps it would be the birds that were more interested in what the night had to offer them, he thought, ironically.

José knew things had taken a turn for the better the moment his Mr. Salsa had told him to turn off the road under the fly-over. Here was a man with money who wanted to spend it. What could be better in life than being paid to drive out to the coast and escape that grimy city to pick up a passenger and take him for a meal? Of course, José knew that the best seafood to be had on the coast was in Valeria del Mar, away from the more high-profile spots such as Pinamar, where even the locals who flocked to their luxurious bungalows from rat-holes in the city were over-charged for second-class dishes. The man has taste, José thought to himself; he's trying to get to know the real Argentina. He was going to have himself a damn good meal and a damn good time, José told himself, and this time his passenger was going to sure damn pay for it.

"Listen, Maria, this is an important assignment, a special one," he told his wife as he was preparing to leave, shaving himself carefully in the bathroom of their two-bed roomed apartment. The children were both fast asleep by now and his eldest son, still only four years old, was tucked up in his blankets in his place on the living room sofa.

"You don't get many opportunities like this where you're assigned to a client especially because he's asked for you."

José had given David the more important of his two business cards; the one which had his home number on it and which allowed him to make some extra on the side without those bastard money-grabbing blood-suckers taking it all away from him. It was something that was understood between himself and his fellow agency drivers, though nobody but *nobody* ever spoke about it or commented on it. That would be giving the game away. It is a little-known but true fact that the flatlands of Argentina play host to one of the largest gatherings of vampire bats to be found anywhere in the world.

"If you ask me," continued José to his wife, who was berating him for waking up the entire household at this unlawful time of night, "This guy's somebody really important but he's trying to keep a low profile."

He tapped his nose.

"I knew it the moment I was sent to pick him up this morning. What? Of course I'm taking the keys to the estate, you're just going to have to use public transport like the rest of us to get to work in the morning," he hollered. "You can't expect me to chauffeur my client in a marked vehicle when all the poor guy wants is a bit of anonymity. I'm sure he's got some special meeting to attend out at this place and meanwhile he doesn't want to attract any attention to himself."

He tapped his nose knowingly, again.

"I can smell it a mile away," he said to his wife, "They'll be waiting for us there in Valeria, and I'm sure it'll be something special," he said with a twinkle in his eye while he finished the last of the precision strokes against his throat. Then he popped the silver-coloured razor back into its holder, picked up his best leather jacket and his sunglasses and made for the door. His wife had been cursing him silently all the time under her breath.

"So what time do you think you're going to be home?" she asked him, "Or will I have to send out somebody to look for both of you, do you think?"

"No, Maria, that won't be necessary," said José in his most business-like tone of voice, "I'll be taking care of things properly. This is an important job, don't doubt it for a second," he announced in a way which left no further room for discussion. He kissed her on her cheek in a bold, chivalrous gesture as if she was his lady and he was leaving her behind in his castle to go off and fight a holy crusade that would ensure their permanent security.

"Would you like me to bring back some fish?" he asked her as an afterthought as he strode through the door of the apartment in a flourish and out into the cold corridor of the sleeping building. Maria made a remark about him having a thousand mothers and slammed the door behind him as gently as she could.

"Just you wait until I get my hands on you, whenever it is that you decide to turn up back here, smelling of whatever. And what am I supposed to tell the people at the agency, hey, when they ask me where the hell you've got to?!"

She thanked her lucky stars again that he'd been born a son of many mothers and went to comfort her youngest son, who had woken, and who only had the one of them.

"One of these days she's going to understand what the life of a taxi-driver's all about," José thought to himself, "And then I'll be well and truly done for."

But José knew that there was a killing to be made this night; he knew also that his part in it was a vital one. His Mr. Salsa was waiting for him tucked in a lay-by a couple of hundred kilometres from here and he wasn't about to let him down. Taxi-drivers in Buenos Aires, as in most big cities in the world, are often rascals, but by no means more so than the people that feed off them. The role of the driver, the one who takes passengers from one place to another, is just as important as the role of the person who has to get to his or her destination. This is just the way it is with other workers elsewhere, simply carrying out tasks they are asked to perform in many countries and cities the world over.

CHAPTER FIVE

"Wake up, Mr. Salsa, it's me, José," said the voice.

It was three o'clock in the morning and David had been sleeping uneasily in the car for the last four hours. At one point he'd been disturbed by some noises in the bushes, against which he'd pulled in the car in an effort to camouflage it, but then he'd remembered the half-eaten hamburger he'd tossed into them. Each time he woke up he'd turned one eye towards the clock inside the car and had been comforted to be able to measure his anxiety in minutes and, more slowly, in hours as the night wore on. David was used to having schedules and although this didn't necessarily mean that he knew what to do within a certain time frame, it did mean that he knew where he was supposed to be at any given time. The hamburger van had obligingly trundled off elsewhere soon after David had dispensed with its services, and its magical fairy lights, which had signalled a kind of refuge previously, had been replaced with a thousand fairy lights in the sky. He heard the scurryings and scamperings of many night creatures as they brushed against the dry vegetation and curiously they seemed to have a particular relevance to him. He was reminded of his own close brush with the law back on the highway. But he was certain he hadn't been doing anything illegal.

"Wake up, Mr. Salsa, I'm here," said José and in an instant David was staring him in the eyes. It took him a while to recognise the man but then he remembered where he was.

"I heard voices further back down the road, whispering. Come on, it's not safe to be hanging round a place like this at night. You never know who might be prowling about," said the driver.

"José," said David, thankful that his driver had finally turned up.

"What do you want me to do with the car?" asked José.

"Drive it," answered David, earnestly, "I'll pay you, of course."

"I mean the car you're sitting in," said José.

David had a spot of quick thinking to do and into his mind came the idea of driving the company car further down the road, perhaps close to the sign for another town or village if they could find one. But then he realised that he wouldn't be able to explain it to José.

"Oh, we'll just leave it here," said David, not quite sure that it was the best thing to do. In any case, he couldn't explain every detail of his exploits the previous day even to himself.

"Say, Mr. Salsa, what are those marks on your forehead?" asked José. David glanced up into the driver's mirror and realised with horror that he'd not completely erased the marks he'd put there as he'd been fleeing the hotel.

"Oh, I cut myself in the bathroom," he answered, not untruthfully and then he added, "Quite badly, actually."

José was looking at the man's shirt as his passenger climbed into the car. Something didn't quite add up, but who was he to ask questions? The man had obviously had enough of the city and quite frankly, he couldn't blame him.

"You're in safe hands now, Mr. Salsa," said José.

"David," said his passenger.

"Yes, of course," said his driver, "Just you lie back, we'll be there in time for breakfast," and with that David closed his eyes.

One hundred kilometres further on as José caught the first breezes of the sea wafting into the air, he pulled over the car and stopped to light up a cigarette. Night was still over the sleeping plains but there was a sense that further out across the coast to the east, dawn was already stirring. It'd been a while since he'd been to the coast; in his line of work he barely got the chance to go anywhere these days. Time had become precious to him even though he didn't have enough of it to realise it. The foreigner had soon fallen asleep in the back of the car and from then on he'd taken his driving steadily, slowing up and enjoying the drive. There were about another fifty kilometres between here and Valeria. He switched the engine off so that its dull purr faded away.

'It's always morning somewhere else,' he thought to himself, surprised at this understanding. Although it was now approaching five

in the morning, José was more awake than ever. He preferred sitting
and watching the dawn grow big into the sky from out here in the
countryside than waiting for the noise of traffic to stir him in the town,
out there on the coast. In truth, José's real alarm clock back in the big
city was the early morning rumblings and machinations of the traffic.
People there seemed to get up earlier than ever these days but he wasn't
conscious of just how much his own body had grown accustomed to
responding to the city. As the commuters swarmed into their hives in
the city, everyone desperate to beat the rush and without realising it
contributing to it as well, so they obliged everyone else to break their
night-time reverie.

'Night's a good time,' José thought. He hated the mornings.

David woke to the whistling of his driver as the scent of the sea
flooded his nostrils.

"I hope you're not too cold there in the back," said José, "I thought
you might like to get some of this fresh air."

The breeze streaming in through the car's slightly open window
was pleasantly chill on his face. At some time during the night José had
put a blanket on him. As a matter of fact, whilst José had done so he'd
thought of his own child wrapped up back at home on the living room
sofa. He'd been glad of the company although his passenger had been
asleep.

"We'll soon be into the town," said José, "It's a pity you missed the
dawn earlier on, but I didn't want to disturb you."

"Thank-you," said David.

He was starting to feel like his old self again.

"I love these mornings," said José, enjoying the conversation,
"It's like you don't know what's coming round the next bend until
you see it, but in a nice kind of way."

David felt a glimmer of recognition but said nothing. The driver's
words were having a soothing effect on him and he let him continue
talking, glad of the man's company.

"You should have seen how the skies turned orange, but far, far out
there over the sea. You can't see the sea, of course, but you can feel it
coming nearer as the morning gets lighter."

He stopped, slightly embarrassed.

"No, go on," said David.

"Well, what I mean to say is," said José, but his words and his poetry were disappearing as he became conscious of them. Still, he was happy.

"So, Mr. Salsa, what are we going to have for breakfast this morning?" he asked his passenger, rubbing his hands on the wheel.

"David," replied his passenger.

"Oh, right, yes, of course," said José.

"Well I think a new shirt and some trousers are in order," said David and as he did so José wondered what it was they'd been talking about.

As they approached the still-sleeping town the car started to go downhill. You wouldn't realise it if you'd spent many hours driving over the vast plain that constitutes for the most part the geography of Buenos Aires province. But as you start to go down towards the coastal towns that lie fringed on the shore, you suddenly become aware that other landscapes also exist. There must be many other plains and many other coastlines in the world, but it's easy to forget that as you drive across the Pampas of Argentina; it's just simply that your perspective is further out to sea at night. It was hard to tell which were the lights of the town gently being switched off and which were the dull fires of the still-smouldering night sky as they drove down into the town. The dry grasses in the sand dunes whispered words of morning and all about the arm of the coastline grew bigger.

"I've got some spare clothes in the back," said José, "I didn't know how long we'd be staying. You must be about my size."

They were the first clients in the restaurant and had time to appreciate the fullness of the morning's arrival with the waves crashing on the beach just in front of them. José had kindly let David change in the car whilst he got out to smoke a cigarette and survey the town from above, savouring the last remnants of the journey before the town was finally upon them. The clothes could have been almost made to measure and the jeans, casual shirt and smart sweater that David now wore almost made him look like an Argentine, albeit an Argentine on holiday. The thick leather belt at his waist in particular made him look like he'd been in the country for some time; the gold-coloured buckle in its centre was almost a badge denominating national status.

"Thank-you, José," said David when they were seated in the restaurant looking out to sea, "I'll replace this stuff for you. We'll do some shopping, okay?" he said.

José wasn't totally convinced that he'd be relinquishing ownership of his belt so easily, but the way his passenger said things wasn't in any manner presumptuous and José decided there and then to make him a present of it. After all, the American would be paying for his meals as well as his clothes, he'd decided.

Smells were wafting in from the kitchen, the boat had long-since been emptied and only the gulls and other sea birds picked around its edges.

"La Ventola" read both the paint on the boat and the sign above the entrance to the restaurant. The place was renowned for its fish and the exquisiteness with which it was prepared. They took their time to choose from the menu, José stopping to explain as best he could exactly what each dish consisted of when David asked him. José was enjoying his new job of translator and part of the work definitely consisted in helping to explain his beloved Argentina to the foreigner. This more often than not included comments about the landscape in front of them.

"This sea is a big sea," José explained to David, stretching his arm out to match the slightly curving sands, "From back there on the way down you can see that the whole area," here he made a gigantic sweep, "Is actually one big bay, but from down here it is difficult to appreciate this fact."

José was pleased with himself. David, in turn, felt like he was beginning to understand. There was much truth in the man's words and it was possibly this that had led him to have confidence in him in the first place. Two strong aromatic cups of black coffee had been brought to replace the two they had already finished, this time with some fresh croissants and butter. They hadn't even really got down to the job of choosing from the menu yet. David finally decided on the 'lenguado a la basqua', with the help of his assistant, whilst the other man asked for sea bass. It wasn't unusual that the restaurant owner came to their table to attend to them personally, especially as morning was the time that the owner liked best, when he could take his time over things, prepare his dishes they way he liked to and exchange a friendly word with his morning regulars. These included, of course, the town's chief police official, the council delegate for the area and one or two other assorted professionals such as the doctor, the dentist and an occasional hotel manager. He knew that they came to spy on his recipes and they knew equally that they couldn't compete with them. Neither was it unusual that the restaurant owner, Don Pepe was offering them a bottle from one of the finest selections of white wine to be found in the area; those that had the money to spend it in this town did so gracefully. The police chief never failed to tip heavily, for example.

"So, what brings a gentleman like yourself to our modest fishing village?" Don Pepe asked David as they were tucking into their food.

"We're here to make a film," said David and José was blown away.

"Ha, you had me there for a minute," said José later as David and he were strolling into town to look for clothes and other provisions.

"No, really," said David, "I'm here to choose locations and you're going to help me," he said with confidence, "If that's alright with you, of course," he added.

José made a quick phone call from a public telephone booth to his wife in which he could hardly contain his excitement, and then fell in silently with David as they walked down the town's main avenida.

"I noticed back in the car that you had a fine eye for landscapes," David was saying to him, "And that's when I decided that I was going to ask you to be my assistant on this case."

David had never been more imaginative in his life.

"Before you ask, it's to make an advertisement; publicity, you know?"

The words were falling like grains of sand tossed dizzily into the sunshine before José's eyes. He'd immediately put on his sunglasses the moment David had informed both him and Don Pepe that the two of them were making a film.

"I decided that I needed somebody who understood the area," he made a sweeping gesture of his arm, "And I realised that the one man I knew here that could help me with all of this was you," he said not untruthfully.

"Maybe one day they will make a film about all this," he thought to himself. He knew that he could count on José. He had plenty of money in his wallet and he knew that money or even the slightest hint of it bought loyalty the world over.

"We're going to have to replace your clothes," said David to José with his hand on his belt buckle. They were standing in front of one of the town's preposterously expensive boutiques, the kind of place which there was no more room for in one of the flashier places to the north and south of the coast from here. José had thought that his leather jacket was more than up to the task and felt a little insulted, but he said nothing. He checked his sunglasses in the shop window before entering the boutique and David entered after him, on his heels. It didn't take long for José to decide on a replacement outfit, but here and there he consulted David as to his choices. David nodded in agreement as José produced a slim new pair of jeans with a conspicuous label, a flowery shirt of the type that only the tourists wore and a sweater that was almost identical to the one that David was wearing. David himself bought a replacement pair of sunglasses.

"That'll do just fine," said David as he handed over the cash for the merchandise, making sure that the beautiful young sales assistant didn't get a look at exactly how much he was carrying. José noticed the gesture and kept his normally chivalrous remarks to a girl like this to a minimum as he paid her for the garments at the counter. David had learnt by now that his Argentine friend liked to pay the bill wherever they went and he'd taken care to make sure that his money went into José's hands back at the restaurant before it was given to the restaurant owner. He did exactly the same thing here. Both of them needed to feel good about their roles.

José had decided to change into his new clothes immediately, it transpired, and suitably attired he and David left the shop and the smile on the lips of the stunning young girl to go and look for an appropriate location here on the coast.

"It's a big country, this country," José was saying as he flung the boutique bag containing his old clothes into the rear of the car, "We may have some travelling to do," he said.

"Then let's get out of here and go and find it," said David, "Where do you suggest we head for?"

"Well, I have a cousin a bit further down the coast in Mar del Plata," said José, "And he knows everything there is to know about Argentina. Perhaps he can put us up for the night, we can save costs that way and leave a bit more money left over to really see the place properly," said José who was getting into his role.

"Plata means money, doesn't it, José?" asked David.

"Yes it does," said José and both of them laughed at the joke.

It was a long drive that afternoon but they'd tacitly agreed to make it longer and stop at places that caught their fancy along the route. They stopped to enjoy an ice cream at an ice cream parlour along the way, having first made a detour into the exclusive little town with timbered constructions and guards at the entrances to the even more exclusive residential areas.

"What about this place?" said José as the car was already turning off the main coastal road towards the wooded town of Carilo.

"You're the one doing the driving," answered David and from that moment on José knew he'd done the right thing in accepting the job. 'The agency be damned,' he thought to himself as they were nearing the outskirts of the splendid little town, 'I can get a job anywhere I want to. There are thousands of agencies that need good drivers in that tinselled town. I'll choose whichever one I want when I get back.' José was starting to realise that there was more to his job than just the driving; his skills as a translator of local customs and culture were important to his clients and he knew how to dress properly for the big jobs.

"Here they serve the best ice cream in the world," José informed David as they pulled up outside the ostentatious-looking ice cream parlour where over-indulged housewives and their over-fed husbands languished at the counter.

"And of course the place has one of the best sweeps of sand on the coast," he said, tapping his nose, "We can take a look afterwards, if you like," added José, courteously.

"Yes, I think that'll be most agreeable," commented David, wondering which of the many, many flavours he would choose from.

"If I might suggest," said José, demurely, "They do an excellent raspberry ripple at this establishment."

"Yes," said David, "That'll be just fine. I'll take a raspberry," he said in his best Spanish, "What will you be having yourself?" He enquired.

"I've already tried the raspberry," replied José, "I think I'll try something else for a change, perhaps a rich dark chocolate one."

He thought of his wife back home in her tattered carpet slippers

74

and curling-rolls and decided that he'd definitely be trying a dark chocolate one this time round.

"Are there many people of, you know, colour, back where you come from?" he asked David.

"You could say that," answered David.

"Yes, I see," said José, realising why it was that his boss hadn't been interested in the chocolate ice cream.

His thought of that morning in the early unguessed-at light that it was always morning somewhere else, came back to him now as he bit into a particularly rich vein of chocolate chip. His boss seemed to be enjoying his ice cream just as much as he was his. He wondered how many days you would have to travel in order to catch up with the sunrise but then something inside him sensed that you could never catch up with it. It would always be there, one step ahead of you. José had a profound philosophical insight which made him flush as red as the veins of raspberry sauce rippling through his client's ice cream.

"Ha, that's funny," he said, disguising the real reason for his blushing, "I've just realised, your name, Mr. Salsa; Mr. Sauce, just like your ice cream," temporarily forgetting his role.

"Or just like ketchup," said David, ominously, "The kind of stuff they smear on meat to make it more palatable."

His line had a resonance to it that killed the conversation dead. David hadn't been particularly offended by José's words; it's just that he, too, had had a profound philosophical insight.

Back in the car José sensed that it was going to be a long journey. They had tacitly agreed to leave the viewing of the beach to another time. Soon they would be on their way to Mar del Plata. As they sped away from the sleepy woods and the chalets hidden in their midst, a few toppled pine trees could be seen in the clearing, lying like spent matches on the sandy track where David and José's car had thrown dust into the air. An observer perched in the treetops would have seen the sun's echo on the dark blue rear of their car before its presence there was nothing more than a memory and the hum of its engine had disappeared once more into the distance.

Back on the open road the breeze streamed through the windows.

"So, where's it to be, Mr. Salsa?" said José, already knowing the answer to his question.

"I think Mar del Plata might be what we're looking for," said David, absent-mindedly. They were in this thing together, now.

"Yes, I know some great places there, you know," said José, "And my cousin will help us out as well," he added, "In any case, he owes me a favour or two," he said.

It was a long time before either of them spoke again. The miles passed and stretch after stretch of road swam through stretch after stretch of open flat land. It wasn't until they were nearing the faintly rising line of hills that rose barely tapering out to meet the sky that they became aware of each other's presence in the car again. José had resumed his role of taxi-driver and with it his customary way of speaking.

"I'd better pull in at the first gas-station we reach," he said, "The tank's getting empty and I have to make a call."

David nodded his consent and soon the air of the open road was replaced with the smell of gasoline and the worn rubber on the tyres of trucks that had travelled long distances. David got out to stretch his legs. They'd been driving for a long time and he was beginning to feel the miles. José ignored the emblematic sign of the cigarette on a white background with a red cross painted over it and instead lit up his cigarette and drew on it heavily, the smell of its smoke and the fumes of diesel mixing in his lungs. The drivers of the lorries were doing the same whilst lounging in their cabins reading newspapers or propped against the open doors of their vehicles idly chatting to one another.

"I won't be a minute," he said to David as he went inside the adjacent cafeteria. The waitress inside went about her work piling up plates and mopping up the mess on the tables without seeming to notice anyone. She had earned her anonymity through long hours fading into evenings and a stream of faces passing hers' that now seemed not to notice her, nor she them. She was quite pretty but the look on her face had become as vacant as the tables at the windows, where previously departed occupants had left behind their half-empty polystyrene cups and plastic knives and forks slopped with the remains of food. She could tell the character of a person from the way they left their utensils on the tables, but this was knowledge that served her little in her place of work and which she was barely conscious of recognising. Had you asked her, she would have been able to provide you with details, but nobody ever did. The only way she applied this knowledge in real life was to insist that her young daughter and her even younger son finish all the contents on their dinner plates and leave their knives and forks crossed on them.

"There's no problem," said José on emerging from inside the cafeteria, "My cousin will be glad to have us."

"No problem," repeated David, confirming what he'd heard.

"But mind you, that one is a real ladies' man and he's a devil for a party," continued José, "We'll have to watch him when we're out with him," he said with relish.

David wasn't really interested in José's cousin; not out of disrespect, but once you've seen one face when you're on the road they all become the same. Even the pretty ones in the roadside cafeterias seem to lose their sparkle, somehow.

David was thinking of his wife, but soon that thought was thousands of miles from him. He'd have to keep up the act somehow, he was thinking to himself. We'll, he'd got money and José didn't seem to be in too much of a rush to get back to the city. In the meantime he was safe. After all, what happened next was up to him and so long as he could present a convincing story no-one would suspect anything. The future was his to decide. He himself, however, was beginning to suspect many things.

"Jump in, Mr. Salsa, we've got some road to cover before dusk and our man is waiting for us."

The diesel fumes gave way to dust and the dust gave way to dry vegetation. When night comes in these landscapes it is often cold, especially so when the day itself has been warm. This is so much the case that the plants which dot the plains dry up and their leaves and stems become brittle with the cold at night. Nothing is ever completely unaffected by its environment. Everything lives in its own present; it is just a case of perspectives.

Thus David and José, both wishing to escape the city, found themselves back on the road leading them to another one. Soon the shining lights of the coastal town lay ahead of them.

"We can get anything we want here," said José to David, "We can stock up on provisions and look round the town a little to get our bearings."

"Yes," said David, "It's always important to know what you've got and where you're going."

José suspected that David wasn't talking simply about the location they were searching for, but the thought was too deeply buried in his conscious to trouble his immediate concerns. For his part, David's thoughts were occupying too much of his mind to allow him to focus on the details of the moment. David and José were both looking forward to arriving at José's cousin's place, but for different reasons.

"I'm not sure how much this is going to cost us," said José as they pulled up outside the apartment building where his cousin lived, "But I'm sure it's going to bring us some progress."

There was a wolfish grin on his face, but he was turned away from David and was looking up towards the window of his cousin Ramón's apartment. It had begun to get dark but José was still wearing the sunglasses he'd had on all day. He turned up the collar of his leather jacket and strode off purposely towards the ground floor entrance to the building. David followed him.

"Wake up, Ramón you son of a thousand bitches, it's me, José," he said in the usual manner, with his finger jammed on the buzzer to his friend's apartment. "Wake up," he said, "We're here."

On the intercom David heard the growling sounds of a man who'd either been fast asleep moments previously, or who was recovering from some terrible hangover.

"Your cousin sleeps at this time?" enquired David, slightly taken aback, "Is he an elderly gentleman?"

"Gentleman?! Well, I've never heard him called that before but I'm sure he won't mind if you do so. Lazy son of a bitch, he's probably got a steaming hangover!" he said and with that they were inside the building. David wondered what he was letting himself in for as the glass doors to the entrance closed shut behind them. He had a brief but faintly disturbing notion that he'd been here before, but before he'd had chance to dwell on it too much, they were already travelling up in the lift.

"Ramón's been waiting for us," informed José, "I told him a little about what we're doing but I thought it best if you explained things properly to him yourself."

"Thank-you," said David, not quite sure of what he was thanking him for or what he was going to explain.

The chain to the door rattled and then a key was turned in the lock on the other side.

"Come in," said the voice.

"David, this is Ramón. Ramón, this is David. We're making a film," he said, matter-of-factly. He was still wearing his sunglasses. The amber of the streetlights down in the street was beginning to glow against the windowpane.

"I see," said Ramón, unimpressed, "What do you need my help for?"

"David here will take the spare room- you still have the bed in there, don't you-," more of a statement than a question, "And I'll take the sofa," he said authoritatively, "This is an important job, Ramón, and I need to be able to count on you."

Ramón's index fingers and thumb came together in a crisp movement designed for José's attention.

"Of course, Ramón and plenty of it," said José.

It was apparent that a business transaction had taken place but David wasn't sure of the precise details, although he suspected that he'd be the one doing the paying.

"We're going to be in town for a few days and you're going to take us where we need to go," said José, puffing heavily on his cigarette, smoke curling into the fading light of the fourth storey room.

"My man Mr. Salsa here is American," he said, tapping his nose, "He's only after the best," he added remembering their meal of that morning in Valeria del Mar.

"What kind of film…?" said Ramón, becoming interested.

"About meat. The whole thing's about meat," said David explaining the reason for their visit with a dismissive gesture of the hand. Understood by Ramón. Big business. An American in Argentina mixed up with beef; got to be important. José, in command of the situation, exhaling smoke-rings the shape of zeros floating towards the windowpane. Ramón and David both seated, eyeing each other cautiously.

"David here will tell you what we need, when we need it," said José prescribing; in the driving seat, "What *do* we need, David?"

David, trying to find his words.

"I'll tell you what we need," said José, saving the situation, inventing it, "We need to see the real Mar de Plata. We need to get out there and look for the places that people don't normally see. It's no good taking us to the entrance to some flashy hotel that's been plastered on the tourist brochures…"

David becoming relieved. José continuing to explain,

"We need the harbour early in the morning where the fishing boats are. We need real faces and real people. We don't want the beach, do we, David? We want the refuse truck on the road beside it. You see what I mean?"

"Yes," "No," reply David and Ramón in unison.

"What have fishing boats got to do with cattle?" Ramón, the upstart, too clever for his own good.

"Precisely, what have fishing boats got to do with cattle?" asks José, more tentatively; silence in the air, questioning. José and Ramón, turning to David. The image of a boat drifting across a big, wide river swimming through David's mind. He's not quite fully formed the picture yet but he's beginning to grasp the idea. The distance between Uruguay and Argentina isn't so great. The boat is big; it can carry cars and trucks, as well as cattle – perhaps the cattle are in the trucks on the boat drifting across the river. Perhaps the boat isn't leaving Argentina but arriving there. David is sweating, begins to panic. He fights an urge to escape from the room. Ramón and José are now both sitting on the cramped sofa, one either side of him. José removes his sunglasses and carefully slips them into the breast pocket of his jacket. David feels for his wallet and his passport. Everything's in place.

"It's a difficult one," said José, answering the question himself, "Either we keep the boats in, or we keep the boats out. What do you think, David; in or out?"

"We've got to keep the boats out of it," said David, "I can't think what the hell good is going to come of us messing around with these bloody boats full of cattle."

The conversation ends. Night fades in. The three of them are left sitting on the couch staring at each other in the darkness.

All this talk had made David rather nervous and the discussion of the film they were supposed to be making had been a bit too realistic for comfort. José was a bit too perceptive, David thought and he wasn't sure if Ramón was to be trusted.

"So what line of business are you in?" David asked Ramón, breaking the tension. In the shadow Ramón looked at David but didn't answer him.

"You could say he's in the import-export business," answered José for his cousin as Ramón looked at him like he was going to slit him, "In any case, we're all in this together," said José.

"How about a drink, for starters?" asked Ramón.

"That'd be great," said David, "What have you got?"

"Whisky," replied Ramón gruffly.

"I'll have mine straight," said David, who hated the stuff, and José knew he was with the right man.

"It's Brazilian," said José by way of an explanation. David stuck his tongue into the drink in the heavy glass tumbler. It tasted like mouthwash.

"Whisky from Brazil, whatever next?" he said to them. And with that the image of a stream of boats full of trucks, all bearing snorting cattle from across the waters to Argentina's shores flooded back into David's mind.

"We definitely have no need to go down to the harbour," said David, authoritatively.

"Then it's settled," said José and the three of them simultaneously took a sip from their glasses. By now the room was in total darkness.

"What do you think of my idea about the refuse truck?" asked José, genuinely.

"I can see us ending up in one, but I'm not sure that that's where we want to be heading," replied David, "We ought to leave Ramón out of this," he continued, "It's not right to get him involved as well."

So the American was trying to leave him out of the picture, was he? However stupid they looked or acted, these Yankees were subtle bastards, he thought to himself; one could never be sure of their real intentions. He was the first American he'd ever met in the flesh, but so far he was living up to all the preconceptions he'd had of them.

'No wonder they own half this country,' Ramón thought to himself and then he decided that he'd sooner be part of the thing than not and smiled graciously at David,

"Please count me in," he said, "I've got expert local knowledge and there's no one who knows the ins and outs of this place like me," he said choosing his words carefully. The words 'ins' and 'outs' struck a chord with David and from that moment on he decided that Ramón would definitely be working with them. Now the image of the boat came to him again, but this time it was leaving the country.

"You might be of some use," David said more to himself than to the others and Ramón and José took another swig from their glasses. So subtly had David taken charge of the scene that Ramón, at least, felt his assessment of the man had been accurate. David looked at the contents in his tumbler. Whisky wasn't his drink at all and he let it slam down hard on the table without meaning to.

"How many boats would you say left this port every day?" he enquired. Ramón was embarrassed that the man was used to finer tipples. This man obviously knew his drink.

"It all depends on the day and on what's coming in," responded Ramón as he was returning from the kitchen with a bottle of the real stuff.

"It's not what's coming in but what's going out that I'm interested in," said David, flatly and somewhat tetchily.

The others mistook his anxiety for impetuosity and José too thought that there was a side to David that he had not fully revealed. There certainly was more to this man than met the eye. Meanwhile, David was thinking that his luck might be changing, at last.

It was around midnight when they staggered out of the small apartment. José had suggested they get some fresh air and David had readily agreed. He needed to get a perspective on things and the liquor was clouding his judgement. He needed to think but at the same time he dreaded the consequences of doing so. The more he'd thought about things up in the apartment, the more he'd wanted not to think about them. Ramón, too, had fire in his belly. Ramón didn't like people who drank too much and this American was downing everything that was put in front of him. David had confused Ramón's anxiety for hospitality and had felt obliged to drink what had been served to him. His host seemed a little dangerous but David had already realised that his passage out of the country might involve some degree of danger. If this was what he had to do to gain the man's respect then he had no alternative left open to him but to drink what was served to him like a man. Ramón for his part had vowed to milk the American for all he was worth; the man's shame knew no bounds and he'd drunk the best of his whisky. He said nothing to his cousin, José, but vowed to make the most of this meal ticket. Who did he think he was? He was trying to show how tough he was and drink him, Ramón de Alcátrada under the table. He didn't stand a chance. If he didn't have such a hangover from the night before he'd already have given the man a pasting. Ramón was determined to give the man his comeuppance in public; he'd show this American what Argentines were made of. Besides, he needed the fresh air, too.

So it was that the three of them stumbled into a club at midnight just outside of town where cheap drink and cheap women could both be easily purchased. They spotted David immediately. He was dressed in the clothes of a tourist and one of his sidekicks was wearing an identical sweater. The other they all knew but he tipped heavily and was able to get hold of cheap electrical goods without having to pay for import duties. The apartments of quite a few of the women there had the latest television screens, DVD players and powerful mini-stereos. The place was crowded with people and music and there wasn't room to sit at the tables.

Ramón calmly strolled up to a man and two women sitting at the best table near an open window. He bent towards the man's ear with a smile on his face and said something to him. It seemed as if he knew the man. Ramón was smiling good-humouredly and gestured towards both of the women. The man stood up immediately, beckoned to his friends and the small group soon departed, leaving the space to be occupied by Ramón and his friends. One of the women cast a disparaging look back at the group of men coming in to muscle in on her table. The man who had vacated the table was already outside with a grim look on his face and was turning his keys in the ignition of his silver Porsche Turbo as the woman with the mini-skirt and long tanned legs bent down to get into the tiny back seat of the car. Her companion tossed back her raven hair, spitting in the general direction of the three men as she stormed out of the door of the building, having stopped to pick up her fur coat from the bartender.

"Phew, would you look at that car?" José was grinning, "So what'd you say to the guy sitting at our table?" He enquired of his cousin.

"I simply told him that if he didn't move, I was going to offer his girls more money than he could and take them along with us for a ride afterwards," he said nonchalantly.

Ramón laughed out loud, loud enough to attract the attention of most of the people near-by who'd witnessed the incident.

"Hey, Rosa," he beamed across the room, "Come here. This is my cousin José and here's in town to make a movie with us. Order whatever you want to drink," he said, flashing one of the large denomination bills that José had passed on to him, "It's on the house!" He shouted with glee.

The girl ambled over to their table and was soon joined by two of her companions. Rosa removed her chewing gum and fixed it securely to the underside of the table as she was squashing up onto the bench beside them.

"So, what are you, American?" She said, addressing David directly.

There were more eyes on David than he wanted; even in his semiconscious state he was aware that they were attracting too much attention to themselves, though not through his actions.

"Sure he's American," answered José on his behalf, "He's here in town to explore all its charms. He wants to get to know the real Argentina," he said, slapping David on the back as he did so.

José fondled the breasts of the dark-haired woman sitting on his lap through the smooth wool of her jumper.

"So, what are we going to have, my friend?" drawled Ramón into David's face. David had had a notion long ago that it was time to get off the whisky, as he was feeling distinctly groggy.

"Coke," said David through the haze of the cigarette smoke and the whisky-induced torpor.

'Son of a thousand bitches,' Ramón thought to himself, 'He's not had enough with the whisky, now he wants to get stoned! Well, if he's the one who's paying…'

José had drunk steadily through the night but had been under no obligation to prove himself like the other two had and therefore was slightly more coherent. He clutched the dark-haired woman sitting on his lap and thought how difficult it was to find what he really wanted.

The American was obviously having a good time though and had really decided to let his hair down. David for his part had decided that he mustn't look too conspicuous and had handed over a bundle of notes to José soon after they'd entered the club, so that he wouldn't be seen to be paying for everything. Of course the women and Ramón had noticed it all. Inwardly, Ramón was fuming.

Rosa had attached herself to David; Ramón had been left with the oldest of the three women who had badly-bleached hair and whose ancestors must have never had a blonde hair between them. Ramón cursed out loud and ordered himself a double whisky.

"You want some coca, Da-vid?" intoned Ramón in English, showing off his prowess with the language. The girls were turned to him.

"I get you what you want, is no problem for Ra-món! I get ever-body what they want!" he said, in a magnanimous gesture that barely disguised his frustration. He tossed a fifty-peso note onto the table with contempt as he lit up a fat cigar.

Most of his goods came via way of the states, from Miami and had to be paid for with real cash: with dollars. Those who were privileged enough could simply fly their purchases back on the plane; if you travelled first class you paid no taxes, except, perhaps, a bottle of scotch you might inadvertently leave out on the counter at customs. Ramón was fed up of people who didn't have to pay taxes.

"So, David, you're making a movie are you?" asked Rosa in her syrupy Spanish. She might well have been from one of the other Latin American countries. David didn't look like he was in films and Rosa liked his quietness; he wasn't brash like that one who sat puffing ostentatiously at his cigar. He seemed to be trying to think something through. They were seated with their legs pressed against one another due to the cramped conditions of the table. As yet, though, he hadn't laid a hand on her and Rosa liked his politeness. For this reason alone she decided she would take his hand in her own; after all, she wasn't going to be left out of things. She looked straight into his eyes. His fingers were moist and warm and then he looked at her and he seemed to be really looking at her. This one was different. Most of them looked through you as if they couldn't really see you.

José by now had got his hand inside his partner's blouse and Ramón was so stoned on whisky and cigar smoke that half the contents of his glass were dripping off the table. He was running his finger along the wood where he'd spilt the whisky and was dabbing the end into the bleached blonde's mouth. He had one eye cocked on David and Rosa but he was determined to be seen to be having a good time. He whispered something into the mestizo woman's ear and she laughed raucously, turning slightly towards Rosa and David as she did so. Rosa was aware of all this and reading the unwritten language which she and her companions spoke she saw the jealousy on the face of the blonde woman. The foreigner remained wrapped up in his thoughts. She squeezed his thigh and made a comment about how nice the breeze coming in off the sea was. As she did so she slipped a finger inside a button of her pink blouse and undid it.

At the doorway to the nightclub the woman with the raven hair who had spat on the floor as she left earlier had returned and was signalling out David's group to a man who was with her. Rosa leaned further on David's thigh and suggested that they go upstairs where they would be able to enjoy the sea breeze a bit more. David looked into her green- brown eyes again and then found himself being led upstairs by the hand to an airy and not altogether disagreeable room. The girl threw open the windows to the sea down below and David allowed himself to lay back on the bed for a while.

"Here," said Rosa as she passed him a mirror with two white lines on it, "Ramón said you'd like some. This is for both of us."

Hardly realising what he was doing, as if in some vague dream of another place, the scent of the woman and the scent of the sea mingled together and David inhaled his share. The stars spun webs out on the ebbing tide and David reached into this woman's arms to find the peace he'd been looking for. He'd misunderstood Ramón yet again but none of that seemed to matter now. Nothing but the scent of the woman, the scent of the sea ebbing away before him and the vast open panorama that is the Argentine sky at night entered his thoughts. The stars had come out to witness this night and David could see how they changed in intensity, getting brighter and brighter.

He leaned over and was sick violently and couldn't quite get the smell of the cattle cramped and confined in their pens on the boat out of his nostrils; the air blew in their warm sickly-sweet odour and then David was making love to the woman beside him. Soaked from the water from the sink in the room and soaked from perspiration, David made love with the woman as if it were for the last time in his life. Thoughts raced into his mind and died with the same intensity; the stars pulsed and vibrated out on the sea and the snarl of the waves grew louder. Though the sea was flowing away from him and with it his passage to safety, the waves were clamouring for attention. The words the girl whispered in his ear grew louder and louder and for one moment, just one moment, David and Rosa allowed themselves to believe in the power of each other to undo the wrongs that had been done to them. Rosa was breathing softly now and her words were incoherent, still she looked like the child she was although she'd long since been a woman; for one moment, just one moment, David allowed himself to believe that he'd finally, finally found her. The child in David crept closer to Rosa, nourished his body against her; the sweat starved on their lips and eyelids and the night and the sea shook them to sleep.

CHAPTER SIX

The water was drumming in his eyes.

"David!" his wife was shouting to him on the other side of the curtain of water. As he fell to the ground with the force of it a huge rock that had been dislodged from above crashed into the pool in front of him, missing him by a only a few metres. His heart was racing, thumping in his chest. His wife's voice echoed in his mind and across the shattered surface of the pool, where only a steady torrent of water had penetrated it previously. He'd been slightly underneath the overhanging boulder which formed the lip of the waterfall and which had narrowly protected him from the rock-fall above. He gouged the stinging water out of his eyes but he couldn't see his wife for the force of the water that was beating down on him.

They awoke to the force of the minor explosion that ripped through the lower storey of the building, shattering the glass chandelier close to where they'd been sitting with Ramón and José only hours earlier. The bar had been practically drained of its customers when the explosion went off, but Ramón had succumbed to the lure of the whisky and the lure of his anger, which had grown like a hammer into the night. José had left the bar to take his girl to the car just moments before, the fox in him having decided that the time to leave was right. He hadn't wanted his cousin to muscle in on the action and had thought that he'd return to wake him up from his alcoholic slumber when he'd finished with the girl back at the apartment. At the same time, he'd pick up his client from upstairs. Ramón was slumped over the table with gashes to his head where shards from one of the chandeliers had ripped through the air. He was bleeding profusely and didn't look like he'd be regaining consciousness.

José had heard the blast seconds after turning his key in the ignition and for one instant had thought that the car had been wired. The whore opened the passenger door and ran away from the car screaming. Inside, the few hard drinkers that had remained in the club had been made sober by the force of the explosion; one or two had cuts on them and were walking around in a daze. A girl was sobbing to herself softly in a corner.

David gouged at his eyes but the aftermath of the explosion was still ringing in the air. Rosa was clutching her blouse to her breasts as she sat up in the bed, trying to cover herself up. Their hearts were racing, thumping in their chests. It was not quite yet dawn and the stars were struggling with the sea, wrestling with their light on its surface. Then there was the sound of sirens that seemed to come at them simultaneously from all sides; a whiff of smoke or something resembling gunpowder with a dull burning smell was being blown back at them through the open window.

"Come on," said Rosa, "It's time to get out of here."

They leapt out of bed and raced to put their clothes on. David was still wearing his pair of jeans although he had to zip them up and fasten the belt. He hastily buttoned his shirt at the middle as Rosa scooped up the rest of her belongings, stuffing bra and pants into her handbag. They left the room as Rosa was closing her handbag with the snapper, now out of the room and briskly walking down the stairs at the opposite end to where the blast had shook the building. She quickly teased down her skirt over her thighs and checked herself with one glance in the stairway mirror. Everything was in place, at least mostly it was. Trotting behind her David heard the moans of the all-night drunks getting louder as the wails of the sirens approaching became louder too. Rosa kicked open a door at the foot of the stairs and the smell of the lingering night flared up at them. José had been standing at the door of the car, one of the last still remaining in the gravel car park. His hand was glued to the door, the motor was running and the right-hand side passenger door was wide open to the night.

"Jump in," he said, "Ramón won't be going anywhere else tonight."

Rosa squeezed in through the gap made by the folded-down seat, pulling down her skirt over her bare legs as José's foot hit the gas pedal and the wheels of the car spun kicking up gravel.

"You okay?" he said, glancing up into the driver's mirror to meet the expression on Rosa's face, then glancing over at his passenger who seemed to be wrestling with something that was darkly floating out to sea.

"She broke her leg," said David, blindly.

"Woman, are you okay?!" José asked Rosa urgently.

"I'm fine, I'm fine," she responded and both she and José were left to ponder on the silence left in the wake of David's outburst.

Back in the car park at the entrance to the smoke and debris-filled nightclub, a waiter made a mental note of the license plate of the car as it spun out of sight and crashed headlong into the night. José's hands were locked on the wheel, his eyes penetrating the road ahead in an act of supreme concentration. Rosa was applying lipstick and touching up her hair, though here and there she jabbed it a little carelessly and had to wipe it off her expanding lips with the sleeve of her blouse. David was floating out to sea. The water was drumming in his eyes and his heart was screaming; she was nowhere to be seen, nowhere at all. Like a deep swell that grows and travels mysteriously with the urgency of the ocean, the blank space in his mind was gathering weight and pushing outwards at his skull.

"She's gone," he said blindly.

"What? What!?" Snarled José at the grip of the wheel.

And then silence, again. The black, widening expanse of the road grew into David's mind and forced its way into his reckoning. The sky of the night and the sea of the road flooded into one another and all that David could hear was the crash of the waves on the shore of the pool, delivering him back to himself.

"It's my fault," he said to no-one, "All of this is my fault."

"Shut up, man, will you?" José spat out and then softer, releasing one hand to squeeze David's shoulder next to him, "It's not your fault, Ramón had it coming to him I guess; he was drinking too much of his own whisky and not leaving any of his goods over for the rest of them. They don't like that," he said, shaking his head in an effort to comprehend exactly what crime it was that his cousin must have committed to offend them so much.

"I don't think we should go back to the apartment," said José, "Have you got everything with you?"

"What?Yes," replied David, checking his jeans to find his wallet still sitting there miraculously like a stone in his pocket and checking the girl behind him. His passport had spent the night in the boot of the car, along with José's bag of clothes.

"Where are we going to drop her off?" asked José as if the girl in the back seat couldn't hear them.

"I'm coming with you," she shouted back at the driver who had interposed himself between her and the American.

"She's coming with us," repeated David, blindly.

José swiped round at his passenger with his glance but David was staring straight ahead into the darkness.

"I'll have to pick some things up first," she said, relieved but also shocked to find herself volunteering to go on the run like this. But what it was she was running away from, or what it was it she was running towards she didn't know. Her heart was heaving and one look, just one look from the foreigner had suggested to her that here was a man she might be able to trust.

They pulled into a side street as they were approaching the outskirts of the town again and stopped to let Rosa go up and get her things. Quite what she was doing she didn't know, but it had to be better than running from one client to another, night after night seeing the same sad faces. It had been something on the face of the blonde who'd been with Ramón last night before all hell had let loose that had pushed her towards this decision. Her family members who were back in Buenos Aires weren't aware of what she did for a living, or perhaps they were and it was the shame of what she had to do, coupled with the shame of their being barely able to feed their own mouths, that kept them from speaking about it. The rent was long overdue and only the other night she'd had to move around the tiny flat in silence like a criminal when the landlord had come thumping on the door demanding that she pay him, or otherwise she'd be in trouble. Perhaps her sister suspected because Rosa never told her about a boyfriend or a love interest in her life, and her sister's husband was a hard-working, religious man who hustled the streets by day trying to sell sandwiches. The engine of the car was gently purring and Rosa looked anxiously out of the window to make sure that they were still waiting for her down in the street below. She quickly slipped on a pair of panties.

Throwing her life's belongings into one small suitcase and leaving the television set as payment for the landlord when he returned, she dashed out onto the outside staircase. She'd scraped her key in the lock on entering the flat and had had trouble opening the door because of her nerves. Now she simply left the door wide open so that the landlord would see that she'd moved on when he returned to demand her head on a plate; or worse. As he'd once tried to do when he'd had the stench of drink on him; insinuating himself against her and trying to creep his way into her room. It was no longer her home now, though, and it no longer mattered.

"I hope someone comes and steals the television set so that that pig can't make use of it," she thought to herself as she clattered down the staircase. Any second thoughts she'd had about trying to justify her place in the car by using it as collateral were swiftly dismissed. She had on her person a very small amount of money and one small suitcase, but as she was entering the car through the driver's entrance where José had stepped outside to smoke a cigarette, it occurred to her that the American hadn't yet paid her for her services. One look at him again sitting forlornly in the passenger seat told her, however, that it'd be unlikely that she'd be asking him for the money. He seemed to have much more important things on his mind and this was both a source of concern and a source of relief for Rosa.

"You can throw that thing in the back of the car," said José, stubbing out his cigarette with the sole of his shoe, its blue flame suddenly and insistently smothered as he watched himself do it.

"I'm not parting with this case," said Rosa, viciously, "It's staying right here where I can keep my hands on it."

She cradled it in her lap as if she were a child cradling a teddy bear.

"We've lost enough luggage already," said David, out of nowhere, surprising them both. The most logical thing to do seemed to be to return to Buenos Aires; José was anxious to get back and check up on his wife and kids. He was also anxious to get out of this damned port before those that had done what they did to Ramón realised they were related and tried to extract their revenge from him for whatever hideous crime it was that had been perpetrated. The pretence of looking for locations had suddenly worn thin, although it was by tacit rather than explicit agreement of the two men in the car. In any case, it was an alibi that both José and David could resuscitate whenever they felt like it; independently of each other and for different reasons.

Out on the side-road leading off from the road to Valeria del Mar, the abandoned car had been found. Back at the nightclub just down the coast from Mar del Plata, police were now questioning the waiter, who'd faithfully passed on the license plate number of José's wife's car. The raven-haired woman had gone back to the scene of the crime and was most helpful in her descriptions of the American and his sidekick who'd been wearing identical sweaters and throwing money about. This last detail was noted dutifully by the officer and subsequently conveyed to his commander-in-chief. If there was one thing the people in these parts had disdain for, it was a foreigner who thought he could circumvent the law by throwing money at it.

David was feeling tired with the excesses of last night and the weight of the day dawning on him. He'd climbed into the back seat of the car by accident after a brief stop at a gas station along the way and Rosa had taken it as a sign that her presence in the car was justified. She put her arm round David possessively as José regarded them in the mirror and Rosa brought her gaze up defiantly to meet his. José was once again the driver and his passengers were their customary silent selves in the back seat. He'd known all along that his brief escape from the city would have to end sometime. He'd only been gone a little more than a day and a night, but he could feel every single kilometre under his wheels. He wondered what his wife would be up to and how he'd explain to her about his cousin Ramón, and indeed whether he should attempt to do so. Rosa didn't know what kind of life she was heading to, but she was the luckiest of the three people travelling in the car; she knew what kind of a life she was leaving behind. She smoothed down David's fair hair over his temples and allowed herself to believe that only the moment existed, then another moment and then another moment. He was curled up to her, sleeping soundly with his head resting on her shoulder, curled up to her like he had done last night in that glorious bed with only the sea and the stars before them. Last night, Rosa had let herself believe; for the first time in a time longer than she could remember, she'd flirted dangerously with hope. That was before the explosion had killed all that, along with the one who paid for things with electrical goods, perfumes and alcohol; but then she supposed that he had to be paying his own kind of duties and maybe he, too, had failed with his payments. Nothing in life was free, everything had its price. Everyone had somebody they had to pay, she reasoned.

Now though she performed the greatest trick of all once more. She tricked herself into believing that she'd taken this decision to be here with these unknown men in this car, right now. She tricked herself into believing that she had no past and that her future was only the sum total of her present moments. She tricked herself into believing that her place in this car travelling along this road had been offered to her. She tricked herself into believing that the foreigner was a good man. She tricked herself into believing that he, too, was running away from something. She tricked herself into believing that what each of them was running towards but neither of them knew was something they shared together. It was a very dangerous game to play, but under the circumstances Rosa had very few other occupations with which to pass the time as the kilometres faded into memory and memory itself faded into nothingness.

José's alibi was wearing thin even to himself. He'd brought nothing back for Maria and the kids and the memory of the discovery of the sea that morning, so long ago now, was fast slipping away from him. He'd understood something on the drive down from the plains into Valeria del Mar, when he'd tucked his passenger up in a blanket on the back seat of the car and the mystery of the sunrise had held him entranced. For one brief moment, just for one brief moment, he thought he'd begun to understand something about the way he lived his life in the city; or rather, about the way it was being lived for him. That discovery was slipping away from him now and the harder he stepped on the accelerator in an effort to regain it, the faster it seemed to slip away from him. The more he tried to recall what it was that had made so much sense to him, the less sense it all seemed to make. And there was guilt, too. There was guilt at having left Ramón to his own devices just a few moments prior to leaving him forever. The dark-haired woman whose breasts he'd enjoyed had fled from the car in terror; he doubted he'd ever see her again. His passenger had come looking for locations to make a film and all he'd got for his troubles was excess baggage he'd have trouble explaining and membership of a club that would be harder to explain still. Maybe that's what it is to be Argentine, thought José. In this day and age an Argentine was lucky if he didn't have to sell his soul or hide out somewhere for having accepted somebody else's soul in payment. José thought for a moment about an article he'd read about the population of Vampire bats in the Argentine Pampas; or perhaps he was mistaken and it was Romania or somewhere else he'd read about; one of these under-developed countries. Didn't they have a dictator there as well?

David was dreaming in the back of the car. He was dreaming that he was taking a shower and that he'd suddenly had an inexplicable urge to flee, as surely as if his life had depended on it. He was dreaming that he was underneath a curtain of water and that his wife had been calling to him from the other side. What she was shouting at him was important but he only knew that it was important and not the reason why. He dreamt that he'd been in the arms of a beautiful young woman whose green-brown eyes flashed like the stripes in a piece of Tiger's Eye. He dreamt that he'd held her in his arms before the water had parted them and that the scent of her perfume had mingled with the scent of the sea. He saw the tide ebbing away from him and the cattle on the boat escaping safely to Uruguay before the explosion had caught up with them. As the tide drifted out many beautiful shells were left glinting on the beach behind; they were all different colours and sizes and each was more beautiful than the next. He stopped to pick one up and lifted it to his ear. It was the voice of his boss back in the office in New York, informing him politely that they were going to shoot him. He put the shell down and looked for another to listen to, hoping it would have another message he could hear.

"David, yes. I want to get out of here right now," and with that the line went dead. When he tried to phone his office back, he couldn't get through and the girl on the end of the line told him that his office no longer existed.

"That's impossible," said David, "You might as well be telling me that I no longer exist," he retorted.

"I am," said the efficient young woman on the end of the phone and then she started checking off a list of his character defects on a paper she had attached to a clipboard. His Spanish wasn't up to much so he could only answer 'sí' or 'no' and in any case he'd been led to understand that that was all that was expected of him.

"David, are you awake, darling?"

"Sí," he answered.

He was looking into the eyes of a girl as the car rolled along in the approaching storm. He had his head in her lap with the suitcase at their feet and she seemed to know him and to know where they were heading. He had a vague notion that they were carrying a small baby in the suitcase, but he dismissed this notion and drifted back into sleep back to his dream, which made altogether more sense. Sometimes, the further away you are from something, the more sense it seems to make.

He awoke again to a heavy sky above the metal of the car. As he looked out of his window, he could see cows lying down in the field they were passing. Brown bodies littered the grass as if they'd been tranquillised. He looked across Rosa to the other window and more cows were lying still in the fields; either they were asleep or dead. Seeing the spark of light flash into the sky before him he realised a storm was on its way. Under the weight of thunder the skies were amassing, menacing as they did so with their heavy buoyancy. The car travelled on in its eerie half-light filtered through the clouds.

"We should be there in a couple of hours," said José as a glint of light showed up the roof of a farm far off in the fields on their left hand-side. Of the three passengers in the car, he was the one who was most anxious to get back to the city. None of them spoke about what they were going to do when they reached it. For Rosa to do so would have meant uttering a future which was beyond her present grasp. For David to do so it would have meant relinquishing a past that he'd not yet caught up with. José was intent on focusing on the road ahead. Then the rain was pattering on the car, slowly at first with the first caresses of the storm. Now it was falling in heavy waves, rivulets running down the windows where David and Rosa looked out, and through it they were made increasingly aware of the other's presence. José, meanwhile, became less and less aware of his passengers. Flickers of light struck out in the landscape like silver tongues.

Rosa felt for David's hand and found it still there, pressed moistly against her own. She wasn't sure whether to press it tighter with her own hand or to loosen the grip altogether; she didn't want David to think she was cheap or that she was still pursuing their transaction from the night before. In any case, she had decided not to request the money that he owed her; it wouldn't have been right to do so under the circumstances. The agreement between them hung in the balance. It had shifted slightly, imperceptibly, without either of them having uttered so much as a word about it. As for the agreement that José had with David, that had altered too with the addition of Rosa in the car; though José knew that David would pay him, he couldn't help feeling cheated out of something. What it was exactly, he wasn't sure and if he had stopped the car to get out and think about it, he would most likely have laughed out loud at his foolishness. Ramón was dead, though and it was no time to be laughing about anything. He'd never really trusted him and there'd always been an uneasy tension between them, but the two men had often sought each other out in the past and José comforted himself with the deceptive thought that it had been because of friendship. As he slipped on layer after layer of memory, remembering the laughs they'd had and the scrapes they'd got into, José managed to convince himself that he'd lost a friend in life; one who was tied to him through blood. He wondered what he'd say to his wife when he got home.

David wondered whether to grip Rosa's hand tighter or loosen his grip on it altogether. He didn't want her to think that he was under the impression he had purchased her companionship, or anything of the kind. He didn't want the girl to feel that she was under any obligation to him, or for her to feel that he considered this to be the case. For a brief moment he thought that the right thing to do with the money he had left would be to divide it equally between the three of them, but then a sense of the absurd struck him; they weren't partners in crime fleeing a bank job, after all. They would be offended at such a foolish act, (he was forced to remember, once again, the policeman that first day in the city) and he was offended at himself for having thought such a mean thing. The relationship between people and money was different here and David was only just beginning to understand its complexities; he was beginning to learn that it wasn't all just a question of money. For José, all of this had never been just a simple question of money. For Rosa it was the issue of money that she was trying to forget.

"When we get back you're welcome at my place," said José in a gesture he knew he couldn't live up to and he hoped wouldn't be accepted.

"Thank-you," said David, "But I think I've caused you enough problems as it is."

"Don't be ridiculous," said José, "My wife and the children will be delighted to meet you and hear what we've been doing."

There was a long silence in the car.

"I don't want to go back to his place," said Rosa, finally, realising the untenable nature of her predicament. David had known anyway that it was time to say good-bye to José. José, disguising the fact from himself, had wanted his two passengers to collude with his alibi. In any case he'd known that it was time to say good-bye to David. It seemed like he'd been saying a lot of good-byes recently.

With the storm still pounding incessantly on the roof of the car, José suggested they make a stop so that they could go to the bathroom and he might make "a call." In half an hour they were pulling into a gas station with the customary adjacent cafeteria, yesterday's newspapers from the city and the touristy trinkets desperate to sell themselves to people equally desperate to remember their holidays. You couldn't get away with selling such cheap bric-a-brac on the coast itself, but here the whiff of a sea shell claiming allegiance to some left-behind coastal town was often enough to tempt a traveller who was still in holiday mood, or trying to be. David and Rosa went to the bathrooms whilst José ordered the obligatory cups of coffee and got some coins to make his call. "Ladies," said the sign on the door through which Rosa had walked. Slowly she assessed herself in the mirror, touched up her sagging hair which immediately flopped down on itself again, repeated the action and applied her bright pink lipstick with art. She didn't necessarily like what she saw looking back at her in the mirror, but she was comfortable with it; comfortable, because it was familiar to her. David, in the room marked "Gentlemen", went through similar actions, although his rituals involved the fastening and unbuttoning of his shirt button and flattening his hair with a splash of water. David and Rosa left the toilets at precisely the same time, meeting behind the screen that deflects one sex through one door and the other through the other. There was no partition in the middle, (presumably to allow those who wished to make a last-minute alteration to their courses the possibility of doing so) and they were embarrassed when they met face to face.

"David," said Rosa.

"Rosa," said David.

They walked back through the cafeteria ignoring the cups of coffee José had left them on a table close to which he was phoning from and walked straight out to the car.

"Everything okay?" José was asked when he came outside to find Rosa and David resting on the car on opposite sides next to the rear doors. The rain continued drumming on the glass roof above them.

"Nobody's at home," said José, "I thought it was strange as Maria doesn't work on Thursdays, so I phoned my mother-in-law and she said that Maria and the kids have moved in with her."

"Oh," said David.

The storm continued savagely as they made their way closer to Buenos Aires City. The silence in the car was greater than ever as José, David and Rosa considered what to do next. Rosa and David sat with the maximum space possible between them on the back seat of the car, each with their faces determinedly looking through their passenger windows. José had his gaze fixed on the road ahead of him, but had reduced his speed slightly now. It was possibly due to the increasingly poor conditions caused by the weather on the road, but equally so it might have been because he had nobody with whom to discuss what it was he was going to say to his wife. David and Rosa said nothing either; not because they had nothing to say to each other, but rather because they had too much. They were both feeling embarrassed out of a sense of inadequacy. José, meanwhile, envied them their togetherness.

"Well, things certainly have changed," said José, breaking the silence.

"Yes, they have," answered David and Rosa in unison, only further serving to heighten their sense of isolation. What she had meant by the phrase, David didn't know, but he was frightened that he might have detected irony in her voice. Rosa was just frightened; in an act of supreme self-survival she pushed her thigh boldly against David's and grasped his hand in hers. David was relieved but at the same time taken aback, so that their close physical proximity and bodily contact had to make up for the lack of conversation between them as they continued to stare into the rain out of the window. This uneasy marriage had started this way in the first place, so perhaps it was fitting that it continued on this way.

"When we get to Buenos Aires," David eventually said,

"Yes," responded the other two together in anticipation, but David had run out of words to say.

"We're on the edge of town now," said José in an attempt to lighten the mood as they were approaching the outskirts of the city. But all three of them were aware that their uneasy collaboration was shifting and none of them at this point in time thought of the city as home – Rosa because she needed to preserve the feeling that her home was the back seat of the car; David because he'd already tried to escape the place and José because home was now, quite simply, no longer home. It is curious to what extent our notions of security are determined by our attachments to the people we are involved with, but it is more curious still how often we continue to cling to those attachments long after they have ceased to be. We cling to people and structures that bind us in our places; not knowing, in fact, that in the very act of liberating ourselves from a feeling of isolation we also relinquish our means of achieving liberty.

"Look," said José, "There's the ring-road that leads to the port," and David remembered the borrowed car that had brought him down the same road, incredibly, it seemed, only two days before. He sunk lower into his seat, attempting to screen the profile of his face. Rosa mistook this as a sign that he was uncomfortable with her company and whilst she released the pressure of her thigh upon his, she would not relinquish the grip of her hand in David's.

CHAPTER SEVEN

They said their good-byes at one of the turnoffs along the Pan Americana Highway, allowing José to proceed to his apartment alone. The taxi-driver had plenty to do and it was only right that he should be the first to break up the journey. David enquired how much the fare would be and José grossly undercharged him. He waved David away with the toss of a hand; David of course had learnt by now and hastily pocketed the remaining cash he'd been holding out. He had no reason to want to offend José after all he'd done for him. Cursing himself under his breath that he'd not taken more of the gringo's money, José drove away from them.

"José, you sad son of a mother," he said to himself, "When are you going to learn?"

David and Rosa looked at each other in the drizzling rain. They could have been any of a number of couples coming back from a short seaside vacation; Rosa's case was at their feet and David wore the outfit of a man who was still on holiday. The only thing missing was one of the graffiti-stricken seashells that they should have picked up from their last stop at the service station. Rosa smoothed her skirt over her thighs, relieved that she'd had time to dress herself back at the flat and then suddenly remembered that she was wearing no bra. Realising what kind of a picture they made, David picked up the case in his right hand and thrust his left arm through Rosa's. Neither of them knew where they were but they strode confidently across the street to the other side. Once there, David turned to face where they'd come from and was startled to see the name of the French supermarket chain his company was involved with, pulsing on and off in large neon lights.

"Where are we going?" asked Rosa, who had been reassured by David's lack of temerity in taking her arm.

"I've no idea," he replied, "But wherever it is, it's not here," he said.

Rosa turned to check when she got out of the car, but the eyes of the man who met her green-brown eyes were the same as those she'd looked into last night. For a brief moment, imperceptibly, she looked into his eyes again rather than just looking at them. She was with the right man.

"I'm tired," she said, trying to buy time, "Couldn't we rent a little room for the evening and take things from there?"

It seemed like a perfectly sensible idea; he'd already grasped the idea that whoever might be looking for him would be concentrating on looking for a single American male dressed as a businessman. The trick with the clothes back in Valeria del Mar had been a stroke of genius and now he'd got himself a woman whom he could pass off as his girlfriend. He gripped her arm tighter. They'd have a hard time finding him now. Hailing a taxi just opposite the supermarket, they climbed inside and David instructed the driver to take them to the nearest hotel.

"It's just round the corner," said the taxi-driver and then he added, waking up, "Would you like me to take you on a short tour of the area?"

"We'll get out here," said David as they rounded the corner, "How much do I owe you?"

"Three pesos," said the man as he bent to check in his tariff book.

"Three pesos!" exclaimed David, "We've only come just round the corner," he said, indignantly.

"Well, that's what it says in my book here, but if you want to dispute it we can go to the local police station and check with them," he answered, having barely batted an eyelid all the while.

"That won't be necessary," said David courteously as he provided him with a five-peso note, the man winking at Rosa as she was exiting the car. Rosa smoothed her skirt over her thighs again.

'Obviously a foreigner with a good-time girl just back from the coast,' the driver thought to himself, and then he thought no more of it.

Feeling tired and getting wetter by the minute, David pushed through the door to the small suburban hotel. The receptionist passed them the hotel registry to sign, barely looking up as he did so.

"It might be better if you don't sign your real name," whispered Rosa gently, out of habit rather than foresight, seeing what David was doing.

"That's a very good idea," said David to her, so he signed the registry 'David Smith.'

"What's your name?" he asked her as they were climbing the stairs to their room, "Your full name, that is."

"Rosa," said Rosa, "Rosa De La Peña," and they shook hands at the door of the room before entering.

When José got back to his apartment he was met by members of the local constabulary who were anxious to talk to him and any other occupants who'd been in the car he'd borrowed from his wife. They'd conveniently arrived just a couple of minutes before he did and thus were able to welcome him home when he got to his door. Over long distances the telephone undoubtedly has its uses. Though of course it is better to speak to people face to face.

The room was well aired and now the rain was finally beginning to abate. It dripped off the end of the over-hanging roof and onto the metal shutters that Rosa De La Peña now opened to encourage the memory of David Salsa. She wanted him to remember the night they had spent by the sea. She wanted him to remember how he'd slept curled up to her looking into her eyes. She wanted him to remember that he'd been the one to offer her a place in the car, and she also wanted to forget. David, however, had just had a nasty reminder of why it was he was here. He put his head in his hands and rocked gently back and forth on the bed, trying to wash the memory from him.

The sound of running water could be heard from the shower as Rosa stepped into it. She knew she wouldn't be taken advantage of by David and she had also just seen the quantity of one hundred-peso bills he had stuffed in his wallet. She wasn't going to take advantage of him, either, but being next to money made her feel safe for the moment. She came into the room drying her hair with another, larger towel provided by the hotel wrapped round her body. It wouldn't have been in her nature to go towards him naked, but she was sufficiently conscious of her assets to know that a little more time could be bought if she wasn't wearing her clothes. She sat down on the bed next to David and tentatively put her arm round his shoulder.

"Are you okay, darling?" She asked him in her lilting Spanish.

"What? Yes, of course. I'm just trying to work out what to do next," he said. A pause.

"Do you love me?" She asked him.

"I, I don't know…, Rosa," he stammered.

"That's okay," she said, reassuringly, "We have plenty of time to get to know each other ahead of us, don't we?" She asked him, sweetly.

"Yes," said David turning to her, "I suppose we do."

With the issue resolved Rosa went back to the bathroom to dry her hair, as David Salsa watched her from behind walking from the room he was sitting in. A memory of the dream he'd had while he'd had his head in her lap came back to him; a warm memory of her soft green-brown eyes and a feeling almost like being on vacation.

"I feel like I'm on vacation," he called after her as the towel was dropping from her in the doorway to the bathroom. For one fleeting moment she was naked as she walked away from him. Out on the balcony the struggling sun was challenging the rain for the right to bring home the night.

"That's good, honey," she called back to him, "Then why can't we be?" She said.

David Salsa had never been with a prostitute before, though Rosa was unlike many other prostitutes he hadn't known. She was at work now, though she wasn't aware of working and unbeknown to her she was doing everything in her power to make David think she wasn't. The means by which she had supported herself previously would continue for a time to be the means by which she broke free of such an existence, until she was able to do so. David turned to look at her as she re-entered through the bathroom door. His escape from the bathroom of the other hotel came back to him in a flash. There was something about the demure movements of Rosa, coyly making her entrance, which made him vaguely aware he wasn't the only one feeling vulnerable. She stooped towards him as she approached, but David was embarrassed that he'd caught sight of her and he didn't want to feel ashamed in case she'd noticed him doing so. He looked up towards her with a plea on his face. She sat back on the chair beside the small lamp table in the room, one elbow balanced as if she might just have finished drinking a cup of coffee, or be in the process of applying her makeup. The rain had now finally stopped dripping from the roof and shutters. Her face was angled towards his with the light that peered in through the window reflecting on one side of her face, the other half of her in slight shadow as she turned into it. She was leaning towards him, the towel loosely tucked round her. The departing sun was fleetingly brighter within the oncoming advance of evening, drawing itself into one small corner of the room before being extinguished piece by piece. Rosa inclined herself minutely closer towards David in the growing silence with the sound of the waves from the night before echoing in her ears. Or perhaps it was her heartbeat. Then she sat up straighter again and turned to face where the night had installed itself on the wall between the hotel and the next building.

"I am a prostitute," she said eventually, breaking the silence.

David said nothing, nor was he expected to. A silence between two people who have much to say can grow if it is left unchecked, until it has taken every last word from their mouths. But before it has done so if one of them is brave enough the truth will be spoken.

"For three years I have lived on the streets and in bars. When I went home to my apartment I always felt guilty, as if the moments I had to myself should have been spent in the company of men. I never knew what to do with myself, so I would put on some music that I wouldn't listen to or flick on a program on the television that I wouldn't really watch. Sometimes I used to turn down the volume of the television completely and imagine that the words being sung on the radio were the real words to the program. Like that I could sit for hours, until I became afraid that the men in the bars would forget my face. Then I'd take care of my makeup and rush out onto the street just to make sure that I hadn't been forgotten."

David was listening intently but he dare not speak. Rosa was looking towards where he was sitting but she wasn't looking at him.

"I had friends but they were in the same business as me; they never really knew me." Softly, into the darkness, her face now completely in shadow.

She was crying but the tears slid down her cheeks silently, as motionless as the room in which they sat. David could see her so he averted his face to the window through which she had turned to look, afraid that she might suddenly stop speaking altogether and that he might be left with nothing to say.

"I,…" started David, "I had a woman once." Silence. "Now I no longer have her."

"It's okay," said Rosa, "I understand."

And the two of them let the night fill up the room.

Rosa loosened the towel about her slightly. Now that she had undressed herself she couldn't bring herself to put her clothes back on. She was acutely aware that David was still fully dressed and that he was making no signs of being about to change.

"How did you lose her?" she asked him.

"I don't know," answered David, lying to her, "I suppose she just went. There were problems between us," lying still, "It was my fault, too," he said, finally.

"Yes," said Rosa, agreeing with him.

"I shouldn't have come to Argentina in the first place," David continued. Rosa was staring harder out of the window. Had she been sitting there totally naked neither of them would have been aware of it.

"I had a job to do," said David, "I was going to present a report which would help some people to demonstrate that the cattle in the north of the country had foot and mouth disease. Over in Europe they've been tremendously worried about the disease. Then our clients were to introduce beef imported from Europe that they'd be able to sell at a cheaper price."

"Doesn't the price of the meat fall if it isn't of good quality?" asked Rosa, not understanding.

"Yes, it does," said David.

"I don't understand," she said.

"Like I say," said David, "It was a simple question of economics. Besides, I didn't think it was fair that people in this country weren't able to afford a product they exported. Doesn't that make sense?" he asked her, genuinely desiring her answer.

"So why was the meat from Europe cheaper?" she asked him by way of reply. And David knew the answer.

"I didn't think I was doing anything wrong," he said defensively, "But then I lost my briefcase and the Director I was to meet with said our business was concluded. I couldn't work out why that was the case, unless he also thought that what we'd been about to do was wrong. Maybe he did," said David, resignedly, "That's when I knew I had to get out of the city and buy myself some time to think. I worked hard for my company," David went on, "I thought I was making an honest living."

"The worst thing we can do is fool ourselves," said Rosa, "Sooner or later the truth always catches up with us." To both of them.

She was beginning to feel the cold now but she dare not get off the bed to close the window. David, too, was rooted to his seating place.

"I'll sleep in the chair," said David.

Rosa understood that things had changed between them but she was frightened of the morning she might wake to.

"I'm frightened to go to sleep," she said.

"It's okay, I understand," said David, remembering the events of last night.

"You don't need to sleep in the chair," she said to him in one last desperate attempt. The moment was fast running away from her but she refused to let go of it, "It'll be cold," she blurted out and softly the tears rolled down her cheeks again. She stepped underneath the sheets with her back to him, her towel now falling completely away from her. David felt uneasy and remained sitting on the bed as if nothing had happened. Quietly as the dim night came about them he slowly lifted his side of the bed covers and got in next to her, taking care not to touch her. He was still fully dressed, except for his shoes, which he'd eased off carefully, leaving them next to the bed. He put his hand out tentatively towards her shoulder, but just as he was taking his hand away she turned over onto her back.

"I can hold you, if you wish," she said to him.

David retracted his hand to his side and as he did so she bent his head to her breast as David curled his knees up underneath him.

"You don't have to sleep in your clothes," she said, removing the sheet against which her body had wrapped itself. She began to undress him. Carefully she removed his trousers from along the length of his legs and then she helped David undo the shirt he was unbuttoning mechanically. They laid together like that in the darkness for a long time. The breeze after the rain was cool and filtered in through the window.

"I was wrong," said David, finally.

"Yes, darling," she said to him and pressed him close to her.

In the morning when they awoke a dove was perched on the window ledge outside the room. There was no sign of the rain from the day before. The dove opened its wings stretching them in the sunlight and flew off with them ruffling in the air. Rosa and David were still holding hands. Rosa had lost her shyness from the evening before and now the morning was on them it was she who busied herself about the room. She was wrapped once again in the towel and her clothes hung idly from the back of the chair as if in a permanent state of abandonment.

"You can't be very old," said David to her as he watched her moving about the room.

"Older than I look," said Rosa, but no self-flattery had been intended and she had taken none from David words.

"We can't stay here for ever," said David.

"We'll stay as long as we like, darling," said Rosa, colluding with him.

"Yes," he said and the matter was resolved.

In the morning sunshine they were eating the croissants out on the balcony. From where they were sitting in the two ornamental metal chairs they could see down into the leafy gardens of the houses adjacent to the hotel. The morning rush had passed unnoticed by them and the gardens were empty of people except one elderly lady who came out to leave some scraps for the birds. She looked up at them briefly watching her then returned indoors with her plate. David took a sip of his orange juice; it was freshly squeezed and cold in the glass. There was a paper on a small tray that had been left by the chambermaid but it had remained there unread. In the morning light David could see how the green of Rosa's eyes clouded over when she became lost in thought. In some lights they appeared brown but there was green like the morning's grass in them.

"What are you thinking?" asked Rosa as she buttered her croissant and took a large bite out of it, bending her head to the plate slightly as she did so.

"I was thinking," he said, "I was thinking that we can stay here as long as we like."

He'd wanted to say to her that he thought her beautiful, that she was beautiful and that she must see it, too. Rosa, meanwhile, had not allowed herself to think any such thoughts, it was enough that the man she was with was looking after her. A person is only as beautiful as they are made to feel by the people who accompany them; for Rosa to feel that she was beautiful, she would have to stop remembering the men she'd been with before. It was enough for her to be here, now.

"Do you have any family here?" David asked Rosa.

"I have a sister but I haven't seen her for a long time," replied Rosa, "I don't think her husband likes me much." Eyes cast down, sheltering.

"I hear that the mountains in the west are beautiful," said David, wanting to prolong the conversation.

"They say that," said Rosa, doubting. And then, "I have some cousins, half-cousins they are. I've never seen them." A pause. "They live in a small town in the hills in Córdoba, but I don't know the place at all," she added regretfully.

"I was wondering," said David.

"Yes?" asked Rosa expectantly.

"I was wondering if you'd like to meet them," asked David.

Had he been conscious of the boldness of his offer he would have retracted his words immediately, but he had phrased the question in such a manner that Rosa wouldn't have to offend him by refusing his suggestion.

"They're the only family I've got in this country that I might turn to," she said, wanting to believe that what she had heard was true, though still uncertain as to whether the foreigner was genuine.

"Perhaps we could...visit them," David uttered with a weight bearing down on him.

"That would be lovely, my darling," she said, and her hand searched for his hand across the table. Down in the gardens a patch of white jasmine blossom caught the light of the sun upon it.

"What are you reading?" asked David, watching Rosa read her newspaper.

"There's a story here about the explosion in Mar del Plata," she said, "De Alcatráda was killed." She added, "The police are looking for some suspects who escaped from the club we met at in a getaway car."

She'd missed the story about how a briefcase had been found by a shoe-shiner and in it was a document that detailed a conspiracy of national importance.

"I can't phone my boss," said David.

Rosa didn't understand all that David said, but this man with the money moved in circles that Rosa did not. She'd met men before, a few men, who needed to talk and had used the excuse of sex to do so; then again she'd met men who were incapable of speaking but harboured so many stories of their secret lives. They were the dangerous ones. Ramón de Alcátrada had been one such man. David took an orange from the plate and peeled a portion of it. He bit into a juicy segment and let the taste rest against his tongue.

"I've sold out," said David, "And what I thought I had to offer has been taken from me now. I can't see how I'm going to resolve all this."

He put another segment of orange into his mouth, letting the juice seep through the flesh until the fibres of the fruit had to be chewed.

"My position is untenable," he said, "I can't go backwards on this one but I can't see how I'm going to proceed with the matter, either. What I need is somebody to explain to me exactly where I stand," he said, "The Director who was to be the head of the operation here doesn't want to know about it any more, so I guess I'm on my own," he reasoned, "I guess I just feel that I've been sent on a wild goose chase. I kind of feel used, if you know what I mean," he said, lifting his gaze towards Rosa to see if she was listening. She took a short sip from her glass and avoided the contact of his eyes as she tried to guess what was in them. David was squeezing the round ball of fruit in his hand; the same type of fruit whose juice Rosa was now drinking. He placed the orange on the low iron guard that protected the balcony, balancing it there.

Rosa's chair was positioned in such a way that she could just get past the table to get to her seat, but the hotel staff that had placed the furniture there had made an art of fitting it onto such a narrow balcony. As David reached to pick up the fruit again its dismembered wholeness was accidentally sent spinning down into the garden below and David watched it as the plump fruit rolled to rest beneath the dark green leaves of the garden foliage. Something about its position there and the manner in which it had fallen suggested to David that it would soon become rotten; that only the fibres would be left and that then they too would be pulled down into the stream of the soil.

"It's a terrible thing to feel used," said David, "And that's exactly how I feel right now."

All the while Rosa kept her eyes averted from David's. She was listening intently, she was listening very carefully, but she felt implicated in what David was saying and didn't like the feeling that was dawning inside her. The man bore his share of guilt, too. Rosa was feeling intimidated. Following David's gaze, she peered down from the balcony to see where he was looking and they both saw the fruit which had fallen like a stone, splitting its carcass on impact and spitting out its pips as it oozed with the juices which would cause its flesh to rot. For a brief moment, the thought of rotting flesh filled David's mind, and for a short moment it filled Rosa's also.

"There aren't many people I can trust," Rosa said to him.

Now she was as naked as she'd ever been in front of him. But the foreigner's mind was elsewhere.

David had paid for this balcony; temporarily the view belonged to him and whomever he chose to share it with. It was a privileged view in a privileged neighbourhood, giving out onto rose bushes, jasmines, a sundial and a small swimming pool. One of the first things visitors to Buenos Aires will notice is the smell or smells which are altogether particular to it. Climb up the steps to the church on the rare hill in the San Isidro district and the nostalgic smell of the river yearning for the sea it so resembles from this point is inescapable. There is the smell of books, too, musty but full of knowledge, and there is also the smell of the wood that has been fashioned into clocks, some of them large, which tick and tock with the rising sap eternally trapped inside them. The scent of the flowers wafted up to them on the morning breeze, for in Buenos Aires even in winter certain flowers choose to show themselves. But David couldn't get the memory of the rotting fruit out of his nostrils. Rosa was poised on the balcony at her most exquisite, fragile and beautiful as a sculpture, her eyes playing guessing games as they flicked from green to brown and back again in the distilled light of the morning. David smiled at her and as she saw the warmth in his eyes something stirred in her also.

"I can't phone my boss," David repeated.

It was understood by Rosa who had grasped the precarious nature of his position; though David hadn't directed the words at her. It was said for other people he might look at from such a balcony as the one he was sitting on. Rosa, though, had survived by living precariously, and if either of the two of them might lose their footing on the balcony and fall to the gardens below, it was most likely to be David.

At this point, he noticed that Rosa was wearing a watch; or rather, he became conscious of it and for one insane moment he questioned her wearing it round her wrist while he himself had no band round his. A memory of the handcuffs they had put on him after the meeting at the police station came back to him, so that he rubbed his left wrist again in a circular motion whilst he continued to look at Rosa. Had anyone been observing all this at that moment in time, they would have noticed David's envy. He thought Rosa like the bird on the window ledge that morning, able to fly free whenever she had need to. He strived to make her feel at home all the time in his most gracious manner, but at the same time challenged her to prove that her life was simpler than his, that she had less freedom than he did.

The closer one is to another person, the easier it is to say something that might hurt them. It is not always through a desire to hurt that one human being will engage with another in a kind of unconscious verbal warfare; it is simply that the possibility of it happening is more real. With the attachment to somebody comes the possibility of expressing a lack of regard for self as a lack of regard for the other. The more two people are attached, the greater their possibilities of rejecting one another. Such was the nature of David and Rosa's relationship. Neither of them fully trusted the other yet, though both of them had need to share secrets that were damning to them. Their need for each other was not so much driven by choice, as it was born out of necessity.

After finishing breakfast, David watched the girl with the long dark hair move about the room. Here and there she repositioned an ornament, straightened a picture that was slightly askew and folded the covers neatly on the bed. Then she went into the bathroom to comb her hair.

She had slender shoulders and when she lifted her hair up at the back to comb out a tangle her brown skin glistened almost white. She dropped her hair down over her neck again and applied her lipstick as sparingly as she was capable of. All this she did in view of David, but the four steps that had taken her the three metres or so from him still stood between them. She was conscious of him watching her and needed his approval. David caught himself looking at her and pretended instead to be looking out of the window, ashamed at finding her so beautiful.

"Was your woman pretty, too?" she asked him not without false modesty when she went to rejoin him and sit down on the bed. David was sitting with his feet on the floor but Rosa curled her legs up on the bed next to him. The distance between them had been carefully measured by Rosa and she had calculated in her walking back from the doorway of the bathroom that there was just enough room for her to squeeze onto the bed, without actually bringing herself and David into physical contact. With cat-like simplicity she now curled her legs up in a seated position, her left arm holding the weight of her body and her blouse one button more open than when they had been out on the balcony. David was conscious that Rosa was a very beautiful woman.

"Yes, she was," he replied, "She had hair somewhat like yours and was very intelligent. She knew her own mind." A pause, "I met her at a party in New York, but it was a while before I'd plucked up the courage to ask her out."

"Where did you take her?" said Rosa, with stars in her eyes.

"Well, we were at a seminar together some time after the party and she asked me if I'd like a coffee, so I accepted and things all started from there." Another pause.

Rosa shifted the weight of her body down the length of her arm.

"Would you like a cup of coffee now?" asked Rosa.

"Yes, that would be nice," said David and Rosa made another call downstairs to hotel reception to bring them up a fresh pot.

She returned to her place on the bed after making the call, carefully shortening the distance between herself and David so that she was within touching distance if he desired her. She wouldn't make the first move and she was clear in her mind that it was his prerogative, not hers. David noticed the slightly closer physical proximity between them and gently acquiesced to it.

"You are divorced now?" Rosa asked him.

"Yes," he responded simply and Rosa inwardly breathed a sigh. She shifted her weight onto her right hand, arching slightly further forwards as she did so and gently extending her left hand towards David's shoulder. Her fingertips made contact with the material of his shirt but David had been unprepared for the gesture and did not respond. Rosa retracted her hand so that it fell with a casual embrace onto her own thigh, touching the smooth nylon of her tights where her fingertips now rested, skin on skin.

"So we can go to meet your cousins in Córdoba, then?" David said, clarifying in his mind that this would be nice for Rosa. He would not have suggested anything he thought might be against Rosa's wishes or undesirable to her; he comforted himself with the thought that he was to some extent offering her a service. He comforted himself by thinking that he could provide this for her. Rosa's finely tuned instinct told her that she could count on this man, at least for a while longer.

At his local police station, José Afortunado was recounting to the police how he had driven down to Valeria del Mar with the American and then how they had gone on to Mar del Plata. The details of their meeting with the dead man, his cousin Ramón de Alcatráda, he kept to a minimum, not wanting to incriminate himself further. When asked about their business down on the coast, José had responded faithfully and with much insistence that they were in the process of making a film. Not him, they were to understand, but the man he was driving around. The room in which he was speaking roared with laughter for a moment and José was offended. He tried to defend his good intentions in having gone out to the coast to help the American with his work, but the staff at the police station had seen through the masquerade and delighted at entertaining a celebrity in their midst.

"So, you say the car is your wife's?" he was asked, "Where is she?"

A faithful response from José informing them that she was staying at her mother's temporarily brought the house down again. When asked why he and his passenger had been in such a hurry to get away from the night club where the explosion had occurred, killing de Alcátrada in the process, José dutifully informed them that he had had not one, but two passengers in his car. The girl's name was Rosa, he informed

114

them and his passenger had been talking with her during the night.

"Yes, it was probably to do with making a film, of some kind," said the staff sergeant on duty to his grateful audience, stressing the word '*some*' as he did so and bringing the house down again. José was asked if he and his cousin Ramón had got on well together, and summoning up the memories he'd invented for himself on the way back to Buenos Aires in the car, almost in tears José struck his hand on his heart to signal the bond that existed between the two men. His performance was so convincing that one of the officers removed his hat. Everybody turned their gaze downwards for an instant.

"You say this man had a lot of money on his person?" enquired the staff sergeant, taking the lead again.

"One might say that," said José, regaining his composure, "But it was probably no more than anyone in his position would normally have," he stated, trying to defend his friend.

If there's one thing that had been clear to José from the start of driving the American around, it was that in spite of the cultural differences that existed between them, there had been a kind of friendship between them. Though of course under no circumstances would he admit this to the police. Those seen to be friendly with people of other cultural persuasions were not necessarily welcomed in society; this was the same regarding those of Bolivian or Peruvian descent as it was regarding Americans. Befriending them was a matter of necessity, not choice. The fact his friend was an American made the crime doubly heinous.

José went through the account of the raspberry ripple and the chocolate ice cream in Carilo.

"It was you who had the chocolate ice cream, you say?" enquired the staff sergeant, making sure to note down the American's tastes with care. "Do you think this man has anything to do with the nefarious document that has recently come to light?" the staff sergeant enquired, looming, and precise with his vocabulary.

"I don't know of any such document," replied José faithfully and after some questions more the policeman decided that the taxi-driver was absolved of any guilt.

"Just take care whom you pick up in future," the sergeant admonished him and with that José was let off the hook.

The car had been impounded for further examinations and the

police did not extend the courtesy of their previous offer of a lift to the police station to offering him a lift back to his apartment. So José was left to take public transport to make his way back home to his empty residence.

At the train station across the road-bridge that straddled the Pan Americana, José's wife Maria was standing with two large suitcases in her hands. One of them had been full on her way back to the apartment, but on finding her husband still not returned from his trip, another suitcase had been prepared and was now heading on its way, together with the first suitcase, back to her mother's house. As she looked across the platform to where a couple were buying their train tickets from the vending machine, she was surprised to see her husband's jumper on the man putting the coins into the slot. It surprised her for a moment but then she reasoned that the man had every right to be wearing a jumper that was the same as José's. Downcast, she boarded the train which had approached the station and which would take her back to where the children of her husband were still waiting for her.

The train would take them to El Retiro in the centre and from there David and Rosa would be able to walk the couple of blocks to the coach station to take the bus to Córdoba. Rosa held David's hand tightly and thought of New York. She'd only ever seen it on the television, but everybody seemed to live in huge apartments in districts with names like Manhattan and Rosa was conscious of being with a celebrity. She protected him fiercely as two young women with short skirts and dark hair rolled into tails swished by them, one of them turning her glance towards David. There was a look of recognition on the face of the girl with the smile playing at her mouth that alarmed Rosa, so she pulled David's arm round her waist so that there could be no grounds for misinterpretation. The girl responded by sliding her own arm round her companion's waist and off they went, two dark ponytails flicking as they sauntered down the platform.

"I suppose that's how they get away with it, two of them together," Rosa thought to herself and pulled David's arm round her closer still in a tight embrace. Two by two the different parties disappeared from one another's sight, the girl with her arm round her companion's waist casting a glance back along the platform like a line cast out to a silvery stretch of water. David and Rosa, the holiday couple, boarded the train that arrived at the platform. It was a train coming from the same station as the one that had been boarded forty-seven minutes previously by José's wife, Maria. It was a train whose final destination had been the same as the final destination of the train on which José's wife, Maria had been travelling on towards the centre. Had they travelled in the same compartment together, the two parties might have made better acquaintance and learned something more about José. But as it was this was not destined to be and both parties would have to conform to making do with the meagre details they had concerning José's present whereabouts. Maria rode her train back to her mother's in silence. David and Rosa also rode along in silence, fiercely protective of one another in the unfamiliar territory. Rosa was imagining New York.

"We'll soon be on the bus, darling," she was saying to him with stars in her eyes, "And then we'll be able to relax properly."

She reached further across behind David and out of habit squeezed her client at the top of his thigh, but although David was taken aback by the gesture he increased the pressure of his own arm just underneath her bosom in a reciprocal response. Thus two travellers were flung into closeness by the demands of the journey while another passenger on a train passed theirs, flung against the side of the compartment where her husband should have been.

Rosa had butterflies in her stomach and they were fluttering where David increased the pressure of his arm on her as they went through the tunnel.

CHAPTER EIGHT

David's child, Hannah was calling to him at the side of the pool. Across its shattered surface her mother was lying motionless with a part of the rock that had splintered off crushing her leg.

"David," she said again.

Her left leg wasn't moving. Hannah was whimpering, a few metres away from her mother.

"It's alright," said David lying to her, "It's alright."

"It's your fault," she said feebly, "Maria told us to be careful when there were storms in the mountains."

David was just able to prise off the shattered stone that was crushing her but through the blood on his hands he could feel his own burden grow.

"We could all have been killed!" she screamed at him in agony, "You're going to have to leave me and take Hannah with you to get help. I can't move."

David covered her with what spare clothing they had, dropped their daughter into the child-carrier and went off at a sprint back to the hotel to fetch help. He thought of bending down to kiss her before he left, but she was remote to his touch, her teeth clenched together with the pain of the assault.

Rosa had forgotten to take her emergency contraceptive pill the morning they'd been disturbed by the blast of the explosion.

David's mislaid report had reached the newspapers, the newspapers had been read by the police and now government officials were demanding an enquiry into the contents of the report.

There was no one on the end of the phone at Maria's mother's flat. Probably they'd gone out for the day, José thought to himself. Then he hung up.

The train emerged through the tunnel on the other side and Rosa and David were still holding on to one another. It thundered on past the station where José's wife Maria had already made her exit into the crowds of people spilling onto the platform. They had with them one suitcase with a couple of changes of clothes for Rosa, a hair drier and a couple of photos; an amount of money in David's wallet and documents each which denoted that although they were seemingly a couple, they were from different cultural backgrounds. So long as David had the money and Rosa was discreet, their semblance of being a couple was vaguely acceptable. Now that they were out of the tunnel they pressed even closer together.

"How long will the journey to Córdoba take, have you any idea?" David was asking her.

"I…don't know. Argentina is a very big country," she said, repeating a phrase she had heard many times. But in her mind the United States was infinitely bigger than Argentina. Like so many who have lived their lives in abject poverty, the idea of a country whose riches outnumber an entire continent was too immense for her to understand.

"I'm sure we'll be there soon," she said, referring to the station; which was really the same to her as getting to their destination. It was only marginally less significant to her at this moment in time than disembarking from a plane that might touch down in David's home country. She had seen it in the films and in the sports programs they showed on television in the early hours; though Rosa had often wondered what the significance in a coastal town in Argentina was of a ball game being played by foreigners on the other side of the world. She had also wondered why it was that she needed to translate the language they spoke as if she were supposed to understand it. But the people that ran the programs had no such doubts.

As they drew closer to the centre, the train on which Rosa and David were travelling was increasingly plunged into darkness as it ran the gauntlet of the many tunnels the engineers had been forced to construct in order to facilitate its trajectory into the city. Peoples' faces stared back at them as they flashed through the inner-city stations, the train only seeming to stop randomly at those places the driver felt inclined to. Men with accordions and a swagger in their step beckoned towards buckets positioned at their feet. The incantations of sisters struck their monotone metallic syllables with outstretched hands; dark gypsies in rags who had escaped the persecution in Europe to find themselves unwanted here as well. Babies clung to their mothers' teats like slugs slung underneath them, a flashing brown breast sometimes enough to shame passengers. Many looked away but some gave coins to appease their guilt. The songs sung out of tune and without a note of hope in them were the ones that profited most - a few coins at best.

The helter-skelter journey of a thousand myriad faces was repeated day in, day out until travellers and commuters recognised each other and knew at the intonation of a note which people to tip and which not. They'd stopped collecting the fares on the train itself a long time ago, for obvious reasons when the conductor might have been mistaken for the man with the accordion. Ghosts flashed out of the darkness and swayed leeringly towards Rosa and David, grimaces on their faces and hands weighted down as if by chains. 'Crickety-crack' the helter-skelter train went as it plummeted headlong down the track. And when they tried to turn and flee, their reflections sneered back at them from within the confines of the tunnels. Opposite them a man was pretending to read a newspaper. He bought his anonymity daily by lying behind his newspaper, pretending he was deaf when the leprous hands of starving children scratched against the black and white surface of his world and even poked a finger into it. He pretended he was blind when the hip-high children cupped their hands together expecting to taste the shower of gold coins in them, brushing past their heads with a stride anxious as a last-minute hop. Not of my world, not of my doing, not of my world, not of my doing, not of my world, not of ....crick-crack.

The little monkey discarded the newspaper he'd picked up from the man but could not read, tossing it aside with an irreverence that declared it unfit for human consumption. It fell open at the page where the Minister for Agriculture in his black and white jump suit was demanding an enquiry into a treacherous foreign conspiracy, jostled by reporters thrusting lollypops. Rosa glanced down to read the title and David glanced at it too. He saw the screams on the faces of innocent children; he saw the words being stolen from their mouths. He saw their dry hands cupping air instead of water, he heard black flies buzzing round their heads, he heard the moans of the ghosts in the tunnels they whooshed through and the spaces where empty words were falling like bombs. A soldier climbed swiftly into the carriage at the next stop.

"I've got to get out of here," said his wife, killing him, "I've got to get out."

"David, are you okay?" she was saying to him. But David was caught in the reflections in the tunnels, his gaping mouth sucking in air, his eyes as wide as the train. He was in a lift and he was falling, the betraying smile of his wife fading on the glass.

"David," she said to him. He was holding her hand with his heart pumping furiously, "We're here, we're at the station."

The carriage had emptied of its turbulent circus, the accordion deflated round the neck of the shuffling man, its convalescent weight moaning the next train. They got out at the back of the stream of passengers, the children mingling unnoticed at the security gates.

"Ticket," said the man in uniform with his hand outstretched, "Ticket," he said as David held out his hand.

Out of the station they walked with the sun on their limbs, past the ranks of taxi-drivers clicking at Rosa, past the sweet-selling stalls where children were bought for fifty cents. Out into the street with the flashy glass buildings remotely steering the people towards them, over the park where men and dogs and children slept, through the parade of market stalls where women were plying their wares. They were part of the clatter they left behind them, up the ramp to the fortress where buses left. The slick of the oil a part of the roadway, only those with tickets allowed access. Across the park in the breeze the buildings were swaying, their mirrored surfaces dark on all sides; bowing to the people lounging idly all day until home time who followed the newspapers back to the trains.

Fast behind the closing glass doors at the bus station, David and Rosa shook off the crowds, into its deeper silence with engines purring they set down their bags. But the newspapers flapped limply like pigeons, their wings weighted down where oil slicks were cast. No pictures, not yet.

"Are you okay, darling?" as if out of a dream of the past.

Strangely he took her hand in his, pressed it close to him. He opened his lips and the words sailed out spinning, bubbles puckering in the air.

"I've got to get out of here," he said to Rosa, "I've got to get out."

A soldier eyed them suspiciously. In his trance of dreams of the future they traipsed up the stairs, Rosa trailing him uncertainly, combing the locks of her hair. They bought their tickets and hid them in their pockets.

"It's alright," he said to Rosa, lying to her, "It's alright."

In the slumbering bus that shook the station, they stretched out into the invisible night. Her arm was wide around him, she was cooing like the pigeons on the tarmac; her face turned towards him - heart fluttering like the wings that dodged the traffic. He was back in his dreams of the present resting his head on her shoulder. Slipping down further into the seat, the city slowly pulled away from them, let its fingers slip as it left its grumbling traffic. Then they were clear of the noise of the cars; the boats slipped their anchors at their docks in the port; long-distance buses stole off for the night; children whose faces were etched in the ashes and dirt of the city were left behind. In Rosa's belly the wheels were rumbling; butterflies tracing paths through the dust of her skin, flying obscurely-looping patterns like stars.

They were heading west out towards the distant promise of mountains like ghosts. Rosa was reading a paper she'd picked from the floor where rumours floated of foot and mouth disease stampeding in the north; in Europe to the east sheep and cattle were being burnt in piles. Where the rumour had come from nobody could tell, it trawled its mysterious dread in the pages of the public and crept into their imagination.

"Listen to this," she said to David, "In the south in the Pampas cows have been found with parts of their brain missing, dead. One man is suggesting it's the work of aliens; he's serious about it. Somebody else is saying that it might be the government carrying out tests."

David had also heard the rumours of CJD having spread to South America. Up to now they had been just that; rumours, which his company had traded on in order to undermine public confidence, cultivating intentions of releasing hushed-up secrets. Nothing spreads faster than an intimation that has been deliberately released and vehemently denied. If it is covered up at the same time that it is allowed to surface, then it will spread as surely as fire charging through a forest.

Through the soft material of Rosa's blouse one undone button rumoured the sullen promise of her breast. The journey would be a long one, long enough for her to find herself again. Her actions had been unconscious when they'd finally boarded the humming darkness of the coach; but an animal that senses danger will always do the bidding of its instincts, just as surely as stampeding cattle will charge away from fire.

When the sprawling city could hold them no longer they were suddenly ushered out into the land. Infinite pastures grew alongside the road they were travelling on; miniature fences dotting the horizon. Rosa got up and went to the back to pour herself a cup of the sickly-sweet orange they had on tap. Bitter tasting coffee in the other tap steamed when it was released. As a man went to go to the cramped bathroom, Rosa was forced to press herself into the headrest of the seat next to her, feeling herself crushed for a second. She walked back to her seat and instinctively offered David the plastic cup with its sugary juice.

"No, thanks, Rosa," he said.

She'd done what was expected of her and now she could sit back and relax. It was going to be a long journey, but Rosa and David were tolerant enough of each other's company to pass the hours well. He inclined his head gently towards her shoulder and she held onto him as if he might float away from her. Comfortable, now, David allowed himself to drift into a deep sleep; though later on it would be peppered with images he could not understand. Rosa welcomed the man to her shoulder and the sleep that came to him as her eyes began to drink in the landscape. She did not know the country she had been living in, she thought to herself. They were playing a movie on the overhead video screens, but Rosa did what she had always done back in her apartment. She let the noise of the sounds wash over her while she watched the panorama of the landscape unfolding. Into her eyes washed the fields shimmering in their coats of green, the solitary majestic old trees were sentinels to her thoughts, the cattle chewing at the cud in the fields were her feelings inside her, growing.

The man was sleeping at her side. The journey by train into the city earlier on had disturbed him and his words to her in the hotel about what was bothering him were somehow connected to what she had read in the paper. Rosa thought back to when she had met David, two nights and what was stretching away of the present day ago; she thought of the sad fate of de Alcátrada who had pushed his merchandise like a pirate in the clubs near the city on the coast. This man was not at all like him and perhaps for this reason she had chosen him that evening, instead of the free-spending Ramón. Her instincts about people were very seldom wrong, though instinct had often tricked her into believing most men were the same. Her life had been a succession of streaming faces, most often seen in the unreal light of the cavernous bars and clubs she worked. She'd preferred the ones that were directly next to the sea; there the noise of the waves allowed her to think. Córdoba was still centuries away and rose up out of the landscape in her imagination like the unforeseen hills which she knew must be out there, but whose existence she had only ever guessed at. How this infinitely flat landscape would summon up hills of the magnitude that she imagined, she did not know; the vastness of the plains was like the ocean that beat on her in waves. There was something child-like about David; the fact that he and not others had the cash to get them here made perfect sense to her, his still-sleeping form cushioned against her body. The nervousness she had felt in her gut was disappearing, and in its place was the grain of the pastures. Everybody had their price to pay, she reasoned and David's must have been a high one. She was feeling light-hearted and allowed the green flowing tides to drift into her.

Sometimes she chanced upon a hidden homestead, tree-clad under its watchful boughs. She tried to imagine the life there in them, contented herself that there was a place where a man and a woman farmed for their food together. Somewhere that place must exist. She looked at the white skin of David's face and the brown of her arm that held him, she felt her previous life glistening beneath her skin and the watchful stir of the hours that had crept under hers. She would not allow the thought that was forming in her mind to fully take shape yet, though its outline was hazily visible like the far-off horizon that could never be reached. But night always falls wherever we are; pushing us under the day we have lived. There were different trees marking different homesteads, different roofs over those different houses and though the landscape of the plains was endlessly similar, there were subtle differences if one looked hard enough. Rosa watched the landscape take shape in her mind; let it fill her imagination. The widening skies still betrayed no mountains, but her imagination had already guessed at their presence and though she could not see them, she allowed herself to suspend disbelief 'til they were almost real and hovered there on the fringes of her mind.

When David awoke the night that had been growing in Rosa's mind was over them like a blanket. Still she held him as the last candles of light were snuffed out, the velvet cloth of its cooling surface drawn over them as night came to rest. The conspiracy was safe between them.

"Where are we?" David asked Rosa and then, "How long have I been sleeping?"

Rosa concentrated herself for a moment, pulling her thoughts out of the darkening sky,

"Where we are is how long you've been sleeping," she said.

CHAPTER NINE

Patience is a virtue. When we most want something is often when it is furthest away from us. When we have something close to us we overlook it, take it for granted. When we own something, we no longer value it. Rosa was playing a difficult game. She must appear to be within David's reach but at the same time be beyond it. She had never been on such an extended journey before, not since her now-dead mother had travelled down from the high plains of Bolivia carrying her in her womb twenty-six years ago. She had died, leaving Rosa and her sister to fend for themselves in the sprawling metropolis that grew like a hungry spider drawing insects towards it. Once you were caught in the city it was almost impossible to break out of it, it trapped you in its invisible web and anaesthetised you so that it was years before you realised you were stuck. A man on the landing outside Rosa's mother's grim apartment had once called to her,

"Buenos Aires, I was trapped in that hell-hole for twenty-five years! Don't ever go there," but she had disregarded his words and scraped enough money from the floors she cleaned and scrubbed to buy her passage. Although she had heard what her neighbour had said to her, she couldn't allow his words to penetrate, not unless she was prepared to abandon all hope she had. And she was pregnant. Her husband would stay behind for a while to attend the small stall in the market where he handed over the vegetables they scratched out of the tiny patch of land. That was until it was safe for him to leave the market stall and come down. The land was not theirs' and they had to pay rent on it. Their five year-old daughter would go with her mother to help her if necessary. She had an address in the city of a woman who was a friend of a friend of hers.

When she got there, however, she found a man waiting for the woman while she attended the door.

"Yes, yes, you can come in. Hurry up, I have a client waiting."

So her mother whose belly was growing did what she had done in Bolivia, she scrubbed floors for those that had them and Rosa's sister helped. As luck would have it, she gained a job cleaning for a family who gave her and her young daughter a roof over their heads and paid their wages in food. There was a little money given, too, but this she usually had to spend on buying cleaning implements for the house and clothes for her daughter. Rosa was born in a city hospital and taken home to where her mother and sister worked when she was a few days old. Her father had written to her mother that he couldn't leave the market stall; although his wife had somehow scraped together just enough for his coach fare from Bolivia, she could offer him no place to live and no work. Then the owners of the house had discovered her little nest egg stashed away one day. They wouldn't believe that it was money she'd saved over the months and threatened her with throwing her and her two young daughters out onto the street. From that moment on, Rosa's mother kept her head bowed to the floor when scrubbing and the years had ebbed away. One day on her mother's birthday a letter arrived telling her that her husband was living with another woman. Rosa had never seen her father, but she never forgave him for breaking all hope in her mother. The two girls had grown up in the house and Rosa's sister had gone into domestic service, too. But Rosa grew too big for her pinafore and she left her mother and her sister in search of a better life. Finally, after years of menial jobs and even working as a supermarket checkout girl once, she had skipped the bright lights of Buenos Aires for the bright lights of the coast, only to find that one city was the same as the next.

Now she was on a bus again, owned by the same company as the one on which her mother had travelled twenty-six years ago. David looked down where his watch should be. He'd been missing it sorely and the hours spent on the bus and the distance they must have covered only further served to disorientate him without its compass to help him. Rosa's answer to the questions he'd asked when he'd woken up eluded him. The countryside all seemed the same to him, pressed flat under the rolling sky that went on interminably, even in the darkness.

Rosa's eyes were as wide as the moon, which hung in its fullness out of sight, its face shadowed in thought.

Time is a human construct; we build with it in order to make advances towards our desired possessions more real. When David lost his briefcase, he'd lost that part of him which had a sense of purpose. David's impatience at wanting to know where he was at this point in time was a measure of his loss of purpose. Rosa's ability to imagine where she was was a measure of hers'. She turned towards him in the darkness.

"Are you hungry, darling?" she asked him.

"No, no thank-you," he said kindly.

They'd not eaten since breakfast that morning on the balcony of the hotel room, but neither of them was feeling hungry now. Rosa's belly was as content as the green of the pastures the cows had been chewing and which rested there like a thing growing. David was empty inside. The smoothest pebble found at the roar of the ocean is enough to content a child and it is possible for them to see treasure in the fields around, while an adult may see nothing.

David looked towards the stars that were shining and tried to calculate his position. The half-forgotten names of stellar configurations came back to him, but he was unversed in their tongue.

"Like the stars over the sea," Rosa said to him, whispering, her eyes wide awake upon their motion. David said nothing. He was thinking of how it was that he came to be on this bus when he normally travelled first-class in jets. He was thinking of how it was that he was with this woman instead of being with a wife, like other men.

"What will we do when we reach Córdoba?" he asked Rosa.

"We'll look for my cousins and introduce ourselves to them," she answered with certainty, although the family members she had never seen and who had never seen her were only half-cousins, members of the family of her father who had betrayed her. She was, after all, her mother's daughter and hope is something you are either born with or are not. David thought about the wife he'd not seen for more than a year now. In his mind she was more beautiful than ever, but correspondingly his own self-esteem had suffered. He would not betray the ideal that made the memories of their perfect togetherness complete, but in doing so he had betrayed himself and forced himself to believe that he had been at fault in losing her. To admit that they'd lost each other was just too much for him to bear.

Their daughter, Hannah would be celebrating her birthday soon. They'd had her whilst they'd still been at college together, daring convention and then having to grow up around it. He wanted to tell his daughter how much he missed her. When he picked up the phone to say happy birthday the words came out meaningless and empty each year. He wanted to say that she meant more to him than anything in the world, he wanted her to know that she was still his little girl, he was desperate to tell her how much he loved her, how the times with her close to him were the best times of all, how the discovery of ice on the frozen river together had enchanted his heart. He wanted her here with him now. David was crying softly to himself. Rosa felt his tears like the tears her mother had cried to her, but she said nothing, nor could she have done anything to offer him comfort. So David cried softly into the darkness and the dream of his daughter grew with those tears, the distance that separated them broke his heart and under the spell that was created a seed took root in the black gentle night.

Dawn had not yet broken when they disembarked from the bus in the city of Córdoba. They picked up Rosa's suitcase like a baby they had stowed in the back and wrapped their arms round it as they gathered themselves on the platform. It was cold and their holiday clothes were insufficient. A soldier stood chomping in heavy leather boots, his green jacket fastened up to his chin. Rosa couldn't work out why they were not yet in the mountains but sensed their presence on the horizon of the still-sleeping night.

"I have the name of the village," she said to David, "And the surname of the family."

They went to the cafeteria whose lights were blinking in the hours before dawn, whose staff moved round like sleepwalkers in their uniforms. Rosa went to the bathroom to remove her make-up that had smeared in the night. The dream of his child was upon him and David guarded the suitcase like a still-sleeping babe. In a part of his mind still stirring, David was holding onto the suitcase as if onto his life. Rosa emerged from the bathroom without her make-up, wearing the jumper that David had leant her over her blouse, though still her legs shook long and dark beneath her tights. She smoothed her skirt down over them as she sat at the table with David; the two of them perched on the tiny metallic chairs. They were too ornate to hold their residents seated comfortably, but their outsize coffee-cups had been served brim-full in compensation. This was not a place for people to sit for long, more a place for people who needed a quiet moment of comfort on their long journeys, temporarily offering them respite before other passengers were tempted towards them. An insomniac pigeon strutted on the platform pecking at crumbs.

David left Rosa with the suitcase and went to purchase their tickets. His Spanish was still groggy in the time before day had broken and his accent was encumbered by his stay in Buenos Aires. They were in a new province now, one where the people spoke in a thick-lilting hush and curled their rr's as if to make the promise of the mountains a secret shared between themselves. The boy looked up when David pronounced the name of the village as best he could.

"That's over the other side of the hills," said the boy, as if enquiring whether David was sure of the place.

"Yes," said David, simply, and paid for the tickets.

"It's two hours until the bus goes," said David as he approached Rosa at the table, "I'm sorry there's not another one before then."

"It's not your fault," said Rosa, simply, and put down the coffee-cup so that she might make it last longer. David looked at the suitcase they were carrying and then looked towards Rosa again.

"I'll sit down a little, then," he said, as if asking her permission.

"Of course," she said.

The all-night pigeon was still at its tricks but its bleary-eyed antics diminished as dawn rubbed its eyes on the glass. The soldier, still chomping, reduced another cigarette in the darkness. So they boarded the bus in slumberful wakeness as the sun of the morning switched off the lights that had shone through the eyes of the cafeteria. The metallic seats were left vacant behind them with the space that was empty of the suitcase.

On the bus that chugged out of the watchful morning passengers were popped around like smarties, snoring in their multicoloured village fancy dress. The red-hatted beret burped in its sleep, steep toes of brown cowboy boots flaunted convention, pointing over chair-backs to the west. The suitcase came on board with them, a passenger on the empty seat opposite. The luxury of the decrepit village bus reserved for the villagers was showing off its largess. So half a dozen passengers assured of their comfort snored away the blue morning that was creeping up all sides of the vehicle. The fingers of the hills were showing, jauntily poking at the last trails of morning or at the city still chomping on platforms. With the air climbing between them the passengers stretched out their limbs.

David put a hand on Rosa but her skin was cold and he retracted it quickly. The pale fingers of morning were retracting their promise on the broken skyline of the day; the teeth of the mountains were suspended in cloud. Deep in her sleep Rosa was still dreaming, the silhouettes of morning riding towards her. David patted the bag by his side and breathed in the blue morning air. He wondered whether her family would look like her, or if, at all, like the villagers on board asleep like horses. Was the soldier on the platform nonchalantly saluting? Why was he there at all? Only the driver gathering in the muscly energy of the vehicle was awake with David as they bounced up the precipitous road. He was glad that the village lay on the other side as they pushed their way through the green slumbering hills. He watched Rosa breathing deeply. He dare not touch her to wake her from her sleep as he saw how the blue canopy of the sky's ceiling reached high above the mountainous walls. But when at last Rosa awoke to the valley below her dream of the mountains had fled.

"Wake up, Rosa, it's me, David," he said.

In the growing morning two lovers shifted silence between them until the sun had filled the air with words they had not spoken. Rosa had shaken off the narcotic of her dreams and was pressed against the glass, the skin of her face inching into it with her fingers enlaced in David's. She wondered what her family would have to say to her, what they would ask her about the foreigner whose hand she was holding.

"You've been asleep," he said.

"Yes, I know," she replied curling up.

In the intractable sunlight pale shadows of day were creeping down to the valleys, the bus and its accomplices moving silently. It wouldn't be long now until they reached the village. The wakening chatter of the villagers made David and Rosa feel like foreigners. So they interlocked their fingers, but the white of David's fingers in the brown of Rosa's was incongruous as rivers.

"You could pretend that I'm your friend," said David, at last.

Rosa looked into his blue eyes and kissed him on the cheek.

"You are," she said to him, smiling.

The bus was fidgeting as they slid down the twisting road. Boots that had pointed out west on the climb up were realigned on the way down. The red beret straightened itself and a throat was cleared down the throat of the morning.

In the crispness of the sun with the hills nestled in behind them, Rosa and David climbed down off the bus. There was no-one around them and the other passengers had all disappeared. Rosa and David had no need to hold hands now but they were smiling deeply at one another. 'Candelaria' said the name on the signpost.

'What a handsome couple,' thought the old woman as she pressed the notes into the cash till behind the desk at the bus terminal. A man dressed in a jacket tied round his bulging waist with a piece of string told them that they, "Lived over there, somewhere." A small tan-coloured dog cocked a leg at them in welcome on the kerb, its tongue lolling out in good-natured largess. David looked at Rosa and saw what she was wearing.

"Perhaps it would be a good idea to change your shoes," he said, "Those high-heels are going to be no good on these dirt roads, don't you think?"

As yet no money had changed hands between them and for one blindingly - stupid moment he thought of taking a bundle of notes from his wallet and giving them to her. But he stopped himself from reaching for his wallet just in time.

"What are you smiling at?" asked Rosa, smiling back at him.

"I was just thinking how much I'd like to buy you a pair of shoes," he said.

"I'd be delighted," said Rosa.

They made their way to the small-town shop selling fancy dress and came away with a cowboy hat for David and a black and red poncho and pair of the finest calf-length leather field boots for Rosa. Outside in the small circle of greenery that served as a village square, they put on their new clothes; David taking José's jumper from her in exchange for the poncho, Rosa pushing her shoes into her suitcase before putting on the new boots. They fitted her as if they'd been waiting for her on the shelf. David looked at her; she was still wearing the mini-skirt and looked very sexy.

"It's okay," said Rosa, "I've got a pair of jeans in my suitcase. I can put them on if you want," she said.

"How long do you think we're going to be here?" asked David.

"I don't know, honey, that depends on us, doesn't it?" she replied.

She was still smiling. He smiled warmly back at her and in an instinctive gesture she threw her arms round him, kissing him on the cheek.

"Thank-you," she said to him.

"For what?" he said.

With a cowboy whelp that sent the amiable dog that watered the public kerbsides running, David took Rosa's arm and walked down the dirt road that led out of the town in the general direction of where the old man had pointed. The woman in the shop where they'd bought their new clothes had informed them that both the taxis that operated in the town would be busy taking passengers over the hills to the capital, as today was Saturday and people would be travelling to see their families.

"Why's that?" David had asked.

"It's National Independence Day," said the woman shopkeeper, "Out at the ranches they'll have killed their steers and will be barbecuing them tonight for the feasts. Are you going anywhere special?" asked the woman good-naturedly.

'Ah, but they can't be,' she thought to herself, as the American with ready dollars and the strange accent and his strange partner walked out of her shop.

The neon lights of the French-owned supermarket were flashing on and off in the district of Loma del Peludo. It was Saturday the ninth of July and the most patriotic day in the Argentine calendar was being celebrated. The supermarket was open for the morning only; its workers were allowed only half their independence today. The pretty girl at the checkout desk dropped José's groceries into a bag for him as he flashed her a fat smile and opened his wallet.

"Celebrating with your family today?" the girl asked him.

The money David had given him would be enough to tide him over for a couple of weeks, if he was careful with it. In the meantime, it was enough until he got his bearings again and was able to find another agency willing to take him on; his job at the old place had already been filled by one of the waiting cars which had pulled in when José's had pulled out.

'Those thieves were always robbing me, anyway,' he thought to himself and slid his bag down the slope of the cash-point before hanging it on his wrist as he walked out of the supermarket.

In Buenos Aires there are more taxis and more kiosks per head of population than in almost any other city in the world. The services of a 'remise' or agency taxi which will come to pick you up at your front door can be proportionally cheaper than a bus fare if you share your car with two or more passengers. So while there is boundless work to be had and a group of people going out for the night will often call upon the services of such a taxi, there are also boundless numbers of drivers queuing to wait their turn for the privilege of picking them up. This is where the service of the multitudinous kiosks comes into play. The culture of the trains, (a legacy of the English as payment for services rendered to the sceptred isle, measured out in grain and cans of corned beef) is literally falling apart. But this is no surprise since the person who decides to pay for light entertainment on the train or who is feeling charitable will often relinquish more than they have for the meagre price of a ticket. It isn't that passengers are particularly generous on the trains flowing into and out of Buenos Aires city; it is simply that the train company is generous to them. Now, the links between the cans of corn beef and the tinny compartments stuffed with passengers are only circumstantial, but one has to draw one's own conclusions.

They had quizzed José until they were sure that his role in the affair was only that of an unsuspecting driver. The name of the American they had got from him and were now scouring the hotels for a certain David Salsa in the area where José had dropped his passengers off. José had made a remark about the joke with the raspberry ripple sauce to the police but they had decided it was not funny. A photo-fit description of the man had been distributed amongst the constabulary;

the Minister for Agriculture had been in touch personally with the Chief of Police and together they were looking for a scapegoat. This man Salsa seemed to fit the picture. In a curious twist of fate, it was exactly at this time that the banks had decided to freeze their customers' assets due to the value of the local currency being readjusted with that of the dollar.

The Director's boys had traced the car left abandoned by the roadside on the turn-off along the main road to Valeria del Mar. There were no signs of its occupant, but what particularly displeased the members of the Director's party who had been sent to retrieve it was that it had been vandalised, with the window smashed and the stereo ripped out. You just couldn't leave a car anywhere these days.

At about the same time as Don Vittorio de Lasagña walked down his stairs and ducked into his local kiosk to pick up the morning papers, he encountered José Afortúnado buying his packet of cigarettes. José had changed for another brand of tobacco instead of the Marlboros he usually bought.

"Wife and kids alright?" Don Vittorio enquired.

"Yes, I suppose so," said José.

The suitcase they had been carrying along the dusty road in their party gear was getting heavy. They knew that distant members of her family lived out here somewhere and that they had a small estancia where they farmed. David's gallantry had been wearing thin and he'd half considered suggesting dumping the suitcase at the roadside. Then it got the better of him and he decided to persevere. They'd been told that the estancia was a few kilometres down the dirt road when they'd asked a man who came whistling by on a lilting bicycle, but the man had been in party mood himself and it seemed like the whole of Argentina was on holiday. The kilometres had come and gone.

"Are you sure you've got the name of your people right?" David asked Rosa.

"Yes, David," Rosa replied curtly.

It was winter and out in the west, winter is the dry season. However, there is snow to be found on the distant peaks of the highest mountains, which may often last into September and the first flushes of spring down in the valleys. David was reminded for an instant of the ice cream he'd shared with José back in Cariló when he looked at them, but then the thought was gone from his mind. The sun pricked but the wind blew fiercely, bowling down the dry road and forcing dust into their eyes. When another man passed them on a bicycle with a woman perched on the handlebars, long after the first cyclist had ridden by, David and Rosa feigned to ask them directions and merely cursed instead at the clouds of dust they left churning into the air. Presently they came to a fork in the road that was devoid of any signpost or signal. Instead, it had a large algarobbo tree at the place where the two roads separated.

"What do you reckon?" David asked Rosa.

"I reckon the cyclist was lying," she replied.

The dry breeze was burning at their throats and David wished they'd taken a car instead. He looked down at Rosa who was sitting on the embankment beneath the tree.

"Don't worry," he said to her, "I'm sure it can't be too far away by now. Here, let me help you up."

He gave her his hand and helped Rosa to her feet.

"But where do we go from here?" she asked David.

He looked down at the ground and rubbed the dirt out of his eyes.

"You decide," he said.

Rosa played a game on her fingers and stopped at the ring finger of one of her hands.

"We'll go this way," she said, pointing to the right-hand fork.

"If you say so," said David, although he now strongly suspected that the left-hand road was the one to take. They had not bothered to bring any water with them, David having thought that it would merely weigh them down, but now the wind tore at them and they were thirsty. Rosa, however, had been astute enough to save the two packets of curled-up sandwiches that had been pressed into her hand by the co-driver of the bus leaving Buenos Aires and which had been subsequently toasted by the heater near their legs.

"Here," said Rosa, "Have one of these."

"Great," said David not without irony and they sat down to eat them beneath the tree. They unwrapped the cling film bandaged round them like those cheap lose-weight-quick packs. Rosa nibbled a crust sparingly, chewing at each dried-up morsel of sulphurous egg and lifeless tomato. David devoured his in three or four quick bites. Rosa was still nibbling at hers when David wiped his mouth with the back of his hand and let out a noise that galloped down the road, disguising its noise by cupping his hand.

The dust storm that had died down when they'd been eating their sandwiches picked up again. David cast a gritty glance back at the left-hand road like a child in a sweet shop who's just paid his money and is unable to take his eye off the sweets he didn't buy. Truculently he followed Rosa and said nothing. She was lugging the suitcase but he caught up with her and tried to take it from her.

"It's okay, I can manage," she said holding onto the case.

"No, don't be so silly," contested David and wrenched it out of her grasp.

"Thank-you," she said.

Two hours later they were still on the dirt road of their choice, struggling with the obnoxious suitcase as it banged against their legs. There was a faint smell of burning in the air, probably from one of the fields higher up in the valley where the farmers sometimes burnt off the pastures to encourage new growth. Noon had come and passed and the farm was no nearer in sight.

In a big country, especially where there are mountains on the horizon, the longer you walk towards them the further away they get. Argentina was such a country and it was taking them much longer than they'd anticipated reaching their destination.

"Are you sure we're going the right way?" demanded David, holding onto his hat in the wind that was blowing as he shielded the sun from his eyes.

"No, I'm not at all," Rosa retorted sullenly and carried on ahead.

After about another hour or so the road bent towards the left and began to climb a little. It sauntered past one or two thorn trees that had decided that the width of the narrow road was sufficient and had encroached upon its space, leaning over into the bend at the start of another slight incline, out of the way of the wind. Rosa snagged her new poncho on one of the thorns when she got too close to them in her weariness, leaving a strand of black and red wool tugging at it.

"Look," said David pointing.

The road they had decided not to take had companionably

rejoined their road at this point. Along its clear straight length which rolled back down the hill and out onto the plains, they could make out the crown of the algarobbo tree at the fork in the road where they had sat down previously to have their lunch.

"It looks as if it's a more direct road," said David, but distances were difficult to judge and he might have been wrong. Rosa was on the point of tears through exhaustion but she hid her face from David's.

"Are you alright?" he asked Rosa, but she was turned away from him. She sat down under the thorn trees where they were tugging, jabbing their branches like fingers pointing in the breeze. The odour of smoke was unmistakable now.

"They've started their feast without us," said Rosa sobbing as she pressed her head into her knees. The wind carried on its capricious dance in the thorn trees, impervious to Rosa's tears.

"It's alright, darling," said David, cautiously kneeling beside her.

He cloaked her against the irritating branches with his arm, pulling the soft wool of the poncho about her.

"I want to stay here," she said.

David thought for a moment then realised that it was futile to make Rosa try to go on any further.

"Do you think that my family really exists?" she asked him at length, when the warmth that had seeped from his arm into her shoulder had slowed down her tears.

"Yes, of course, darling," said David without hesitation, "You've got their name on the piece of paper."

So she rocked in his arms like her ancestors before her, remembering the dry, solitary air of the high plains in Bolivia which she'd never seen. She thought of how her mother had been forced to leave her father; how she herself had been carried down from the plains inside her across the vast tract of land that must have been so open and so terrifying to her then.

"I have a lighter," said Rosa later when they had allowed the sun that had stung their eyes in the afternoon to climb down into the shadows of the hills in front of them, piecing out its infinite memories until the day was whole again where they looked.

"Where did you get that from?" David asked her.

"I picked it up from the floor of your friend's car before we got out in the city," she said, "I thought it might come in handy and I didn't think your friend would miss it."

In truth it might have been her only souvenir from amongst the rubble of tacky seaside paraphernalia and the coast she'd left behind, but she'd slipped the lighter into the pocket of her blouse and then, later on, into her suitcase when she'd been at the hotel with David. It was easier to leave the past behind if one still had some hold on it.

"We could make our own fire," she said, "Just a little one to keep us warm."

So they gathered some brush together, held the fragile twigs tenderly in their fingers, heaped dried mounds of grass into the centre and managed to poke some fire out of the ashes. It was winter and the sun was dimming on the slopes of the fading hills in front of them. David went to gather some more twigs and small branches now; Rosa keeping the heart of the fire alive by occasionally stirring into it, puffing out its hollow seams through the white smoke like wool that nestled there, blowing a ring when the flames tricked the tinder and the grass snapped crisply in the air. Gently and with patience they teased out the sparks until a small fire clamoured in the air, devouring the thicker twigs that David had gathered and then roasting small branches that he snapped. It was an act of love, crafting flames out of the hollow dry grass. They allowed the skill of their work to tempt them to linger over it, feeding its nuzzling mouth as it flicked at the air, drawing the light of day from it, sucking the rays of the sun into the seeds of its ashes. As the day grew still in the twilight, the fire burned as precious as a jewel. Rosa was still sitting with her arms wrapped round her legs, her chin resting on her knees. Her eyes were trying to divine the existence of the fire and glowed green and brown in the dance of its embers. She poked at it with a charred stick as if peeling back the layers of her memory as she floated there. Far out into the dawning night and across the valley their fire was as visible as a star floating on the blackness of the sea.

In their reverie David and Rosa had forgotten about the time as it settled on the land around them. The whiff of smoke was stronger now and came to them in gusts on the night air. They did not hear the thunder approaching, its swell in the land under them travelling until it was nearly upon them. The clatter of hooves on the long stretch of road trembling like silver, climbing until the air round them shook.

"What's that?" said David as Rosa stamped out the fire, blackening the soil with the sole of her boot, so that only telltale wisps of smoke fluttered off in the darkness. Lying low, David and Rosa crept into the grass. And then the horses were at the fork in the road. One reared, flashing its belly at the night, its hooves crashing back down hard on the road. A soldier shouted, drawing about his men and their horses that had the hills galloping in their hooves and the dread of the night on their faces. They snorted and pounded the stampeding land.

"This way!" said one, "We've got to tell them at the farm before the fire spreads to them. Come on!"

And with that they were thundering up the road towards the farm where the cousins Rosa had never seen waited.

"What did he say?" said David, his heart trembling.

"There's a fire," said Rosa, "That's what we've been smelling all afternoon. It must be spreading out of control and the military police have come to warn them. There's a farm up here, it must be my family."

The capricious wind blew in again, this time Rosa and David could taste the roasted earth brought to them by the air in their nostrils.

"We'd better get out of here, fast," said David and they got up from their places in the grass and ran out into the road.

"It can't be far," said David, "They might need a hand, come on."

The lick of the smoke was about them now, thicker branches than those they had burned must be snapping like twigs out of sight. It was imperative that they get to the farm as soon as possible.

"Look," said Rosa after they had been running for some minutes, "There it is."

There was a sign hanging at the entrance to the track leading to the farm. It was the same as the name that was written on the piece of paper.

'Well, I guess we can get through the introductions later,' thought David as they scurried down the track. Already the night air was tarnished with smoke and the stench of green things made pulp was thick.

"I can see it over there," panted Rosa as she pointed off towards the fields on their right-hand side and David, too, saw the billowing clouds of smoke retching into the air. The orange of hidden flames flickered underneath clouds that passed high above the plains, indifferent to the fate of the land.

"What about the military?" said David as they were approaching the first of the out-lying buildings.

"They'll probably have gone on to other places to warn them as well," said Rosa, and then, "Maybe one or two of them have stayed behind to help out if they're needed," she said.

A dog snarled and snapped at them as they approached the largest building. They could hear noises inside and the stamp of hooves was pressed into the land. The dog sallied out to defend its property, half in fear and half-full of bravado, its tail wagging as it lowered its head and barked at them. But Rosa had already steered David by the hand out of its path and they were plunging into the courtyard where the geese were straddling. The horses tethered in their stables were uneasy, nudging one another, their tails swishing at imaginary flies. A woman was ushering some children inside, her back turned towards the fugitive couple so that she did not see them at first. Rosa called out to her as she was climbing the steps to the farmhouse.

"Lady!" she called, "There's a fire on its way."

"Who are you?" she answered back, and then, "Yes, I know. The military police have just been here to warn us. My husband's out in the fields with the rest of them, trying to round up the cattle."

"We've come to help," shouted Rosa, still running towards her. And then, more softly, her steps getting slower, "I'm Matilda's girl. My mother told me she'd written to you a couple of times but that she'd never got to see you."

The woman's face widened in recognition; a ghost from the past who'd travelled the same long journey down from the plains as her mother had.

"I'm Mercedes. You'd better come in," she said to both of them, "Right away."

CHAPTER TEN

Inside the farmhouse Rosa and David stood panting. The children were huddled against their mother and two other women, one older than Rosa's cousin, were quietening the dogs.

"What can I do?" said David.

"The men are over there," the mother of the children pointed through the window, "They're rounding up the cattle from the north field. You'd better take one of the horses," she said to him.

"I don't know how to ride," answered David.

"Then we'll go together," said Rosa leaving no room for discussion. When they were outside in the courtyard David asked Rosa if she'd ever ridden a horse before.

"It's in my blood," she replied, "I will remember."

The younger of the two women was standing behind them, watching as Rosa untethered a brown mare with its dark tail swishing.

"Take the track that runs alongside the stream," she said to them, "You'll find them across the bridge in the top field."

She heaved across a saddle and helped Rosa fasten it, steadying the horse for her as they did so. They drew the horse to the steps at the entrance to the farmhouse from where they were able to mount. The sky was thickening and Rosa sat in front of David, holding the reins firmly. They trotted up the dirt track to the right of the farm buildings and were soon alongside a small stream that disappeared underground into an open pipe flowing towards the farmhouse. Clouds of smoke were twisting uncontrollably; the wind, uninvited, strode out in the fields as the horse shied and smoke lashed at its nostrils. But Rosa steadied the mare, firmly pressing it between her knees as she patted its neck, whispering to it softly. David steadied himself, putting his arms round Rosa's waist. He marvelled at her skill with the mare, how she caressed it into obeying her will. As they rode over the small hump-backed bridge where other waters joined the stream, he felt her body rock back against his.

They could hear the shouts of the men on horseback in the far corner of the field they were crossing into. The gate had been left open and they entered without stopping, dogs barking as the men shouted, all the while the thick sickening plume of smoke swirling into the air, choking them. Rosa and David drew close to one of the men who had cornered six heads of cattle with the help of a dog against the side of a fence. They bellowed and tried to break free but the young man rode backwards and forwards tracing the figure of their movements.

"Stay where you are!" he shouted at them as Rosa drew their horse to one of the corners where the cattle were trapped. The mare reared slightly and David jumped from its back, landing at its hind legs before Rosa ushered it to the ground again. He ran with the dog that was snarling at the cows where they bulged and threatened to break free, opening his hands wide and clapping them together when they got so close that the dog was forced to nip one on the legs. The young man on horseback and Rosa each traced a figure on either side of him, drawing closer and closer until the heifer was penned in against itself, rubbing against the wooden posts of the fence. They heard a shout off to their right, slightly higher up in the uneven field.

"That's it, we've got them!" called a man's voice, as animals were urged on and suddenly came streaming down beside them, followed by four riders who came down the field at their heels. Rosa and the young man they had been helping moved to one side as David and the dog took the rear, letting the cattle they had cornered move with the irresistible flow that shuddered past. One of the men galloped on to the head of the procession, accompanied by another dog, whilst other riders took up positions along the flanks.

"Up you get," said the voice of the man they had heard before, helping David hoist himself into the saddle behind him with a strong hand. Rosa rode to their right, slightly ahead. She flicked a glance across the swelling cattle at the rider who was riding opposite her, his face darkened with the grime of the smoke. He was wearing the uniform of a military policeman, riding bareheaded.

143

Back in the courtyard with the livestock safely in the barns and some of the horses back in their stables, David arrived with the husband of the woman they had first met earlier. He helped David to the ground as the soldier who had been riding on Rosa's left helped her dismount. Her eyes shone with excitement as her feet reached the floor.

"Go on into the farmhouse," said the man with the thick moustache to Rosa and David. He looked across at the policeman, "We'd better go back and open the sluice gates into the fields, just to make sure," he said, and the two men's eyes met before they turned back out of the courtyard.

"That was a lucky escape," said Mercedes as David and Rosa trooped back up the stairs. The younger woman, Montserrat, was tethering the horse they had rode out on. Presently she came back into the building. Mercedes pointed to the direction the smoke was now drifting.

"It looks as if the wind's blowing in from the east now," she said, gesturing in the direction of the mountains that Rosa and David had crossed earlier on that morning on the bus.

"It looks as if it's going to miss us," she said, relieved.

"Yes, but the flames were only a kilometre away across from the top field," said one of the men who'd been out in the field, "They were starting to lick the pastures where the woods are, and if they catch hold there, there's no telling what will happen," he said, mopping his brow.

David looked at the man whose eyes were dark and obscure. There was something in him that reminded him of Rosa, but he wasn't sure what it was. Mercedes caught him looking at her youngest son.

"Manuel," she said, this is Matilda's girl,"

"Rosa," said Rosa, supplying the word.

"And this is…." said Mercedes, looking at them both.

"David," replied Rosa.

"David," said the woman who looked too young to be the mother of a man that age. Manuel looked unrecognising at the couple.

"Matilda," repeated Mercedes, "The wife of Alonso."

He looked hard into the face of the dark-haired young woman and then a faint smile of recognition crept up both their faces; a smile of people who had never met each other nor known of each others' existence, but who recognised each other.

"Welcome," said Manuel, beaming at the pair, "That was a good job you did out there. We're thankful."

He drew up two seats to the table for them to sit down.

"My father's still out with my older brother and some of the others, checking up," he said, "They'll be back soon, I guess."

"Put the kettle on the fire," said Mercedes to Montserrat, "They'll want some coffee."

Manuel went off to wipe his eyes of the smoke that had got into them while Montserrat took the heavy black kettle to the fire. She set it down on an iron ring that was glowing faintly over the embers.

"You must be tired," said Mercedes to David and Rosa, "Have you come far?"

They looked at each other and then Rosa said,

"It's taken a long time," and the journey down from the plains that the mothers of both the women had made was before them.

"Montserrat," said Rosa's cousin, "Put the children to bed but read to them for a while. We don't want to let them go to sleep until Juan is back and his father says everything's okay."

"Okay," replied the girl and took the bright-eyed children off to their room where the night and their imaginations were glowing.

"Say goodnight to David and Rosa," said the older of the two women.

"Goodnight," said the children leaving the room, the obscured stars climbing in their eyes and their minds hazily awake with the pull of them.

"You must tell me about your mother," said Mercedes as they were seated at the table together.

"She's no longer with us," replied Rosa, speaking the words in a way that would help her to avoid the pain of the memory coming back to her, "She would have liked to visit you, to have known what little family she had here in Argentina, but she never made it," she said sadly.

"I'm sorry to hear it," replied Mercedes, "But I'm glad that you did," she said sincerely. The old woman who had been in the house when they first entered was sitting rocking in her chair; she was the older sister of Mercedes' husband, Pedro, who had lost her own husband and moved in with them some years ago.

"I heard about what your father did to your mother," said the old woman to Rosa, with the rumour of a river flowing down from the dusty plains in her, "It wasn't right," she said simply.

"Shush," admonished her sister-in law.

"No, she's right," said Rosa.

Her father Alonso had had a half-brother who was dead now; the two of them sharing the same father but not the same mother. Mercedes' mother was one of the sisters of that man, and had come down like so many before her with all her hopes resting in the skill of her hands, more than forty years ago. She'd been one of the lucky ones, she'd been industrious and not without her share of luck. She'd married wisely, trading in an earlier romantic dalliance with a poor man for security with an older businessman from the province. When Pedro had come one day looking for work as a farmer or carpenter to their homestead, he'd found both employment and a young girl who would become his bride. Besides, Mercedes' mother had left her country with money in her pocket, which made all the difference. Mercedes was only ten years older than Rosa, but had had the first of her sons when still a girl.

The men were back from the boundaries now, the sound of hooves skidding over cobblestones in the courtyard.

"The wind's blowing the other way," said Pedro as he entered the room, "There's no knowing what started it. Probably some fool setting fire to his pastures with too much liquor in his belly."

He looked where David and Rosa were sitting.

"Thanks for your help," he said, "We were short of a couple of hands."

Mercedes introduced Rosa as Matilda's daughter; the daughter of the woman who'd written to them once or twice from Buenos Aires. Pedro looked into her face and saw there the same smile as the smile of his sons.

"I guess you've come for the feast," he said, "That'll have to wait until tomorrow now."

He took off his hat and went to shake David's hand.

"And you are…"

"A friend of Rosa's," said David.

Rosa smiled at Pedro and shook her hair free. At the entrance to the door the young military policeman who had stayed behind to help them was standing watching.

"I'll be going now," he said.

"Come round tomorrow in the afternoon if you can make it," said Pedro, "There'll be something to eat, if you want."

"Thank-you," said the young man, "I'll see if I can," he said, looking at Rosa.

He closed the door on the night and the sound of his horse was heard clattering back along the road in the distance. Pedro, his oldest son Juan, his wife Montserrat and the younger son Manuel had remained in the room with David and Rosa and the woman who'd first welcomed them to the farm. Pedro's older sister had risen to her feet and taken herself off to bed when she'd heard the sound of the men approaching again.

"Mercedes," said Pedro, "Let's get these people something to eat." Mercedes and Montserrat went to the kitchen and returned with a plate of cold meat and potatoes from the fridge. Pedro pulled down a bottle from off the shelf above the table and poured a large glass for himself and David, and a smaller one for each of his sons and the three women.

"To your health," he said lifting his glass to the newly arrived couple and then sat down to eat. They ate their meal slowly, the exertion of the evening ringing its silence in them. The couple from out of town had their plates heaped with food again when they had emptied them. David protested but ate it anyway.

"You'll be wanting to sleep now," said Pedro when the meal was finished. Mercedes showed Rosa and David to one of the boy's rooms that had been vacated for the night. She paused at the low, uneven entrance to the room with bedding for the two of them in her hands.

"Thank-you," said Rosa, taking it from her and kissing her cousin on the cheek. Mercedes' doubts were dispelled and with the glow of her new found cousin's kiss on her face, she returned to the dining room where her husband sat smoking next to the fire, staring into the embers that were dying down.

"Matilda's girl," said Mercedes.

"Yes," said Pedro without taking his eyes from the fire.

In the morning Rosa woke before David did. He was still asleep on the floor with a thick blanket wrapped round him and the pillow that Rosa had given him from the bed propped under his head. She smiled amiably at his still-sleeping form and watched as he turned in his sleep. She wondered at the journey that had brought them here, the endless road on which they'd walked yesterday when she'd doubted that all this really existed. She remembered too David's words to her on the bus as she woke to find the hills she'd been dreaming of upon her, the blue sky hanging over the valley where they'd finally found her family's home.

"You could pretend that I'm your friend," David had said to her.

"What are you looking at?" asked David good-humouredly when he woke to find her watching him, straightening his hair with his hand and rubbing the sleep out of his eyes. He sat up wrapped in the bedclothes, still wearing the clothes he'd been wearing the night before. He tossed the pillow at Rosa playfully and she flung it back at him with a squeal.

"That was some evening," he said to Rosa.

"Yes, wasn't it?" she said, looking out of the window which faced the lower range of mountains in the direction they'd come from. Behind the mountains was the city of Córdoba, and beyond that the endless plains that stretched all the way to Buenos Aires and even beyond to the city on the coast she'd left behind.

"What do you think will happen now?" asked David, suddenly serious.

"That depends on us, doesn't it?" replied Rosa. She took her jeans out of her suitcase and put them on while David looked through the window. Out of modesty she pulled on her T-shirt quickly then took two steps towards David, then paused.

"I was thinking," she said.

"What's that?" he said turning towards her.

"It's nice to have a friend," she replied.

He beamed a smile back at her that was as warm as the fire they had kindled together the day before when they'd seemed lost.

"Thank-you," said David, "I haven't had many friends like you."

"You could use something a bit warmer while you're on the farm," said Pedro to David when they'd finished their breakfast. His two boys

Juan and Manuel were accustomed to rising early and had already gone out to the fields. He got up and went to fetch David an old leather jacket that was hanging in the passageway.

"This should be about your size," he said, handing David the garment.

Rosa looked at him.

"Perhaps you'd like to see round the place," he continued, "In any case, I guess the ladies have a lot of catching up to do," he said, rising from the table. "We'll be back in a couple of hours," he said to Mercedes and Rosa as the two men walked out of the door.

"It's a beautiful day," said David when they were out in the courtyard and he was breathing in the clear cold air of morning.

"The wind changed direction again last night," said Pedro, "The fire caught hold of the woods just a bit higher up. They burned like a box of matches; set fire to the field where we'd rounded up the cattle. We're fortunate we've got the stream on this side and it's been full with the melt-waters coming off the tops. You wouldn't think it," he continued to David, "But the water that flows through this place comes down all the way from those mountains over there," he signalled to the line on the horizon that David had seen with Rosa the day before.

"It certainly is a big country," said David, taking it all in.

"There are many big countries," said Pedro looking at him, "It just depends on which one you happen to have been born in."

In the kitchen, Mercedes was holding Rosa's hand.

"Your sister?" Mercedes was asking her.

"Oh, she's still there," replied Rosa, then she added, "She seems to be happy."

Though Rosa had only been alluded to in her mother's rare letters from Buenos Aires- only two had ever reached the farm- and the two women had never met before the previous evening, they had much to talk about. Their parents had fled the place of their birth because it had become a living hell to them, but a person will always look to that unknown place with longing, searching out a past in the grains of the soil.

"I'm happy here," said Mercedes, looking out of the window at the mountains on the skyline, "Pedro is a good man, and my sons have a future. Back there," she signalled to the far-off distant north in the direction the flames had come from last night, "They had nothing."

"Yes," agreed Rosa, though she couldn't help but wonder what it would have been like to meet the father she'd never seen and been a part of a family in its own right. The memories she had of her time in the big house with her mother and sister were still present, but she'd pushed them away from her with each of the years of her leaving, so that by now the memories seemed to belong to someone else. Recollections of waiting at tables for people she didn't care for, dolled up in clothes she didn't want to wear were blurred now.

"And the American?" asked Mercedes.

"He's a friend," answered Rosa.

"How long have you had the place?" David asked Pedro.

"This has always been my place," Pedro replied without irony. He pointed to the pastures in front of them, up to the big mountains beyond. "I was born in a little village up there in those hills," he said, "I came down when I was sixteen to make a life for myself and have been here ever since. It's hard country up there and the grazing is difficult. Me, I prefer it down here. What about you?"

"My town's small, too," he said, "Some people think it's a big city, but you only realise how small it really is when you get outside it."

"Yes, a lot of towns are like that," said Pedro, "So how come you never learned to ride a horse?" he asked the American as the man followed him uneasily on his mount. They went down to the edge of his lands, land he'd had to buy when he and his wife's herd had grown and needed more room for grazing. When his family had grown too, he'd had to extend the original building. Pedro didn't think of himself as the owner of a big estate, he thought of it more as the size that was necessary to accommodate those that he was responsible for and which grew with every passing year.

"The police were up here again last night," he commented, "We tried to put out the fire in that forest but what can you do out here?" he asked to the winds, "We've got no resources to deal with a blaze like that. Some people just don't appreciate the luck they're born with," he said as they turned back towards the farmhouse.

The wind had begun to pick up again and David and Pedro

stopped at the side of a fence where the barbed wire was singing with the wind. A little way off from it was a small tree that was stunted on the otherwise open field, its leaves still clinging to slender branches that whipped under the force caught in it. David watched how the whole weight of the tree bowed with the force of the wind, from the bunched up leaves down through the elasticity of its trunk into its roots, it seemed. Pedro was disentangling the barbed wire of the fence, twisting it in his leather gloves as he tried to pull it tighter.

A flock of birds spiralled in the sky, fanning out as they turned on a gust before coming together as one darkening mass, lifting into the sky then swooping down towards the tree. As the tree settled after the flurry of wind that had passed over it, so the birds settled too. Their wings were almost indistinguishable from the dark leaves that rippled on the tree in the aftermath, like fingers that had been caressed by something and were now letting its force dissipate through them. David thought of Rosa and tried to understand what it was that had brought them together. The tree shook again and the flock of birds shook in it. The sun-bent boughs of the tree strained, then it shook in its upper branches, the birds holding on as the wind rippled through their feathers. David saw all this and felt it inside him also.

"Time to get back to the house," said Pedro.

"Yes," said David and they motioned their horses into the wind as it glistened on them.

Rosa, Mercedes and Montserrat were in the kitchen preparing dinner when Pedro and David returned.

"The boys will be back soon," said Mercedes.

"Ramiro said he might be along later," said Pedro eyeing his wife, as he recalled the words of the policeman who had helped them last night and David wondered whom he might be referring to. Rosa seemed relaxed and smiled at him briefly as he entered, though he could not help but feel it was the smile of someone who knew they were playing a game together; of one who wished to keep it secret.

"The wind's picking up again," said Pedro to his wife, "It's to be hoped it doesn't rekindle any sparks that might still be smouldering in the fields out there," he motioned towards the direction of where the wind had been tugging at the tree and further beyond. He had noticed the blackened, scorched earth where the fire had passed over it, had held his breath as the memory of the fire and the rounding up of the cattle from the night before passed through him too. David had been too preoccupied with mentally establishing the boundaries of the farm tacked against the open fields in barbed wire and the occasional stone wall to notice what Pedro had noticed further off. To Pedro it was the stuff of his daily life that changed only as the seasons changed it; though one winter was never the same as another and this year the snow had not yet fallen deep in the valley. No spring was the same as another, either, but one had to see many springs and many winters pass on the land to understand this. He was aware, without ever having voiced the thought to himself, that even as he had found the boundaries of the farm expanding with the purchase of new lands to feed the growing population of cattle, their place was small compared to all the lands on the valley floor. This huge corridor opened up all the way from La Rioja in the north, through Córdoba, down to the open lands of San Luis in the south. There it met the central system of the same province like an island castle surrounded by the widening seas of the plains around it. On the west side towards where the wind had ridden, the hills of a mighty chain came down from immeasurably remote places where the snow lingered even beyond summers. Like the spine of an animal so huge that few had ever glimpsed the jewels of its eyes in the remotest places, or even guessed at them, the chain of mountains stretched down from the high plains from whence Rosa and Mercedes' families had issued. Proof that in distant lands beyond the imagination people also lived.

David looked again at Rosa, who seemed to have been silently accepted into the bosom of a family which had only the day before been as remote as the two letters penned by the imagination of her mother, and who had dropped into Mercedes and Pedro's world just as unexpectedly. Rosa and Mercedes had not spoken much about how it was that the younger woman had found her way here across so many miles and so many unspoken years. It was enough to them both that she was here now, for both of them understood that some things from the past were better left covered up, out of the way of the present. People may share many secrets with one another in their lifetimes, though secrets may remain unspoken even between the people that share them.

So, too, might a person keep a secret from him or herself through the course of many years; though it will stay there to rot until their life is not their own. But those who can see beyond the place they are born, who carry with them knowledge of the lands their families have come from even though they have never been there, understand. To them the present is not a moment lived in isolation that hurls them into an unknown future, but the natural inheritance of a past which might be painful but whose future has a familiar face. David understood in that moment that he was the outsider here, and that just as fate had led him here unexpectedly, so would his leaving of the place become inevitable. He did not yet know whether Rosa would follow him, but he had understood that it was her choice to make and not his.

The image of the tree out in the fields welled up inside him, so that for a moment he understood something of how he was part of the tree himself; or how it was part of him. In his mind the wind was tugging at its leaves and at the birds that rested there amongst them, until one by one each bird became a leaf which was pulled from the tree by the wind; or which shook itself free of it. David felt himself falling like one of the leaves as it was gathered into the eye of a darkening storm, but somewhere, still hidden from him, was the growing knowledge of his own power of flight. Crouched like a cat inside him it had not yet flashed its precious eyes.

"Sit down, David," said Pedro to David as he glimpsed the coldness that was forming on the eye of the foreigner. It was something that he himself had felt that afternoon, when it had come to touch him with the knowledge of the wind's capriciousness and of how the fire might so easily have ravaged the farm if it had chosen to do so. Rosa looked at David and he smiled dimly back at her. He could at least be thankful for the safe deliverance of a soul other than his own that had reached a place where it might manage to shake off the fetters of a long journey.

"The boys will be in soon," said Mercedes repeating her sentence of some minutes before, and calmly like ripples on the surface of his skin David understood how all people are bound to others with a love that frees them from the isolation of themselves. He stroked the grain of the wood of the chair against which he was leaning. Only the wise ones and the mystics know that isolation is self-imposed by minds too blind and too caught up in themselves to understand their attachment to that which is around them. The heart cherishes its freedom and nurtures knowledge of this even at the same time in which the mind has dispensed with the means to achieve it.

"We will eat soon," announced Pedro to the silence that had fallen on them all. Montserrat stirred the embers of the fire in the hearth to life, as much perhaps as anything to abate the fire which was neither of their making nor under their control and keep it at bay. Rosa peered into its crackling flames and for the first time allowed herself to understand that from its ashes may come new life even as old life was being consumed. She smiled across at Montserrat warmly, the two of them silently at peace. Mercedes understood that her family was now complete, though neither of her two daughters had come from her womb and the two boys, Juan and Manuel, were not yet fully men. The girl that had stirred the fire was the wife of the eldest of her sons and what had not yet been sanctioned officially by them having a place to call their own had at least been sanctioned in Mercedes' own heart with the births of her two grandchildren. This girl Rosa, who was not of her own flesh and blood and was so at the same time, had found a house where she might take lodging, but would never be bound to stay.

Just then Juan, followed by Manuel, strode into the house. Rosa looked up at the younger of the two brothers as he entered the room and the smile of the one matched the smile of the other. Manuel recognised the sister he'd never had and though Rosa had left behind a sister a long time ago, she was at last beginning to feel that she was no longer an only child; or worse still, an orphan. Mercedes saw the smile of people she'd never met but who were part of her family in the face of Matilda's girl, Rosa.

"Set another place for dinner, mother," said Manuel to Mercedes, "We saw Ramiro back on the road from a distance off and he'll be here soon."

Mercedes and Pedro exchanged glances but David was still held by a meaning that eluded him in the tree that shook in the lonely field on its own. Pedro saw the ice that was forming in the man's eyes slowly

154

freezing his gaze at a distant point across the fields, back towards where they'd been together that morning.

'It doesn't matter where a man comes from,' Pedro thought, 'Deep down they are all the same, though some have more good in them than others.'

The young military policeman eyed David suspiciously as he took his place at the table opposite Rosa, but with their heads bent towards the soup that was served them, only Pedro and Mercedes, the older ones, noticed how the young man darted glances at Rosa. It was doubtful that Rosa could see herself smiling in the gaze of the young dark-skinned policeman. This much about love Mercedes understood; it took people unawares and without them wanting it to.

"Tell me, Ramiro," said Don Pedro, inwardly grateful to have so many people seated at his table, (although it was also in his nature to worry over providing for them), "What's the news of the fire? We've not had enough snow yet this year and the ground is brittle with the lack of it. The stalks are dry and hollow and this wind is thinning them to no good. I couldn't be sure, but when I was out with David," (Pedro was using David's first name before the young policeman even though in his own mind he addressed Rosa's companion as the 'foreigner', drawing them both into one conversation), "I thought I could see a few wisps of smoke blowing in the air towards the hills."

He froze with the memory of it and how the manes of the two horses had wafted in the same direction before he had decided he could do no more to guess the trickery of the flames and had turned back to the house with the American.

"Fire's still burning," said Ramiro, taking the slice of bread from his mouth, "They say it's started snowing up in the mountains, there was a man who had come down from Dos Rios for the fiesta. This wind's going to keep the snow over on the other side, though, and in the meantime it's anybody's guess how much tinder there is out there still smouldering."

"That's what I'm afraid of," said Pedro, suddenly feeling himself much older than any of the other men present, "We've hacked down what bush we can and put it on the opposite side to the wind in the fields, but the trees out at the boundary were shaking today. They were restless."

He looked across at David,

"Isn't that right?" he asked.

"Yes," said David, "I noticed it too."

"So, what's your business here?" asked the young policeman of David in a manner that surprised all of the people seated, except for the elder son, Juan, who knew Ramiro better than the rest.

"He's here as my escort," said Rosa boldly, "If it wasn't for him I don't know if I'd have ever made it out of that damned city," she said.

David felt the quizzical gaze of the dark-skinned man on him and then he remembered why it was that he and Rosa had fled first Mar del Plata in the first place. David felt himself reddening, but the policeman had been taken aback by the strength of the conviction in the beautiful dark-haired woman's response to his question, and he knew very well why it was that he'd decided to make the trip out to Pedro's ranch again. It wasn't in his interests to pursue his line of questioning. In his own mind the apparition of this dark-haired beauty and the American together the same night as the fire was significant and his only doubt was to what the connection between the young woman and the foreigner was.

Rosa couldn't help but steal a glance at Ramiro when he was turned towards Manuel in conversation. The excitement of the fire the night before was still inside her and a memory of two trees by a small farmstead on the long road in to Córdoba had taken root unexpectedly.

Ramiro and Manuel were engrossed in conversation, they took the fire seriously but they also allowed themselves to feel the excitement of the night before burn in them as well. The recklessness of their youth hadn't yet been tempered by a fear of ultimate disaster; they were both good horsemen and should the impetuous wind steal up on them they both felt equal to riding it out. Manuel had yet to fall in love and feel himself tied like a man trying to ride away but getting nowhere. Ramiro had felt more than anyone on the farm the previous night the relish of the flames and the relish in his pride at feeling able to outride them. Though his horse, too, had shied when he'd stolen too close to them. Now he was back here eating with the family in a place where he'd ridden both dangerously and in hope. There was something about the girl and the way her eyes flashed that would make him ride even more dangerously next time, without thinking too much about the consequences. Her long hair flicked to one side when she spoke but there were also times when she held her head slightly bowed, as if in contemplation, or when she would hold it steady and raise her eyes to meet the gaze of anyone who might dare challenge her. Mercedes had also noticed this in her and something of Rosa's mother's old pride, before the distance between her and her employers and her and her husband had grown too deep and solitary in her, was in the young woman. In the place that Rosa's mother and her own mother had come from there were mountain peaks whose summits were too high to see, whose highest reaches moved away from you as you approached them.

Mercedes had no need to question Rosa much about her past, nor did she feel she had a right to. Whatever misfortunes had been cast on her when her mother, Matilda had felt it necessary to abandon the only family she knew in the vain hope of establishing a better way of life somewhere else, Mercedes felt that the girl had done well in seeking to free herself of hers. It was impossible for her to refuse the girl the right to a new life. The hopes their mothers had cherished in their hearts when they had left the high plains of Bolivia hadn't been fully realised; it was her duty to help their tradition so that her own children might not have to undergo such a long and arduous journey, nor their children after them. In her heart Mercedes always knew that one day she would have to say goodbye to the younger of her sons, Manuel, before he might return one day grown a man. Matilda's girl was sincere and good, and she had already made the journey that had made her into a woman. This much she had glimpsed in Rosa's eyes, and the young woman's smile echoed the smile of the son she could see fast growing into the young man he needed to be. He would return to them, when he was ready to do so. Mercedes understood that her children's children would become her children as well.

"Give me your glass," said Pedro.

He would serve the man before he served his sons and the other young man who had helped them last night. That too was tradition. David chewed the meat in his mouth slowly, savouring it like an animal that sensed that there might be harder times ahead. The American was even quieter than he'd been when he and Matilda's girl had first arrived at the farmhouse. Sometimes Pedro also kept silence with himself when the burden of knowledge that had been tempered by responsibility to his family forbade him from speaking. Juan, the elder, was much like himself in this respect. Pedro envied his younger son Manuel the ability to be untroubled too much by situations beyond his control, but he was the first to pour scorn on him if he saw that the boy did not quite understand the world just yet. That would come when Manuel had a wife and children of his own to look after. Pedro understood the American's silence and they had travelled much of the day earlier on without the need for speaking. It was not so much that what he shared in common with the man was something of their own choosing, rather than a path taken which he had crossed and recrossed many times himself, on which the American himself now also walked. It is easy for a man to walk in isolation even when he feels surrounded by his own family; especially for a man like Pedro who is born to a world where the responsibility of decision-making rests on one set of shoulders alone. Tacitly, Mercedes and Pedro's marriage had worked because she felt it both her responsibility and her right to share some of that burden, but this was an unspoken secret between them in the harsh lands where they lived. No whisper of it was spoken outside the walls of their house, nor would Mercedes belittle her husband in the eyes of others by challenging him for this right openly. That they would discuss matters of the farm and that their children were often part of the conversation was proof enough to Mercedes that her husband was man enough to understand his own limitations.

Rosa could see that David was locked in contemplation of something far beyond the confines of where they were; just as in her own mind a memory of two trees proud under moonlight had taken root and was growing. She caught his eye as he raised the wine to his lips and the ice that had formed on his gaze melted as David remembered the familiarity of her look. Instinctively he cast a glance to where the policeman was sitting and though Ramiro and Manuel were locked in hearty conversation, their laughter framing the canopy of the room where they were all eating, Ramiro felt the man's presence on him. It was the conversation of young men who must prove to the rest of the party that they are so, and as such Ramiro was aware of the effect that they were having on those around them. Rosa looked where David was looking and found herself embarrassed, settling her sight on Ramiro. She looked straight back at David but though the companion of her recent nights was dimly smiling, she could no longer see into the depths of his eyes. They had frosted over again with memories of his own, memories that she wasn't a part of. The American had told her fragments of his life with his daughter and with the wife from whom he was separated; she too had told him fragments of her life. Somewhere inside Rosa a seed was growing swathed in moonlight. She had begun to feel it on the bus so that it shaped its own dreams within her dreams. The American would never know, nor must he. That would be unfair to him, she realised.

David saw how the wind swept up the dry leaves that had fallen against the window of the kitchen. He heard the young policeman when he told of the snow that was falling in the mountains on the other side and probably high up on this side also, where they lay out of view.

His daughter was not with him now but in reality it had been many years since she had been. His wife, perhaps, had never really been with him, although their temporary union had brought them a child. He imagined first his wife and then his daughter taking steps across imaginary snow that was falling in mountains he'd never been to. In his mind their steps left deep imprints where they walked but it was only these that David could see; not the bodies of the two people that had gone on ahead of him and made the indents into it. The footsteps of his wife were deeper than those of his daughter, and those left by the little girl he had carried once on his back on the slopes of an unknown country seemed to fade before him and disappear before his sight. He could hear her voice calling him, and his own voice calling her, though the sounds came from some place far off from where her tiny footsteps retreated out of the boundaries of his imagination. He could taste the food on his plate and he ate it as if it might disappear. He could see the smile of the young woman he had shared a bed with coaxing him out of his reverie but felt how it was moving out of his reach; how it, too, would become nothing more than a memory. He smiled dimly to the warm-hearted man who sat at the head of the table when he passed him the plate laden with meat without utterance. David in his turn passed it on to the elder son, Juan who was sitting beside him and he took his share before passing it to the mother of his children. David chewed each mouthful carefully.

He had taken his place in the house as a temporary guest. He spoke little and watched as the woman who had brought him here took her place in the house. He could see how Manuel and Ramiro competed for the attention of anyone that would bear them witness, and he felt apart from them. Rosa would never betray him, he knew, just as he would never betray Rosa's past to those present in the room. But he knew that his own steps would lead him away from her in the future; not out of choice, but as if her voice would also call to him from further and further away as time passed. Perhaps it was he that had walked across the snow and made the imprints he thought his wife had made; perhaps he had always been walking away from her. No man in his right mind would ever consciously walk away from his own child, though; perhaps he had taken the footsteps in his sleep.

After dinner David found himself making excuses and putting on the leather coat Pedro had lent him before turning out into the wind that was sweeping the valley. David could taste something on his lips and on his tongue that he couldn't see, that was only hinted at in the far reaches of the upper-most clouds that passed overhead as the night sky drew in. Up the valley to the north the sky seemed black and ominous, where it slid down to meet the mountains to the west as they cut a diagonal path towards where Pedro and Mercedes' farm lay.

'A fox will always turn back on its tracks,' David thought to himself. Though why this thought should leap into his mind now was a mystery to him. He had not yet voiced to himself the thought of his leaving the farm, but with each step he took further into the increasing darkness the farm and all its inhabitants seemed to float further and further away, on a sea whose mist his eyes were veiled in. He eventually found himself at the tree by the patch of barbed wire fencing that Pedro had unsnagged the day before. The birds were gone from it though and David found himself surprised at the naïve but up to then unconscious expectation that they would still be there. It had lost some of its leaves too, curled into the black eye of a storm that had swooped down like the gathering of the birds but had passed over the farmhouse without sweeping it. David turned up the collar of the leather jacket to keep the wind from funnelling down inside it. He saw one black leaf snatched from a branch, imprinted against the crisp outline of the sky as the clouds were momentarily parted. Then another as it was pulled upwards and away. Then almost immediately another. He touched his head and felt the first thin flakes of snow that were dissolving into water. Then the flakes and the ice they transported within them had disappeared and a sleety rain was being whipped against his forehead. The drops began to thicken and out of the ice he felt on his fingertips and the snow that had dissolved, the chill rain of a winter evening began to beat down. He hastened to get back to the farmhouse now before the full brunt of the storm was on him, more out of a question of habit than decision. In his native city when it rained you ducked into the nearest café, or into a shopping mall, or the lobby of your apartment. Here there were no such places to be found and the lights of the farmhouse glowed like a beacon inviting him, but which also reminded him of its isolation in the midst of the massive valley.

When he got back he hesitated slightly before opening the door. He almost knocked on its heavy oak frame but stopped himself from doing so just in the nick of time. He turned round to face the wet sleet that was dissolving into rain on the stones of the courtyard and then he understood the importance of the news he had to give Pedro and the others.

"It's raining," he said as he entered the kitchen and those that still remained in the room turned to look at him, "That should put the last of the fire out," he said turning to Pedro.

The man nodded as he took a puff on his pipe and the smoke rose up into the rafters of the ceiling. Pedro was relieved of the weight of the burden he'd been carrying but as the night had gone on, with the American's absence, he had allowed the mantle of another one to settle on him. Manuel, Rosa and Ramiro sat chatting in the corner in the glare of the fire. Rosa looked up as David entered with the news and he began undoing the buttons of the leather jacket, but Manuel's voice pulled her back into the conversation with Ramiro who had been making them laugh.

Pedro drew up a chair at the table for David and the man sat down with him. They left the three younger ones to their own conversation. Now and again Rosa looked up to where David was sitting but he had his back to her and was chatting now with Pedro.

"You must have come a long way to get here," said the owner of the farm.

"I guess I have," replied David.

"Your life in America must be very different to ours' here," said the older man, more as a statement than as a question, "What brought you here in the first place?"

David thought hard for a moment before answering him,

"A misunderstanding," he said.

Pedro nodded and took another puff on his pipe, drawing in the American's response to him as he did so. What was left unsaid in the man's answer was food enough for Pedro's quiet imagination. The distance that separated them was not so great in the older man's mind and the friendship they had garnered rested not so much on what they had said to each other, but in what they had left unsaid. It was the quietness of the American that encouraged Pedro to let the man into his world. Juan had Montserrat and the children to think about and Manuel was still in the flush of youth that made serious conversation with him difficult. The American was different.

"I hadn't really thought much about where I was going or what I was doing," said David as an after-thought.

Pedro assented with his head but left David space to carry on what he was saying, peering into the smoke which rose from his pipe.

"I mean, I didn't really know anything about this country," continued David. He stopped in mid-sentence and paused. Somewhere at the back of his mind was the dim realisation that he'd been talking about something else, or had been about to, but Pedro was staring into the distance and not at him and David found himself retracing footsteps in the snow that had seemed to belong to him. He had needed to leave the house after dinner and had found himself taking refuge in the solace of his own company. But when he'd reached the tree where he'd been earlier on that day, a sense of his smallness out in the vastness of the plain had overcome him. He'd felt how the first flecks of snow had fallen on his head, how the coldness they encapsulated disappeared as they dissolved into water in his hair. He'd set out on his walk without knowing where he was going to, but the tree marked a boundary in his mind and his thoughts were snared on the barbed wire fence that sang in the wind where Pedro had twisted it. The smoke from the older man's pipe hung lazily in the air and filled the ceiling.

"The land goes on much, much further than we can see," said Pedro out of the dimness of the smoke. He moved towards the bottle that had been resting on the dining table and poured both himself and the American another glass from it.

"The grapes that go into making this need both the sun and the chill from the frost," he said, "Without the sun they will not ripen but without the chill a quality in the wine is lost. This particular grape, the Malbec, grows best at a certain altitude, and although it is difficult to realise, the valley we are in is much higher than the city back there where you have come from."

David thought at first about his hometown; the Big Apple, they called it, but then he realised that the Argentine had been talking about Buenos Aires, the city he'd left with Rosa. The names of both cities were misleading, it occurred to David. There was hardly a green leaf in the whole of New York amidst the skyscrapers that closed in on you from above, except of course for the manicured parks where executives in expensive suits strolled by day and delinquents prowled by night. As for Buenos Aires, he had not felt the crisp air that he breathed out here in the country, and on his trip past the long curling arm of the brown river there was a sluggishness that slowed down everything. Then a story from the bible about Adam and Eve and the snake, and the temptation they had succumbed to, came back to him. The name of the capital city of Argentina was ironic too, he thought, probably deliberately so on the part of its founders in the same way that the name of his own city was designed to entice people within its confines. It was curious how different life in both cities was compared to the lives these people led out here on the farm. It was curious how different his own life seemed to have become to him. At times it was as if he was observing someone else's life out here, but then he wondered whose life he'd been living before fate and Rosa had delivered him to the farm. Here he was, dressed during the day in a leather coat that wasn't his and which had no place in the city; the cowboy hat he had left on the peg when he had been out on his walk.

"The life of a man is the same as the life of a wine," said Pedro, drawing David out of his thoughts, "Too much sun without the chill and a man becomes too full of himself; too much chill without the sun and a man cannot mature enough to understand what it is he's working for."

David thought again of the imposing towers of concrete and glass and steel of his hometown, how the shadow of the day was cast early on the people that scurried along its floor. He remembered too how he'd once been one of their number.

"Take my son, Manuel over there," he pointed to the young man engaged in boisterous conversation in front of the fire, "He's not yet fully felt the winter upon him, but when he does I hope he won't feel it too cruelly. Of course," continued Pedro, "Solitude and wine are the privilege of old men," he said allowing a wry smile to curl upon his face.

"Here," he said to David, "This bottle needs finishing and you're the man to help me."

With the bottle finished and set down firmly on the table, the conversation of the three people by the fire faded. Manuel stretched his arms in front of him and yawned.

"Work to do tomorrow," said Pedro to his boy, "Of course, you're welcome to stay," he challenged Ramiro, and the policeman hastily made his excuses to his companions and rose to take his coat against the night.

"You'll be here for a few days more?" He enquired of the beautiful dark-haired woman whose cheeks were bronzed by the fire but whose guileless smile was now turned away from him. She looked up at David and Ramiro shivered in anticipation of the journey he had to make back down the road to the village where he lived. But David was seeing something else while he saw all this unfold in front of him and the snow that had begun to fall out on his walk that evening was falling in his mind also. Pedro saw this too; just as he had seen when they had arrived the night before, and he stood up from the table. The farm-owner was always the last to bed; this too was his privilege.

"Ride carefully," he said to Ramiro, and with that the younger man was gone out of the door into the dark night that rushed in to meet them.

"Goodnight," said Manuel cheerfully as he left the room for one of the backrooms that was sometimes used for storage.

"You two okay then?" asked Pedro as he was snuffing out the fire with his back turned to Rosa and David.

"Yes, thank-you," said Rosa for both of them, "We'll manage fine."

David followed Rosa down the corridor to their bedroom and as she was going through the doorway she reached for David's hand and pressed his fingers gently in hers.

"You don't have to," mumbled David struggling to see Rosa in the darkness.

"I know," she said, "And you don't need to remind me."

She stood for a moment by the window where the curtains were undrawn. The night rain pattered against the windowpane and up on the horizon heavy clouds could be seen forming where they were gathering in solidly. Rosa pressed her lips against the glass and for a moment thought of saying what had been on her mind ever since their journey on the bus, but she could not bring herself to do so. David stood motionless in the doorway.

"Come in and close the door," she said to him.

There was light coming in through the window that reflected on the underside of the amassing clouds where the curtains had not been fully closed. She shook her long hair open and turned towards him, the distance that had formed between them not of her making and uncertain of its purpose.

"You should have a woman that loves you," she said to David.

"I," stuttered David, but he did not know what to say.

"You," answered Rosa in the second's silence that ensued, "Have been my first friend in a long time. For that I owe you."

"No, Rosa, it's not like that all. You don't owe me anything."

He was on the defensive, wanting her to see that he valued her more than that. A part of him admired her, but a part of him resented her past life; though he was resentful of himself also for having succumbed to something that was so contrary to his nature.

"I must leave you some money," said David, hating himself for saying it.

"So you will be leaving then?" Rosa asked, voicing the fear that she had known all along would overtake them both; "I knew you would want to leave me eventually."

"No, it's not like that; I, I," he wanted to tell her that he loved her

165

and that she was beautiful, that her past didn't matter to him and that they could make a life for themselves somewhere here where both of them could forget their pasts. But he could not bring himself to say it, though he struggled with the emptiness of the words in his mouth and hated himself for this also. Something within him had changed and was gliding away from him, as if against his will. The rain had changed to snow and flakes began to stick on the windowpane; the darkness of the world outside that had been intruding on the room where Rosa and David stood was being papered over.

"Come to bed," she said to David as she undressed by the bed where she had slept last night, modesty about her and her back turned towards him as her skin slipped into its undress in the cold of the night air. Her neck was long and curving; her beauty moving out of his reach even as he moved towards it to embrace her naked shoulders. She would give herself to him completely if he required it of her.

"We," David tried to say.

"Yes. We are," replied Rosa, "I need to know what it is to feel love before I am to lose it again. Those men, they…,"

"I know," said David and he wrapped his arms tighter around her. She owed him this and she would not let him go without feeling that she had given him something that was of value, as he had provided her with the chance that would enable her to offer herself again. A chance for the possibility of love to enter her life again.

"I don't want to leave you, Rosa," he said.

"I know. But you must," she whispered.

She felt the child that was inside her, her child that would grow up without ever knowing its true father. This night at least her unborn daughter would feel her father close to her.

"My mother came down from Bolivia when she was with me, with my older sister accompanying her," she said in the quietness, "With the years that passed my father found himself another woman and my mother's heart was broken because she could not bring him to her, or offer him anything that would make him want to come and look for her."

There was a pause before she continued,

"Then I left her, too," she said. "My children will know that there has been love between their parents."

"Of course they will, Rosa. You will have beautiful children," said David. They held each other tightly and the nakedness of their bodies rocked each other to sleep. The snow fell blindly, covering the window like a blanket.

CHAPTER ELEVEN

In the morning when he woke Rosa was already dressed against the frost that had crept into the room. She smiled at David but her smile was already retreating from him, her eyes were somewhere he could not quite follow, though the memory of how they had lain together the night before was still on his skin.

"I must go and help Montserrat dress the children and prepare the breakfast," she said, her words travelling towards him across the distance that had formed in the room where they had been sleeping.

"I think I'll see what Pedro's up to," said David, and already his mind was racing across the snow that had been falling in the night and out towards the tree on the dim horizon at the boundary of the farm.

When he had dressed he went to the kitchen and found Pedro seated at his place at the table. The children had already eaten and Mercedes busied herself in the kitchen with Montserrat.

"Rosa's outside with the children," said Montserrat by way of explanation to him through the open door. David could see their imprints in the snow and beside them those of the woman he had held the night before. Pedro was gazing into space, quietly ruminating in the same position he had been in last night. It seemed as if he'd never been to bed.

"Sit down," he said to David, "You must eat something."

"Thank-you, I…" said David, but before he had time to finish what he was trying to say Pedro's words cut through his own.

"There's no need for thanks," said Pedro, "It is I who have to thank you for helping me save the cattle the other night. Do you know what one head of cattle costs?" he asked David, turning towards him.

"No, I have no idea," said David, but already the older man's face was curling into a smile and the wrinkles that showed his age had spread into the corners of his eyes.

"I want to show you something when you've finished your breakfast," he said to David, "Eat up."

With that he stood to his feet, slapping David on his shoulder as if suddenly roused from his reverie. When they had mounted the horses and David was following gingerly on the one Pedro had let him ride the day before, Pedro signalled for him to look up. The breath of the horses steamed in the cold that had condensed about the courtyard and their hooves echoed on the hardness of the cobblestones.

"You see?" he said to David, pointing up at the skyline.

David looked to where the farm owner was looking and breathed in the ice of the air, as mountains he had not been able to see the day before glistened under their new-formed blanket. It was cold, as if the heat of his journey on the long dusty road two days before with Rosa had been erased at the flick of a switch by some giant's hand, but the sun was shining thinly on the newly christened mountains.

"Beautiful, aren't they?" said Pedro.

It was true, David hadn't been able to see their full shapes before, but now that they were heavy under their white blanket they cut a hole in the sky where before they had merged with it in the day's haziness. The whiter the mountains shone, the bluer the sky around them grew, until the day was hard and shone as they rode out to the farm lands, before the chill of the morning was stamped out.

"There's more snow ahead," said Pedro as the farmhouse blurred into the distance.

"How do you know?" asked David who was surprised at the growing fierceness of the rays striking them from underfoot. It seemed to him that the ubiquitous sun was a constant in the landscape in this part of Argentina.

"Don't be fooled," said Pedro to him by way of an answer, "The winter here brings snow and in the summer the rains come. The air is dry, but at night up there where I was born," he signalled again to the mountains, "It freezes the land until it becomes a solitary thing."

Presently they came across a group of molle trees to the south of the farmhouse on a patch of land where a few dry stalks of brown grass pushed through the covering of whiteness. The horses stepped crisply in the snow and here and there dark holes were left where it had fallen unevenly, clinging to the long stalks and amassing silently. Pedro stopped a few yards from one of the larger trees whose limbs had shattered the rock out of which it had grown. The gnarled trunk of the tree twisted out of the rock and David wondered that any living thing might have the force for life to push through anything so solid.

"I've never seen anything like that," he said to Pedro, still looking at the tree.

"Ah, they're older than you or I," said Pedro, "Part of an ancient forest of which this is only the remains."

David had read articles in magazines before about how, if cities were left unattended by their inhabitants for a number of years, the trees would take over and organic life would force its way through pavements and even topple buildings. But he had never seen anything such as this, where the might of a single tree was enough to split the very rock against which its seed had been sown. Somehow he'd imagined that it would take the force of many trees to break through concrete, break through solid matter. He looked at the trunk leading down to the rock and imagined how the rock must also serve as an anchor for it in the winds that blew down the valley in such an open place. The trunk that flowed through the stone and down to where its roots must hold it seemed almost to have merged with the same substance it had broken.

"A man can learn many things by looking at the land," said Pedro, "The trees and the mountains are more than adornments on the landscape; they are the land," he continued, "And when the water falls from the sky and is frozen into this soft whiteness," he gestured at the snow field whose surface was now pock-marked by the stepping places made by the hooves of the horses, "If it holds fast and night and the wind come to freeze it, it may split the trunks and limbs of trees itself."

David reached up, letting one hand free of the rein that held his horse, running his fingers through his hair where it fell against his temple. The wind picked up small pockets of snow where it gusted gently and David remembered how he had felt the first flakes of snow, the first whisper of the winter, fall there and dissolve; clearing his mind as they did so.

"These trees break through stone," said Pedro as if reading David's thoughts, "But it is useful to them also and provides a base on which they can grow for many years, longer than you or I," he said.

David stared into the depths of the small forest where it had shut out light and seemed to hold its own council, making the snow dance round it in small gusts but not seeming to penetrate into its heartland. Again his mind was drawn back to the solitary tree by the barbed wire fence where the birds had swooped down in a black rush which had then settled into individual birds, calming, as the tree became a multitude of individual leaves rippling in the wind.

He had carried the knowledge of the existence of his daughter and of the wife who had produced her with him for a long time, though he had not always understood how they had come to exist and form part of his world. Many times it had seemed to him that they were giants, shadows in his memory like the sleeping giants on the horizon which now let through, now blocked out the sun. He had used them. His own existence was dependent on theirs', but his wife had never been the woman he had supposed her to be; and he had not been the man she had supposed him to be.

He wondered what Rosa would be up to with the children. He thought of her having gone out with them into the newly fallen snow in the morning and how Montserrat, their mother, had stayed behind in the kitchen to help Mercedes. Something Rosa had said last night while they lay like silver in each other's arms had made him think now about children. She was older than he was. She had the ability to meet people on their own terms and to recall an innocence in herself, forgetting her own past. David had knowledge of his past all along, but he'd shied away from it all these years. He lifted his head and let his wife and the image of her go now, and wondered whether he had love left in his heart for his daughter, love enough to let her grow.

He was thinking of Pedro's words to him as they retraced their steps back towards a fallen out-building in need of repair where his host was eyeing the sagging roof. It struck David that those things in life that were hardest to repair were those in which one's perception of oneself were bound up. But it wasn't until one was free of the demands that one placed on the self that one could truly begin to move forwards.

He'd been living the life that he thought he was supposed to lead, but it had betrayed him. He had betrayed himself.

"It's the wrong time of year to fix this," said Pedro looking at where the roof of the small barn bowed with a timber that could be seen through a gap in the slates. Amazed that he should have missed it before and brought into a realisation of how the farm had been expanding even as he had strived to contain it, Pedro whistled a sigh in the air.

"Your sons will help you," said David to the farmer.

"Yes," said Pedro, "Until they have also reached their limits and their families need them more than the farm does. I am getting old with this," he said.

"Nonsense," said David, reaching over and slapping his friend on the back, "A man is only as old as he lets himself be."

And with that both of them smiled as their horses trudged off across the snow.

In a field to the side of the farmhouse, Rosa and the two children, Miguel and Natalia were throwing snowballs at each other. Although only young they were familiar enough with the snow to know that it had different faces. They knew that there was the snow of daytime in the sunshine like this that was good to play in, even when the wind caught it in little flurries and tugged at their hair. But their night times also hinted at the snow that lay up in the mountains, when they pulled their covers round their necks and their hairs froze on the back of them with the cries of an owl. Or worse. For Rosa the snow was a new thing, a dress she had never worn and the children delighted in her delight at soaking herself to the skin in it. But when she looked at the able young girl and her alert brother, she found herself taking stock against the winter when solitude might keep them pent-up in the farmhouse. A horse flashed down a clattering road into the village that she and the other occupants in the house might be cut off from. A horse that had ridden away before the snow fell.

"Come in, you'll freeze to death," Montserrat stood outside the house calling to them.

"We're coming in now," said Rosa catching snow in her hands and throwing it over her companions, into their grinning faces, "Come on, my loves, I don't want you getting cold," she said.

Rosa put her hand to her body and felt the chill that permeated her clothes where a well-aimed shot had hit her. She took the girl by one hand and the boy by another and they walked towards the farmhouse, leaving the snow to gather again where its undulating form would freeze over. It had stopped snowing before they had made their way into the pastures, but when they were gone it would gather itself together again, smoothing over the indents they had made in it while playing.

"Will you always be here?" the little boy holding her hand asked her. She squeezed his hand gently and led him and his sister to where their mother had walked out to meet them.

"Rosa has never seen the snow before," said Natalia to her mother as Miguel was swept up in his mother's arms. The two women looked at each other and Natalia held on to Rosa's hand whilst Montserrat carried the boy. The two women walked side by side and the snow behind in the field stretched as far as the mountains. As they neared the building where smoke was drifting from the chimney, Pedro and David could be seen approaching from the lower slopes where they had been out on horseback that morning.

"You go ahead," said Rosa to Montserrat, "I'll catch up with you later."

Montserrat took the children up the steps and into the warmth of the farmhouse while Rosa waited for the two men on horseback.

"Good afternoon," said Pedro to Rosa as he and David approached her.

"Hello," said Rosa to both of the men, "Did you have an interesting morning?" she asked.

Pedro geed up his horse and turned away to the farm.

"I'll be getting along," he said.

"Want to give me a lift?" Rosa asked David when the farm owner had gone. David took his foot from the stirrup and stepped down, helping Rosa up onto the horse. She patted its neck and spoke softly into its ear as she hoisted herself into the saddle where David had made space for her, taking the reins in front of David as she had done on the night they'd arrived.

"Where are we going?" asked David when he had adjusted his position and given over control of the horse to Rosa.

"There's a pond that Montserrat told me about," answered Rosa, "Have you seen it?"

"No," said David, "You show me."

With that Rosa guided the horse down a track whose outlines were still visible where the snow had fallen into its furrows.

"It's beautiful here, isn't it?" said Rosa after some minutes when the farmhouse had retreated behind them and the warmth from their bodies was suffused like the silver of their skin from the night before. The way Rosa carried her body made it easy for David to hold onto her. His arms reached round her waist and when their bodies rocked together with the motion of the horse, neither of them was uneasy with the presence of the other.

"You're happy here, aren't you?" David said to Rosa as the needles from an outlying tree on the edge of a small patch of woods brushed past them. She took a path that turned down a slope where water could still be seen running through the snow that had collected on the banks of the stream. They were amongst the trees now and a quiet murmur rustled through them. The sun of the afternoon still bathed the fields behind them, but down here they were hidden from it, so that the place they were in seemed quieter.

"What day is it today?" asked David, suddenly alert in the hush of the little river valley.

"Monday, I think," said Rosa, who was thinking back to the day they'd arrived at the farm. It had been the ninth of July, National Independence Day. Quite appropriate, Rosa thought to herself.

"A week," said David, "I've been here for just a week," he said.

It seemed incredible to him that it had been such a short time since that morning when he'd stepped off the plane at the airport. The events of the last days were a blur to him. The escape from the hotel, his night at the police station; it all seemed unreal to him. And now they were nearly six hundred miles away tucked in a valley whose sides were guarded by mountains.

"I did wrong," said David, "They'll be out looking for me."

"Hush," said Rosa.

The peace of the little river valley was cloaked about them. For her, the pass through the mountains on which they'd travelled was the end of a world; for him, the start of another.

"Nobody will find you here," said Rosa, "We're safe now."

David thought of Rosa out playing with the children in the snow where he'd seen their footsteps leading off that morning. Her family had recognised her and welcomed her. She was at home here.

"I envy you," he said to her as they followed the meandering stream.

Presently they reached an opening in the land where the trees parted on the riverbank and the ground opened out in a hollow. One or two willow trees hung down by the edge of the pond that was in front of them. Higher up on their left the bank rose more steeply and the trees at its top were stunted by exposure to the wind. They were smaller than the trees down in the hollow and the leaves upon them were scarcer.

"I can't stay here, Rosa," said David.

"I know that," she said.

They dismounted the horse and tied it to a tree by its reins. They stood looking at the pond where the snow had banked up on its sides and frozen the water over at its edges.

"Have you ever been fishing?" David asked Rosa.

"No, I haven't," she said, and then thought how curious it was to have lived so many years on the coast in Mar del Plata without ever once having been fishing.

"Have you?" she asked him.

"Once," he said, half wistfully and half-smiling.

"Your life is not over yet," Rosa said to him, looking into his eyes.

"I know that, Rosa," he said to her.

They stood gazing at the pond for some time and watched how lumps of snow were tugged gently free from its banks by the current in the water which they couldn't see, but which flowed in from the side they had entered, thawing at its southern end. At their side water dripped into the pool from the melting snow.

"That policeman," said David.

"Yes?" said Rosa, not quite certain of what he was going to say, "Do you think he suspects anything?"

"Ramiro? How could he?" she answered him.

"Word will travel round that there's a Yankee staying out on Pedro's farm," said David, "We may think that we're cut off from things here,

175

but in a small village such as the one we passed through anything different is news. I don't want you involved in any of this," he said to her.

"I already am," she replied.

It was true, she thought to herself; news was bound to spread of their arrival and whatever it was that David was running away from would eventually catch up with him here if he stayed. But whatever it was he'd been running away from, he was a good man and had been generous with her. He was no criminal, she knew that. He'd just got mixed up in something he shouldn't have. He was no different from her, really. In any case, Rosa knew it wasn't just the men back in Mar del Plata he was trying to escape. She, also, was leaving the ghosts of faceless men back in the city behind her. There was no crime in that.

"When will you go?" she asked David.

Her words surprised him but he realised he'd been building up to this. His leaving had been inevitable from the first night they'd arrived at the farm.

"So you don't think Ramiro…?"

"I don't," she answered his half-finished question, but the eyes of the dark-skinned man flashed at her in her mind as they had done the night of the fire.

"Pedro says there's more snow on the way," said David, "I should leave before I'm trapped on the farm."

They saw the tracks of an animal that had circled round the pond and then disappeared into the clump of trees at its bottom edge.

"A fox, probably," said Rosa.

David followed the tracks into the trees and wondered whether the stream would pass through the grove of molle trees where he'd stopped earlier in the day with Pedro. A map of the farmland was forming in his mind and he guessed that given the lie of the land the stream must at least pass pretty close to the woods. South would take him back closer to Buenos Aires, but a cunning animal always turns back on its tracks to outwit its pursuers.

Afterwards they dismounted in the courtyard and Rosa led the horse into the stables. She filled a bucket with some oats that were in a sack by the wall and brushed the coat of the horse before closing the gate of the pen behind her. Pedro's horse was chomping on some hay but Juan and Manuel's horses were still out.

"They must have a lot of work to do," Rosa said, "I hope I can be of some use to them here."

David hesitated a moment to take in the panorama of the fields and the mountains that were glinting in the sunshine of the late afternoon. He was reminded of the hills he'd once seen with his wife from the window of their room in Mexico. It was only at night that they loomed large and took on the shape of an impassable barrier. She'd broken a limb and had had to be carried by the old man, Patricio and himself down the path back to the hotel. They'd had to cut their holiday short after she'd been treated at a hospital in the nearest city.

He let Rosa go in ahead of him and paused a moment on the steps that were smooth from the passage of the people into and out of the farmhouse. The room was warm inside but David was already steeling himself against the cold. His job had brought him to this country but already it seemed to him that it had all been a mistake. How long was it since he'd spoken a word in his native language? He stopped to think and found himself marvelling at the way he'd been able to converse with Rosa's people on the farm. Why was it that they'd misunderstood him so much at the police station? Why had he felt so compelled to flee the hotel room? He remembered the shouts that had come from the corridor outside the room, the clatter and jangle of keys as somebody fumbled with them at the door. And then he'd scraped through the skylight in the bathroom and dashed headlong like a madman onto the roof of the hotel and jumped down on to the gravel, where the car that had brought him from the centre still had its keys in the ignition. He wondered if it had been his own impetuousness that had subsequently triggered the events that had followed. He half-expected Ramiro to be seated in the corner by the fire, his dark eyes inquisitive and uncertain of him. He was, after all, a foreigner, and it would not go unheeded in the mouths from the village that funnelled up the valley into the farm. Pedro was a good man and he would not put his family at risk, nor would he Rosa.

The children were freshly scrubbed and had changed out of their wet clothes made soggy by the snow. Mercedes sat knitting in the rocking chair where the older woman, the great-aunt of the children,

177

had been sitting the night he and Rosa had arrived. The garment she was knitting was small, and David wondered if it were intended for the child of a friend or another relative of hers.

"Where's…the old woman?" asked David, reminded of her existence by the backwards and forwards motion of the rocking chair made by Mercedes.

"She's in her room," Mercedes said to David, "She's shy around strangers and in any case she feels the cold more than we do in winter. She sleeps a lot during the colder months."

Rosa had gone in directly to the kitchen and in the absence of Pedro, David was left at a loose end.

"Where's Pedro?" he asked the man's wife.

"He'll be back soon enough," she answered, and with that she returned to her rocking and her knitting in the chair that eked out the syllables of its wood against the wood of the farmhouse floor.

"After he returned with you early this afternoon he went out with his shotgun," said Montserrat to David, "He said he'd seen the tracks of a puma close to one of the barns where the cattle are wintering and he wanted to catch it."

"But he didn't take his horse," said David, who had seen Pedro's black mare through the door in the barn.

"No," said Montserrat, "He says the only way to catch a cat is to sneak up on it without it getting a whiff of another animal. The horses give off the scent of fear when they are near one of the beasts, so he goes after them on foot. And he should know, he's shot enough of them in his time."

David thought of the solitary tracks of the animal that he had seen with Rosa circling round the pond, and something in him froze over like the hard steps of the fox that had trotted round searching for something, but had then wandered off.

Rosa returned from the kitchen where she he'd been helping and saw what it was that was in David's mind. She came up to him quietly and sat down by the table.

"You won't get far without a horse," she said to him discreetly, "And in any case, the horse will know its way better than you do. I'll speak to Pedro when he gets back in," she said, "We'll say that you've got urgent business to attend to. They'll understand."

"I have the money," said David, "Or at least thereabouts," the plan forming in his mind. Though he wasn't sure that Pedro would want to sell him one of his horses, or indeed that it would leave him enough money left over to survive. Perhaps he could borrow one of the horses and leave it somewhere where Pedro could pick it up. Perhaps he would just take one out to the edge of the farm and send it back on its way from there. Maybe that way he'd be less conspicuous when he arrived in a place he wasn't known and was looking to remain unnoticed.

"I've made up my mind," said David, "I don't want anybody else being mixed up with this or held to account for things I've done."

Rosa turned away from him, resolute, like the drip of melt-water into the pool.

CHAPTER TWELVE

It was dark when David crept out of the farmhouse. He had with him an old blanket he'd taken from the room and the leather jacket that had somehow become his. He carried a little food with him too, which he'd wrapped up in a cloth taken from the kitchen. This he'd bundled up in an old backpack, which he'd found in a corner of the room when looking round for anything that might be of use to him. The house was silent and the ground was crisp underfoot as he stole out into the courtyard. He left the people sleeping, hitched the bag over one shoulder and made his way gingerly out in the direction of the molle trees where he'd stood that day with Pedro.

Rosa had slipped into bed while David sat perched, still dressed, in an old chair by the window. They had not spoken for words were unnecessary now, and David had waited patiently for Rosa to fall asleep. But Rosa had not been properly asleep and when David had picked up the bag from the corner where it had been hidden under some cloth, she felt the kiss he left on her forehead as he was leaning over her. He closed the door silently behind him, the only noise he could hear was the snoring which came from the room where Pedro and Mercedes lay. But Rosa discerned the creek of his boots across the floorboards; she guessed, too, at the rustling of the rough material of the bag against the smoother leather of the jacket.

"Good-bye, my love," she said, but David was already opening the door at the entrance and was stepping outside.

The sky was clearer and although he could taste snow in the air none was falling. He figured that if he could pick up the stream where it must flow down from the hollow where he and Rosa had been that afternoon, he could follow it southwest to where he'd been told the valley opened out on the other side of the mountains. He didn't know what he would find there, but he knew that eventually it should take him towards the province of San Luis. After some time walking he stopped to look back in the direction of the farmhouse. He imagined them sleeping there, safe in their world, and fear shook him so that he wanted to turn back and steal into the bed where he'd left Rosa sleeping. He knelt down in the snow and put a hand into the bag to check his provisions. The food was there wrapped in the linen cloth, so too was his wallet and passport and the woollen blanket. His hand closed upon something hard and drawing the object out into the light reflected up from the snow, he saw that it was a lighter. It was the lighter that Rosa had used to start the fire they had made that night on their way to the farm. In the bottom of the sack was a bundle of dry straw.

He threw the bag over his shoulder and left the people and the farm behind him. He was alone, but no more so than on the day that he'd arrived at the airport; no more so, either, than he'd been all these years. He wrenched himself away and hastened his steps in the direction of the forest. After some time walking one of the outbuildings began to loom in front of him and as he approached it he thought he caught a whiff of something sharp and acrid. Inside the barn the cattle were restless and one called out to the night. He passed by the barn without looking into it and carried on over the open field. He felt vulnerable out here in the cold, so he pressed on faster still in an effort to reach the clump of trees. The clouds parted above him and for a moment an eerie light was reflected back up from the snow, so that all the landscape before him and around him seemed one thing. If he held his breath he could feel the chill of all the valley seeping into his lungs.

Just as he was despairing at ever finding the woods out in these crazy open fields, a glimpse of something darker on the horizon began to appear and as he walked closer towards it, a shadow of something clustered together became apparent. The molle trees were whispering in their silvery cadence, their hard leaves rustling in incessant chatter. He ran towards them and found himself exhausted by the effort of having to lift his legs out of the snow where they sank into the deeper drifts. He took hold of a branch with his heart pounding and bent himself underneath the tree. Sitting down on a rock at the base of it, he turned back in the direction he had come from and allowed his toes to feel the cold that had been cramping up in them, where the snow had gone in over his boot-tops.

He rested for a moment like that, until the cold in his feet reminded him where he was and he prised each boot off from his feet, shaking the snow out of them. The rock under his fingers was cold, so cold that the tree which split it and under which he rested seemed to be swelling with ice trapped in its limbs. The farm and all its people were as distant to him as the people scurrying to and fro' in a city which no longer belonged to him. Only this was real, only here where he was now. He nibbled at a piece of cheese where his fingers had crumbled it inside the bag, and scooping a handful of snow into his mouth where it had dried out his thirst, he plunged headlong into the forest.

He found himself being led downwards where the land dipped, then sometimes rose up again, though the way invariably led down further. In the night air a smell filtered out from the molle trees and the bitter perfume of their hard leaves penetrated his nostrils. He felt his bowels loosening and wondered if it was fear that had crept up on him, but Pedro had forgotten to tell him that the leaves of the molle were used to relax the intestines. David could hear the passage of something pushing its way through the snow down below him, he could hear the drip, drip, drip of water unclogging itself from the snow. Faintly at first, a force felt rather than heard, and then growing louder as his path and the path of the stream became bound up in one another and neither the quiet solitude of the stream nor the solitude of the walker could remain undisturbed. Uneasy companions walked together, inextricably the footsteps of the one and the current of the other grew more coarse so that neither of them were quiet together in the forest and with each movement onwards their noise grew. Rudely they trod a way through together, and any animal that might have been watching would have seen them there, would have felt their mutual fear of being imprisoned in the woods.

Out in the fields by the barn where the cattle were, the moon was skulking. The farm pushed up its assemblage of dreams and the dreamers that dreamed them breathed inwards and out. The screech of an owl was catapulted across the valley, but it was coming from other woods, not those where David was sleepwalking.

The stream and David staggered on together, so that as the legs of the man grew wearier, the breadth of the stream grew. It became heavy and heavy with water, until the stream became a slow river where the banks it cut through were deep with snow. Lazily he lifted his legs to carry him on, hoisting himself over fallen branches rotting by the stream-side, hoisting the pack that rested on his back. Sleep wanted to come over him but he would not let it carry him yet. Obstinately he made the branches give way for him, the tall-growing grasses bend under his boots. The swollen river led the water and the man; in its mouth it was letting solid elements flow in it, lumps of snow that dissolved where quietness and the man were parted from words.

On the edge of the woods something was sniffing at the night air, tasting an unfamiliar scent. The fur on its neck ruffled in the breeze and it plunged into the woods and into the darkness. It lapped at the ice-cold water that was shaken from the snow and two half-closed eyes began to prowl.

The man was tiring and in his solitude had begun to babble. Sharp thorns tore at his trousers and rocks cut up out of the river- bank so that he had to clamber over them in order to carry on in his course. The dim swish of water was more raucous now and the man was determined not to lose its scent. He took hold of an overhanging root that projected from the slippery bank but his feet slipped from under him and he was left facing the earth trembling. He grabbed at the root with his other hand and was spun round suddenly, his feet sliding in the mud until he was looking back up the river where he had entered.

An animal lifted its ears and paused as frozen as the moon that shone on the hard round leaves of the molles. Moon and animal left their trace of silver gliding over the snow.

David saw the darkness of the space he had left behind closing in on him. He stood paralysed for a moment with the futility of it all and then scrabbled at the water's edge, slipping one foot into it before wrenching its ice-cold force out of him. He smacked the boot onto dry land and trailed the other one like a slipper in the snow where his toes were unfeeling. The numbness in his boot was pleasant for a while, a narcotic trick on his senses, but it began to seize hold of his leg, too, so that even the material of his trouser leg stiffened. He sat down in the naked snow and shook the water from his boot, but what liquid there was left in it had been sponged up in his sock, so that he had to remove this too and wring it out with fingers painfully slow.

On the brow of a hill something glinted. The darkness accumulated in its eye was gliding with the revolving of the world, the stars rushing in where its paw scraped at the flimsy velvet of the night, tiny fireworks exploding on its retina. It slunk down and dragged stars and velvet after it, the slippery cloth of its underbelly flattening out against the landscape.

In his mind the man's world had stopped turning and everything had frozen in the cramped hollow in which he lay. He could feel the numbness creeping through the seat of his trousers, sticking him to the spot, his leg recumbent like a fallen trunk. Thorns scratched the side of his face when he tried to turn his head. He let his eyes close on the world for a moment and drifted into its seeping blackness. Suddenly, without warning, his will flexed in him and against his wishes he found himself struggling to his feet through the vegetation. His slumber shook from about him and the trees whispered for him to move on. He stared across the water and intimated further below him across the other side a clearing in the land where two trees had been toppled, their slender sticks poking through the snow. In one last elastic effort of will he propelled himself onto a log on the near side where it protruded, its far end scraping the other bank.

It moved when he moved so that he could feel the current in the water brushing against him, then in oblivion he leapt from his balancing place and feet unexpectedly found purchase in the soft snow of the opposite bank. Scrambling up on his hands and knees he found himself sitting where the trees lay toppled.

He looked back at his trail through the forest along the water's edge and a faint glimmer of recognition at how he'd almost let himself fall asleep on the opposite slope of the bank flared in him. He pulled at the blanket in his sack, but had to tug at it to free it, so that his bundle of food and the lighter, which had once been José's, fell onto the ground. Pulling at the last lumps of the blanket with his swollen hands the raw stalks of dry straw scratched at him numbly. He retrieved the lighter, clumsy pain swelling in his fingers with the minuteness of the object. Struggling to wrap himself in the blanket he took a bite out of the cheese and pushed the end of the loaf of bread into his mouth. He felt the lighter again in his pocket. Fingers fumbled for the dry bundle that was stuck in the bottom of the sack. Taking a handful of the painful stuff he brought it out and smelt it. Taken from the stables, no doubt.

He dragged himself up as the idea glowed in him and he dug for small twigs to start a fire. But when he clutched at their protruding forms in the darkness they came away wet in his hand. Some he pulled up from the bough of another fallen tree whose slender trunk bruised the lip of the hollow where he'd left his belongings. But these were moist and rotten and turned into powder in his hands. As he trod back down the slope his knee knocked against a hard limb so that he cursed out loud. Rubbing his knee and cursing at the tree, his leg moved against a patch of something drier. The grass and weeds in summer must have grown against the trunk of the tree and been pushed against it by the wind. As David pushed into the tangle he found a hollow space underneath where the snow had not been able to reach. He flicked at his lighter clumsily and after three or four attempts managed to get some light from it. Holding it close with one paw where his other had penetrated he saw two snapped branches, whose ends, at least, were relatively dry to the touch. He dragged first one then another of the long, slender branches with their attachments of twigs and grass out of the tangle down to where he had left his sack.

Frantically he trod at branches that bounced back up at him, but with hands that were bleeding now he managed to somehow make a wigwam shape and stuff the clump of grass inside it. He jerked the lighter at the ends of it. A spark burned orange then died down. The next time he caught a spark and blew at it, retrieving the grass and cherishing it in his hands. Smoke tufted from its folds and he blew wind into it again softly before placing it back inside. Rosa would be sleeping. He prayed that she, at least, would be safe. A thin twig snapped with an orange glow and David rested two sticks delicately against it over the tinder. Desperately he pushed his hand back into his bag and pulled out another clump of hay. He pushed it intrusively into the twigs so that they collapsed, but blowing with all the air that was left in him, the sticks spat back at him and into life, hissing and bubbling at their ends.

He jumped up and ran to find more wood, pulling anything that would come with him down to where he'd made his camp.

A pinecone still attached to the fallen log suddenly burst into flame, and realising what he had stumbled across, David went to gather as many as he could. He banked some earth up against the fire with his boots, and, wrapping the blanket about him again and resting with his back against the other log, his boots at last felt fire. He took a large bite out of the loaf then bit off a piece of the cheese with his teeth. He sucked at it to get the moisture. His bloodied fingers rounded on the lighter in his pocket again while the sparks of the fire danced before him. A souvenir. Rosa would be sleeping now, at rest.

The animal circled round the fire on the lip of the slope where David had retrieved the branches. The rich iron of blood was quivering in its nostril, but the flames that danced and lit the clearing where the man was sleeping flashed in its eyes also. Even when an animal has never come face to face with fire before, the memory of it is passed through the generations; just as the knowledge that men have sometimes been killed for food also persists.

Exhausted, David was dreaming. He saw the multitude of faces streaming past him on the pavement. Rosa's face was there and Pedro's too, but they went past him. The face of the Director loomed large through an office window high above him but the glassy expanse of the skyscraper turned black as he walked past it, hiding its goings on. There was snow everywhere, even on the signs at the entrance to the subway where it perched piled up on the thin metal. His feet were warm but for some reason he was dressed in a summer suit. Girls in summer dresses and women in short skirts had boys and men on their arms, some of them with ties loosened and some wearing open-necked shirts. A policeman stood blowing into his whistle and urging the crowds of people jammed elbow to elbow to move faster. The traffic of people on the streets was dense, but not a single car or vehicle was to be seen on the road.

"You! What are you waiting for? Hurry up, can't you see the light's on green?"

The policeman shouted at him as David stopped and watched the crowd of people cross the road in unison. The policeman blew his whistle and the group of people recrossed the road back to where they'd started. This crowd of people vanished, then another crowd appeared to repeat the procedure. David went to join them but as he was striding across the street he realised the light had turned red. The car that had taken him from the meeting with the Director slammed in front of him and David had to jump out of its way. The Director leered at him as, turning his head at the steering wheel, he looked back to where David was sprawled in the snow. As the car disappeared from his view his daughter turned round to wave at him and David saw that she was accompanied by her mother in the back seat, though apparently she hadn't seen him. Feeling embarrassed as he dusted the snow off his jacket, he stood up and looked round for his briefcase, but it had gone. He asked a girl who was crying if she'd seen it but she just burst into tears and her boyfriend gave him a scolding look as they passed by.

He could feel the eyes of the people upon him and the policeman was demanding an explanation.

"It's alright," David was saying, "I shouldn't be here."

"Oh," said the policeman, "You'd better move on then."

He shrieked on his whistle and the crowds parted to let David pass. It was half-past three by the clock on the building and David was going to be late for his appointment. When he got to the subway entrance a guard checked his ticket and asked to see his documents. David took out his leather-bound passport from an inside pocket in his suit jacket and the subway attendant looked from the picture in David's passport back to his face.

"Everything in order," said the man, "Is your trip for business or pleasure?" he asked David.

"I'm not sure," replied David and the man let him pass through the gate.

"No luggage, sir?" said the man in the smart uniform as he boarded the subway train.

He raised his eyebrows to his female colleague who was dressed in the same colour. The white gloves of the blue-suited gentleman directed him to his seat after he'd checked David's ticket. David sat down in seat 36D but soon a young woman came who seemed perturbed.

"Excuse me," she said, "But I think you'll find you're sitting in my seat!"

She wrenched David's ticket from his hand and her eyes moved like typewriter print across the page.

"You see?!" she exclaimed, "36E it says here on your ticket. What did I tell you?"

She huffily accepted David's apologies as he shuffled over to the adjoining space and then the stewardess arrived to give her a manicure and a facial and she pulled the hood of the hairdryer down over the woman's head.

"Are you sure you're on the right train?" the stewardess enquired of him, but David meekly showed her his ticket and she spun his seat round to face the window in front of him.

On the other side of the train, seated in a line, were many people who were looking at him.

"Excuse me," said David, and the people went back to their speaking in many tongues. There was a woman of middle-aged appearance accompanied by two teenage sons wearing combat uniforms and expensive sneakers. One of them lounged with his legs half-blocking the aisle so that a woman who stepped over him with her poodle in her arms nearly tripped. He clicked his fingers at his brother and they laughed. Next to them was the waiter who'd swindled David out of his briefcase and who was chatting in Spanish to a man wearing sunglasses. Neither the waiter nor the man in sunglasses seemed to recognise him, though, and they continued with their conversation, oblivious to David.

"This is your captain speaking," said the voice on the Tannoy as the steward who had checked David's ticket on boarding came round checking people's seatbelts. He winked at a male passenger who made a comment to him, then frowned as he got to David.

"Is your wife accompanying you, sir?" he asked.

"No," responded David, "I'm divorced."

"Ah, in that case you'd better use the phrasebook that you'll find under your seat…emergency exists to the left, (he winked again at the man sitting three seats down from David) and to the right."

The train shuddered as it picked up speed and somebody groaned at the back as the train veered round a corner.

"Not this damn film again! I must have seen this a thousand times," the voice was saying. David turned to see who it was that was moaning but his seatbelt was fastened tight and he could barely move. The girl in seat 36D had changed her hair colour and through her fake eyelashes she fluttered a smile at him. She seemed to have forgotten about the earlier incident altogether.

"It's so exciting," she was saying to him, "Do you do this often?"

Then the screen opposite them on the window flicked into view and the movie started. It was in black and white, unfortunately, and was set in some old country where everybody rode on horses. For some reason the film had been dubbed in Spanish and the landscape seemed to go on forever.

"Oh look," said the girl, "That's you, isn't it?"

A posse was chasing a cowboy on horseback and as the face of the man being pursued came into view, David saw that it was indeed him. The girl put her arm through his and rested her head on his shoulder. The stewardess smiled at them and pointed to the skylight. But David was feeling uncomfortable and was starting to sweat. He'd read somewhere that it wasn't good to keep your shoes on on long journeys. As he was trying to kick off his shoes, the Director passed them driving the car again in the movie opposite.

"Rosa," he whispered, but Rosa was far away from him now. He woke up in a sweat with his boots nearly singed, the fire crisply licking the bone of the log. The glare from the fire lit up the mud of the opposite bank where he'd almost given up and David strained to recollect what it was that he was doing here. The girl from the cinema had disappeared and the snow was cold beneath him. He put his hand into his pocket and it closed on the lighter that Rosa had given him.

He put his hand behind his head and was relieved to find the bag made of rough sack where his possessions were. He made a mental check of everything he was carrying there, then picked it up and swung it onto his back. He watched the flames lick the log for a while then set about smothering it and the remains of the rest of the fire with snow. It took him some time and the snow sizzled on the log so that he had to heap pile upon pile of the stuff to quench the flames. By the time he had finished the log was almost totally submerged in it. Instinctively, he decided to cover up the rest of his tracks and set about sweeping his resting-place with one of the branches. Then he kicked some of the charcoal from the burned out fire into the stream and let the current dispense with it. He was feeling giddy on his feet and his throat was dry, but David set out as morning would be on him in a few short hours.

He decided to keep to this side of the river and for a moment considered climbing up to the lip of the hollow and making his way out into the open. But although his way would surely be easier, something of the immensity of the open valley impressed itself on him, so that he imagined himself more at risk and more lonely out there. He stuck to his plan and let his instincts guide him. If fear is an instinct then it is the first truth a person must learn to heed.

Down the long swish of the valley the temperature was plummeting. As daylight clambered up the slopes of the mountains the temperature was in retreat. 'Why was it so cold now?' David found himself thinking, and for a while he continued walking with the blanket wrapped round him. The going was easier on this side of the river as he continued, but his movements were slow and clumsy with the stiffness of the night. How far he'd travelled he had no idea, but it felt good to be on the move again. What he could remember of his dream disturbed him and the harder he tried to recall it, the more elusive it seemed to him to be. But the Director existed. Somewhere. His report in that damned briefcase existed also, but he had no idea where it was or who might or might not have read it. 'How could a few pieces of paper become so important?' Then he stopped for a moment and laid his bag down in the snow at his feet. He fished inside it and found what he was looking for. His passport in its leather holder and his wallet containing his last crumpled up notes were still there. Half the money he'd been carrying in his wallet he'd taken out previously before setting out alone. Pride had got the better of him but he hadn't wanted Rosa to think he was buying her silence, or worse still.

But he had become enough of a realist by now to know that in this harsh world money was worth a lot more than the paper it was written on. It would at least afford her a temporary sense of security, and David was well aware that she would need it. As for himself, David was in the process of understanding that not every security he'd thought he'd had could be bought by money; often it bought the opposite. Presently the land began to flatten out and the trees began to thin out with it. He could see the mountains still laden with snow bathed in the half-light of a morning approaching. The residents at the house would be rising soon and asking of his whereabouts. She'd put the lighter in his bag, along with the clumps of straw. She'd make his excuses for him. Or her silence might speak volumes.

The mountains were bigger closer up, though he couldn't have travelled that far on foot. They were brooding on the horizon and David felt how small he was in their shadow. Ramiro would want to know where he'd got to and David wondered how long Rosa could keep him guessing. He scooped up a handful of snow and washed his face with it, brushing it across his mouth and his tongue. He tasted her lips and her skin on his tongue. He longed to have her with him right now, but he knew that they were both better off this way. There might come a time when she would have to defend herself against accusations. If that time came, so be it; it was better that she might have to betray him without his knowing it than that he should betray her memory. Love is just a lie spoken between two people who knew each other once, or tricked each other into believing that they did.

CHAPTER THIRTEEN

Morning's sleepers would be rousing soon. He wondered at the mystery of the sky as it shook the night from about it. He wondered at the uncertainty of where he was going but then flashes of his dream came back to haunt him as he ventured out onto the snowfields, so that this morning seemed, at last, to be the first morning. In the pale glimmer of dawn a creature stopped in its tracks and lifted to nuzzle the wind. It watched him as he watched it, then trotted off out of his view like a dancer who has stopped for a moment on the stage then passed on to another scenario. The white-tipped brush of its tail flickered in his mind.

Ears alert, David retreated beneath the shadow that was being cast down from the mountains. How long it would take him to reach the next village, and whether he wanted to be seen there was unclear to him.

"I watch you leaving and doubt that you are doing so," the thought echoed in his mind, "Waves that carry you away from me, though it is I who am moving, not you."

The cracks in the mountains had begun to appear. Fissures where light showed steep valleys cut into their forms. David was walking with the sun gleaming under him now, where it rent the snow and burned underneath. The forest had fled far behind him but his mind willed another which stretched out in front of him beneath his stride. Light and shadow walked on the snow, and David walked behind giants who were striding on ahead of him. The featureless plain lay before him, blurred in his mind and sticking to it.

When he woke up there was an aching in his throat and in his head.

The snow was burning in his mouth so that he dare not drink from it. He crawled on his hands and knees in the wetness that would not let him drink from it, and moved towards a decline in the land where a small bush pricked the land like a drop of blood. With his head pounding his eyes were closing through the skins of them which were being pulled tight.

Tight down over the landscape that was shrinking, tight across the infinite whiteness. He stopped and turned his back on the eyes glaring back at him, rested in the shade of the bush that was cool. With one hand covering the mechanical light of the snowfield, he fumbled at the buttons of his jacket. Round coins that slipped under his fingers. He stretched out the coat where he heaped a pile of snow on it in his blindness. Even turning towards the sun although he could not see it through the closed lids of his eyes made him hurt. But he could feel it, though. He dragged his jacket into the light and let the sun bleed over it. He picked up a cake of snow from the jacket where it had started to melt, and bit off a lump. It exploded in him tearing at his lungs making his throat even drier. But he broke off another lump and let it dissolve in his mouth, like swallowing blood, letting it trickle down his throat. He worked at the blanket until he had a piece of it in his hands, tying it round his throat and up over his head. Its material was soft against his temples where they were throbbing against it like a bandage.

He took the lump of bread from the bag and dipped it in the snow. He brought it up to meet his mouth and sucked it like a sponge. He lay there with the crumbs of bread in his mouth until, much time later, the form of the bush began to impress itself on him. It was well past midday, and not a soul had crossed to interrupt the landscape. He drew the fragment of the blanket further over his head to shield himself and sat still until colours had returned. He would have to travel at night, or at least wait until the sun of afternoon was not so harsh.

Rosa woke quietly that morning, trying to make as little noise as possible in the room before the others were awake in the house. She planned carefully what she would say to them. She might tell them that she had woken to find David gone, but this would draw suspicion on him. Alternatively, she toyed with the idea of a lovers' quarrel; though she was against it, it might be the best way to explain away his sudden absence, though something told her that Pedro and Mercedes might not be so easily convinced. She let the people move about the house and go about their business, quietly letting the early morning advance. Then, when she was beginning to feel that her absence from the kitchen and from the breakfast table might attract attention, she left the bedroom and the deceits she had woven there and crept into the kitchen.

"Sleep well?" Mercedes asked her.

Rosa nodded but her eyes were looking out through the window and searching across the snowfields.

"David?" Mercedes asked, but Rosa merely let her gaze slip to the floor and said nothing.

She had found the money placed carefully at her bedside and had guiltily pushed it inside her case. For a moment she had been hurt by it, but then she had pushed her pride to one side and had counted each note as she used to do. She convinced herself that the money was hers, as she had done so in the past; but already a distance had begun to form in her mind and she separated the act of the man leaving her the money from the man himself.

They had sipped coffee and orange juice on the veranda of the hotel in Buenos Aires; she had fallen asleep on the soft satin sheets of the bed and had awoken to find him with her. He'd been curled up to her with his head against her breast and she had brought his head gently closer to her. He was gone, but each day would see a part of him grow inside her 'til she had made a dream of him that would almost explain her existence.

When she sat down at the breakfast table Pedro looked at the vacant space where David no longer was, then up at his wife who was bringing in a pot of coffee. Rosa ate her breakfast quietly, chewing each mouthful of the eggs slowly, her eyes fixed on her plate. There was a space in the house where the American had been and the house was quiet because of it.

David was ahead of them where he sat cowering beneath the afternoon sun. In his hood made from the woollen blanket his eyes were beginning to take in details in the landscape that he had not noticed before. He had left the river when it had seemed to veer too far off to the east on his left-hand side, but now he noticed a sinuous track in front of him across the land where it cut through the snowfield. It was just a faint mark etched into the whiteness, barely visible but darker like a thin shadow; a pencil mark on tracing paper. Water had become a priority to him, more important even than knowledge of where he was going. More important still than both of these things was refuge from the harsh light glaring up at him from the snow. The river might just provide him with these two things, or with all three of them. He resolved to make his way out from the safety of the bush towards the closest point of the thin pencil line, when the sun had declined sufficiently to allow him to find the thin rope in the land ahead of him and not let it go.

They finished their breakfast slowly in the house then cleaned up the plates after them. As the manner of the American's arrival at the farmstead with Rosa had been unexpected, so his departure from it did not come totally as a surprise, to Pedro at least. Rosa's silence at the table told him more than she could have done if she had attempted to explain things. Montserrat saw the fondness with which she looked at the children, understood the longing with which she looked at them when the three of them were together. Juan was often gone from the farmhouse for long periods of time, often without explanation. The nature of their work on the farm forced them into exile, so that she was bound to forgive him his need to find some time for himself, often with the company of other lonely men. It can't have been any different for the American, though the circumstances under which the man had seen it necessary to leave the farm were unclear to her and it was none of her business to know them. She was sorry for Rosa though, although the young woman who had come from the city shunned any thoughts of pity with her defiance.

What had brought the woman to the farm and the hardships she must have had to endure in getting there were secrets she was entitled to keep. Pedro had enough concerns on the farm to keep him busy; if Rosa needed to tell any of them anything, she would find an ear willing to listen, but a tongue not quick to judge. He would make sure of that himself. People were too quick to let idle tongues gossip when their hands were idle too, while their farms were left to ruin. He had not forgotten that his wife's immediate family had been forced into exile by circumstances beyond their control. More reason, then, to consider the girl Rosa family if she was in need of a place where her present actions were to be valued more than any secrets she might have to keep in her past.

Pedro glanced at Mercedes as she took the last of the breakfast things to the kitchen. She smiled at him with a smile at once full of tenderness and patience. It was just like him to try to solve the girl's problems himself, though Mercedes knew that he would never interfere directly and would only offer help if it were asked of him. She loved him for this. She understood him more than most. Mercedes placed her hand on Rosa's arm as she was reaching for the dishcloth in the kitchen, and though the girl was turned away from her, the older woman was able to see her visibly relax. The man was American but Rosa's ancestors, like half her own, had come down from a land where poverty was a way of life from generation to generation. In any case, Mercedes was certain they had parted amicably. Rosa was young and attractive and had plenty of spirit, and now she had a home. She'd have plenty of suitors queuing at her door; sooner, rather than later, she was sure.

David found the bank where the earth sloped down and the water that sped through in spring was weighted down with the dullness of winter. It turned back on itself at the point where David came to it again, and although its journey through the land that was freezing it was longer than walking in a straight line, it would keep the worst of the sun's harshness off him where he was out of sight of it. The sun was a brittle thing here on the landscape, David realised; it shone off the surface of the snow but did not penetrate it enough to completely unlock the river. Its glare was merely the glare of the land bouncing back at it.

At the river's edge once more he stopped to scoop up a few handfuls of the icy water. It had been a serious oversight not taking some sort of container or flask from the house. Something made him turn back to look the way he had come. For an instant he thought he could see something move in the distance close to where he had emerged from the forest. Probably a fox. He slaked his thirst though the cold in the water tore at his throat and lungs. Then he set off again. The loose hood he had fashioned from the ripped blanket kept the worst of the sun's rays out of his eyes when they penetrated into the channel cut in the otherwise monotonous landscape. He wondered why the banks of earth alongside the river were so high, but then he realized that perhaps the volume of water in the river varied at different times of year. It must be a sudden flood that created these steep-sided banks where he walked, though for the most part it was protected from the sun.

It suddenly occurred to David that any village he might encounter further on would probably be situated on or close to the banks of the river. This thought caused him some trepidation; he would have to stock up on his meagre supplies and contact with people would be unavoidable. The snow had fallen in deep drifts where he walked, but exposure to the sun and the glaring whiteness out in the open was unthinkable. He fell into a rhythm, sometimes counting his paces by the hundred as he struggled with the snow. His sense of time became distorted, but still the sun was high and had not yet begun to relinquish its hold. He imagined the people at the farm waking and asking after him, but they were long into their day and had been going about their routine for a long time now. Curiously, though, David felt as if he had travelled many miles since leaving them and the distance in his mind which separated him from them was growing. The mountains had not yet diminished however, and every step that David took made him feel smaller and the mountains bigger. He could see his shadow sometimes ahead of him when he stumbled unavoidably into places where the light broke in, swerving round a bush or shrub that had sprouted at the edge of the water. He had not stopped for a long time to drink.

Ahead of him a rough, furred tongue was lapping at the water in an open spot where the river broadened. Its flat paws were splayed on the bank to avoid it slipping, but the ease with which it retracted and opened its claws was second nature to it, so much so that it had become a reflex action. It leapt up the bank in one fluid motion and was instantly part of the landscape again.

It did not seem like him. This form that moved with such a slow gait, its head flapping, hunchbacked where the bag was slung on his shoulder. It hardly looked human at all. He had to stride to catch up with it, but always it was further ahead than he was. Sometimes he felt like sitting down and letting his shadow leave him behind, letting its black flowing shape disappear as he let himself dissolve into the whiteness. He was stubborn though, and the task of keeping up with it became a challenge that he could not give up on now, even if at times he wanted to. He despaired at his obstinate refusal to admit defeat; he could never give things up, he was forever persisting where such persistence was unwarranted. Such had been the case with his wife; it had taken him years to let her go. He wondered how long it would take him to forget the girl at the farm. It was easier to forget things when one had decided to let them go, it was much harder when they were being taken away from oneself. He wondered for a moment whether he'd really lost the briefcase on purpose, but the thought had occurred to him before and memories of a prison cell flooded with electric light intruded in his mind, so that he wanted to shut them out. It was better to follow the dark shadow ahead of him, let it lead him where it would.

The animal had been keeping one eye on the man and one eye on the sun. The mountains to the west down from which it had been lured in search of food were frozen over in their heights. Nothing stirred in that whiteness, the land seemed to be asleep and all the animals with it. Nothing moved, nothing, that is, except the man. He stumbled on, mumbling to himself, but his words were carried away with the wind that slipped across the fields. Going on in front of him, his shadow stretched to the shadow of the mountains that was inclining towards him as they reached out to the tiny flicker he made in the landscape.

David was sitting hunched in the snow, staring at the black moving shape of his hood as it haunted the snow like a raven picking at it. He had climbed up from the banks of the river when the sides had become too steep and his footsteps too heavy to carry. His bag was asleep on his shoulder and its contents long forgotten. Now the man was falling into a kind of sleep too. His eyes, half-open, were content to let the movement of the hood lull him into inertia where it flapped with the flapping of the wind. The long shadows of afternoon rocked him into idleness.

The animal saw the man sitting with his head inclined upon his chest, slumped where the effort of movement had left him abandoned. The animal's cubs had been abandoned too, left temporarily in their cave whilst their mother had slunk out in search of meat to still angry appetites. In winter everything was confined to spaces, each one smaller than the last as it tightened its grip and refused to let the land or the animals on it grow. The animal and the winter were locked in a battle, but the animal was cunning and could prise meat even out of holes made small by the blowing powder. Its scent was sharp and it had learned to smell life out of the land even when death hung over it. Now, though, its cubs were growing and they growled in the cave and became hungrier as the days grew shorter. Memory stirred in the cat and she padded softly forwards towards the sleeping form where it rested like a dark smudge on the landscape. It seemed smaller the closer she drew towards it and it stank of fear. It was huddled with its arms wrapped over its knees, its head turned away from her. She slipped into the stream of the wind down from the man just as she had slipped out of her cave on the slopes with the wind glistening across the ice. Her shadow grew under her as she moved flattened against the snow and then stretched out from the tip of her head to the length of her tail as she cut in silently towards the man. Her jaws opened with the claws that pierced the snow like needles and she was bounding towards her prey now, long teeth protruding like the icicles that had formed on the ridge that overhung her cave.

He saw the shadow too late as it was closing upon him. The black flapping shape had taken on a life of its own and danced on the snow where its whim carried it. He turned just as a huge bird or one of the mountains itself was toppling over him and looked into a darkness that was deeper than any he'd known. Instinctively he put up his arm to shield his face and a piercing light split through his bone. Claws raked his skin and he glimpsed the lightning in them where they tore down his curtain on the world and parted day from the night that had been resting there. They had caught his hood and it limped flatly in the air before falling in front of him.

He was falling backwards, staggered by the blow and torn out of his separateness with the landscape. The world turned underneath him as the mountains crushed him, surprised that they had caught up with him so quickly. Suddenly his head broke through water and then his boot caught the underbelly of something soft as the needles in the water penetrated his skin and he was being dragged away to his death. He caught sight of something prowling at the edge of the river for an instant before his head went under for a second time and all the world turned black. Death was in its eyes and scowled on its lips. His lungs were rushing with the ice that had entered them and in panic he drew in a gulp of the terror that was staring back at him from the other side.

He kicked as hard as he could, kicked again as he had done when the terror had been on him. He was digging at the snow where it gave in and was soft to his hand but it was pulled into the river with him. His head went under for a third time as the shape on the opposite bank stood awaiting the outcome. The scent was in its nostrils again but it was wary of the animal in front of it and would not chance a leap into its jaws. It saw the man being pulled away from itself and let the dark animal that never slept drag its capture to its lair.

Something disappeared on the horizon and David found himself snagged on a branch where the water tugged and tugged at him but could not pull him downstream. The weight of water was in his clothes and his right arm was shocked with the cold that had grabbed hold of it. He was gasping and ice pressed against his lungs so that he had to fight to open them up underneath the water. He skewed his head round with a vision of being trapped there permanently and some other terror beating down on its wings to pick at him out of the darkness. He was snagged by his backpack, which had remained on one shoulder and whose material had been pierced by the branch. He flung his left arm round expecting to find something soft and unpurchaseable but instead his hand found the log that held him fast. In one last, brutal effort he spun round with his full weight and hauled half his body out of the water as far as he could, twisting out of the strap on his back sack as he did so. He ripped it from its moorings and hurled it into the snow, not looking to see whether it had hit land as he pulled each leg, and then his feet, out of the wet skin that was holding on to him.

He clawed into the snow in front of him but his right arm would not do his bidding and hung limp and useless and heavy. It was stained with red and red was flowing out of it but the man looked at it as if it wasn't his. He twisted his head round while snaked out in the snow, one heavy skin falling from him but another growing as the teeth of the breeze cut through the wetness and exposed his clothes and his skin as separate things. The terror had retreated and he laughed out loud with the last half-gasp he had left inside him. His shook his fist at the devil, cursed at it with a howl that rasped his lungs and made the savage in him shake. It echoed out across the other side for a second so that the animal bounding away across the snow heard it also. Then spasms shook his body and he sobbed.

He lay there until the cold was threatening to sheer his skin from his bones and the pulpy mess of his arm had made him sick. He wished he could cut it from him and looked at it like a dejected thing, a thing that made him feel pity and disgust. He disowned his savaged arm, but it dragged after him obstinately and swung heavily when he struggled to get up.

The only thing to do now was move; it didn't matter where to, so long as he kept moving he would eventually find people. He struggled to rip off another piece of the blanket and bound it as tightly as he could round his arm to hide it from his view. The adrenaline was still pumping in him and he plunged into the snow and away from the terror that had nearly drowned him. He kept his gaze fixed forwards, away from the mountains with their impenetrable stillness. He wrapped what was left of the blanket round him, over his sodden clothes. At one point he started marching away from the river but the knowledge that it had saved his life as well as almost taken it was with him somewhere and he resolved to follow it as far as he could. He could not allow the thought to form that night might steal up on him and find him still exposed in the wilderness. That was too terrible to contemplate. The ache from the mangled mass in his forearm reminded him of his need to get to a village or a house as soon as possible, when it swung down uselessly and he had to carry it patiently like a sick thing. He was on one side of the river and the thing that had done it was on the other side. Death lay between them. It was still afternoon, but the patient light of day was fading where longer shadows stole in from the mountains and when David looked across at them their faces were gleaming. Unspeakable darkness and the terror that had flung itself at him dwelt there and he was frightened. He wrenched his face away from them but out of the corner of his eye David knew that they were still grinning.

Ravaged and bloody David crashed through the branches where they tore at him. He wanted to shake them off him, he was fearful of them snagging him like they had done in the river where it had forced his head under that blackness. He'd hardly noticed the trees as he approached them, intent only on reaching safety and heedless of what was ahead of him as he struggled towards it. The minute details in the landscape were drifting over him, passing through him like water might pass through a tunnel in the rock. They would wear him down eventually, but for now the snow, the trees, the water and the rocks were passing unnoticed as he hungered for a resting-place. They passed through him like faces he had seen every day of his life in the city rushing past him that meant nothing to him.

He felt his legs going down and at times heard the angry water crashing over rocks when he cut in too close to them. It was not yet dark but under the thick canopy of the trees that lined the river David could hear voices when their leaves rustled. He could hardly feel his legs now and each step downwards jarred his hips. He hissed back at the water and the rocks and the voices that whispered up at him. He hurled abuse at them and dragged the stump of his arm impatiently with him. He knew that the reason he was running to safety was because the arm needed attention. He knew that the arm was also holding him back. He cursed his luck and the interminable woods and the leaves that bled and bled. And when his legs stepped down into hollows that jarred him to his senses he sneered at his miserable arm, wiped the snot from his nose and plundered on and on.

"Stupid damn country, stupid damn country," David stammered, "Ought to have sold it off when they could have."

He could not see more than a few feet in front of him, the noises to the sides and around him were distractions that were slowing him down. He had to keep moving, must keep moving. Blindly he snapped a branch underfoot that sprung up at him and struck him painfully on the shin, making him feel the pain in his arm as well.

He cursed again and spat saliva from his dry mouth. The voices in the river were getting louder and the rocks that cut up through it which were damming up its banks were becoming increasingly difficult to negotiate. He scrambled back up the bank uttering obscenities in a fury, breaking through the cover of the trees. The noise from the river where it broke into a fall was humming in his ears, tormenting him as he tried to escape it. He leant against a tree for a moment then steadied himself as the world spun away from him, dizzy and out of reach. As his legs moved under him a sickening whisper of leaves coming from the molle trees shook him. The black congealed mess of his arm was growing heavy and he felt he might slip into darkness again. With one last effort he staggered down the ridge, his legs jolting him sick to his stomach. He bent double as he reached the flatter ground and heaved at the air that was escaping from him, legs disappearing from under him as he hurled himself on the house.

"Joaquin, help me get him inside. The man's hurt bad."

They carried the wild man who was soaked and bleeding into the hearth where the fire was burning. Gently the old Indian woman removed the blanket from round his arm and saw the gashes where the marks of the cat were. His arm didn't seem to be broken but his flesh had been ripped open and it would have to be sown after they'd disinfected it. The man's eyes were wild and staring as if the horror he had experienced was still frozen there. He was sweating profusely and other parts of his body were lacerated with cuts too. She cut his clothes from him while the old man went to get the flowers she had asked of him and which she kept dried in a jar. They moved him a little further away from the fire whilst the woman applied the tincture to his arm. As she did so she spoke a few words and circled the man's heart three times. The sweat was burning into a fever and David's naked body was shaking along its length.

CHAPTER FOURTEEN

The man slipped into and out of consciousness all that night and into the next day. Sometimes he uttered things that Matilde and Joaquin didn't understand, in a tongue that was strange. It was obvious a puma had attacked him, but how he'd come to be out on his own in the snow they didn't know. There was much trouble in the man and it was written in his face. Matilde had put his bag to one side of the makeshift bed and there it had stayed untouched.

There was a scent of herbs burning in the room where they'd rigged up his bed and Matilde had opened the window although it was cold. She was sitting in a chair that she had pulled to the bedside. The old man was drying the stranger's blanket and his boots in front of the fire but Matilde had insisted that the clothes were washed before they too were hung up to dry. The water that fell over the fall some way up from the house could be heard through the open window, above the sound of the man's moaning.

The passengers on the train glared back at him. The doors of the compartment were shut fast and morning was repeating its frenetic ritual. Down here the light of day was blocked out and an intense, surreal light grazed the somnambulant passengers. Although the subway train went fast, the passengers were anxious to get to their destinations on time. The compartments were crowded and their occupants were thrust into forced proximity. Men in suits jostled for the openings when they came in the tunnels. There was nothing they could do to make the train go faster though they willed it do so with a collectivism unparalleled in other facets of their daily lives. This day, as every day, they stood and watched the time slip by as they anticipated the dash up the stairs, their minds racing ahead of them as far as the exits out onto the streets and sometimes as far as their offices where tasks were left uncompleted.

David thought hard of the task he had to do that day. The report had been due in two days ago but the work wasn't yet complete and it was impossible to meet the deadlines. He depended on other people in the office feeding data to him, though they worked independently of him, and of each other too. He was on first name terms with most of the people in the office, but he knew little about their lives outside of the work place.

They were constantly working ahead of themselves, anticipating the completion of a report although the information coming in changed from day to day and frequently contradicted that which they'd previously received. The markets were subject to fluctuation and it was difficult to predict with any accuracy where they might be in a week or even in a few days' time. They had become accustomed to expecting the unexpected and the rising stars in the office were often those who had the knack of breaking the rules in terms of the extent to which they ignored or took on board the most recent statistics. One of David's colleagues even boasted that he never read the most up to date sources before a meeting, as they were likely to cloud his judgement too much. Instead he preferred to rely on his own gut instincts rather than the market analysis. Sometimes he got it spectacularly wrong, as had been proved in the infamous case in '93 in Columbia. That had been all hushed up though and when Bill had proved everybody else wrong and himself right five years later in '98, the company had struck rich. Ever since then Bill had been riding on the crest of a wave and he was one of the very few employees who was not formally required in the same manner as the others to submit his ideas in writing before a meeting. Of course he always carried in some scrap of paper or other, (the more rough-looking and loosely-bound the better), but the casualness of his dress, (a deliberate ploy on his part) and the easy manner with which he addressed his superiors unnerved the more junior members of staff. Their attention to detail was inversely proportional to the extent to which their research was taken seriously, though of course their superiors couldn't allow them to know this.

These fresh-faced students just out of business school at Harvard or elsewhere were resentful of Bill's prowess in predicting the market. It seemed to them that his open shirt and loose-necked tie were not compatible with the degree of accuracy and acumen required in the kind of negotiations the company was involved in. It went against everything they'd been taught on campus, much of it too subliminal for them to even notice that they had learned it. They were intimidated by the man because of what he represented; like some freak sudden drop or rise in the ocean he cast aspersions on their notions of security, diligence and well-constructed arguments, simply by his very existence.

One might have wondered why it was he'd not been elevated to the higher echelons of management within the company, but the truth was that his bosses were also scared of him. He himself preferred to propagate the illusion that in the position he was in, he was freer to surf around and do his own thing, (which in reality was precisely what he did), than if he'd been regimented into the higher ranks. But the precarious nature of his existence within the company served as a reminder to the more diligent, hard-working members of staff that they themselves could not imitate him, nor should they try to. That was exactly the way their superiors preferred things. Bill was an exotic; a luxury the company could afford to have who had once brought the company luxuries. Neither he nor the younger, more junior members of staff were aware that he was being preserved as an endangered species in a sort of experiment that the company had unwittingly engaged in. Like a whale swimming round in water that was too shallow for it, he would one day find himself run aground.

David envied Bill, though they rarely socialised outside the office beyond the few drinks at Christmas, which was in itself a kind of office formality. There was a party for the generals, one for the lieutenants and another one for the foot soldiers that was the best party of all, although it would have antagonised the generals deeply if they had suspected this. David was in awe of Bill even though they had a similar number of years' experience working in the company. They were both of a similar age and divorced. Though their passions in life were wildly different, the statistics were against them and they were forced to acknowledge each other's existence against the grain of their different personalities. Unconsciously they sought each other out at lunch times when the staff descended to the canteen and chewed things over. Bill would salute the bosses as they came down locked in their quiet, serious conversations, seemingly oblivious to the other workers. One or two of them would salute him back and break the spell that was cast over the canteen that had become hushed, though they would do so out of a reverie, as if granting the man a royal pardon dropped casually like an invitation to a ball through a letterbox onto a mat. Bill represented their contact with the workers and their distance from them as well. The others bowed their heads and pretended to ignore the favouritism.

David attached himself to this, and Bill was patiently generous of David's admiration of him. In any case, the man had proved on more than one occasion that an apparently lost cause could be won back by the right blend of integrity and innocence.

"So tell me, David," said Bill, "What do you think of the new redhead over there with the big boobs?"

Only Bill could ask such a question in such a direct manner. Regardless of the fact that everyone was besotted with the new female member of staff in Market Investment Research ever since she'd arrived two weeks ago, he feigned a lack of interest on the relative merits of the girl's beauty. He was irritated by Bill's comment and the lack of subtlety with which his own romanticised notions had been instantly degraded, but he was, however much against his wishes, envious of his colleague's ability to speak his mind.

"It's time for your appointment, Mr. Blanco will see you now."

"Thank-you," replied the tall gentleman in the pinstriped suit as he rose from his seating place on the cream-coloured leather couch to enter the man's office.

"Thank-you, Eva, that will be all," said the man with the platinum hair as he showed the taller man into his office.

"It's been a long time, Huberto," said the taller of the two gentlemen as he was extending his hand.

"Yes, it has, hasn't it?" said Mr. Blanco, "Thank-you so much for coming."

"So, David, what's your assessment of the situation?" His boss was asking him. He took some time to consider his reply and then answered the question as best he could.

"I think it's quite a straight forward operation," he said, "The size

207

of the country and the distance of the capital city from the north should allow for the rumour to generate itself."

David's boss considered this and then considered that perhaps he'd underestimated his worker's intelligence.

"So you don't think there'll be any problem in trying to get the evidence sorted out which will prove that the cattle up there are contaminated?" His boss asked.

"That'll be the easiest part," David answered, "All we've got to do is get the results down from Brazil and bring them across the border. Mike's contact in Brazil has told him that the studies are already in place. It's being held tight by the buro's there, (it was a term that the members in Foreign Latin American Negotiations had coined themselves – it was short for 'bureaucrat' but meant 'donkey' in Spanish if pronounced properly), all we need to do is put in the money. The evidence is not a problem, it's how that evidence travels to Buenos Aires," David concluded.

"So who exactly found the briefcase?" the white-haired man with the long curling moustache was asking the representative from the Ministry of Agriculture.

"That's not important now, Huberto," the man replied, "What's important is that a fairly precise version of the report is due to appear in the papers even though Ministro Trevillo does not want it published. These damn freedom of speech advocates, they're going to end up ruining things and causing a bigger scandal than the one that's already out. If people actually read the report, it'll cease to be just a story, you know, Huberto. It's one thing to read about how some damn Yankee has supposedly been plotting a conspiracy against the country and its interests; it's another thing altogether to read the actual bloody document itself."

"Hmm," said the Director, taking a puff on his cigar.

"Of course, you know that Ministro Trevillo himself is implicated?" said the taller of the two gentlemen.

"How's that?" the Director asked with genuine surprise.

"He's a friend of the Brazilian regional minister, Osvaludo, the one who accepted the money in the first place. Only the other week they were photographed together with their arms round each other after the

Mercosur conference in Mar del Plata. Ministro Trevillo's got a place up in Rio Grande in Brazil, you know."

"It's not related to that bomb thing I read about, is it?" The Director enquired with growing concern.

"No, separate incident, apparently, though Carrasco the Chief of Police is keeping his lips tight on the subject. This Yankee's cleverer than you'd thought, you know, Huberto."

His friend thought back to his meeting with the American and how he'd been convinced the man was stupid. How deceptive appearances could be.

"You could be right Arnaldo," said the Director looking out of the fourteenth story window. There was the escape from the Hotel Espléndida, after all.

"This thing isn't about beef at all, is it?" he said to his friend from the ministry.

"It's a plot to discredit the Government," said the man from the ministry emphatically and the Director took another puff on his cigar.

The evidence travelling down from the north of Argentina and the evidence travelling out of Buenos Aires had somehow met in the middle. Whether or not the facts travelling southwards and the facts travelling northwards out of the capital were the same was of little importance now. David had indeed been right in his assumptions concerning where the real issues lay. His boss hadn't received a telephone call from him since he'd gone missing in Argentina and at this rate it was unlikely that he'd be receiving one. Salsa was separated from his wife so there was no immediate concern in terms of informing his next of kin. He had a daughter somewhere at college but that could be sorted out in due course. The office had adopted standard procedure since the news had broken last week in the Buenos Aires Tribune and their correspondent had been in touch with his man from the New York Standard. Salsa's desk had already been cleared and there was a rather promising newcomer, a woman, who'd entered into the Market Investment Research Section who'd temporarily taken over the post whilst they assessed her suitability. Quite promising, she was. Personally, it was a sorry story as far as he was concerned, he'd liked Salsa. But it was the nature of the game and David must have known what he was getting into. They paid him enough money to do so. Operations in southern Brazil were also on hold for the moment while they were cleaning up the mess and it was possible that their clients would be demanding a refund. Nothing he could do about it, anyway, so it was best to turn his attentions to the longer-term projects.

He turned away from his desk at exactly the same time as Huberto Blanco was doing the same in his office thousands of kilometres away in Buenos Aires. It was a delicate operation and it would require skilful handling.

David mumbled something but the woman could not make out what it was he was talking about. She mopped his forehead with the towel and the man glistened under the stars that were now shining in through the open window and along his feverish skin. She'd asked Joaquin if he'd stay on at her house that night while the man needed attending to. They were old friends and after the death of Joaquin's wife they'd become closer, though not close enough that either of them had ever considered exchanging their own house for that of the other. The old man lived a little way further down the river, alone now that his sons had left for the city. He was often in and out of Matilde's house, exchanging his solitude and reticence for that of the quiet words of the Indian woman which dropped like the river over the falls at the spot where her family had lived for generations. She was quiet in her manner of speech, but when she spoke those that knew her listened, for it was seldom she said anything if it was not worth saying. She was tough too, through years of keeping her own company, so that it seemed like the earth spoke in her when she spoke. She had been garnering up its energy year after year, never having married and therefore never having to concede too much to anyone. But she loved all things that moved on the earth and was at home with them. People in the area often went to her to cure them of their ills and women who were troubled in trying to conceive would ask her help in calling the powers that would grant them a child. Matilde had never had a child herself, nor heeded the desire to have one. She was, therefore, better equipped than many to understand the sufferings of those who came before her, those whose lives were in need of something they did not possess.

The stranger was weak not only from the attack by the beast and from his journey. This much Matilde saw. What it was he was fleeing could not be flung off until he had wrestled it within himself. She rose to light another broom of herbs at the fireside where old Joaquin sat. She put her hand on his shoulder affectionately.

"Make yourself comfortable in the armchair," she said to him, "The clothes will dry by themselves."

She smiled warmly, showing the wrinkles that time had etched into her face, though if one looked closely one might see a light in her eyes that was younger by far than she was.

She returned to the room where the sickness was all about it with the lit broom of herbs in her hand. This she circled the air with and cast words that had come from the river, words that had drifted into her from her long time spent by it and whose meaning, though indecipherable to most, was as constant as the water that flowed there.

"Who are you?" she said to the man who lay in the bed at her side when his fever had begun to subside hours later. It was the dead of night now, and all this time Matilde had sat in patient watch, letting the dark hours ebb away as she listened to what the river might tell her.

"Who are you?" she asked again, addressing the man, and there was firmness in her voice.

"David," the man replied feebly, not sure of where he was nor whom it was that addressed him.

"You have come a long way," the woman said, though David could not properly see the woman's face in the room near by him.

"Yes," replied David now that he could hear her words more clearly.

"You have need to talk," said the woman simply after a time and she left David to ponder the silence. All around the room smelt of something sweet. It was not an over-powering smell, but its fragrance had a gentle insistence that somehow made him feel less tired. Thoughts were crowding David's mind and a rumour of suspicion trembled in him before his gaze at last settled on the face of the woman and he felt the peace that was in her.

"I am not who I seem," said David with an effort, though when he had said this to the woman he immediately felt relief.

"Yes, I know," she said to him patiently, "You must not let your fear allow you to misjudge that which is truly important to you at this time. I can listen to you, but it is you who must name the thing that you fear to speak of."

"I was attacked," said David as the memory of the pain that had come flooding into his arm troubled him again. Now the sensation was more of a dull ache, but in his mind the pain was glowing. He tried to move his arm and found it sore, but when he rested it the pain flowed away a little.

"You are lucky," said the old woman, "Your arm is not broken though you will bear the scars of the wound all your life, to remind you of what you have fought with."

For an instant David felt as if the old woman was reaching into him, reading the events of his past in a place further away than his mind could deal with. David felt afraid for an instant that she should know his life without his telling her of it, but the manner in which the Indian woman spoke to him was calm. She was not hurrying him. She had authority in her voice, but she did not make David feel threatened by it. The questions she asked of him, however, seemed to demand a lot of him.

"You are safe here in my house," the woman said to him, "You will be healed if you allow yourself to be."

David didn't quite understand what it was the woman was saying to him, she seemed to be speaking in riddles. Though her assurance that he would be safe here was said with such conviction that he could not help but trust her.

"How do you know who I am?" asked David.

"You have told me yourself," she replied, matter-of-factly.

"You said something," David said.

"Yes," said the woman, waiting for him to speak.

But the silence of the night intruded on them.

"I was lost," said David after a while, attempting to answer what he thought it was that the woman was asking him.

"You have been lost for a long time," the woman said to him, "But your spirit brought you here and it is for a reason."

David lay back in the bed and felt the power of the water that was running in the echoing night. The old woman said nothing more and David thought of how it was that he had come to be here in this strange place, so far from the place he had travelled from. He could feel the woman's presence strongly in the room and he felt compelled to speak some more.

"You must rest now," said the old woman, putting a hand on his forehead and gently restraining him from sitting up. With that she got up from the chair and left the room. David struggled after her but saw only the flicker of the candle burning in the glass jar on the shelf before he finally drifted back into sleep.

There was light streaming in through the window when he awoke and the patterns the trees made on the wall reached diagonally across it. David felt the sun on his bedclothes although there was a chill breeze that blew in through the still-open window. He thought back to the desolate waste over which he'd crossed, how the sun had taken his sight while the wind blew angrily across the snow. Then out of nowhere the beast had seized him and he was falling backwards, backwards towards the noise of the other beast clutching at him.

It seemed to David that he'd been watching it happen to somebody else, but then he remembered the long night in the forest after he'd left the farm and he knew that these things must have happened. Where was he now? Someone had put him in this bed and the smell of soup simmering was wafting in from another room somewhere else in the house. Presently the woman came in with a bowl of the broth that she'd prepared.

"Drink this," she said to David, "It will make you stronger."

David took a sip from the bowl as she brought it up to his lips, then lay back in the bed again.

"How long…?" he said.

"You have been away from the world for many hours," Matilde said.

"I remember," said David.

"Good," said the old woman, raising the clay bowl to his mouth again, "It is good that you do so."

"Was I … attacked?" David asked her, though he could feel the marks streaked on the arm that was now covered by bandages. The woman nodded in assent.

"Those who are faced with death and survive are fortunate if they forbid themselves from thinking it just a dream," she said.

David heard the words but did not understand them, but there was honesty in the woman's voice and it was indisputable.

"Drink," she commanded him, raising the bowl to his lips again. The soup tasted strange, and the herbs that were in it were unfamiliar to him. He drank as much as he could as the woman had bade him to, then she took the bowl and what was left in it and placed it on the floor by her feet.

"You will sleep for some time now," she said to him, "When you awake it will probably be night but I will be here all the time in the house, and if I am not I will not be far away."

"Thank-you," said David, and for a second the woman placed her hand on his heart through the material of the shirt he was wearing before she walked out of the room.

A strip of the blanket he had taken from the farm and had wrapped himself up in when out on the snow had been placed on top of the other bedclothes when he woke up. He was feeling much better, though when he stupidly tried to sit up quickly in bed he was reminded of how long he must have been laying there. He was feeling more cheerful and his mind was clearer and less confused, even though his body struggled in its efforts to catch up with him. He pulled the blankets up close as a sudden gust blew in through the window. He must have laid there for an hour or two more before he could hear the sound of voices in another room quite close to him and he came to completely. There was a question on David's lips when Matilde entered some minutes later but she spoke before he could address her.

"His name's Joaquin," she said to him, "It was him who helped me carry you in last night when we found you."

"Is he…?"

"A friend," Matilde answered him, "I have known him a long time."

She went out of the room, but not before she had relit the large candle that had been glowing in the room since the previous night on his arrival.

David could hear Matilde and the man discussing something in the other room, but when the man asked her a question that David couldn't quite hear, David was consoled by the fact that the woman's response seemed to satisfy him. The man's voice lowered and David heard a door opening and closing before Matilde came back into the room again.

"You are safe here," she repeated, "Who are you?"

"Haven't I already told you?" he asked her, slightly on the defensive and perturbed by the noise of the door that had closed and the sound of the footsteps that had walked away from the house.

"You have told me many things," the old woman said to him, "But not yet this."

Her words were forceful but the smile on her face coerced him into reassurance.

"I was with a girl but I had to leave her. I didn't want them to hurt her," he struggled.

"Good," said the old woman, "That will do for now. My name is Matilde. Before we can talk you must promise to listen carefully to what I have to say to you. I fully expect you to answer my questions."

David was taken aback by what seemed to him the woman's sudden change in tone. She got up to close the window as David looked towards the candle that spluttered on the shelf on the wall.

"Why are you here?" the woman demanded of him when she had sat back down in the chair. Authority and assurance reigned in her voice. The light cast by the candle on the wall made him recall the light that had crept onto the wall of his prison cell that dreadful night so long ago. He was sweating. What did she mean? He was beginning to panic.

"They locked me up," said David, unable to guess what it was the woman wanted of him, "But then they made a mistake and set me free," said David, unable to look the woman in the eye, suddenly fearful of her betrayal.

"You say it was a mistake?" said the old woman, accusing him, or so it felt to David.

"It was all a mistake," David stammered, "I shouldn't have been sent here in the first place, they should have sent somebody else."

"Who sent you?" the woman asked him, emphasising her words.

"My company in America. There are many others who could have done the job properly, they should have realised that I wasn't the right person for the job," David gushed, "It's their fault I'm in this mess. I didn't want any part of it, I ran away."

"From whom?" Matilde enquired.

"From the people in Buenos Aires. Don't you see that I didn't want any more part in it all?" David was pleading with her.

"Yes, David," she spoke to him addressing him by his name, "I can see that. Have you harmed anyone?" she asked him, her voice still as calm as the unruffled trees that withstood the wind outside the window. The image of his wife trapped by the boulder that had come crashing down on her thundered back into his mind and he started to cry as the woman continued to look at him so that he could stand it no longer.

"My wife, I … I let her down, there was an accident. We had a child, a daughter."

Matilde reached towards him and unexpectedly stroked his hair as she eased him into a more comfortable position, arranging the pillow behind him.

"Your daughter was born because *she* wanted to be," said Matilde interrupting him, "You may feel that you have lost her, but you will find her again."

David was astonished.

"How do you know…?" he asked her, abruptly dragged away from his self-pity.

"I do not," said Matilde, "You are telling me. All I can do is listen to what you have to say. I can never tell you what it is you must do."

David looked fully at the woman. He had stopped crying.

"I didn't hurt her deliberately," said David forcefully, "I tried to warn her but she didn't listen to me."

"Perhaps she couldn't hear you," said Matilde.

"Hear me," said David, "She couldn't hear me for the sound of the water, it dislodged the rock and…"

The fatigue of his ordeal and the pain of the freshly awoken memory welled up in him again.

"We have all let people down," said Matilde, removing her hand from his head, "The one person you must never let down is yourself and I sense that you have done so. Neither my pity nor your own will help you recover. But you are not willingly a bad person," she said, "This I know."

She said the words with a conviction that bordered on the absurd in David's mind. How did she know what crimes he had or hadn't committed?

"I wouldn't have gone through with it," said David, aggressively asserting himself and, curiously, his guilt in the matter. "Once I realised the full extent of the plan to dupe the public and sell them meat which was unfit for consumption I no longer wanted any part in it."

Silence.

"Now, though, it seems that everyone wants a part of me."

And as he said the words he realised what he had done. He wondered at the time it had taken him to see that what he was doing was wrong, and why it was that he hadn't realised that he had a choice in the matter. Only now did he understand this.

"Good," said the old woman, "Now I can help you."

The light that had seemed to emanate from her face before was drained from her now and she was no longer threatening. She stood and turned to the window, peering through it, with her slightly hunched back turned towards David.

"You must remember when you are gone from here that the most important words you have heard underneath this roof are your own. Learn to forgive yourself David, and then the world may begin to forgive you," she smiled, "I myself will forget our conversations easily if anyone ever comes knocking at my door enquiring of you."

She wafted her hand round her head in an affectation of forgetfulness. She turned to face David, fatigue in her face as old age resumed its stance in her body again; more so than ever, it seemed to David.

"I know what you are thinking," she said to him, "You are thinking that I am old, but I have lived for many years and have a right to be. You are still a young man - your life is just beginning, but before it can do so you have to live out your past."

The Indian woman was speaking in riddles again, but a tension had cleared in the room and the sound of water volleying into the night could be heard again clearly in the stillness. David cleared his throat and even though the conversation with the old woman had been at times fierce and, he thought, he'd even been momentarily frightened, he was glad of it.

"I don't know what to say," said David.

"You have nothing more to say and any further words would be an effort for both of us, me especially," said Matilde with a certain air of indifference as she let the force of her years lower her into her chair again.

"I am tired, young man, and many there have been with problems far greater than yours."

The words hurt David but her sincerity was implacable.

"You are not the only one who needs to sleep!" she said some moments later with a gleam in her eye again. Whenever he had felt that the old woman had been reaching out to him she had pulled away from him; and when she had been at her fiercest with him was when what he had been made to say had helped him most. David could never understand her, but he felt a kind of taciturn love on her part towards him; as if somehow she'd made him her child.

"Too much self-pity is the worst kind of cruelty," said Matilde after some time, "It is not my business to indulge you further," she said, "In the morning I will come and we will have breakfast together with Joaquin. He was worried about you but I told him he had nothing to fear."

She turned her head towards the window.

"I knew you were essentially a good man from the moment you first looked at me."

"I,...have money," said David, feebly.

"Ah, yes, no doubt you do," said Matilde, "But that doesn't necessarily make you a good man. Good night, David."

And with that the door of the room closed behind her. The tiny room was trapped in the transparency of the darkness that impressed itself. Water volleyed into the unfathomable night somewhere outside. In a distant wood an owl flies silently from one branch to another. Eyes open. Eyes close. The night leaves its victim and in a blink the world has turned.

CHAPTER FIFTEEN

Sometimes the desire to uncover one's past is as great as the need to leave it behind. A web hangs between the two points of our eyes and what we see is little more than what we have allowed ourselves to, caught up in false preconceptions of ourselves.

The sound of water is in my ears and stones murmur and chatter as from within the early morning fog in which I walk the tinkle of goats' bells is heard and I begin to realise that I am walking. Down they come out of the fog in a flurry, first one then another and then somehow the whole flock slides past me as the acrid stench of their coats and their droppings penetrates. My boots are caked with their sludge and I can't breath under the weight of my pack and the weight of the hill, but as I am thinking this to myself I realise that I am, actually, breathing. Perhaps for the first time since I got off the bus and craned my neck to peer up at the glimmer of rock way up above. Perhaps I have been holding my breath ever since and only now have begun to breathe again. 'Pasos Malos' they call it: the 'bad steps'. No way up for horse or mule and probably not for the Spanish who swelled like sores down in the valleys below. The Indians must at first have looked out at them with the same trembling curiosity with which I now approach the fortresses of their ancient rocks perched high above. The earth pulls away from me as I strain my head again to see them through the sun in the early morning mist. Then I bend to the weight of my pack and the weight of the hill and bow down to the huge hummocks of grass and scree hanging over me. Now the chanting of the flies intones itself like a prayer as I leave the stone corral behind me with the river approaching. It is winter but winter has not yet reached here, except where the rivers have been gifted by the melt waters of the snow that have fallen on the peaks above and found a footing in some hidden valley. The rocks on its shores glint with white crystal; once across the precarious stepping stones which spit and chatter I scramble up the bank and find myself beneath the first molle tree. No stranger to the elements, these trees seed themselves and split open boulders when first shoots stretch out to meet the spring. There they remain, anchored in stone for centuries after.

The voice of my daughter, Hannah calls to me. She is seven. We brought her to the mountains when she was just eight months old, and we marvelled at the winter sun and the swelling mountains which glowed purple as night rushed in and the chill of the air replaced the day's chatter and laughter. I am thinking this now because I need to be with you and you are far away from me.

How much of our lives do we spend simply waiting for things to happen to us and then when they do we find that we cannot free ourselves of things imposed on us by forces beyond our control? Not you, child; you were no accident, you are the most precious gift ever bestowed on me, though here, now, I find myself amazed that I should be a father and that you should be my child. I choose to climb this mountain because I am forced into exile; I need to draw breath; I choose it now.

The sun is blinding as I step out from underneath the cool shade of the molle tree. It reminds me of a painting in the taverna back down in the village where women with dark sun-kissed faces in long dresses are seated beneath a similar tree that grows alongside a thick stone wall, heavy with sun and lightened by it also. Between the women in their colourful dresses, the baby crawling, the tree and the wall there is a harmony and a restfulness that stills me when I see it. I can't remember the meals I have eaten in the dining room of this beautiful, dark-beamed hotel while I have been here recovering but I can remember every detail of the painting. I thought at first that I would like to buy it; to own it, but now I know that I would merely like to be able to look at it when I please, but not take it from the place that it belongs.

It takes a lifetime to cross the clumps of grass where the cows have idled, left their dung and loll about swishing at flies that have forgotten that the noise of the river has rushed on down behind us and left this place quiet. The weight I carry feels heavy and I am bathed in perspiration under the early flints and blows of the sun as I inch my way to the hummock that I have outlined as the starting place for my ascent. That weight, sometimes, is good though, so long as we are going forwards with it and not merely bearing our burdens and suffering under them. The weight I am carrying now feels good to me.

Hands reach the first wet sods, limbs lift. The warmth absorbed by the rocks is absorbed by my fingers and, weightless now, I can feel myself stretching. The pain in my arm has begun to disappear, ever since I left the Indian woman's house. Already the goats seem like insects below and the clear breezes of wild thyme and rosemary have filled my nostrils, replacing the quarried animal labour in the corral. The ridge on which I am climbing is narrower than it looked from down near the river but that in itself is part of the feeling of joy I have; no thought of turning back, committed to the task in hand; only one way forwards and it is I who have singled out my route. The bushes and grasses that grow between the stones are tough and leathery, sometimes it is necessary to take hold of them to pull myself up and I taste them as their powdery scent is disturbed. After an hour I have become an insect that crawls amongst them. Occasionally I come to a place where I can pull myself upright against the laws of gravity, boots solid as the rocks themselves, steadying me. I live side by side with the fear of falling and I am big but small at the same time. The mountain can teach us how to live within the shadow of doubt and even to prosper from it also.

As I move on there are places where I am protected from the sun's fingers scouring the slopes for things to claim as their own. I am not sure whether I am part of its prey or whether it is my destiny to meet with it on the tops of the mountain. The water tastes good, the more I drink, the cleaner I feel inside. The ridge on which I climb becomes narrower, twisting out of my reach at moments, sometimes making me feel bigger than the valley itself as I swing out unprotected above it. So I toil with myself as I look for ways up towards safety. Here and there a loose stone is sent crashing down to the noise of the gully and the goats and the river below; thoughts rolling from under me, some of which I free myself from deliberately. A hunger is in my lungs and only thoughts of Hannah steady my giddiness and make me check my handholds carefully as I scrabble at the rocks. It is easy to believe that I am immortal sometimes, and in that instant be sent crashing to the world's slow turning below.

The river's anger is funnelled up the sheer sides of the valley; the opposite side seems almost within touching distance, and more so the higher up I am pulled. Somewhere up there must be snow but it is lying crouched like the cats I have been told stalk the heights above. The water from my new canteen soothes me again, some I tip over my head and almost at once my vision steadies itself and the flock of images all around me becomes one crisp view, blue and true as an eye. The nostrils and the eyes are one. The wind rakes them.

At last the ridge has opened out; left the land dips, pulled irresistibly into the bosom of gold, sun-drenched grass which meets another col, before plunging down into a dark obscure ravine; to the right brutish green slopes are trampled on by clouds hurrying past. I have come to the top of this ridge to find a hump in the land; the first finger joint beneath the knuckle on the sun's spreading grip over these hills. Just up above me there is a buttress.

I approach with caution for some sense that is not mine but which is with me bids it so. I am wary of other beings but have no reason to believe that any are about. The wind idly plays with a solitary tabaquillo tree whose bark, like strips of tobacco left out to dry, flaps on its trunk. I pull myself up onto a great flat stone and brace myself. The scurrying of the leaves just out of the right corner of my eye tricks me and makes me start. Here the wind soars and the sweat begins to grow chill on my body. As I move up to the left a dark opening begins to grow and I bend on my hands and knees to peer into this low cave. Some material on the floor has been disturbed and, as I examine it with a stick, I realise that although the faeces I've found are dry, they are not those of a goat. Puma, though something tells me it is far off now and, at least for the moment, has left this place. At the back there is a small opening, big enough to crawl through and rather than it being completely dark there, there is a dim light, with the wisp of a breeze running through it. Something compels me to crawl my way in and as I do so I realise that this is just an anti-chamber to a much larger cave, partially open on the right-hand side and tall enough for me to stand up in. On the left as I turn round there are what might serve for rough sleeping places, two ledges at shoulder height tucked underneath an overhang, of which the first, (the second is partially obscured in the darkness) must be about two metres wide and three metres or more long. The sun breezily filters through on the right and underneath this huge boulder is another low chamber that appears to run almost the length of it. In front of me now as I stand with one hand resting on the sleeping area, I notice a small opening at the end of the system that looks back down towards the valley. Here a draught tugs at the air and the wind moans through it, coming in sudden gusts as it does. The dust beneath my fingers feels dry and old and I no longer feel welcome here. Up onto the first ledge with a swing back out to the right through the roof and suddenly I am standing above the cave, on top of a huge crazy boulder which forms its right flank, with my gaze directly tilted back out across the valley. But it is not the valley I have climbed up. It is the sweeping valley that separates this mountain chain from the plains that reach down from La Rioja and the open expanses of patchy farmland leading towards the central mountains of San Luis; a grey island swathed in misty sunshine, mysterious and imperial.

I move away across the top of the boulder and only have to jump a short height to reach the ground that has risen up behind it, grass rustling at its base. Something in the shape of these rocks, (or is it one rock?) attracts my attention as I move away to get a more precise view of the whole. The ground is suddenly steep and I am drunk on the sensation of height as the stone beak, huge and angled towards the impenetrable slopes off out of human vision, stern and foreboding, takes shape. The head is tilted to the right and there is a rock that forms an eye, perfectly in proportion to the rest of the head, which is catching the rays of the sun. The ruffled feathers of the eagle's chest are mirrored exactly in the pattern of rocks. The whole head must be at least the size of a small cottage. I have quite forgotten where I am and the great valley underneath suddenly seems precipitously far off; as if I had strayed into some strange territory to which, very consciously, I feel I don't belong and I should be back down there with the people in the village. And yet I have been allowed here, it is both my duty and my right to take all this in. I run onto the bridge of the beak itself and rejoice in the feeling of weightlessness. I feel that I am flying simply by being there, simply by existing.

Back on the grassy slopes stirring in the breeze the chanting which comes back to me on the air is my own, though the words are a language beyond my meaning. I am singing. People have lived here, children have played. The darker, greener fields which were to my right on the hump on top of the ridge immediately below the eagle's head seem softer and less foreboding now. They even seem less steep than they had first appeared on nearing them. I am back down where the solitary tabaquillo tree stands half-hearted watch over the children playing, at a patch of grass which is softer still than the fields which are slightly behind me now to my left, where small mountain flowers bloom and the air is quiet and peaceful. In front of me in this small garden is a long oblong table-rock, berries crushed into it by the birds or by the ghosts of a tribe in hiding. I rest here while I share my simple food with them. What I spill will become the earth itself. The words are not my own as the chanting recommences itself within me, but the meaning is; the singing is all around me moving off up the greener slopes. The language is older than my own, tumbling down over the mountain's flanks.

I am not less but more than I was before, but the heart is a hard task-master and I am not, often, tutored to hear its wisdom. The time was, maybe, when the heart was a fiery stone as fierce and as proud as the sun and the ancestors of my ancestors lived within its glow. Perhaps, once, there was only one heart and those tribes that understood this took up its singing. Life goes on around us, even though we sometimes will it otherwise. But some of us are made stubborn, even though that stubborness is a rock against which we beat ourselves.

There is water underneath the land that moulds the shapes and colours above it; even where it can't be heard it must still be present. Off to my left on the greener slopes there must be a constant trickle of water which has oozed down over the centuries and caused the grass to be greener and taller there. I make my way over and begin the steep ascent of the hummock which rises behind the eagle's head, continuing the line of this huge incongruous ridge which seems to grow in its dimensions the further up I climb it. I must set out from this refuge I have taken against the vertigo the mountain throws down at me. The wind whispers that it is time for me to leave; I feel uneasy both staying and carrying on. There is no way past this exposed hump and I feel vulnerable and strangely alone again as I proceed to climb it.

Snatches of a tune imagined in some thin street of a deserted high mountain town far to the north in the altiplano drift towards me. The music is both solitary and comforting, as if its creator must also have experienced the solitude of the high lands in the same way that I now experience it. The mountains are like a shout whose echoes draw closer and louder the higher up and the further into them I get. For I do not walk upon the mountains, I walk inside them. As if to intimidate me, now the massive stone outcrop of the first visible peak lumbers into view, bending over me like some ancient giant that has just risen from its sleep. Its heights are black and foreboding; out of the thin dry air it has wreathed itself in mists that swirl about its tops. Out of these mists a pair of black dots wheel into the vacant sky beneath its face and, growing larger, suddenly veer off across the valley to my right.

I turn my head to this hill which blocks my way and, taking handholds of its flowing grass, begin to pull myself up it. I am an insect on the finger of a giant's hand; either the mountain will open itself up to me and take me in its palm or it will close itself into a fist and smash me. I reach the browned knuckle gasping and sweating and have to adjust myself to the newly perceived dimensions of what lies in front of me before I can go on. The grass is coarse and windswept and rather than feeling securer for my having reached the rounded top of this hill, I feel even more isolated. As if in movement I can put my fear to one side- although it is still carried with me- but when I am still the sheer magnitude of the mountain somehow finds space to press itself down on me and expose my fragility.

Stretching in front of me is a line of similar hills, all bigger than the last, leading up to the jagged, grinning teeth of the summit. I have to pass between a passage in the stone where the grass has been scorched with fire and only tough, charred roots remain. A fire here whipped up in the infernal dry dust of the air would soon scorch any wings I might naively have thought I'd grown. Amazingly, cattle must have reached here as there are dried and flattened heaps of dung round the rocks, though how they managed to get here is beyond my understanding. Normally, the sight of an animal close to me serves to comfort me, even if this is their home and I am an intruder; though it is easier to think of the animals belonging to the mountain rather than it belonging to them. Nonetheless, the very visible presence of the cattle in this strange blackened scrub land makes me feel ill at ease, as if the cows must have been ghosted from somewhere else by the hand of the mountain, or as if they had never been here at all. Perhaps the animal whose presence I feel so strongly at the moment but cannot see is the mountain itself, watching from its vantage point and waiting to see how far I will dare to approach it in its den.

The line of the ridge veers off determinedly to the left, away from the steep jaws of the valley I have come out of, but whose walls now begin to preposterously unite. So, blinding myself to the way I have come, I forbid my eyes from anticipating the drop on this side and inch along one pace at a time without daring to fix my gaze on the summit either. As the ridge narrows further my hands and limbs take over, groping at the rocks and boots digging their toes into anything which will hold them, a drunken man staggering up the stairs of some house he's invited himself into in which he no longer feels comfortable. How many of these hills I climb before I can finally see the summit in front of me is guesswork; I only know that my lungs ache from the concentration and my pack is stuck wet to my back where it has been sleeping.

As if carried by some inner, psychological momentum rather than any actual driving force from my body, I do not give myself time to doubt the steps ahead I must take, launching myself at the first real buttress of solid rock I've had to face.

I am not a climber. Back where I am from the acrobats and gymnasts perform fingertip tricks and the applause they get when they stop in the rush-hour traffic is no more at most than some half-uttered flat response to the day's dreaming. I have no ropes with me. The mountain is my only companion and it is my foe as well. I do not eagerly anticipate the next handhold with relish or plan my route ahead; the hands and feet do the work and my mind puts itself like a fragile animal into a glass jar until hands and feet suddenly find the top and the mind can let itself out of the jar again. Hands pull the summit towards me, fractured into a thousand rocky pieces. Lungs suck in air. I can breathe, I'm past the worst.

Ahead of me lies the real peak of the mountain across an undulating plain of grass. To my right and still some considerable distance above me is the first summit I'd seen bending down over me in the valley, though from here I can now see that it should be more or less accessible if taken from the side and slightly from behind. Its face is only for the gods. My lungs are sucking in the wind as it sings over the plain in front of me and on which I now finally stand: the mountain has let me into itself, I have become a part of it, at least for the time being. Cabeza del Indio- The Indian's Head, they call it; well, its scalp will be mine today. This is the vast upper plain they call the Pampa Achala- it stretches all the way from here to Córdoba away in the north where still higher peaks erupt from its midst and a man like me might dally and lose himself for ever. There I too might have dallied too long. I leave the first teeth beneath the plain behind and let the lingering ridge I've climbed stretch out like an indolent hand whose fingers just barely touch the ground, whose embrace I now desert. I think of Rosa, looking at the mountains when she looks out of her window at the sky.

My way up trails below me, but I am giddy with the excitement of first free steps on the mountain tops like a child who has just learned to walk. Back down in the valley an old man said to me as I started my ascent that I had to avoid the gorges as they were evil, but what child will heed an adult when there is play and adventure to be had?

It has taken me much longer than I had thought it would to get up here. You can only really see the outline of this vast and relatively flat expanse of grass from a long way back, away from the overhanging shadow that these mountains cast on the village. The shadows that fall on the upper slopes, the sleeping shoulders, are purple and make the white surface of the church in the square cry out as the sun smoulders behind them and drags night down with it.

It is time to press on and I find myself struggling to gain territory. Quartz glints in the earth and there are places where the earth itself seems to be no more than a thin veil of soil over solid veins of crystal. The sun's light is blinding up here, compounded with the rarity of the air and magnified by the blueness of the sky that now seems to have dispelled the mists that lingered. After about an hour I am suddenly in a shallow rift cutting across the plain and down below me, but not too far below, are a couple of bare, scrawny trees- possibly tabaquillos again- on the edge of what appear to be fields of crystal. As I approach them I realise that they are pools of snow formed round a partially frozen stream that hangs suspended.

The wind has stopped and the closer I get, the bluer the vein running through the snow seems to be, as if some pure essence of the crystals had been extracted and was frozen inside the snow; but not too frozen for a little of their light to flow out from within its transparency. Sensing something held in awe of the moment with myself, I glance up and trace the outline of a small grey fox almost directly opposite me on the other side of the small valley. This hollow is replete with snow but nowhere else can I perceive its muted glow. How cold the mountains where I left the girl sleeping seem to me now. This snow holds the light, keeps it within itself. It does not reflect it like the tarnished light of cities on the snow that falls in them, embroidered with whatever cheap decorations are thrown at it. Perhaps that is what you tried to tell me also, Matilde. The fox is looking inside me and as I turn to look at it it is gone, disappeared without a trace across the soft footfalls of this pure white carpet.

As if to follow the fox to where I feel it must have gone, I am led down further towards the water's edge and off to my right where the water must break free of ice and plummet into the abyss. I am crossing the other side of the gully now with the blue of the mountain spring and the incandescent white of the snow frozen behind me, as if merely turning round to look at the scene again will somehow cause the spell to break and send the water crashing down, bringing noise where there should be none. The sun is hot on my forehead and I am tiring of the effort of concentrating as I go picking my way amongst the stones which have been washed down by the water, or merely been pulled to its centre of gravity. The water is like a magnet that attracts everything towards it then spews it out into the infinite space hanging over the valley. I am being forced dangerously towards the edge of this ravine where I can sense what lies below but not see it. Suddenly I find myself climbing on the edge of the precipice to get out of the ravine but the sweat is running down my face and I am dizzy with the desire of conquering this place. I climb upwards but I am being forced to my right and the silent hanging valley every few steps in order to follow the contour in the rock. Madness takes over and the sweat in my eyes is stinging; the scarf I have tied around my head to keep the worst of the sun's heat off makes me feel like an Indian brave off to poach an eagle's egg on some ritual quest for manhood. It is not until I finally reach a ledge where I can stand up properly and make my way back left along it that I fully realise where I am; exposed and almost on the very face that loomed black in the mist on the way up, but which now thrills with the sun. Do the clouds turn like vultures here and ride the thermals?

I am intoxicated with my accomplishment as I scrabble back towards safety, laughing out loud into the canyon and concerned at my own foolishness also. I have acquired a taste for this weightlessness and even though I am conscious of the madness of it, I can't escape the impulse to go back to the edge.

I have pulled myself up to stand on these dizzy heights and taken a few footsteps when out of the corner of my eye something seems to move. In the moment that I have perceived the shape of some creature lazily sunning itself on a huge slab of rock balanced on the ridge below it becomes not one shape but two. Into the unreal blue of this immense sky two sets of wings have launched themselves. In their blue cavern they embrace the spinning earth for an eternity, interlocked in feathers, then let it loose; drift into it. Sky shifts into earth, earth into sky, mountains draw a pale line glistening in the divide. A precious metal has been invented: snow.

I have been holding my breath all this time and begin to exhale slowly, as if the very air I breathe is travelling out with the condors in their arc encompassing the whole of the valley. Not just the one I have climbed up, but the whole system of the valleys stretching from here to the distant peaks of the central ranges and beyond to the great Andean wall. This part of the sierra is the only place in the whole of Argentina where condors live and breed freely outside of the Andean chain, or so I have been told. Somehow they seem to say: "You have seen how we fly, you may even have glimpsed something of what we ourselves experience; but now you must be content to watch, if we decide to let you, and envy us. Leave the flying to us, the gods." They have flown through the eye of a needle.

I make my way carefully back down the way I came up, step by step, not climbing now if I don't have to. Reaching the contour of the ledge that runs round the left side of the summit head I opt for the easiest route down and eventually find myself at its base on the flat plain of grass, with the valley gratefully hidden from view. I have experienced their weightlessness, rid myself for an instant of my own insignificant gravity, but I cannot stay up here forever. There is no sense in turning to retrace my route back off the plateau, it's far too steep and in any case I am becoming nervous at the prospect of not being down safely before nightfall. I have almost forgotten it is winter, the sun is kind on the mountains here like an old man's hand on a favourite grandchild.

Night must fall at about seven in these western parts; I'd better press on. So, half running, half stumbling across the Pampa, I find a part where the land begins to sag gently rather than disappearing steeply at the edge, which should lead me down onto the first major ridge, past the summit I have just reached. It is on the opposite side of the valley to the ridge I climbed this morning. I have outwitted the mountain and got its geography mapped out in my mind. True, I have to sit on my backside at times and take firm holds of the tufty grass, but there appear to be no major rock faces to have to divert round, at least as far as I can see. I am pleasantly ensconced between the brow of a steeper ridge to my left and the reappearing, looming head of the 'Cabeza del Indio' to my right, so that although my way is becoming increasingly steeper as I inch down, more often than not on my backside now, I do not feel the dizzying vertigo of being exposed on my left and right flanks as well.

The valley floor is now hidden from view. Not to worry, it'll be a steep climb for sure, the closer I get to the bottom, but I can see the village way down below this series of stairs and I know where I'm going. It crosses my mind for a second that I'd temporarily forgotten that I am on the run. I have a sip of water from my flask and decide to use the cheap binoculars I have bought. The magnifying power is reasonable but the focus is not so good; nonetheless, four of these 'lomos' or humps and I should be just about back level with the eagle's head where I stopped on my way up and which I can see glinting in the high evening sunlight. No sooner has my mind begun to start making calculations regarding the amount of time I'd thought it was going to take me to get down, than I realise with a gasp that I've been cheated. What looked as if it were one continuous, sinuous ridge spiralling its way down to the valley floor is in fact broken. The arm in front of me swings in from left to right, re-climbing to an abrupt rocky outcrop after having seemingly surrendered to the scree and boulders of the slope tumbling towards it: that was the ridge I should have followed. I am on a spur that has been chopped off into a precarious over-hang just waiting for some forlorn creature to slip and thus take its revenge. I get as close to the edge as I dare, just to feel the impulse of vertigo, so that I can assure myself that there really is no way down apart from what would be one last big step. Though that is a thought that my body seems to entertain a little too wistfully as far as I'm concerned. Nothing is as it seems to be in these mountains. An impossible-looking ascent might be accomplished by twisting and squirming up it, but an easy-looking descent is surely a trick and rounded hummocks the size of small mountains might lead me to a terrifying impasse on their hidden faces. The clock in my head is ticking away and the foolish thought of backtracking is dismissed as too flirtatious a plan. The face of the rock summit from where I had seen the condors some hours ago is black-bent upon me now and both its weight and the weight in my legs forbid me to do anything so impossible as tread upon its slopes again. How far am I down? –About as high as the resting place of the condors. No, surely I must be further down than that. Eyes check visible landmarks - one found, the eagle's head. Still above it? A couple of hours climbing in the dark inevitable. Clear sky. Hopefully good starlight to guide me down. Don't get caught in the watercourses. Damn it, only way out. Plunging on I slip down through some high, reedy grass into a pool which catches me by surprise, both because of the cold of the water and its depth, which easily comes up to my thighs. Damn this. Got to get back up there. No chance. Want to be losing height at all costs, not gaining it! Got to keep going. Like a child who keeps committing the same mistakes while attempting a puzzle but refuses through obstinacy to give up, the logical certainty that the only way to get back safely is to haul myself back to the top and start my descent again is thrown out in the blink of an eye. My limbs ache all the more because they know that the only way down is to go up but that is impossible.

I know that I am doing this all wrong but it's the only way that my body will let me carry on. Can't stay stuck in this stupid pool all night– what if it's a watering hole for pumas? Damn, this rucksack's heavy; probably waterlogged. I balance it precariously on one shoulder like an outsize shopping bag and take my last two remaining oranges from it. Should some sleek cat come crawling down the rocks wondering where this tangy aroma is coming from, it will find a man up to his thighs in water with his back turned defiantly on the inevitable, slurping oranges which have been slipped from their cases and then been shredded and tossed to the birds in a non-existent high altitude resting place for waterfowl. I climb my way out of it with considerable effort and the water drains from me. Skirting round its edge, I pick my way over an obstacle course of boulders as the serpentine water slashes its way at the hillside. It twists and turns before it is mastered and wrestled down, so that my descent follows its path turning back and back on itself again to lose but a few precious metres in height. The hand and footholds are wet. I'm forced to cross the stream to the right-hand side and then re-cross it lower down too close to the over-hanging rock face. The farther down the chasm of this dark water I get, the deeper inside the mountain I am led. Reason tells me that normally, to get off a mountain would be to both get down it and to leave it alone; to desist from the mutual tormenting and leave it alone. Getting off this mountain means climbing down into its entrails and poking about in places that have not been poked about in before. There is no truce; either the mountain or myself will win, but not both of us. I swing myself round with my back outwards so that my rucksack doesn't push me away from the rock it is constantly getting scraped against; no way down this chimney but to climb it properly. Somewhere in the back of my mind my excuse for having wanted to climb up here is wearing consciously thin. The spray of the water is flowing over the toes of my boots and if it weren't for the crevices in the rock into which I can jam my hands as fists I'd be off here. By the time I'm down into this basin the stream is gushing over me and my hands are bloodied. The obvious, steeper way where the water flows is on the right, but that looks like solid rock, as polished and slippery as an eel twisting down to who knows where out of the corner of my eye. It is closed on the impossibility of it all. The whole damn thing looks steep from here, the left-hand chute opens out into a pool that looks big enough to bathe in and the passage over its lip is wide; vertigo-inducing. Only one way up, out of this mess on to the ridge that cuts from left to right that I thought I'd be straddling in the first place.

Away from the watercourse, climbing upwards instead of down is a temporary relief. I take my bearings as I reach the top of this stony outcrop and realise that I'm still three humps above the height of the eagle's head, catching a fast-disappearing sun at its edges. As I survey the scene in what I know will be my last minutes of daylight, I notice that further down the knobbly length of this spine it truncates into two, then lower down it seems to divide itself yet again. The enormous complexity of these chains, which divide and rise and divide again, is too much to assimilate. I feel pulled towards the left-hand curve of the chain, if only because the valley it bleeds into is well defined and resolute; dark and sheer, yes, but it does look as if it has a purpose. By the time I have mastered the boulder, I am confronted with a slowly darkening sentinel of rock coming at me from my right-hand side; futile and dangerous to climb in the dying sunlight. There the wind seems to whistle and I am not sure if it is birds that I can make out whirling round its heights or the ghosts of my own imagination. I am locked in a fight with the mountain itself now, any unexpected adversary will tip the balance in the mountain's favour; though I know, of course, that it is already substantially so.

I know in my heart that the mountain has got me, it has sucked something out of me as the last echoes of daylight play tantalisingly out of reach on the tops and blackness shuts them out, sealing me inside this chasm. I never thought it would come to this, not here and not like this.

Perhaps you will never see me again. I know that I have not been a good father, but I want you to know that you were never really very far away from me. Why I am saying all this I don't know, I thought I'd left all that behind. The old woman was wrong, or maybe I just didn't understand her message.

The sun dips behind the col and I am alone. I know that I am not progressing down the mountain but limping down into it, further inside it, but I am suddenly stubborn and my stubbornness refuses to let me curl up and wait. I'll decide where my final resting-place is, even if I am unable to decide the time. At some moment in the journey I can sense the angry whisper of water again. Before I know it, as if I was sleepwalking, I am buffeted by the spray of a steep waterfall, water slapping my face and hands that have become pure fingers growing, delving, seeking, sucking in any bit of rock they can fasten themselves to. Toes are as nimble in boots as a dancer's are pivoted in a pirouette. My right leg kicks itself straight against the in-hanging chimney only because it refuses to give up even if I do. Down, back-step, down, back-step into the laughing throat of this monster. It is like lifting my weight down time and again and handing it on to somebody else. I am sick of the necessity of doing so; the intricacy of handing my body down then handing that self on again, as if I had become a fragile but very heavy statue.

On occasions the blurred orange neon of a village I once knew flickers in the darkness and then is gone, tiny singing fires floating out to sea. I do not know whether it is land I am treading down into or dark water. Then the lights are gone for good. At any moment I feel as if I might step down to be submerged and the orange candles flicker above me, drifting out of reach. The mountain is angry with me and has pulled its dark hood on, silence is about to fall, but the starlight above torments and will not let me sleep. The mountain is moving within its robes, shifting as it prepares for prayer. It has not even occurred to me that I am its sacrifice.

I am groping backwards on all fours over the dimly-struck contours where rock has given away to grass, the canyon branching out for the time round an island that has been pushed up away from the spray that flows on either side. To the right the water sounds less fierce but my scrabbling boot gains no purchase on the sheer surface angled back in towards this promontory. The starlight glints off it, shiny and seemingly veined with crystal. As I disturb plants and shrubs their aromas are released into the night; dry, pungent notes uncluttering the air. My hands are getting shot through with the spines of cactus and other stiff spikes. At times I fall and taste the earth, arms splayed out from underneath me as I kiss its red bitterness. I'd supposed that I was to be pushed into some bone-shattering leap but it seems the mountain will leave me for its servants; not kill me instantly but pin me on its cross to wince through the night; perhaps to die of thirst within the sound of water or suffer the agonies of seeing starlight wrenched from me, as its carrion birds consume the last light inside.

Suddenly I am falling with my arm clutching a scrawny bush, it has come away at the roots, torn away easily from the dry earth in a shower of dust. My feet are swimming down through dark night as water churns and churns at my side. Its silvery chute is frozen; it is I that am falling. I do not feel fear; time has ceased to be. How strange to go like this, I think to myself, now that death has come I seem curiously calm. I am watching somebody else die; somebody I know who isn't me. What on earth am I doing here? The rock face is travelling up past me, I am not moving.

Like a cat falling clutching at thin air. How perfumed the night air smells. Why haven't I hit solid ground yet? What an absolutely stupid, stupid way to die. Then my feet come up to meet my knees but instead of a hard splintering sound all I hear is a loud dull thud. I have seen the cliff face slide past mine with a whoosh, its surface cold, shiny in the starlight that has broken the cloud, lit up like some manic stage. Now somebody turns the tap on again, the waterfall unfreezes itself in sickly applause.

I am embedded in sand and for a moment cannot work out what sand is doing up here on the mountain. I cannot work out why I am not dead. Is the mountain playing a trick on me, toying with me so that it might kill me several times over? The pool in front of me seems quite deep, the silver thread of the waterfall narrow but steep above it, bending up as far as my vision will allow me in the night. The starlight bobs up and down on the water. Perhaps I have fallen nine metres, ten: probably the height of a house. My left foot is just in the water's edge and now and again little waves wash over it as the roar of the waterfall becomes more deafening, or perhaps it is just my own heart I can hear, louder and louder in my ears.

There is a dull ache in my right knee and for some reason my wrists feel swollen. I laugh and cry at the same time. I am exhausted but cannot think of bedding down here to sleep for the night. I have less fear of a cat coming than before but the noise of the water is too loud, too crisp; I want a quieter place where I can just go off with myself and keep my shame close by. I know that I cannot possibly go on any further tonight and that the mountain has not deemed me worthy enough an adversary, otherwise I would be dead. I pick my way slowly over the boulders that are encrusted in the land towards one further off with a slightly pinkish hue in the starlight. It is bigger and perhaps flatter than the rest, though quite how I'm going to sleep there and what protection from the elements I'm going to have I don't know. The constant jumping of boulders on the way down has left me numb, shocked by so much lunging from one to another, transferring their hard but eventually brittle qualities to my legs. In places where the river opens up and the sides of the land are less steep, huge, rounded rocks have crashed into the water's path and flattened the land. Or perhaps it is that the water has called them to herself, the bigger the better so that no fool would be tempted to spy into her secret high pools and tread where the wind and herself are lovers.

I don't know why I am climbing this boulder after all the climbing that I have done. I don't know why I am lying down on its cold hard surface under the starlight. I don't know why I am here. As I press myself against the blanket, too tired to wrap it round me, the dull orange of morning fires stirs in my eyes, playing with me. I turn on my other side to shift the weight from my right hip, which is beginning to feel bruised. As I shift onto my left side I can see the neon fires of the village lights burning not that far below. I understand that the game is over. I also understand something of forgiveness.

Down boulder past boulder I jump though my knees and hips are shooting with fire. It is at least another hour 'til I am standing by another pool and sit down to take a rest. I swing my legs over the side of the wall in an effort to stretch them and then realise that the structure on which I am sitting is, in fact, a wall. Hope stampedes in me and soon I am across the other side. I see now that it is a small reservoir with water swaying under the shadow of molle trees. I set a tentative foot on the twisting path which leads down through the grove of molles bristling in the starlight, the air rushing towards me as a huge white stallion with the moon on its back comes charging down it, inches past me. I can hear the sound of its hooves clattering down the track as the wind whistles in the grove after it.

Paralysed for some moments I turn back to face the mountain and hear its angry shout bearing down on me. It has removed its robes for an instant and stands with the moon upon its shoulders. I walk down quietly to the village, fearing the gallop of the white horse at any moment.

CHAPTER SIXTEEN

"What the hell are you looking at?!" screamed Bill McKenzie as the occupant of the car that had just slammed into the nearby crash barrier on the bridge glared at him, "It was your damn fault, you ass hole. Whoever gave you a license ought to be shot!" he ranted as he turned to look at the damage to his Buick. The cars were piling up behind on the freeway and honked like geese.

"And you, buddy!" Bill shouted in return as the car behind him edged onto the curb and crawled its way past him, all eyes. Now the other cars filed past in procession as each of their occupants looked at him, silently and with hatred. Bill was shaking his head from side to side as he looked at the side wing of his car. There was a dim mist caused by the intense heat above the river and Bill's eyes were beginning to fill with a mounting rage. He yanked at his tie, loosening it with a violent jerk and looked through the stream of cars to where the owner of the other vehicle was looking intently ahead, still seated at the wheel.

"You're gonna pay for this you dumb mother!" Bill yelled, waving his fist in the air. He turned his back on the driver who had remained silent, and ducked inside the open window to get his insurance details. The owner of the other car was reversing up against the traffic and had pulled round to face the opposite way he had come, pulled up onto the kerb.

"Oh no you don't! You son of a.." Bill turned to look in horror as the realisation that he had been shot in the chest struck him and he crumpled to the ground. The scowling wheels skidded off the tarmac and the burnt-orange Oldsmobile powered its way off the bridge and into the anonymity of the highway going the other way.

On the dashboard of Bill McKenzie's car a half-read copy of a newspaper with some trashy photo of a murder investigation was soaking up the contents of the spilled carton of Coca-Cola he had purchased at the drive-in earlier. His fries were scattered on the passenger seat with the burger slopped out of its bun. The list of his appointments in the black leather journal tossed onto the back seat would not be completed. An obituary, a death, a mourning.

"So, do you think he did it?" said the police chief as they surveyed the car at the compound.

"There's no doubt about it," said the tall gentleman in the dark pinstriped suit, "We're dealing with an extremely dangerous man here. You've seen the report on the damage at the nightclub: that was a sophisticated explosive. There's no doubt at all in my mind that we're dealing with a highly-trained individual here."

"What does the Minister have to say about it?" asked Chief Carrasco.

"Ministro Trevillo's of the same opinion as myself," answered the tall, slightly balding gentleman, "The document's become public knowledge now and the public will want justice to be seen to be done, the same as you or I do. This one document could cripple the nation's exports; just on the strength of the rumour alone. If you ask me, Eduardo," said the taller gentleman indulging in the intimacy of first-name terms as he inclined himself towards the Chief of Police, "If the scandal's allowed to grow unchecked and this man remains at large, one or two people's positions might be made insecure." He raised his eyebrows.

The Chief of Police fired a dart back at him.

"What are you trying to say, Arnaldo?" he asked, fiercely.

The Secretary for the Minister of Agriculture dropped his head in deference, taking a slight involuntary step backwards as he did so.

"Nothing, nothing at all…except that I wouldn't like to see the Minister at all," a pause, "Inconvenienced. The present situation could become increasingly embarrassing to him," he answered.

"The foreigner's got to be stopped," said Chief of Police Carrasco beginning to grasp the situation.

"Yes," said the Secretary for the Minister of Agriculture slipping his arm around the shoulder of the other man as they walked back inside the building,

"At all costs."

Six a.m. The alarm goes off and wails its fire-frightened shriek at Monday morning's ghosts, passengers dropped off by the weekend. Bill is staring into the space between his night's uncomfortable sleeping and the morning's insistence at wakening. He paws his head and draws the circle of loose hair over his balding head, massaging the nerve fibres like a light bulb that is dimly but resentfully starting to shine. Time to get up. Knock the dust off. Keep clean. He stumbles into the bathroom where the mirror, its flashes of light bouncing off its face, humbles him into sucking in his guts and straightening up. Six-fifteen. In no time at all. His briefcase is slumped on the sofa with its contents bulging out of its seams where the papers from the night before forgot to order themselves back inside. Pushing up walls and breaking them down again. Six-thirty. Thirty, twenty-nine, twenty-eight, twenty-seven,... twenty. With some effort he straightens up from his exercises while the iron rays of the shower prod him away from the coffee that is starting to hiss.

The television screen laminate is painting on its faces, addressing the public. Politicians, publicity, stunts. The cool smatter of their words drowns out the rays of the shower and the water is turned off. They are a rallying call, all of them. Sleekly tanned, just on the right side of golden, not a muscle out of place. Their words are selected, collected, chosen, exclusive; executives executing with precision. The choice is clear, either become one of them or die trying in the attempt. Bill scalds himself with the coffee and his blackened tongue swells in his mouth. Sticky fingers stick to the pages of the newspaper while the sun is already clamouring for its subjects out on the streets. Word is that there's a crash about to happen, and he'd better be there when it does. The coffee is already getting to work and it's about time he does too. Forty-five, just in time. The door is shut behind him and the keys to the ignition ignite, the radio extends its greeting with a jump start as Bill slips unnoticed into the filter of traffic all headed down-town, all determined to beat the rest. Again.

When he arrives at the office he takes pride in casually parking his car to the side of his superiors' slots, just close enough to the line so that if they scratch his bodywork they'll know about it. They have their own forecourt, they are an important company. He checks his wing mirror before stepping out of his car, runs a finger along the inside of his shirt collar where sweat is already beginning to prick and tucks his newspaper under his arm like a loo-roll, sheets of which have already been thumbed, discarded. Imports and exports, the flavour of the day. Today Bill is wearing his brown shirt that shows up his sweat stains magnificently. He wears Armani cufflinks, black patent leather shoes and a trouser in an unusual beige colour by Cagliarse. He would like to make the world a better place and enjoys eating, television. He has always wanted to be in this kind of company but nobody would be more surprised than him if he made it to the top-spot. Genuinely. The other contenders are far more attractive than he is and he knows it, but he has his charm, which he exudes without discretion. The secretary gets a wave as he sweeps past her, the smile on her face and the usual remark about being first to come in lasting one instant longer than his deodorant has. Seven forty-five, a full fifteen minutes before the riffraff are due, the paparazzi, the pretenders. Bill is in cheerful mood now, on top of his world. His apartment is mortgaged, his car is on higher-purchase and the shirts on his back are laundered. The fat cheques he dispenses are a sign of his largess, post-dated. He spreads the contents of his briefcase in careful abandonment on his desk before the others arrive and is confidently optimistic that the crash that has been predicted will not occur today. Why? Bill knows something that the others do not, and it is a secret that he will keep to himself, carry with him. It infuriates both his superiors and the office junkies alike, but then this is part of his game plan, indeed, it is his game. Speaking of which, his team is playing tonight, major league, and what better way to admonish his colleagues' unnecessary Monday-morning anxiety than with a sandwich and his pre-booked tickets tossed on the desk enticing them? They're so dreary, so confined in their ties and their newspaper-informed views, so eager to please.

At eight o'clock the people arrive. Bill is an actor, consummate in his skills, the ham sliding out of his mouth. Still chewing he looks at them irreverently while shaking his head measuredly from side to side. They are stunned at his audacity, at his commanding address to them that singles none out in particular but greets them all without distinction. Slowly and without a word he ponders the cup of coffee that has been poured from the jug he lifted. It is an Objet d'Art, a talisman around which fingers cling when it is given over for communal possession. Bill is cherishing their reflection in it, counting the seconds in his head before he must deliver his opening, triumphal line.

"It won't happen today," he says to everybody and to nobody, then swigs back his coffee in haughty reverie and turns to embrace them with his smile. He laughs, (reading their mood superbly) to this one and that one and lets his audience appreciate the Comedy. They are flustered, whisper amongst themselves, disingenuously disengage themselves from the spectacle and become once again aware of the theatre in which they are seated. A triumph, and the day could not have started better.

"Going to the game tonight?" Bill enquires of one of his neighbours in tones just audible enough for the others to overhear. The response is undetectable, unimportant in so much as the others do not need to hear it and should not be concerned, but of course they are. A daring finale; the ribald, the unexpected, even as the audience were waiting for the lights to come on.

'PLEASE ENTER YOUR PASSWORD…
IT IS NOW SAFE TO TURN ON YOUR COMPUTER.'

Bill's gratification knows no bounds. He places one of the tickets on his neighbour's desk and struts off to preen himself in the florescent lights of the lavatory. No more words needed. The fingers tap-tap on the keyboards, tap-tap, tap-tap, tap-tap.

At eight-thirty precisely the floor manager arrives, reeking of designer after-shave and a designer breakfast. His secretary, (for he is almost invariably a *he*) comes to relieve him of the burden of his coat which he has been carrying outstretched over his arm, full of neglected pathos. She is an attendant merely, not the leading lady. She herself sits red-haired and besuited, engaged behind a pair of spectacles that she felt inclined to purchase on joining the company, denouncing her usual attire in favour of a more demure and, (at least to the observers involved), carefully concealed expression of her sex. It is this woman our two protagonists fight over. The manager has already spotted her and has ear-marked her for promotion to a place recently vacated by a man on permanent leave abroad. Bill of course cannot declare his interest in her, for reasons which are the following: one, he cannot be seen to provoke the jealousy, (in a professional sense, of course) of his superior; two, it would be tantamount to hypocrisy to forgo the method of his acting and cease to play the fool.

A Few Notes on Playing the Fool

N.B Whilst Bill's interaction with his audience depends on highlighting many of his fellow characters' shortcomings, it is his position, exclusively, which allows him to do so. Nonetheless, a direct challenge to their privileged social position would make him bereft of the grace that automatically accompanies his tenure as a player outside the social context. This role is by its very nature a tenuous, transitory and temporary one. No man is an island; not even a fool. His jokes must be cutting but not too personal, his remarks provocative to the society as a whole but not too challenging to the individuals who inhabit it. Furthermore, he must walk the line between those of the social class to which he, (secretly) aspires and those of the social class to which all concerned suspect he belongs, but which he must somehow seem to be aloof from. He must seem to be engaging to the society he criticises but not engaged by it. Those around him should perceive him to be disinterested in the economy and yet extremely knowledgeable about it; dismissive of the fairer sex as mere objects and yet capable of winning them over. Undeniably, it is the case that he cannot call his superior an asshole to his face or state to his red-headed colleague that he *really* wishes to get his leg over with her; even, worse, that he is actually *in love* with her. Both scenarios would undermine the pretexts on which his character is based, resulting in its implosion, with the ultimate and (ultimately human) fear of being made to seem absurd.

'YOU NEED NO LONGER HAVE ANY FEAR OF TURNING OFF YOUR COMPUTER. IT IS NOW SAFE TO TURN OFF YOUR CONFUSION.'

The floor manager's mouth is open for an exquisite second. The clock is striking eight-thirty and a sound emits from it.

"Have you heard from David?" Bill asks him.

"No, actually, no," says his superior.

A silence, protracted, in which Bill feels on the verge of exploding. A moment, gathering moments to it with an untimely, sticky mass; gaining momentum, becoming momentous.

"You know the procedure. David knew the risks."

"Crap," says Bill shaking his head. For a moment the windowpane sandwiched in between the forces of gravity and the steel encasing the swaying building is about to implode and shower everyone in the office with buckets of blood.

"The stock market," says Bill, by way of explanation, "The crash won't happen today, you can bet your last dollar on it. It won't happen for a while yet and ..." a pause; back into his perfectly rehearsed routine, avoiding the use of the personal pronoun with something bordering on the obsessive,

"Something suggests that it's not going to happen at all."

Hazy, alluring. Executives executing a relationship. No pain no gain. Nothing ventured nothing gained.

"Keep up the good work, Bill."

At lunch in the recess Bill is perturbed by something. He knows it's not going to happen today, he can feel it in his bones. That's something they don't teach these goddamn rookies; gut feeling. It is twelve-thirty and the birds are twitching outside. They're kicking up a babble in the dust and in any case they didn't ought to be here, right now, in the middle of this intense heat in this goddamn intense city. He is sitting in a bar with an inexplicable need to be away from the others, the rest of the crowd, the lingerers-on. So many empty faces with their puppy-dog puke. Jees, where did they find them these days? Perhaps the company had formed some kind of committee and had got a neighbourhood watch scheme to watch out for the biggest jerks on each block. God it was hot in here. Couldn't the bartender be a little quicker? He has to be back at work in an hour and he still hasn't eaten. Perhaps he won't do so today. He doesn't know why, but there's a growing sense of uneasiness and it's coming from his guts. He doesn't know if he's hungry or lost his appetite altogether.

Twelve thirty-one: he's thinking about the moment between him and the boss, remembering it. Remembering it. He was going to say something to him, wasn't he? Damn the son of a - , ask him what the hell's going on down there that they haven't heard from David in so many days. What the hell is it?! Over a week now and still the guy's not keyed in. No mission statement, no project completion targets. What the hell's he up to down there?! There's something uneasy forming inside Bill and he isn't quite sure if he's being angry at David or at his boss; even worse, he isn't quite sure why he's getting angry. He catches a glimpse of his face in the metallic clock on the wall behind the bar and he's not sure if he likes what he sees. Twelve thirty-five. He wouldn't usually have come to a bar, normally he would have gone to a diner or to one of the drive-ins where there's a bit more air, but today he doesn't know what he wants. He is opening his mouth to shoot the goddamn waiter off but as his mouth opens the waiter's does too and all that comes out is crap.

"I'm sorry, sir, I didn't quite catch that order."

"Crap," repeated Bill, "Crap! Crap! Crap!"

He's throwing himself into his car and steering like a madman to get the hell out of this stinking place. He's soaking with perspiration and his shirt is gluing itself to him.

"Got to get a little air in here," he's saying to himself, out loud, in the mirror; the mouth is opening and closing like some goddamn puckered-up fish.

"You bastard!" he shouts out loud in the mirror with the fish-face suckering up, puckering up, gulping out its obscenities. "You always were a liar!" he blurts out, spitting at his reflection in the wing mirror through the open hole of the window. "Ha, it's me you're after next, isn't it? Isn't it? I knew it, all along," he spits again, disgusted, exhausted. " 'No, actually, no.' It's me next, isn't it?!"

His heart is thumping and he's feeling like he's gonna puke but he's still somewhere thinking that he ought to get something to eat, maybe he's going to get something to eat; some meat.

"You're just a coward!" he scowls out, looking at the mirror again. And now he really isn't sure if he is speaking to his boss, or to himself, or to his shadow, or what. Every time he opens his mouth, it's like there's a delay, or something, or nothing at all. Maybe it's him. "Crap," he says.

The closest he's got to the truth in a long time. He's calming his speed down, he's getting some fresh air. These RUV's are like tanks on the road. What the hell are they trying to prove? He's swerving round one up onto the sidewalk hell-bent on getting to the drive-in.

"The whole damn thing disgusts me," he says out loud to no-one in particular. He's checking his eyes in the mirror. He's still angry, furious in fact. "They don't teach anybody to rely on their instincts anymore."

It's high time they did, what were people like him supposed to do? There's something not quite right going on down there. The man's in trouble and he's next in line, he knows it clear as daylight. They've soon filled the space, look at that goddamn redhead and how he's grooming her for the job. The hell he will! She's only been here a couple of weeks and already he's lining her up, who the hell does he think he is? If David got back the smile would be on the other side of his face. So many years' loyalty and the bottom line is they don't give a damn; they care more about their filthy investments than they do about us. Didn't they say it was just like a family? Liars. How many years' service did he have? Cheap skates, money minders. His tongue was hanging out of his mouth, enraged and swollen. He was good at talking crap but not at cutting it. And in the end, he'd changed the conversation, diverted the body blow, hadn't told the guy what was on his mind, what he was feeling or was starting to feel. For one insane moment he almost turned the car round again and thought of storming up to the office to tell the man what he thought of him and where he could stick his new employee before the old one was even dead yet. He was going to tell them what he thought of them, what he thought about the whole situation, the whole damn mess they were in.

His foot hits flat down on the floor just for a split-second, just to feel it, and swipes past a woman who has a look of panic on her face and her baby in her arms. The car's steering itself out of control and he makes an important decision, realises there is one for him to make. It's twelve forty-five and although he's got to be back at work in fifteen minutes he isn't going to be. Before he gets back there with more of his lies, or questions; or whatever they are.

This heart is thumping like a gun. This old boy has had just about as much as he can take for now and he ain't gonna take it for much longer. Who the hell d' they think they are? Messin' around with people's lives like that, mixing them up and spinning them round. That time he'd been to Columbia had been enough for him, they'd been spun round more than enough then and the poor damn peasants looked at them like they were gods with their black glasses and false smiles. In and out of pick-up points and stop-off sites. One move-of-a-muscle-twitch and you've bought it. The don't-you-fuck-with-me flight brigade, in and out of little planes like they were medics, or something. A meeting here, in full suit with side-packages on their hips in the middle of a goddamn jungle landing strip with naked mothers giving tit to children and praying to heaven that the little white birds don't come swarming out with ants, and fake smiles, and a glint in the eye. Shit, he'd seen it, he'd seen enough to last him a lifetime.

Where the hell was he going now? The mirrors are blinding him as he goes with the stream of traffic. Suddenly he's turning into the shopping mall along with the RUV's on either side. The people are hurrying inside and there's an incessant chatter clogging up the air. He stops in front of a giant television screen where a man with sunglasses and a golden tan is beckoning him to come forwards.

"Did you know that over 55% of Americans haven't planned properly for their futures? Don't you find this a frightening statistic, living in an age when it's so easy to invest in the future?"

'TAKE OUT AN INVESTMENT POLICY TODAY AND MAKE SURE THAT YOUR FUTURE'S IN SAFE HANDS. OURS'.

The mouth is opening and closing but nothing sounding like sense is coming out. His eyes are lost in the eyes of the speaker and the monotone drone is lulling him to sleep. It's stifling in here. Then he feels the swish of electricity where the pools of sweat are and his skin goes numb under his shirt. 'Maybe I'll catch a cheeseburger,' he thinks to himself and stands on the escalator with the rest of the passengers. He checks his watch. Twelve fifty-five, only five minutes to go. 'Fast is good,' he's thinking to himself, but he's running out of time.

"Hurry now! First come, first served. Only while stocks last!" The voice of the slipstream. Stripscene. Women are coming out with carrier bags full of fake-furs. It's so goddamn hot out there he wonders what the hell they're doing with all this stuff. It's cool inside, though. His eyes are glazing over and his watch is jerking itself to one o'clock as the sweat trickles down his brow. He catches himself in the mirror in front of him and can't believe what he's seeing. He panics as the eyes on the door eye him coldly while fake-fur brushes past him. Then he's falling back down the escalator with no whiff of a burger in sight.

Now he's racing on to the drive-in. He's flinging some coins at the poor mother who has to take his money. They fall from his hands through the hands of the operator and onto the ground. He'd watched the Indians like that, once, scrabbling around in the dirt one time after one of the white birds came and crapped on their village and the ants came swarming out of it. He was amongst them, he was on that plane. There was some kind of an argument going off to one side with the man at the village post. He was waving his arms in the air and he wasn't happy about it at all. He was in no fit state to bargain though and the laughing guys thought it was funny. They made him dance then they shot him. All the little beggars came and picked him clean while the ants roared with laughter before we were bundled back hastily inside the bird. I was angry with them and sad with them at the same time. The kids.

"Would you like an extra-large coke or double fries with your order?"

"What?"

"I said, would you like an extra-large coke or double fries with your order, sir?"

"Just give me regular fries and regular coke," the image from the bathroom coming back.

"I'm sorry, sir, you've got to either have double fries or an extra coke," says the attendant.

"What?!"

"It's the promotion, sir. Look, it says so up there," says the woman in the hut pointing to the poster.

'TODAY'S SPECIAL, BUY A REGULAR SUPER WHOPPER
AND GET DOUBLE FRIES OR AN
EXTRA-LARGE COKE FREE.'

"Look, I'm sorry, I'm late back at work and I don't have time to be messing around with more fries…"

She flashes a smile at me but it looks like one of the smiles the peasant women gave us when they hoped we weren't going to shoot them. Probably.

"Just give me the goddamn parcel and I'll be out of here, okay?!"

I wanna get the lid off this thing but the lid's on tight. There's a hole where the straw should go. I give a snort, pouring half the coke through the window onto the tarmac. 'I wonder how long *she'll* last,' I think to myself. That's the whole problem; people can't think for themselves these days or take the initiative.

The sun's glinting off these mirrors and the flood of traffic on the bridge is huge. I can't get the lid off this thing properly, they only give you some stupid straw to suck, suck, suck through but they give you an extra-large cup as well. Damn it's hot. I'm heading back for the office now but my watch stubbornly refuses to give me a minute to get there. Can't get the picture of the man singing in the dust out of my mind. I've got an excuse, who the hell would have thought that the traffic would be so slow today? Of course I goddamn didn't get back to the office on time! What do ya think?! Nobody told me the movement was gonna be so slow.

"Come on, jerk, get out of my way. I've got a job to do here!"

I fumble for the coke 'cause my collar's beginning to twitch and it topples over before I can get my lips to it, gently soaking into the newspaper. I jab at a fist full of French fries and the salt burns into my tongue. Gotta get the goddamn lid off this thing, why the hell'd they stick it down so tight? That's funny, that is. An extra-large one just so as you can't drink it. All those women carrying all those fakefurs; don't they know how hot it is out here? Suckers. Something explodes on the side of the car and glass is flying out. "What the hell…?!" Silence… "What the hell are you looking at?!"

"Come on in Miss Slicker, please take a seat. Just close the door behind you first. Now, I've been observing your work personally and I think you're just the person we're looking for. We need someone bright, someone new, someone with a future. We're prepared to offer you that future if you're prepared to give us everything you've got. It means no holding back, you know," a pause, "But I'm sure that you realise what kind of an offer you're being made here."

Her head was swimming; it was more than she'd bargained for – at least, not yet.

"Good, so I'll pick you up around nine then, that's settled."

CHAPTER SEVENTEEN

David was standing at the edge of the forest on the track where the bus had dropped him off. The bus had stopped on a bend in the road on the top of a steep hillside where the road and the track to the village met and parted company. He watched it disappear down the left flank of the ridge humming down into the darkness and out of sight. His way led curling down turning back on itself, zigzagging through the pine trees. A plantation, but the trees had grown so much that they obscured the view down into the village now. They'd been planted more than sixty years ago, when the first European settlers came to these parts fleeing the overtures of war back in the Old World; they were dense, bushy pine trees that didn't lose their foliage even in winter. The village was located in a sort of bowl in the bottom of a small valley, he'd been told, situated between a mountain to the north and a lower-lying but extensive chain of hills to the west. There was only this one track into the village, but it remained unsign-posted even though you'd easily miss the village all together if you didn't know it was down there. It was supposed to be a wealthy community with good amenities, but it was curious to David that a community that was supposed to be wealthy had neglected to put a proper surface on the road, like the one on the route that the bus had taken. Still, it couldn't be far down there, he thought to himself. And with that he was comforted with the thought that a white-skinned westerner like himself wouldn't look out of place among people of European descent, if it so chanced that someone undesirable should turn up.

The bus on which he had left the province of San Luis had headed out west originally. But then it seemed to David that it had changed in its course, turning north. Then as he had begun to fall asleep it began snaking its way through the densely wooded slopes of the mountain range amongst which they had journeyed for the last three hours or so.

Now he strode down the track, kicking up stones with his boots as he went. The scent of the pine trees under the black canopy of the night was strong and now and again he caught a whiff of snow where it tugged at him from mountains farther away. As he descended another zigzag he suddenly caught sight of what remotely appeared like a castle perched on a high rock face where snow from the high peak behind it clearly shone. He had to concentrate to see it but then a cloud drifted in front of the mountain and the silhouette that had suggested itself disappeared and became trees once again. He crossed a small stream that ran freely across the road from an opening in the rocks on his left-hand side, and again he wondered at the lack of provision of the villagers. Surely it wouldn't take much to dig a furrow transversely in the track so that the water might not hinder any travellers to the village when the flow was heavier?

Nonetheless, he found himself remarking on his good fortune and clicked his black boots against a stone that lay obstinately in his way. He was feeling strong from his days of walking in San Luis and his rucksack rested jauntily on his shoulder. In any case, should his pursuers have reached any of the villages he had encountered since leaving the farm in Córdoba, they would be hard put to determine just in which direction he was heading now. "Ha!" he laughed to himself, thinking as he did so that the zigzagging track on which he was walking was curiously auspicious in this sense. He felt the material of the red handkerchief that he had purchased and which he'd tied, as was the custom amongst the locals, round his neck. The mountain across the valley certainly was high, the more he got down into the valley lying snugly below it the more it seemed to tower over everything. Like a sleeping sentinel with the hook of its peak preposterously angled, it guarded the village from the fiercest of storms that could rage outside the valley. Indeed, in the severest of winters, the wind must howl across the valley from its uppermost reaches, and the villagers look up and hear its cries.

Perhaps he would find agreeable company and choose to lodge himself here for a few days. He could just imagine the tinkle of goats' bells as he entered the surrounding pastures and the prospect of a soothing glass of beer to refresh his parched throat.

He still had two s-bends to negotiate though, a length of road that

251

had finally succeeded in tiring him, even though the original descent from the top of the hillside hadn't appeared to be that far when he'd set out. It was curious just how fatiguing it was to get to this village. Well, it had better be worth it! With a smile of self-satisfaction on his face and a spring in his step, he rounded the last zigzag and heard the churning of the waters below him in the river that ran alongside the village.

The village itself was separated from the mainland by a glorious wooden bridge that traversed the foaming mouths of water in a graceful arch. It was as fine a piece of engineering as David had seen during his time in Argentina, a magnificent structure held together with cast iron bolts that had been painted black. Its sides culminated in two highly ornate, carved wooden handrails that must have required considerable skill of the carpenter who'd crafted them. On this side of the river there was a quaint wooden seat attached to the nearside of the bridge, big enough for two people and roofed with smaller logs. It must be a lovers' seat, thought David, and from there its occupants would be in full possession of the fine view back up the hillside that he had just traversed. Here were a people who obviously put a premium on their surroundings, the elegance of the craftsmanship on offer was undoubtedly proof of their nobility of spirit.

It was good to come across people who had made time to incorporate art into their lives. And how couldn't one marvel at the majesty of such surroundings? It would take a dull mind not to be inspired by such a magical place; it was just like something out of a fairy-tale. It summoned up images of castles and princes, of princesses and golden summers in David's mind. Now in winter the river ran swiftly, bubbling and ducking beneath the bridge. He whistled a tune to himself as he set foot on the bridge, feeling the fine texture of the wood beneath his hand as his boots struck out an accompaniment.

A passer-by on the other side raised his hand in greeting as David neared the far side. The gentleman's hound came bounding towards him as David greeted both man and dog with a smile.

"Halt! Who goes there?" commanded the man who had reined in the dog that was snarling at its leash. Taken aback, David put up his hand in greeting also, after the fashion of the man, and the stranger seemed to relax.

"You have come for the festival?" the man asked of him in a rather demanding tone, "Where is your instrument?" he enquired.

David slung his rucksack down off his shoulder, almost in a reflex action as a means of putting something solid between himself and the teeth of the dog that snapped at him.

"Ah, I see," said the man, "You will come with me, please."

Unfamiliar with the customs of these remote people, David trooped alongside the man in the direction in which he was led off. Taking care not to get too close to the fangs of the Alsatian dog, which was still snarling but which was by now held on a tight, short leash by its master, David matched the man's strides across the field.

"You are late," said the man.

"I am?" said David.

"That is correct. We have been expecting you for some time now," he said. "Everybody is waiting in the hall," he added, "I see you have already come dressed in your costume. Good, that is very good."

David looked meekly down at his attire. His cowboy hat had become so familiar to him that he had ceased to be aware of its presence. He put his hand to his improvised neck-tie and loosened it as best he could with the finger of one hand, though as he tugged at it the knot tightened even more. The misunderstanding could be cleared up in due time. Presently they arrived at a wooden door to one side of a huge communal building where laughter and music could dimly be distinguished behind closed doors. The building had several windows along its side, but they were all high up and relatively small given the size of the building and this prevented David from seeing in on events.

"You are to wait here," the man informed him, and then added in a manner that left David wondering as to whether he'd heard the man correctly, "You would be wise to do so."

In an instant the man returned accompanied by another man and they both greeted David in the fashion established earlier by the first man. David responded in kind.

"You are late," said the newcomer, echoing the remark of the man with the dog. "Your name, please?"

"I beg your pardon?" said David, afraid that his cover was about to be blown.

"You will give me your name, please," demanded the man.

"David," said David.

"Yes?" he enquired in thinly disguised tones of impatience.

"Salsa," responded the traveller.

"I am sorry?" said the man. "This is your type of music?"

David looked at the groomed moustache of the man in front of him, his polished boots. There was an uneasy sense of expectancy hanging in the air.

"We are not expecting the Latin music, no, no. Here our tastes are somewhat more," he considered his word, "Refined. You will give me your name in full please." A command.

"Salsa…Salzburg, David Salzburg." There, it was said.

"Good, this is good," replied the man, clapping David on the shoulder. The villagers looked in satisfaction at each other and David was ushered into a side room off to the side of the hall. "You will find refreshments being distributed amongst your fellow musicians."

And with that the men were gone, neatly paring off as they got to the end of a corridor, the more senior of the men turning curtly to the right-hand side whilst his colleague stepped smartly to his left.

"You look exhausted," said a frail voice behind him, "Where have you come from?" David could do nothing but gesture weakly back in the direction of the hillside down which he'd descended.

"Hmm," said the man, "Take this."

A pitcher was thrust into his hands by a man with a miniature guitar and he was urged to quench his thirst. It was beer, after all.

"And you are..?" said David to the first of the musicians.

"I am the singer," said the old man with the drooping moustache.

"Yes, of course," said David.

"And you are..?" enquired the old man.

"Salzburg!" said David, "David Salzburg."

The musicians said nothing but both of them raised their eyebrows, looking from one to the other with surprise.

"Forgive us our ignorance," apologised the old man, attempting a bow with arthritic flourish, "We had no idea you were coming."

By now the turn of events had contrived to mystify Mr. Salzburg to the point of delirium, so much so that he took the pitcher in both hands and succeeded in downing most of the remains of its contents. He wiped his mouth with some relish with the back of his hand; it was good beer, about that he'd made no mistake. As the distinguished Mr. Salzburg had not eaten since very early on that morning, the contents of the pitcher were inclined to lend him a forthrightness and a robustness that he may, under other circumstances, have otherwise been lacking. A man in leather shorts too small for him promptly appeared with a violin on his shoulder which he sawed at whilst the wiry strings of the miniature guitar were plucked in accompaniment. The cat-like tremble of the old man's voice insinuated itself amongst them, climbing like a tenuous vine, while Mr. Salzburg swayed back and forth in time to the rhythm.

It was no good attempting an exit now, and in any case, David was enjoying himself far too much for this thought to merit any serious consideration. There was a rustling behind the curtains and the star of the show, Miss Hilda Von Slappencracker was ready to take her bow. The musicians bowed in deference to her. Vaguely aware of his lack of compliance with social etiquette, David doffed his hat and bowed down as far as his knees, coming up swaying on the third beat of the bar. It was indeed a wonderful place and the magic of it was in David's eyes.

A man in a long overcoat sashayed into the room and the singer nodded politely to him. They were being led down a long corridor towards the rumour of noise and merriment. The musicians parted to accord David his just space and Miss Von Slappencracker barged into him from behind, thus forcing him up the short flight of stairs. There the ensemble stood trembling on the edge of the curtain with their wiry singer clutching at the balustrade. The old man hummed, the violinist sawed at his crumbling cheese and the man with the miniature guitar plucked at his moustache. It was time for them to take their bow and the clamour from the other side was increasingly boisterous.

"Meine Damen und Herren, it is with great pride that we present to you the illustrious, the magnificent, the one and only...,"

David lurched forward onto the stage and involuntarily extended his arm with his hand flattened out to shield his eyes from the burning strobes of the spotlight. Instantly the crowd roared with approval and stood to their feet to salute him. Von Slappencracker burst onto the stage behind him with crimson cheeks glowing as warm as the reception that had been given to the band. David jolted one pace forward and, like a cat caught in the headlights of a speeding car, jerked

255

his hand up to shield his eyes again. The response from the crowd was deafening and they stood up again to salute him. The wiry timbre of the singer wrapped itself round the ropes on which the stage lights were suspended and climbed higher and higher into the air. The fiddler played a mean rhythm as if sawing off one of the slender pines that stood on the lower slopes of the valley, leaning ever more to one side as his velocity increased. The miniature guitarist plucked at his strings 'til one of them snapped, but nobody seemed to notice. David staggered down the staircase into the welcoming bosom of the crowd as Hilda Von Slappencracker burst into full bloom, causing the glasses on the tables to vibrate in sympathy.

Before he had time to fall an empty chair was stretchered under him and a mug of foaming beer thrust into his fist. The crowd was ecstatic and the band had never known anything like it. How they played! How they cheered! The violinist was in danger of sawing himself right through the stage and the guitarist was by now plucking at thin air; there was a fever in their eyes and the old man was on the verge of passing out in his self-induced hypnosis.

Von Slappencracker swelled like an ocean liner in rolling seas and the crowd stamped and stamped. David got up, seeing his chance, and attempted his exit, but the crowd was already about him and had pulled him back down into his seat for another drink.

"Another beer!" someone called and Mr. David Salzburg, formerly Salsa and previously Selborne, was swimming through his past, present and future.

"The best ever," someone was saying, and David collapsed.

When he came round in the dressing room there were handfuls of coins in front of his eyes. They glinted at him aggressively and David remembered the slavering teeth of the dog. He put his hand to his head, which felt as if he had taken a direct blow to it.

"For you, Mr. Salzburg," said the old man who had miraculously survived the squeezing of his soul into strips as thin as horsehair, "We have never received so much in all our time playing here. We felt it only right that someone so," he chose his words carefully, inching them out as delicately as a bird walking on a gossamer thread, "*Illustrious* as yourself should receive the lion's share of the takings."

David looked at him quizzically.

"Please, Mr. Salzburg, we do not mean you to be offended by our lowly gesture. It was you after all that...no, yes, I mean..." he bowed in that ancient manner of his, sweeping his arm before him in a gesture of sublime humility.

"Is it over?" asked David.

"Yes, yes, of course. One or two of the - officials - have been asking after you. They were worried after your unfortunate accident. The doctor has been to see you, too. You've had a nasty blow to your head; he said that you needed to rest. I can put the money in a handkerchief for you if that is alright, that is, if you think..."

"Thank-you," said David and the singer scraped with arthritic flourish once again.

"We'll be leaving on the truck they're providing out of here in an hour. It's been a pleasure meeting you, might I say, and I hope to...," he was still caught in the declining arc of his bow.

"I'm coming with you," interrupted David, "You're not leaving here without me."

"Oh, I, wouldn't want to demean you with our - unsuitable - company," said the ageing singer, gingerly.

David looked at him as hard as if his life depended upon it.

"Well, I, if you say so Señor Salzburg. It's kind of you to want to travel with our lowly company. Of course, we would be, it would be an honour, wouldn't it?"

He looked round at his companions for support. The miniature guitar player raised his eyebrows almost as high as those of the singer; the violinist was strung out nervously through the back of his chair and nodded. Hilda would not be accompanying them. She had her own transport out to one of the nearby farms.

So they sat in the back of the open-air truck, musicians and magicians counterfeited under an old tarpaulin. David still had his hat and his handkerchief with him, and he was inexplicably richer now. His rucksack sagged limply, propped against his leg. The eyebrows of the old man and the charango player were permanently floating above their foreheads. An eagle swooped down with a cry from the jutting peak that towered above them and involuntarily the violinist jerked his chin towards it. It was possible there was an old castle somewhere up there but they would certainly never see it. Not even in another three generations would anyone from outside the valley ever know if a castle existed there or not.

Miss Von Slappencracker would be somewhere warm herself, soon back on her family's farm nestled in the hinterland of the adjoining hills.

At the road where David had dismounted from the bus earlier on in the evening a truck carrying soldiers passed them at the bend with the Argentine flag flying from its aerial. The oncoming truck flashed its headlights at the smaller truck in which David and the other musicians were travelling then disappeared in front of them down the crest of the hill. David lifted up the rim of his hat again and grimaced inwardly.

"That truck?" said David to the singer who was sitting next to him.

"Oh, they'll be on their way to the barracks in La Huerta, I imagine," said the old man tiredly.

"Where are we, exactly?" said David to the singer after some moments.

"You mean you don't know?" asked the old man anxiously, casting a glance back in the direction they had come from.

"No," said David emphatically.

The old man was uncertain of what to say, of what he was supposed to say.

"Well," he said to the foreigner, "We might be in San Juan, or we might be in La Rioja, it just depends on which way you look at it. The boundaries round here are somewhat - unclear-," he said rather nervously, furtively darting a glance at the foreigner's eyes to try to judge his response.

"Thank-you," said David presently.

"No, no, don't thank me," said the old man, relieved, as he attempted a bow from within the cramped confines of his seating position in the truck.

The vehicle was rumbling down the hillside and its motions had soothed the sawing violin player to sleep. He looked even more fragile when not awake, propped against a sack of potatoes like a flowery leaf that had been accidentally tossed in along with them. The charango player was twirling at the ends of his moustache and seemed to be trying to groom them out in either direction, vainly teasing them out before they inevitably flopped down again. There was a dream-like expression on his face.

"I don't know your name," said David to the singer, who was the only one of his companions who seemed to be fully awake.

"I - am - nobody," said the old man, glancing panic-stricken into David's eyes.

"But surely, you must have a name," continued David, unaware at the concern he was causing in his fellow traveller as he gazed nonchalantly into the growing morning light among the trees.

"Balthazar!" said the old man.

David turned suddenly to greet the unexpected force of his companion's reply. David looked at him quizzically, the wind on his face slapping him awake.

"I am Balthazar Rodinoski, son of the Count Rodinoski!" said the old man defiantly, the light of nostalgia burning in his eyes, his teeth clenched in the wind.

"I'm sorry," said David, taken aback, "I didn't know."

A mist descended in the musician's eyes and his long thin hair was smattered on his face. He seemed to see David at last.

"Where are you heading to?" David enquired amiably.

"Wherever the truck takes me to!" said the old man piquantly and he turned his face resolutely away to the woods.

David was left feeling cold and alone. His companions didn't seem to want to have much to do with him and he wasn't sure how or why he had come to be in this truck with them on this desolate road. He pulled his sack towards him, placing it between his knees and rested his head down on it as he fell asleep.

They awoke with a jolt as the truck clattered over a bridge, the violin player struggling to attention before his older companion stretched out a hand to his shoulder.

"It's alright," he said to his friend, "We're just crossing the river. We'll be there soon. Go back to sleep if you wish."

The charango player had a glazed look on his eyes, he was far away somewhere with the strains of his instrument. Balthazar eyed David suspiciously while the latter gazed at the flickering landscape.

"You know," said David, dimly aware of the singer's presence as he turned tentatively towards him, "It isn't right that I keep more money than the rest of you."

The eyebrows on the foreheads of Balthazar and the charango player rose in unison.

"I did nothing," said David, "After all, you're the musicians, the entertainers. What right have I to the money you earned last night?"

Without waiting for a response, David fished inside his rucksack for the red handkerchief that was laden with coins and began to pick at the knot with his teeth. Balthazar and the charango player said nothing but eyed the actions of the foreigner with curiosity. Finally David managed to tug the knot free and as he did so several coins spilled out across the floor of the truck, two or three of them falling through the gap in the tailgate before David could retrieve the rest. His companions sat motionless, full of wonderment.

David bundled the coins together, which were many, and set about dividing them into three equal groups. Balthazar put his hand on David's arm, squeezing it firmly but gently. David was surprised at the strength of the grip of the man; his appearance was that of someone much frailer.

"There are four of us here," said the old man, turning his eyes to the still-sleeping figure of the violin player, Dimitri.

"Yes, of course," said David, raising his head to countenance the faces of the two musicians, "But I can't possibly consider myself..."

The charango player and Balthazar raised their eyebrows impossibly further.

"Stop," said Balthazar, "Put the money in four piles, please."

He looked towards his companion, who nodded at him. The men were smiling and glowing at David. David looked back at them and smiled.

"You are one of us!" said Balthazar, as his normally reticent companion the charango player clapped David round the shoulder. The morning light strode over the hilltops in front of them and the men were suddenly at ease.

David turned his gaze to the still-sleeping figure of the violin player who was propped against the potato sack, and whom the others had covered in an overcoat to keep out the cold. There was a question on David's face.

"Dimitri," said the charango player, simply and it was the first word David had heard the man speak.

"What did you say your name was?" asked the heir to the estate of Count Rodinoski with a politeness that masked his trepidation.

"David Salzburg, Salsa. David Salsa," stuttered David, finally regaining his composure. His two companions beamed at each other in joyful conspiracy.

"I thought that's what I'd heard you say at the door to the hall," said Balthazar, "I knew it all along."

The driver and his colleague in the front of the vehicle were oblivious to the goings on in the back. One took another swig from his hip flask and passed it over to his mate who was driving.

"It certainly keeps out the cold!" said Walther, laughing.

Their cargo, the sacks of potatoes, the onions and the musicians were bouncing about behind them, thrown about by the hard surface of the road. There was a stiff breeze that had picked up with the morning and the early promise of a sun that had shown itself over the tops of the hills was fading.

The road they were on followed the river they had crossed earlier, at times moving away from it but always eventually coming back to it. Inevitably the road would follow the lie of the land even though at times its constructors had burrowed away from the valley floor. Here the waters of many valleys had collected and it was impossible to escape the confines of the landscape. It struck David as improbably strange that the only part of the route that was asphalted was the road leading up to the top of the hill, which passed the turning down to the village and then continued on in its traverse of the hillsides leading down from it. As soon as they had crossed the road-bridge where the chain of wooded hills ended, so too had the asphalt ended with it.

After a period of what seemed interminable cold and wind, with the truck churning up gravel that spattered on the sides of the vehicle and sometimes directly at them, they reached a place where a dog came out growling at the wheels in the dust. The truck slowed ominously and David pushed himself as hard as he could into the sack of vegetables behind him. The charango player, who was still nameless to David, straightened out the curling ends of his moustache that had stiffened in the breeze and pulled them down. Balthazar smoothed the strands of his hair thinly across his head in a vague attempt to comb them. The dog continued to yap and bark in the dust as the truck slowed down almost to a standstill outside the concrete hut from which the dog had emerged. A tall man in a faded grey police uniform came walking out in slow but deliberate strides. He had his hand on his hip where a revolver was resting in its holster.

David slunk down under the rim of his hat, tilting his head into the sack of lumpy vegetables behind him so that he managed to change the hat's angle without touching it, inclining it ever so slightly forwards and downwards. He kept his eyes closed as he did so, screwing them up so tight that they watered.

The driver who had been drinking steadily since the early hours of the morning honked his horn loudly, causing the dog which had backed off a little to renew its snarling discourse with added ferocity. The man in the passenger seat raised his hand to the policeman as he wound down the window.

"Bloody cold, isn't it?" he laughed into the face of the policeman, turning round to share the joke with his mate, who was also laughing. The policeman raised his hand half-heartedly and reached downwards. There he found the lever that released the mechanism by which the metal barrier swung upwards and the truck picked up speed as it passed underneath.

"What was all that about?" asked David of Balthazar when the velocity of the truck had accelerated sufficiently to allow the rapid beating in his heart to slow down. He was as out of breath as if he'd been running to catch up with the vehicle.

"Check-point," said Balthazar, "There's nothing that gets through here without being stopped first. They make the passengers on the village bus get off and show their documents, even the driver. We only got through so quickly because we're with them," he tossed his head in the direction of the driver and his mate who were still laughing and oblivious to them. It was obvious to David to which 'village' Balthazar had been referring; without a shadow of a doubt he meant the village he himself had caught the bus from, not the 'community' he had so miraculously escaped from.

"My name's Constantino," said the charango player stretching forward and taking David's hand in his in an uncharacteristic display of candour. The musician looked to see if the guards were watching.

"Welcome to the band," he said.

"How many of us are there?" asked David, genuinely perplexed.

"Just the four of us," said Constantino in a tone that betrayed his suspicion that the foreigner was not quite as smart as others had supposed him to be. Balthazar leaned over and put a hand to his sleeping friend's shoulder.

"Wake up, Dimitri, we're almost there."

The violin player struggled to a flourish from against the potato sacks and rubbed his eyes in the thin morning air. The others were smiling at him and the eldest member of the group extended a handful of coins in his direction.

"Our good Mr. *Salsa*," he took care to emphasise David's surname, "Has kindly offered to share last night's takings with us." Balthazar and Constantino were beaming.

"Pleased to meet you," said Dimitri to David and the four men settled down to enjoy their ride.

The man sitting in the passenger seat turned round to raise his flask to the band with a smirk on his face then turned round in uproarious laughter with the driver. The general bonhomie in the truck was contagious and the members of the newly established band were smiling like accomplices.

"I said, it's bloody cold, isn't it, Walther?" and the guards burst into hysterics simultaneously.

David put his hand into his jacket pocket and felt the weight of the coins there, letting them slip through his fingers over and over again and marvelling at his good fortune. He retrieved one from his pocket and looked at it, smiling. It did not have the name of the country in which he was travelling engraved on it and it was unfamiliar to him, heavier than the coins he'd been exchanging on his journey.

"That's silver," said Constantino. Balthazar nodded.

"They have their own currency up there," he added, casting a depreciating look back in the general direction they had come from. Again, his companion nodded.

"They brought them over with them on the ships when they came here," interjected the singer.

This time it was Constantino's turn to nod in agreement.

"They've been circulating them ever since, though few ever get out. Usually they pay us in paper, but last night was an exception," he smiled at David, "It seems your presence did not go unnoticed."

"You can change them at the stop where we get off, if you like. They're uncommon but acceptable currency there," said Balthazar. "Of course, you could change them in the capital, in Buenos Aires where you'd get a better price for them," added the old man, "They're considered collectors' items there."

David slunk further inside his jacket and under the umbrella of his hat. It was beginning to rain, a fine gritty drizzle that almost augured snow. David thought back to the circumstances of his leaving the city and was glad that he'd left it. He'd left many things behind on his journey since then.

"You should see this country when the hills are covered with snow and the rivers are swollen. It's a sight to behold," said Balthazar, wrapped up in his own mood of nostalgia and half-remembering, half-imagining the hills of his birthplace where horses stamped freely on the meadows. Though of course he'd only been a boy of three when his parents had brought him into exile from their plundered country. He could only dream of the riches that had once been his birthright, which had been spirited away forever.

"Or in spring," continued Balthazar mostly to himself, "When the fields are carpets of flowers and the last remaining snow glints like diamonds in the high places. Ha! You should see how fierce and how tender the people are."

His own father had been tender with him, as if a father tried to compensate for the material wealth that a son could never repossess in a land like this. Immediately after he'd built the cabin they were to inhabit, built it with his own hands, he fell into a kind of reverie from which he never awoke.

"He died when I was seven," said Balthazar, spitting out of the truck, "He never lived to see what a wonderful country this really is, never had a chance to travel through it."

He gritted his teeth and hummed a tune to himself that he'd half-forgotten, half-invented. It was true, thought David who'd been hearing the monologue, listening to it as one might do a story about one's own past. It was an incredibly beautiful land, it just depended on one's perception of it; on the perception one was allowed to have of it. For the men driving, for example, there was no doubt in David's mind that theirs' was a glorious panorama, a stage set for romance; the kind of romance they were still living in, as if bound up by a spell which made the lives of those who believed in it sweeter. But David could understand the nature of Balthazar's suffering, how his vision differed greatly from theirs'; eternally caught up in a moment in time where tragedy became romantic to the point of excluding all other feeling.

"How far to the stop?" asked David of Balthazar when the musician had drifted back from his remembrances.

"Not far now," came the response, though David could not be sure his companion wasn't referring to some other journey that he had once made, or was perhaps yet to make. "See those trees over there?" the old man gestured to David, "They were planted in my father's time. When we first came here the hillside was just a bare patch of land. A few goats, wild. At least, that's how I remember my father describing it to me."

"So you live round here, then?" David asked the musician after a few quiet moments.

"Yes," came back the response.

"Alone?" asked David.

The old man's brow furrowed and he seemed to be peering into a darkness, lost in an act of supreme concentration.

"There was a time," began the musician, but his words trailed off and either the wind that stole down from the mountains or a carelessness put silence to his sentence. "You should see where I live," said Balthazar unexpectedly when he had wrestled himself free of the distraction of his memory and his mind was flowing out into the pastures again. He was smiling now and David was again taken aback at how quickly the man could throw off previous appearances, previous expectations of him.

"Of course, I expect you have other more important business to attend to," said the man, half- inquisitively, half in deference to a sense of respect to him that David could detect but was at a loss to explain. Balthazar smiled wryly to himself but his eyes had the flame of a fire in them once more, though it was a flame that could be extinguished quickly; put out and left smouldering deep beneath the surface, only detectable if one knew the man. It was a revelation to him to think that how well one knew a person was entirely dependent on how well that person allowed him or herself to be known.

It was even possible that he himself unconsciously practised similar behaviour depending on the circumstances and the company he was in. This new thought came as such a shock to him that he wondered whether all these years he'd been merely acting a role which he'd successfully convinced himself was the truth; as if he'd performed some slight-of-hand magic illusion on himself with such dexterity that he had failed to notice it.

"You alright?" enquired Balthazar from somewhere outside the complexity of the philosophical stupor David had sunk into, and was now struggling to stay afloat in. And then Balthazar added,

"I hope I'm not intruding on personal matters."

"What? Oh, yes, I was just thinking," said David, clearing his throat.

"Yes, it's difficult sometimes, isn't it?" said Balthazar rhetorically.

"It's true," said David after some length, more to himself than to anyone in particular.

"What is?" asked Balthazar,

"Well, no, actually," said David with the newly acquiring wisdom that was forming like still drops of rain on his forehead, "I mean, I do have matters to attend to, a business of some urgency, to be quite honest."

The older man nodded his understanding.

"And yet none of it seems quite so important," continued David, "I should very much like to visit your home with you, if the offer still stands."

Balthazar hadn't so much asked the intriguing stranger to come to his house as he had phrased it as a statement; a sort of categorical assertion to the man that his home was worth visiting and that his father hadn't been wrong to settle his family where he had. Now the American's acceptation of his (up 'til then unconscious) invitation had spun the matter round. The morning mist that had been condensing slowly into rain was dripping from the brim of David's cowboy hat.

"Is it raining?" asked David.

"Yes, it seems to be," replied Balthazar.

"I thought so," said David, and he sank back into his meditations in the folds of the potato sack.

"That's the matter settled, then," said Balthazar presently.

"What is?" asked David, increasingly suspicious of the musician's apparent ability to see into the recesses of his mind. It was unsettling in the extreme; surely he was entitled to some privacy when pondering questions fundamental to the value of his existence. It was his existence surely, and they were his questions.

"You'll come and see the place," said Balthazar.

"Oh, that. Yes, of course," replied David with a flippancy that simultaneously managed to hurt the old man's feelings and failed to disguise the triviality of the matter compared to what was really on his mind.

Balthazar mistook the ensuing silence for a sign that although generous in the material sense and obviously a 'comrade', the stranger was not so generous from an emotional point of view. His own feelings were obviously of little interest to the American and Balthazar desperately tried to recall whether he had betrayed any emotion when talking about his homeland as he huddled into a ball against the sack. And now he was saddled with bringing the man into his home. There was undoubtedly more to the American than he was letting on – he'd seemed such a buffoon in the dance hall and yet he was far from it. Balthazar felt the weight of the silver coins that were stashed in his pocket and wondered at the man. In truth, having newly discovered his ability to mislead people, David was feeling dismayed at the ease with which his travelling companion had picked his mind clean.

The rain continued to drip from the brim of his cowboy hat. He was going to have to take more care of his disguise in the future. There was no knowing who was genuine and could be trusted and who wasn't.

"Do they always dress like that?" enquired David to Balthazar of the drivers who were by now irreverently drunk, pushing up the brim of his hat as he did so.

"What? Oh, yes," replied Balthazar, "What you see is what you get."

This so confused David that he fell quiet for the remainder of the journey.

The truck turned down a side road away from the course of the river and began to heave its way up the winding hillside.

"Not far now," said Balthazar like an echo of the still fleeting ships that sailed on the horizon of the hills. Clouds tugged there and the mood was gloomy and despondent.

"We'll have to get you a horse," said Balthazar.

"What?!" asked David, not sure whether the man had seen too far through his disguise altogether.

"A horse," repeated Balthazar, as David pulled the brim of his hat down further. If they had seen through him completely and were merely humouring him in his pretence at being a fellow musician, then David had better be careful. And yet they had said he was one of the *band*. Perhaps it was a double bluff; they knew but they weren't letting on they did. Although it was dank and cold as they pulled up the hillside, David was beginning to sweat. It trickled down his forehead and mingled with the moisture that slowly dripped there.

"It looks like we're going to be holed up for a few days," said Balthazar looking at the ominous presence of the clouds that were amassing on the skyline.

"Are there many… foreigners… in these parts?" asked David nervously. Balthazar looked him up and down in one glance. He raised his eyebrows like two soaring eagles.

"Well," commenced the old man, "It depends on what you might mean by, foreigners," he said carefully.

The charango player had caught the last part of the conversation and his eyes were peeled like two onions by the wind that whipped over the truck. He and Balthazar looked at each other.

"Well, I'm certainly not a *foreigner*, if that's what you mean" said David, anxious to distance himself from the two buffoons in the front of the truck, and all their species.

"No,…" said Balthazar in his by now familiar half-inquisitive, half-deferential tone, "Of course you're…not," he concluded, as he and the man with the onion-like eyes simultaneously lowered their glance, which they had been holding together like a heavily-strung tightrope.

"That hat?" gesticulated the charango player at the purchase sitting like a tomcat on David's head, snapping the tightrope as he did so.

"Córdoba," said David, as the gravity of Balthazar's gaze forced his companion to lower his eyes back towards the hard metal floor of the truck.

"I bought it in Córdoba," said David, defensively, reddening at the memory of that windy sunny day with Rosa when they'd got off the bus together.

"Yes, yes, of course," said Balthazar resuming his position as band leader and orchestrating his fellow musicians. David turned redder and redder as the memory of the time spent with his neglected, sweet Rosa blushed on his cheeks.

"I was with a girl," said David fighting off his embarrassment.

"Ah, yes," said the charango player, as if this had finally settled the matter. He and Balthazar cast a knowing look between them and the latter nodded. So, he was human after all, thought Balthazar. He was a romantic, just like himself. He would be glad to play host to him under his roof.

"You said we might be needing horses?" said David, uncertain of when his companion might require him to jump from the relative safety of the truck, lest he compromise the group's anonymity.

"Not we, *you*," said Balthazar innocently.

"Ah, yes, of course," stuttered David, "I wasn't for one minute supposing that I might involve *you* in any sort of, or for that matter, or even..."

David stumbled on, the memory of his passage through the forest and the manner in which he'd contrived with Rosa to leave the farmhouse flooding back into him and into his crimson cheeks. The two musicians looked on in amazement as the charango players' eyes were peeled white by the wind and Balthazar's two eagles soared ever higher. And then something most unusual and quite out of keeping with David's character happened.

"I never meant to leave her," he said into the dank air, "I never really intended to get involved with her in the first place," he continued. "It just happened all of a sudden without my wanting it to and before I knew it I was half in love with the girl. You won't tell anybody, will you?" he beseeched the two astonished musicians, fearful that he would be pushed into being an outcast again or, worse still, find himself plunging headlong through some forest where nightmare-dark creatures were lingering and licked their lips.

"No, no, of course not, my good Mr. Salsa," said Balthazar as he embraced the man.

Just then, and at a decidedly most inopportune moment, one of the guards in the front of the truck turned round and saw what was happening. The old man still had his arm protectively round David's shoulders. The soldier let rip with a burst of laughter that could be heard from the back of the truck.

"I said, 'bloody cold for this time of year, isn't it Walther?!'" hooted the guard in hysterics as the truck veered violently off to the side of the road before it was righted with an equally violent manoeuvre which almost succeeded in dislodging its potatoes, onions and passengers alike.

Balthazar grinned at the guards with a smile as thin as cheese wire as the co-driver now took the steering wheel while his mate took it in turn to turn round and view the proceedings in the back of the truck. There was a whoosh and a bump as the truck hit a rock in the road, then a sloshing noise and the sound of a bottle breaking from inside the passenger cabin. Balthazar and Constantino grinned cheesy smiles at the guards as one looked angrily back at them, before he turned back round and looked stoically into the drizzle. The two musicians could hardly contain themselves. Still close to David and trying to comfort him, they heaved out a collective guffaw that might have been a cough should the need arise for it to be so.

"That serves those shitty *foreigners* right," whistled the charango player.

"That's the funniest thing I've ever seen," uttered Balthazar beneath his breath. But David had caught their words even though they thought that they were whispering and he was feeling offended beneath the coat they had draped him in.

"Kick a man while he's down and hurting," he sulked to himself.

But they had said he was one of their band and had put the coat round his shivering limbs.

"I'll be damned if I can work them out," he spat out silently through clenched teeth, "Be damned surprised if anybody can, no wonder there's so many misunderstandings in this country."

A wave of patriotism had swept over him; in his mind's eye he could see a flag rippling gallantly from a building. But there was something wrong. The truck had stopped and one of the guards was walking towards them to the rear of the vehicle.

"You'll have to get out," he barked at them, still smarting at the broken whisky bottle.

Dimitri was woken and Balthazar and the charango player helped David down from the truck as they took their parcels of instruments in their hands. David was stiff all over as the three musicians and their new accomplice stood tensely awaiting the guard's orders. David grabbed at his hat and threw it deftly into the covering trees in sublime panic when the guard's back was turned to them in conversation with the driver. Balthazar looked askance at Constantino, their telling looks sweeping the ground before them. The guard turned and was looking at David's bare head where the outsize cowboy hat had been sitting just one brief moment earlier. He rubbed his eyes in the sulky morning fog and continued to stare at the space. Balthazar bowed before the drunken man and opened his hands as if spreading a prayer book. A conciliatory smile opened in his face like sunlight spreading up the walls of a valley. He was all peace and reconciliation, frail and humble as a piece of cloth blown dry on a washing line.

The others overheard the driver say, "It's the damn axle," but David had removed his hat and his resurgent patriotism had suddenly wilted in the stiff breeze while he awaited the bullet he was convinced must be due him.

"What happened to your hat?" asked the guard as David awaited the fatal shot.

"Blew off in the wind," said David feeling the blood drain to his feet.

The guard looked at him where the hat had been then burst out laughing, staggering back to the front of the vehicle and generously sharing the joke with his companion. The guard laughed. The driver laughed. The musicians laughed. Though not too loudly. The good-humoured guard clapped David on the shoulder as he pointed him and the group of musicians on their way up the rest of the hill on foot. The three musicians were smiling to each other but the joke had been lost on David. If there was one thing that was true, comedy and the causes for it were the biggest cultural dividers that existed, David thought to himself as the party trudged up the hill to where the first houses could be spied, forlornly perched on the hilltop.

"You needn't have thrown the hat away," said Balthazar to David in a gesture of conciliation when they had climbed further away from the truck and its occupants were just two fretful insects pressed against their windscreen at a distance. But the joke hadn't made sense to David, and all hope of retrieving it had been irrevocably lost on him the moment the trees had made the hat their own. David blushed red in the face and wondered what recalcitrant creature might adopt it under the cover of dark, and what creature lurked there to haunt him. He thought again of Rosa and for some reason the grinning face of the young policeman, Ramiro gleamed at him through the flames of the fire in the hearth.

Balthazar and Constantino looked at each other and understood. The American wasn't talking. The matter was settled and no more would be said about it.

CHAPTER EIGHTEEN

By the time they reached the village the rain that had been threatening and spitting all morning had abated, the grey shadows of the clouds overhead rested on the roofs of the houses and along the walls. Out of a windowless opening in a house a middle-aged woman leant on one arm smoking a cigar. Her bare arms were brown and on her shoulders she wore a multi-coloured poncho. David looked intently at her. She caught his glance and held it, firm in her gaze though she seemed to be looking straight through him and at something more distant. David bowed his head slightly, as if to show he'd been looking at something else and the woman exhaled a puff of smoke into the air.

"Up here," said Balthazar, putting his hand on David's shoulder. The latter turned round to take in the bare streets of the village with its crudely whitewashed walls. On either side of the wide dirt street two channels had been loosely dug to facilitate the precipitations that came down from the mountains. A dog was tracing the line of the walls of the houses on the left-hand side, turning and spinning round at intervals as it did so. It stayed close to the walls with its head cowed and its thin tail beating the pavement; Constantino stretched out a hand to it and the dog came scuffling halfway out into the street. David caught the swish of a tail on a leathery rump round a corner and saw as they came into view that three horses were tied to a wooden post strung between two uprights. Ominously, there was a truck very similar to the one they had disembarked from down the hill parked beside the horses. It reminded David of a scene from a movie set, but the truck was parked rudely out of place. He felt the chill of the breeze that was blowing from the mountains on his bare head and reached up to put his hand to where his hat used to be, but then he took it down again quickly. The gesture did not go unnoticed by Balthazar and Constantino.

"Take mine," said Constantino who was not feeling the cold as much as David, as he held out a dark, round beret to him. The gesture was spontaneous, but Constantino and Balthazar froze for a moment in the cold air of the village as David's glower ushered Constantino away. He took the beret anyway, against his will, and pulled it down firmly round his head.

"Thank-you," said David tersely.

"It's nothing," replied Constantino abashed, dimly searching for an answer from Balthazar.

They were more cunning than he'd realised, David thought to himself. He'd been ordered to cover up in no uncertain terms. Crimson-faced, David trooped up the wooden steps to the store behind the band of musicians; surprised to find himself suddenly pushed in before them as the musicians' politeness got the better of them. Immediately a man in a familiar grey jacket got up to greet him and offered to buy him a drink from the bar. David tried to decline but the man insisted and made such a fuss of the issue that David was obliged to accept. He turned round to his colleagues in astonishment; the musicians said nothing but beamed back at David. They nodded politely in unison to the man who had ordered them a round, but who had neglected to ask them what they preferred and had ordered whisky as if it was the only drink worth having.

David's throat was as dry as sawdust and he was on the point of asking for something that would ease the sensation, perhaps a beer. But the contemplation of his companions and the commanding smile of the grey-jacketed gentleman ordering at the bar made him rescind. He'd just have to have what the locals were having. Best to blend in. Smartly the blonde-haired gentleman who'd bought the drinks swigged his down and clinked his empty glass on the table. The band of musicians followed suit as only a group of musicians could do and David was left gulping down the fiery liquid as it burned and tore at his throat. It sloshed out of the corners of his mouth as his glass, the last to be emptied, echoed hollowly on the table. He was unable to swallow the full contents of the glass, and rendered incapable of saluting the gentleman in the same manner as his companions when the former stood smartly and turned on his heels to leave.

As the swinging doors closed behind the man who had stepped into the street outside, David attempted a smile and the contents of the glass were spattered across the faces of his companions in one desperate, snorting gasp for air.

"I'm sorry," he stuttered, struggling to breathe, "I thought we were done for then."

But something about the look on their faces reminded David that they were coolly playing a game of double bluff. They weren't saying anything. So, the disgust on the faces of Constantino, Dimitri and, to a lesser extent, Balthazar, David mistook for distaste at his nearly having given the game away. For their part, his companions took David's ensuing silence as just one further measure of the strangeness of these gringos, and, in particular, of David.

Constantino was regretting having parted company with his beret and kept eyeing it covetously. David took this as a signal that he had almost blown their cover and pulled it down tighter still on his head. Meanwhile the sleepy violin player had sprung to life and was ordering more drinks for them at the bar, where a bald-headed thickset man with an equally thick moustache was handing him a bottle. Balthazar spread his hands in a gesture of appeasement at the clouds that had been gathering and did his best to smooth things over. Constantino eyed the foreigner coolly. At last his contempt got the better of him.

"Was tha matter?" he said, "You don' like whisky?"

Dimitri rocked back in his seat and put the bottle he had purchased firmly down in the centre of the table. Constantino turned away from the group with another glassful, muttering to himself.

Seeing that his integrity was at stake David filled himself a large tumbler with affected bravado and slaked it back in one gulp. He kept one eye on Constantino as if to show he was not frightened. Balthazar looked in wonderment at the man. Constantino affected disinterest out of the corner of his eye but his curiosity had got the better of him. David had already poured himself another huge glass and was knocking it back. He shifted his weight onto his right foot in order to steady himself and the gravity of the moment got to him as the chair he'd been sitting on vanished from underneath.

"Poor man," said Balthazar to his companions as they attempted to hoist the foreigner into his now-righted chair, "You see what love can do to a man?"

Constantino's better nature swam to the surface again and he felt ashamed as he looked at the foreigner slumped over the table.

"You see?" said Balthazar to Constantino, "They're not so different to us after all. In love, all men are equal."

He downed his glass and slammed it on the table. Dimitri now took it in turn to look aggrieved at Constantino and the charango player turned away from them, muttering into his glass once more as he did so.

"Hombre, who got us the money, after all?" said Dimitri in a thinly disguised attack on Constantino.

"Yes, it's true," said Balthazar, who was more perceptive than the others of the nature of the misunderstanding that had occurred, "A man must never be criticised when his heart has been broken, lest we should find ourselves in the same state one day and be in need of some help."

"Yes," agreed Dimitri who had spotted something on the man's trousers, "The man obviously needs help."

Although relieved of his faculties, David had not altogether lost consciousness and something about the tone of the voices; perhaps a dim awareness that they had recognised the error of their ways in making fun of him, lulled him into a reassuring sleep. Dimitri was moved to take his violin from his case and thus commenced a melancholy hymn to the perils of love, to which Balthazar announced his sympathies by accompanying him in his reedy voice. Constantino could bear the tension no longer and, with the weight of inexorable guilt bearing down upon him, proceeded to pluck from the strings of his charango notes so full of feeling as the village had never before heard.

Soon coins began to jingle on the floor beside them as customers attracted by the music began entering the bar. Balthazar, ever perceptive, plucked Constantino's hat from the foreigner's head and tossed it upside down onto the floor. David was dreaming and there was music so pained and so full of romance that, even though he was solidly drunk, he felt it flow inside him in sympathy.

"Who's that?" the barman asked Balthazar when the crowds had finally departed; the musicians' hearts rung to their cores.

"He? He is a great man!" said Balthazar with a flourish, wiping the tears from his face, "And a poet, too."

The barman pursed his lips, turning the corners down in respect, as one might do at a funeral or on hearing the news that one's best friend has just lost his wife to a much younger lover. Certainly, the customers had drunk their fill and the village had descended into a pathos the like of which had seldom been seen in those parts. The whole village was swaying, there on the hilltop.

And so the rumour that had started in the dancehall where men saluted each other stiffly spread wildly to the villages on the hilltops and down into the surrounding valleys. The fame of the musicians swept on before them, and with them the legend of the troubled lover, the silent poet who travelled in their midst. It was rumoured that he was a foreigner and had travelled far to escape the memory of an unforgettable love, but quite where he had come from and how long he had travelled nobody was sure.

"Tie him on carefully," said Balthazar to Constantino as he steadied his horse. It was time to leave his companions and for the time being their collaboration was over. Already there were offers flowing in from the surrounding outposts to play at this or that festival, lead a dance or grace a wedding.

"What did I tell you?" said the son of Count Rodinoski as he turned in the saddle to wave farewell to his friends, "I knew he was one of us from the moment I saw him."

And so Balthazar Rodinoski, the son of the Count Rodinoski, rode to the edge of the hill with the poet strapped on behind him, eager to return to the home of his forefathers.

The snow was crisp on the hillsides where it had fallen in the night and the mountains gleamed like a beacon above the village. Down below lay the valley, hidden inside a valley, where his father had first come seeking a place of refuge; a place where he could raise his young son and watch him grow into a man. Balthazar turned to take one last look at the village that had brought them so much fame, his pockets weighted down with coins.

"Are you okay, David?" asked Balthazar before plunging down the hillside.

"Yes," said David, "I'm fine."

But although he'd retained the beret of Constantino, which had been bestowed on him in an overly ceremonious act by the latter, he was upset that they'd thought it necessary to change his outfit entirely. Perhaps it was part of the disguise, thought David. Again he marvelled at the silent conspiracy of his fellow musicians, who had not only fed him and paid for his previous night's lodging, but had also filled his,(seemingly new) pockets with silver and were now taking care of him.

"What fantastic people these Argentines are," he said out loud.

"Si, hombre," said Balthazar as they cantered down the slope of the dirt road, "My father knew a thing or two when he brought us to this country."

Balthazar was proud to play host to the poet. He knew full well that their extreme good fortune owed more to the man than he might dare say to the others.

"Tell me one thing," said Balthazar to David as the wind raced round them, "You're name's not 'Salsa', is it?"

"No, it isn't," said David simply.

"I thought not," said the singer, "I knew it all along." A pause. "Don't worry," he said, "Your secret is safe with me."

And then they breathed in the silence of the immense valley as they rode into it and it began to enfold them.

"I would just like to know one other thing, if, of course, I am not intruding too much on your - personal affairs. I hope I am not too - presumptuous," he added.

"Be my guest," said David, who had moments previously abandoned all pretensions at trying to safeguard any last elements of his disguise from the man.

"Was she beautiful?" asked Balthazar succinctly.

David sucked in his breath but did not answer.

"The girl, I mean?" enquired Balthazar with a persistence bordering on impoliteness.

"Yes," answered David, as if out of a dream he was somehow a part of but had invented himself, "She was the most beautiful child you can imagine. I lost her when she was very young."

No wonder the man is troubled, thought Balthazar; it was a greater tragedy than even he could have imagined. They rode on into the silent valley and neither a bird nor a living soul stirred to disturb their quiet.

They crossed a stream at a turning through some poplar trees, then began to pick their way up a right-hand slope strewn with loose rocks which looked as if they had fallen there.

"Don't be fooled," said Balthazar as their horse picked its way through them.

"Oh, I'm not, not in the least," answered David, whose head was finally being cleared by the beneficial effect of the pure mountain air, "Nothing and everything is capable of surprising me here," he continued.

Balthazar said nothing but was gratified to be confirmed in his suspicions that the man was indeed a poet.

"Over the brow of this rocky hillside exists something you'd never imagine if you hadn't seen it with your own eyes," said the latter.

As Balthazar's horse laboured up the scree at the top of the incline, David strained himself against the rope that had been threaded through the belt on his trousers. The horse stumbled for a second then regained its footing with agility.

"There she is," said Balthazar when the horse was descending sure-footedly, "This is my father's land."

David took in the fertile green slopes decked with conifers. The sun was protruding out of the mist and here and there it glinted on a silver thread that was hidden, woven into the land where the trees were scarcer and the beige of the earth showed itself in patches. No smoke to whisper of any human presence filtered through the sky. No domestic animal grazed the land.

"Your father certainly picked his spot well," said David when they had come to the flat of the land and the sunlight shining through like the gossamer of a spider's web hung in the space between sky and earth. From this point it was impossible to distinguish any dwelling that might be tucked away there. Balthazar's features had changed, though David couldn't see him, and now he rode with the elegance of a man who knew that the land on which he was riding was his, and who knew every resting place of every stone and every tree on it.

"So you live here alone?" asked David, feeling the tender warmth of the sun on his arms and on his face. His question went unanswered, but the gathering speed of the horse and the spreading silver of the river which occasionally blinded them made David feel that the old man had much to keep him company here; if, indeed, the man was as old as he had seemed to be.

After half an hour's hard riding on the plain they pulled up at a stone-built house that appeared out of nowhere. Close by it and off to one side was a wooden outbuilding of precarious construction with a door that was open and hanging slightly off its hinges. Hay poked out from the doorway and David understood that it must be a converted stable. The older man led his mount to the door of the hut and helped David to untie the knot that had been expertly tied by Constantino round David's belt.

"This is home," said Balthazar simply, bowing ever so slightly as he did so in an unconscious and involuntary movement. David wondered why it was that he should feel the need to act this way before him. It was he that owed him so much. But David had long ago noticed something in the musician's demeanour that led him to believe that he was often on his guard, without there ever really being evidence to conclude that the matter was such. A hardness had been crafted into him, but David was sure that this owed more to circumstances and the unfulfilled aspirations pressed on him by the legacy of aristocracy than was true of the man's real nature.

"This is it," said Balthazar.

"You live in a beautiful place," said David earnestly, breathing in the pure air, the smell of earth and the river and the far-flung scent of snow. The old man's eyes softened and in them David could see a multitude of colours that had been hidden from him before.

"There is beauty in many places and in many things, if you know where to look for it," said Balthazar, who seemed to have thrown off the rigours of the journey almost effortlessly. He was smiling to himself now and his smile was infectious. He strode off past the outbuilding in the direction of the river, beckoning David to follow him as he did so. The water was as clear and as transparent as pure melted ice. Above the stones that shone pink and gold on the riverbed, polished and smoothed, trout swam lazily flipping their backs beneath the surface in imperceptible strokes of colour, separating and then regrouping.

The sun penetrated the water and shone on the creases of

Balthazar's face when he turned round to look at David. In some lights the musician looked pale and this added to the semblance of him being frail, but here beneath the winter sun Balthazar looked darker and altogether more energetic. When you looked into the creases on his face he looked like the gnarled branch of some weather-beaten tree; but it was a robust tree that had toiled with both sun and wind; there was something majestic about him, even. As if prompted to speak by his friend's disclosure, David found himself saying something quite out of keeping with his normal self,

"A man is not the clothes he wears, he is what he is."

Quite why he had said it, he wasn't sure, but he had said it nevertheless. Balthazar grinned widely at him,

"You are a poet," he said to David. David shook his head from side to side, "I might have been, once," he said ruefully.

"Then you shall be once again," said his friend.

David was feeling intoxicated by the landscape. The mirage of tree line and skyline pushed the land back as far as the eye could see. Bare patches of the hard ground shone like the backs of creatures that were either loping off into the distance or had camouflaged themselves and lay still. Down the bank by the river's edge the water clucked and chimed but just a few metres away from it the absence of noise was almost audible.

"I can't hear the river anymore," said David, perplexed.

"That's because there are too many things to listen to," said Balthazar still grinning. And when he stopped to listen, it was true. The wind crept through the dry branches of the poplars, sometimes detaining itself on a leaf that still clung to its perch. Imperceptibly it whispered, was never still. The flicker of an insect's wings could be heard too, pinned against the canopy of the noise of the water that ran smoothly and chattered to itself, quietly hissing.

"First you must hear the sounds in the landscape, then you can begin to appreciate its colours," said Balthazar who was smiling at his apprentice.

David started to ask him a question but realised his folly halfway through,

"How long have you...?"

"I've lived all my life in this valley," said the musician.

There was an aroma in the air too, now that David had stopped trying to fathom the land out and it presented itself to him.

"I can smell wood," he said like a child who is playing a game and has his eyes bound by a cloth.

"That's right," nodded the older man in assent, "It's the smell of the shavings. I'm making a table. Such a quality of wood there is here, a man cannot help but vainly try to do something with it. Come," he said to David, "Do you want to see?"

David followed him round to the back of the stables and saw the other entrance to the building that he hadn't noticed before.

"This is where I do my work," said Balthazar, no longer uneasy at what his newfound friend might say. The clear smell of pine hung in the air inside the workshop; honey dripping from the rafters. Simply being inside the building was invigorating, it made David think of the forests bristling on the skyline; it made him want to climb through them and reach the tops of the hills.

"They're higher than they seem," said Balthazar reading David's thoughts. David was looking through the open window to where he imagined the timber might have come from. Inside the surprisingly roomy workshop, which was separated from the place where the horse was kept by a wooden partition, Balthazar had a saw mounted on a steel table with his tools laid out neatly on the work surface. Various sized chisels and a hand drill gleamed under his inspection.

"You're a carpenter, then," said David as a statement of fact.

Balthazar spread his hands in a familiar gesture, but his expert eye was assessing his previous labours, calculating the angles of the table he was making.

"It looks finished to me," said David.

"Ah, no, not at all," said his friend as he moved towards the object at the side of the room. The carpenter stroked his hand along its surface as if he were stroking the back of a horse, soothing it after a long journey. "The wood still has to show itself," said Balthazar looking minutely at it, "And the legs need reinforcing in the corners if it is to stand straight for many years."

The patience with which Balthazar approached the table reminded David of the patience and kindness that had been shown to him. One could profit from it, if one allowed oneself to be slowed to the tune of the world. How fast they ran in their degenerating cities, thought David, how fast we run. He turned to Balthazar who was splendid in his solitude amongst the wood shavings and the tools of his labour. Already his host had picked up an off-cut and was examining it. He doesn't waste a thing here, David thought.

"Forgive me, I am forgetting myself," said Balthazar who still had one eye on the piece of wood, "You must be hungry, and perhaps you want to wash yourself after the journey."

"No, no, I am happy here," said David.

"Good," said his companion, "Then we will eat later. It is always good to eat after one has done some work and accomplished something," he said, "I find that the food itself tastes better."

It was an interesting thought, and David was left pondering just how many of the old man's commonplace utterances contained within them something altogether more profound, more at the centre of things.

"*We provide you with the service you need,*" said David.

"I'm sorry?" said Balthazar who was engrossed in his work.

"Oh, it's just something they used to say at the company. Something they used to write, actually, not say. Something for display. I guess it's more difficult not to tell the truth when the words are said; spoken from one person to another."

Ever since the incident with the hat in the back of the truck David had taken to thinking about things in a different way. It was funny how he had not seen it all before.

"I suppose I've never really considered these things before," said David to Balthazar who had his back turned towards him, "You must have plenty of time here to think," he added, continuing above the sound of the man working. Blended in with the noise of the river, the mellifluous sound of the saw seemed to cut through pine like honey dripping.

"There is nothing else one can do," said Balthazar, "But it is *what* one thinks about that is important; not the act of thinking itself."

How true, thought David, and the smell of pinesap filled the air like the resolute sun filtering in through the window.

"Here, hold this," said Balthazar, whose normally ceremonious politeness had been replaced by something more genuine. He handed

David an instrument that was shaped like a miniature snow sleigh with two round polished wooden handles at its fore and aft. It was heavier than David had expected and at that moment he made a connection between the tool and his friend's sinewy strength. Balthazar scuffled the table across to the centre of the room, next to the saw and took the instrument from him without looking up.

"Just rest your weight against the end of the table," he said to David, "That's it, there's no need to push against it, just hold it firm with your arms outstretched."

And with that Balthazar turned his force to the table before him and, stretching his back like a cat arching for its prey or a swimmer engaged by the current, he pushed the device across the table, peeling off a part of its skin in one smooth strip as he did so. He straightened himself up in one fluid movement, twisting as he readied himself for the next stroke. David was reminded of the fish they had seen down in the river, how they swam together, separated and regrouped.

In one inspired moment it occurred to David that perhaps his friend had acquired this supple movement by having sat on the bank watching the fish many times. Perhaps we acquire certain ways of doing things even when we are not conscious of doing so, he thought. Perhaps it was only when one was fully engaged with something to the point of being unconscious of it that the act acquired a special sort of artistry.

"Do you think the fish know that they are swimming?" asked David rather foolishly.

"No," answered the craftsman, "I think that if they did they would drown."

The sincerity of Balthazar's response surprised David out of his reverie, for the moment he had uttered it he had thought the question childish. Balthazar hadn't so much as batted an eyelid. For him, it seemed, the integrity of a person was enough to guarantee the integrity of what they said. How strange, thought David, back where I come from it's the exact opposite: respect is gained on the basis of what is said. The more assertive the slogan or advertising campaign was, the more you trusted the company.

"I guess it's all down to individuals," said David absentmindedly.

"Yes," said Balthazar, "Those fish that stop to think about it are the ones that get caught, of that I'm sure."

David laughed out loud at Balthazar's joke, but the carpenter was looking at him seriously.

"Yes," said David in an effort to afford the man's comment the consideration it deserved, "I see what you mean."

"Do you?" asked Balthazar, and at once David was crudely aware of the insincerity of his response; of its inadequacy. He'd only being trying to be polite. And yet as he thought about it while Balthazar heaved at the wood and shed skin after skin off its surface, his old notion of politeness and the new one that his friend seemed to practice were definitely two different things. In fact, one might say that they were almost complete opposites.

"What are you thinking?" asked Balthazar when he had finished planing the wood and the knot in David's forehead had grown to the size of a whirlpool. All this talk of swimming fish had exhausted him.

"I'm thinking that it takes many, many years to speak a language," said David, "I'm thinking that I probably communicate better in your tongue when I'm silent," he continued, half-jokingly.

"Yes, that is possible," responded the old man, "One has to learn to be silent before one can learn to speak properly," he added.

"Yes, of course," said David, and this time it was said in deepest earnestness.

"So, what do you think?" asked Balthazar when he was standing back looking at the centre of the room.

"I think too much," said David who had rather inhaled too much of the pine sap than was good for him, "Or perhaps I don't think enough," he added to himself as he sat down on a stool underneath the window. Wistfully he looked at the dining table.

"My good Mr.,…David," said Balthazar, "I am forgetting my manners completely. That is enough for today; you surely must be tired by now and in need of some refreshment," he said, remembering himself and taking a backwards glance at the table he had been making.

"You are not used to travelling on horseback, I think?" He looked nervously at the space where David's cowboy hat used to sit. David pointed the toes of his boots outwards. Balthazar stared with supreme intention at the forest wavering on the skyline immediately above David's head.

"Do they have - natives where you come from?" he asked, rather ashamed at himself for unintentionally remarking on David's status as a foreigner once again. He rubbed his hands together as if chafing together two sticks to make a fire.

"Yes, there are Indians there," said David with candour, "But not as many as there used to be, and," he added as Balthazar's gaze involuntarily settled on the spectacle of David's head with the trees growing out of it, "They no longer maintain their customs the way they used to."

Balthazar went to tend his horse and led it down to the water to drink again. David looked trance-like at the river below him and wondered at the old man. There was much he had said to him that was starting to make sense. There was an overwhelming realisation of the futility of his attempts to try and fit in, and the slow dawning of his unconscious behaviour promised to fill his mind completely. Balthazar knew the lie of the land and its customs infinitely better than he himself was ever capable of. If he wanted to blend into the background and not stand out too much, he'd better learn all he could from this man.

"Constantino, you sly fox, I was wondering when you'd finally show up," said the charango player's young wife as she stood in the doorway to their house.

"Be patient," said her husband as he swayed up the path to greet her, coins spilling from his pockets, "We've had some luck," he continued.

"Yes, I know," she retorted, "The whole town's been talking about it, and that foreigner who's kept you away from my bed."

"Let's eat," said Balthazar when he had tethered the horse, heartily clapping David on the shoulder, "You must try a little of my vino," he said as he led David towards the house, "It's not bad if I say so myself. The Count," (he looked skywards) "had vineyards as well."

They entered straight into the dining room, where two plates had been left out and cutlery was immaculately arranged on the tablecloth, knives and forks in perfect symmetry. Not sure whether he was being led to a banquet or an uncomfortable showdown in which his bravado would have to do battle with his stomach again, David sat down in the chair he was offered.

"What - do you eat in these parts?" he asked Balthazar gingerly.

"Hombre, food," came back the reply from the kitchen.

Soon there was the most delicious, (and to David's mind reassuring) smell of meat roasting in an oven. He got up and went to look in the kitchen. There was a work surface heaved on top of loosely cemented stones that hardly seemed capable of bearing its weight. Next to it was a round, open-sided oven made of clay of the kind that David had seen before, but the others had been outside the houses in the yards. Cleverly, Balthazar had joined its chimney to a pipe leading up to the roof, which disappeared through a hole made in it.

"I know what you're thinking," said Balthazar as David involuntarily struggled for a moment with the memory of his escape through the hotel skylight.

"What - might that be?" asked David, somewhat anxiously.

"You see Mr.,..."

"David," said David.

"Yes, David. I feel I have my standards to uphold. My father was a proud man. I am proud too. Everybody else can squat over their asados in the rain, if they wish, but we, that is I, (he looked skywards again) am going to cook mine with dignity indoors."

The meal was clay-cooked rabbit with local herbs; wild thyme and rosemary, and mint too, if he was not mistaken. And there was a hint of something else.

"Absolutely delicious," said David as he slopped a chunk of bread in the gravy. Balthazar was beaming and filled his glass once more with the sweet wine.

"In Argentina we have the best meat in the world," announced Balthazar.

"Undoubtedly," said David who was a little red in the face. And then Balthazar did something that was most uncommon to him and most uncharacteristic; he attempted to speak in English:

"Is the bes' bif" said Balthazar, raising his glass and chuckling to himself at his joke. But no laughter was heard from the other man, who had taken it in deadly earnest.

After the meal was finished Balthazar slopped the dishes in the sink as David looked on.

"No, hombre, don't worry about them. They can wait 'til tomorrow. Besides, around here there's no-one to see what a mess we make," his eyebrows twitched and he looked skywards again, and with that the two men stumbled out of the door. Balthazar relieved himself near the bushes on the south side of the house. He crossed his chest and muttered some words to himself.

"It looks like we might get some of that snow here tonight," he said to David when he had finished. David was watching the trickle teeter down towards the river.

"Oh, don't worry about that," said his friend, "I always get the water from upstream. Besides, only a handful of peasants live further down river, and not in this valley. At least, not to my knowledge."

Then they went to get a fishing cane from the outhouse and an extra jacket in case the weather turned nasty. They followed a path that accompanied the river behind the house, leading back up the valley, although the dry riverbank rose steeply above them and the flat of the land was hidden. The row of poplars began to press in on them so that the path that had been made by Balthazar over years of walking to his favoured spot twisted in and out. After a while they came to a place where the river turned away and the earth had been hollowed out in a basin. They trudged into it and up the other side where Balthazar's path seemed to have disappeared into nothingness. The sun glinted on the sand that had somehow been deposited there and even though it was winter there was a dryness in the air that made David's throat feel parched. Silver of the river met gold of the bleached sand where David saw there was a bridge across to the other side.

It was a simple bridge consisting of two felled trees that had been stripped of their branches and lashed side by side. The trunks, though, were quite massive on approaching them and did not resemble the poplars that were growing on their riverbank.

"How did you…?" began David as he looked to where the larger conifers strutted on the opposite, still distant slopes.

"I didn't," answered Balthazar, completing David's question for him, "Only a fool goes wandering in search of that which he can find in his own backyard."

David was reddening in the midday sun. The weight of the timber for the bridge would have been difficult for one man to haul over such terrain, if not impossible.

"The river brings it," said Balthazar simply, "It might look nothing to you now, but you should see it when it is swollen with an avalanche from somewhere up there," he gestured loosely towards the direction of the village they had departed from earlier, "Or when a flash flood has gathered in the dry rocks above."

David looked back at the rim of the sandy basin they had just crossed, the logicality of its existence slowly beginning to dawn on him. The once seemingly placid water of the river shone under him threateningly as David guessed at the ice that was flowing in it, placing one foot in front of the other like a tightrope walker suspended between two high buildings. A moment of vertigo dizzied him as the glare of a neon sign flashed in his mind. For an instant he considered lowering himself onto all fours to gain better purchase, but the vision of Balthazar who was staring at him curiously from the other side was deterrent enough not to do so.

"The colours in the water are extraordinary," said David by way of explanation when he stood steeply drawing in his breath alongside his guide.

"Hmm," said Balthazar, who couldn't help but thinking that given half a chance his companion preferred crawling to walking. Again the image of the man seated by the open window without his discarded hat came into the old man's head. He found himself staring into the poet's eyes and saw the light that had raced into them.

"You know, David," he said, "They say we all have our animal spirit to guide us. There's only one thing stronger than a person, and that's nature, which is everything," he stated with a gesture that took in the whole landscape. It was true, thought David, the corporations were only great because of the individuals in them; without them they were nothing. And yet somehow the silent and unpredictable will of the corporations seemed to outweigh that of the individual. He scratched his head.

"I've had to build and rebuild that bridge over the years," said Balthazar when they were walking again, "But I've come to realise that it doesn't pay to try and build anything lasting. When the river decides, it smashes it and washes it away again as if it were made of matchsticks. The harder you try, the less likely the bridge is to last. But," and he said this with a gleam in his eye, "It's never long before it provides you with the materials to build another one."

David thought of the meal that they had shared at Balthazar's house a couple of hours ago. The rabbit had been a pleasant change from the beef he'd been obliged to eat many times since his arrival. It was probably more plentiful in these parts, too.

"Where is he?" demanded Ramiro of Rosa when her arms were laden with the washing and hanging it on the line. His horse was stamping at the post next to the farmhouse and the man's eyes were clouded over and brooding. His jaw stuck out in the wind like the rock that David, unknown to the policeman and many days' ride away, had just climbed round on the hillside.

"I've told you," said Rosa who averted her gaze to the still snow-capped peaks, "He wasn't the kind to say what his plans were, and I'm not the kind of person to ask."

"But you said that you and he,…" he interjected angrily.

"Yes I did," she said slightly wistfully.

"Well, then?" Ramiro shouted at her, "Just what kind of a person did you think he was?"

His frustration was growing into a rage that was beyond his control. He'd been attracted to Rosa from the first moment he saw her on the night of the fire; she'd appeared out of nowhere and her long dark tresses had stirred his imagination. He imagined all sorts of things about her that he couldn't begin to confess to himself; her bravery that night had magnetised him and her smile had gleamed in him recklessly. He had seen in her what she was and he could never look at another woman again without desiring it in her also. And yet she was dangerous and he knew it. Now though she seemed to him little more than a prostitute; a betrayer, the perpetrator of a hoax.

There is no greater insult to a man than to defraud him of his dream; to belittle it. Even if he might have been part of that illusion himself. He didn't care that she was crying now or that he was becoming the means by which he shred his own desire into ever-smaller pieces.

"Whore!" he shouted at her, "It's not enough that you and that damned Yankee were…involved," he choked on his words, "Now I find out that you are probably carrying his bastard child as well!"

He rounded on Rosa and there was fear and loathing in his eyes, fear at something unnameable that shamed not only him but every man of his race as well,

"An American!" he stammered, "An American!" The spit was sliding from his mouth and the humility of the rejection was making his eyes bulge with distended pride. And yet Rosa had not rejected him, not until now.

"I promised you nothing!" she shouted back at him, "I promised you nothing at all," she said.

He veered dangerously close to her then swung away again at the last moment. He tried to grab her by the arm as she was leaving but she shook him off easily.

"He's dead, I tell you, he's dead!" he screamed after her, "Do you know who you've been sleeping with, you stupid little slut?"

She turned and looked at him, looked him right in the eye. Ramiro fell silent and mouthed the words to himself, repeating over and over again in his mind what he was going to do to the man when he caught up with him. But the girl was walking away from him resolutely towards the farmhouse across the frozen ground; she was taking away the fire from him as she did so, leaving him cold. He leapt onto his horse and cast a disparaging look at the farmstead. They'd better watch out. All of them.

"Yes, commander," said the man on the end of the phone, "We've had a report of a sighting in Candelaria, in Córdoba. They say the man was travelling with a girl, but is no longer with her. Yes, of course we will, this matter merits our fullest attention. The minister himself is right this minute on board a helicopter travelling to Córdoba. Yes, quite. The man's audacity knows no bounds, and he must be brought to heel. Immediately."

So in the time it had taken David and Balthazar to climb the mountain and reach the pool by the waterfall where the old man had said the best fish were caught, and in the time it had taken to catch one, a full squadron of police, the minister and his bodyguards and the local military had all been put on alert. Right this minute the man who had come into contact with the assassin was personally briefing the regional Chief of Police. A black car was racing across a red desert in San Juan towards the border control with Chile. A helicopter armed with trained snipers was whirring its way to the capital city in the province of Córdoba. The media had sent out its scouts and was already one step ahead at a picturesque village in San Luis where they were presently involved in interviewing the owner of its only hotel.

A kingfisher flashed its orange throat from across the other side of the water. Patiently it watched them as they sat dangling for a fish. Its wings whirred above the sound of the pristine water that plunged into the pool, darting suddenly downwards when it had spied something idling carelessly beneath the surface. It shook off the excess water as its head broke through the surface again and, with its trophy clasped tightly but still wriggling, emerged victorious.

"We have no chance against a machine like that," Balthazar said to David, "It is a freak of nature against which we simply cannot compete. When God designed the kingfisher, he had both beauty and the killer instinct in mind."

The minister of agriculture stepped out of the helicopter, his smile shining on the surface of his elegant patent leather shoes. He stopped for a moment to pass a hand through the locks of his golden hair as the precision lens of a photographer from the local government paper purred and clicked and froze him there for posterity. For an instant the crowds that had gathered at the airport to greet him were dazzled as he held his hand in the air, the platinum of the ring on his finger flashing like the trout in the pool.

"We've got time to catch another one," Balthazar said to his friend, "It'll be dark soon but I could find the way back from here in my sleep; I practically have done, sometimes."

The two fishermen sat intently trying to uncover their own mysteries in the pool. The kingfisher had long since departed and was now devouring its prey with an elegance and an economy of movement that belied the fury of the struggle beneath the water. One of the men, the older one, sat still as the falling daylight and let his eyes adjust themselves to the changing shadows in the water. The other, the younger of the two, sat reflecting on what had brought him here and how it was that in the midst of his journey fate had suddenly decreed that he should go rambling and fishing in the backcountry. For an hour they sat still in silence without speaking to one another. The pleasant glow on the other side of the valley dimmed to an amber hush while all around the pool became quiet and the trees that drank from it did so unnoticed. They whispered their contentment when they were replenished and let the wind caress their needles.

"Time to be going," said Balthazar as he dropped his line one last time into the unfathomable darkness. His companion stirred imperceptibly in his somnambulance. As the older man withdrew his line from the darkness there was a wriggle and a splash that awoke them both and a life gasped for life on the end of it.

CHAPTER NINETEEN

The silhouette of the landowner's house flickered through furry trees down in the valley.

"It was fate that allowed us to catch that fish, star-struck as it was by the promise of night," Balthazar said.

David was surprised that they could make out detail at this late hour in the fading light, at such a distance.

"I thought the sun set in the west," said David as they descended the approach to the rickety bridge that traversed the river.

"So it does," Balthazar responded, "It's shining from the west to the east where it is leaving that flank," he pointed far away at the highest mountains whose shadows dwarfed the valley.

"It's quite easy, if you think about it," expounded Balthazar, pleased to be asked to explain a matter concerning his valley, "If it is dusk and you have the sun on your left, then you are walking northwards to the Altiplano which stretches out for thousands of kilometres. If, alternatively, you are walking directly into the sun, then you will at sometime reach the great impassable wall of the Andes and surely come to Chile. Lastly, if the sun is on your right, then you are travelling south to the great frozen wastes of Patagonia and the glaciers, and still colder places."

"So what happens if you have the sun behind you?" asked David, in a self-congratulatory tone of voice.

"Then you are looking for mischief, man. No bugger in his right mind would deliberately head out east to where the capital is."

"Oh," said David, who had finally come to realise that his western wit and intelligence were of no practical use in this place. His eyes screwed up to where the sound of rushing water could be heard.

"What's at the end of this valley?" asked David when he had braved Balthazar's bridge of initiation once again and the shadowy silhouette of the house was finally made stone.

"Hombre, Mendoza, after a while. The highest mountain is there, and the best wines of all."

In the morning and untroubled by the rumours that were flowing from the east to the west of the country, Balthazar set about mapping out David's excursion. To a man of the son of the Count Rodinoski's standing, imagining maps and plotting them in his head had been a singularly special pastime. To David, it seemed that after an excursion rambling in the hills and an exclusive spot of fishing, there was no finer promise or temptation on hand than a visit to the home of the country's best wines. Whisky might not have been his drink, but David was by disposition cultured and had furthered his education on the fine wines of California and France.

Balthazar was enthusiastic as regards the lands he had never seen. He had too much to do that kept him busy here, but the prospect of this man, his friend tasting such wines as to make the poetry flow from him out onto the pages was an indulgence that had to be sanctioned. No specific time was set for David's departure, neither was a date allotted for his return, but nonetheless it was somehow tacitly agreed between the pair of them that David would of course pass this way again. They celebrated the contract with a jug of Balthazar's sweet but not inferior production, whose taste could only be described as reminiscent of the nostalgic wines of the Old World.

"A cup of coffee?" asked the regional police chief to his guests on the veranda whom had had time the previous night to settle into their lodgings. The Minister was particularly confident of a fine couple of days' hunting and had changed out of his formal attire into something more suitable for the occasion. He had with him a large pair of binoculars in an antique brown colour that perfectly set off the cream of his flannels and the sky blue of his shirt. For his part, the Chief of Police of Buenos Aires had preferred to stay in his traditional uniform but had brought along a large telescopic rifle that occasionally accompanied him on his, (not too frequent) forays out of the city.

"Yes, thank-you," said the Minister taking the fine porcelain cup that was offered him. He handed his binoculars, (a family heirloom) to his host to hold while he sipped at the steaming black coffee.

"Damn inconvenient business," said the Minister, (who secretly rather relished the prospect of the outing) to the two police officials. "I'd rather hoped to be concluding other matters," (he thought of the fishing party his friend the Minister in Brazil had invited him on), "Urgent business, requires attention. But I'm sure you'll agree that our current inconvenience is of some considerable urgency itself."

The Minister spoke with a not overrated degree of eloquence, as befitted his station; it was the refinement in the accent of his voice that could also be detected in the precision of his words that obliged his colleagues to grunt their agreement.

"How long do you think the whole business is going to take, roundabouts?" asked the Minister to the less senior of the two officials. He had only yesterday afternoon been roused from the bed he had acquainted with the fulsome leading lady of a lesser-known but very deserving theatrical company, and her pneumatic bliss awaited him deflated and solitary in their rented apartment. The more senior of the two police officials was horrified at the transgression of rank but too dumbfounded to say so. For his part, the regional Chief of Police turned astutely to his superior without opening his lips and thus gained the unqualified respect of the latter. The man with the telescopic rifle made a mental note of all this and assured himself that on another day the proper channels would be gone through and the matter executed swiftly.

"I should say we can expect a capture sometime within the week," prompted the most senior of the two police officials, taking matters into his own hands. The Minister looked to the sub-official for confirmation but the latter was turned resolutely to his superior who had moved to the edge of the veranda to take in the terrain. The Minister handed his cup back to the other policeman.

"I think we should keep the operation as closely under wraps as possible, don't you agree?" said the Minister who was dreaming of the voluminous drapes on the stage of his leading lady. The poetic irony of the situation struck a chord within him as he looked longingly for her through the lens of his binoculars.

"Notice anything interesting?" he enquired of Chief Carrasco who was sighting his rifle adjacently to him.

"Well no, and perhaps, yes," said the Chief of Police with a carefully aimed smile on his face.

"To the south of the house!" advised Balthazar to David when they had finished another jug and the American had stumbled out into the open, "That way we avoid contaminating our fresh water supplies and keep the fish more or less quarried where we want them to be."

David squinted at the sun to get his bearings, but, being still unfamiliar with the territory, took aim to the north where his ancestors might be.

In the afternoon Balthazar showed David formally round his land. He had vines growing strung between wires on a south-facing slope that his father before him had terraced in rudimentary fashion. Here Balthazar had also set out neat rows of vegetables; potatoes in the blackest earth and onions, sweet potatoes and courgettes. There were a few parched leaves where the cobs of corn had been plucked from them earlier and an olive tree or two helped to hold the soil together. There was a white jasmine on a trellis that was propped against one wall of the house alongside a pot of heather and, in front of the rusting tubs, bushes of oregano and rosemary that gave off pungent smells under the ripening sun. Closest to the house of all the trees was a majestic lemon tree so laden with fruit and flowers that the branches sagged towards the ground. This was Balthazar's pride and joy. It was a four-season variety that had taken a year or two to settle in properly but had ever since served him excellently. He patted the tree with affection and whispered a word to it as he plucked a lemon and cut it open with his pocketknife for David to try. The taste stung his tongue and made his eyes water. Balthazar grinned at him through the blackened lips of their morning's activities.

"It's a medicine," he explained to him, "It's good for aches and colds and it clears the head, too."

Later they rode out to the edge of Balthazar's land, past terraces that were crumbling and neglected where a gnarled old olive tree that had dropped a bough poked blackly at the sky. David was finally starting to feel a bit more comfortable on horseback, even though they were travelling at only a slight trot together on Balthazar's mare. The old man looked up at the sky in the direction the olive tree was pointing,

"There'll be snow tonight, if I'm not mistaken," he said, though how he could tell this David did not know. A thin wind was beginning to blow from behind them and the sun-dry scrub and bushes bowed their heads and nodded in front of them on the open plain. They rode as far as a point in the river where it turned off left and coiled flatly across the plain as far as the eye could see. David could see the end of the mountains ahead of them, still some distance off, with the lazy river widening out like beaten silver shimmering beneath them.

"This is the edge of our land," said Balthazar.

He looked skywards again, "We'd better be turning back," he said.

As they trotted back towards the house the wind began to gust down the valley and tug at them more fiercely. It began to drizzle, and there was ice in it.

"Thought so," said the old man, "It could be quite heavy tonight."

They reached the safety of the house just as the first flecks of snow were starting to stick wetly on their foreheads. Balthazar unsaddled the mare and led her into the stable. He patted her neck and spoke a word so softly to her that David could not hear it.

The older man's eyes were full of a strange light like the light that had descended over the valley as the snow began to fall more thickly.

"Can you hear it?" he asked David.

David turned his ear carefully to the fullness of the valley behind them and strained to listen.

"I can't hear anything," he said.

"Precisely," said his companion.

On a frozen road a lone horseman was riding back from the farm he had ridden out to. They were fully aware of who they had played host to now. The young dark-set man had spent his fury and something in the look of the farm owner, Pedro had prevented him from taking out his umbrage on the woman even more. Faced with the presence of Pedro, Mercedes and the two other women, Ramiro had lost his resolve and been unable to say what he had come all this way to say. He would turn his attentions to hunting the man down now.

As the snow caught up with them and piled up on the roof and on the ground about the house, Balthazar and David settled into a silence of their own. The warmth of his host's hospitality had had an effect on David and he was feeling unworthy of the kindness that had been shown to him. He wished that he could have been kinder to his daughter, even to her mother, to Rosa and Pedro and the people on the farm. There was a yearning inside him to want to repay them all in some way, but here at Balthazar's house he had begun to feel inadequate to such a task. The only sensible thing he could do was to leave Balthazar to his peaceful solitude and not get him further involved.

"I should be going, you know, Balthazar," he said to his friend out of the smoke that drifted round the chimney.

"Hombre, are you mad?" asked his companion puffing at his pipe, "Where will you go to in this weather?"

David thought of the lands to the south that had been described to him in tones of reverence by his host.

"To the place where the best wines are," he said convincingly.

"I see," said Balthazar somewhat crestfallen as he stared into the dregs of the last jug they had finished after their supper, "Of course, a man of your age needs to get out and see the world for himself," he said, "Now if I were a younger man, I might accompany you," he continued with a sparkle in his eye that hinted at adventures past as well as imagined ones that had drifted away from him, "It'll do you good," he said to the younger man, "And you'll have plenty to tell me about on your return. You will," he hesitated, "Be coming back this way, won't you?" he asked.

"Hombre," said David, "Who wouldn't return to the most beautiful place in the province to see his old friend?" he said with sincerity.

Balthazar's smile warmed like the coals of the quebracho that was burning in the hearth, his eyes dancing with the sparks of the fire that was crackling.

"In the morning, then?" asked Balthazar.

"Yes," nodded David, although he had begun to have second thoughts about leaving now that he considered just how perilous his journey might be with all the snow that was falling. He pulled back his shirtsleeve and scratched his arm with his nails. Balthazar noticed the deep scars across the tissue of the arm and raised an eyebrow.

"From a previous - adventure?" he enquired of his friend as he moved his pipe to the corner of his mouth, biting on it as he did so.

"You could say that," said David without further elaboration.

In the morning David woke to find Balthazar busying himself about the house. His friend had been up since very early even though it had been bitterly cold and he had no genuine reason to have abandoned the warmth of his bed so abruptly. There was a smell of ham frying in the kitchen and the sizzle of eggs frying in the grease. David found his sack laid out for him on the table and when he came to lift it to put it on the chair he found it heavier than he'd expected. There was a bump sticking out of the material and when David tapped it he heard the hard response of a jug that had been stashed there for him. There was a huge wedge of cheese folded up neatly in a white handkerchief and bread, olives and other provisions too.

"I can't accept all this," said David, concerned that the old man might have left himself short and might not be able to get out to stock up in the bad weather.

"Of course you can, and you will," said his host in a firm tone that left no room for argument.

When they stepped out into the courtyard, Balthazar bade him wait a moment. He disappeared round the other side of the house and came back leading the horse behind him. It was fully saddled and there was a roll strapped to its back. The snow had stopped falling but its thick carpet had coated everything. David looked puzzled at his host who was not dressed for a journey, but his host answered him before he had time to ask him the question on his mind.

"You can leave her at the store in the next village down the valley," he said to David, "Just let her take you there, she knows her way."

David was overwhelmed by his friend's generosity,

"But I..." he began.

The old man shook his head with authority as he slipped an imperceptible word softly like the wind into the mare's ear. He turned to David and the matter was decided.

"I can pick her up when I'm next down there," he continued, "I have business to attend to there and they know me well. They'll look after her."

Balthazar was holding the horse steady with one hand as he held one of the stirrups out for David to climb into.

"Come on, man, I haven't got all day," he said to him, urging him on.

David was hoisted into the saddle and before he knew it the old man had slapped the mare on its rump and it was cantering away from its owner before David had had a chance to say good-bye. He tried to turn in the saddle to wave to his friend but the horse held steady in its course. Out of the corner of his eye David might have caught a smile deepening like the valley but his host had already turned to go indoors and was disappearing from him.

The horse slowed to a steady trot when it was at a safe enough distance from the house to do so. It seemed to sense the breeze that played across the shimmering river that had somehow pressed silver into David's eyes and pockets. So many partings, so many journeys; when would he be free of them? He thought of his daughter and heard the sound of water flowing alongside him, and in front of him the sound of her laughter.

It took hours to trot out of the valley whose sides sloped ever outwards. The horse stopped when it needed to, to drink and to munch at the oats that had been hung in a bag round its neck, its breath steaming in the air. The pale mountains glistened along the spine of the river and were untouchable. The breeze that rippled off their backs and haunted the river on the flood plain was caught up in the horse's hooves and led it dancing out onto the plain. The horse had scented something far away and she was enchanted by it; it had its own path and its own motion and she was carrying its rider along with it.

It took them all day to reach the staging post that Balthazar had called a village. Horse and rider wore the expression of creatures that had been exposed to a landscape too immense for the mind's reckoning, so that when they pulled into the village they looked as one. The mare stopped outside the only store amongst the sparse buildings of wooden construction and lowered her head to graze on the grass that was growing there.

David exchanged a few words with the owner who was unaccustomed to strangers and held himself in reserve for those he had known longer. The man agreed to look after the mare until its owner had arrived to collect it. He neglected to ask David any further questions or enquire as to the wellbeing of their mutual friend. David purchased a stout hunting knife with one of the silver coins he had acquired and although the shopkeeper was at first suspicious, (biting into the metal to test its veracity) he accepted it.

Outside the store David went to talk to the horse and to reassure it that its owner would be arriving to collect it soon. A sudden thought occurred to him and he went back inside the wooden lodge to enquire of the shopkeeper whether he knew of anywhere roundabouts that he might purchase a horse for himself.

"You leave me ten of those coins and you can ride out of town on the one you rode in on. Balthazar and I are business partners and I can speak on his behalf," said the man concluding the transaction.

"Are you sure?" said David doubting the shopkeeper.

The man raised his eyebrows, "Don't worry, he'll be able to purchase two horses up in the village with the money you leave me. Business is business and Balthazar's not a sentimental man."

There seemed to be no choice in the matter and rather reluctantly David handed over the money. The shopkeeper bit each of the coins in turn before putting them into the pockets of his apron and nodding. David swung his leg high into the saddle and cantered down the only street of the town. His head was held high and the few locals who were out in the streets turned to watch him leave.

He rode for two days and most of the night before he next came across a town of any standing with a store to call its own. There he stocked up on essentials and enquired in a vague way of the south and of Mendoza.

Once he chanced across a tumbled-down shack that had been abandoned on a slope by the river and spent the night there in more comfort than he had become accustomed to. The mare had found itself pastures as they moved away from the snowfall and the mountains declining in the west, receding away from the branching river in ever-growing but ever-distant peaks. She had led him this way and was certain of the way she was heading; David was content to follow her.

One night later on he had spent cold and freezing but had then retrieved the lighter that Rosa had given him from the bottom of his haversack, which was a souvenir of their time together on the coast so long ago. He put dry grasses and twigs together in the manner that he had learnt and pushed small branches into the bundle, watching the sparks grow with delight like he had with Rosa. Later, half-asleep and startled by the cries of some nocturnal creature, he'd fled the scene, with his horse content to idle under the half-light of the winter's night unperturbed by any such imaginings. Finally, with the skies clearer and starlight to lead the mare's way, they had entered into a dry and rocky place where their footsteps echoed stiffly on either side of the narrowing canyon.

The noise of the river that had followed them for more than a hundred and forty miles gushed far down below as it licked at the steep sides of rock, cleansing and scouring them. They were in the province of Mendoza now, but for all David knew, they could have been anywhere.

The sky was clear and the night cold and bright. The track underneath them was hardened and small pools that had collected in its potholes were freezing over with the reflection of the stars in them. David was weary with the journey and his saddle soreness had become a lethargy that was dulling his mind. The horse plodded on aimlessly, pulled as if by gravity to some place beyond her endurance. This was unfamiliar territory for them both and the momentum of the journey out of the valley and across the great flood plain had deserted them.

"We'd better make camp somewhere around here, girl," David said to her, bending towards her and patting her neck. But the sides of the canyon around them were steep and high and the horse had no intention of stopping in such a strange place. He murmured a word of comfort to her and whether it was the wind that funnelled there or the enclosure of the place that brought David's words back to them louder, he could not be sure. They broke through a stretch where the sides of the canyon had become impossibly narrow and its walls vertiginously steep. The track rounded a bend and sloped down in front of them. Perhaps the horse had sensed pasture there, or perhaps the wind had whispered to her of a less confined space where it was playing. She broke into a canter and took David and their provisions down to the river again where it opened out more gently and a small patch of grass grew beside slender trees.

"Good girl," said David as he stroked her, pausing an instant to take in the place before he dismounted. The mare was softly nibbling at the tufts it had found, untroubled as if the passage through the eye of the canyon had become nothing but a memory. David, however, was breathing deeply, drawing in the rarefied air carried down by the river. They were protected from the breeze itself though in this hollow and once David had tethered the horse and settled himself into his sleeping roll, he quickly forgot where he was and fell soundly asleep.

At night he dreamt a dream in which he heard voices calling on the plains above them. A horseman was accompanied by others who lagged behind him and the whole party halted when it caught up with him at the edge of a great cliff. The young rider on his dashing white horse pulled back from the ravine and tried to urge the creature over it, but it reared under his command and shied away from the edge. His cries urging the horse onwards ran away with him over the plains and the night that was smothering them made them distant and smaller.

David awoke to find the mare still tied where he had left her. He looked round for signs of morning but the night was still thick and it had got colder, too. Pulling his haversack closer to him underneath his head and huddling himself further inside his bedding he blinked up at the dark and the sky rained its light on him.

He was stiff when morning and the mare woke him and his throat was dry. He hobbled down to the waterside to scoop up a handful and filled up his water canister from the fast-flowing current that was cold and greedy. The horse snorted as David nibbled at a crust of bread, as if anxious to be untied and tired of waiting for the man. He untied her clumsily and hung on tightly to the reins as he did so; perhaps it was the cold that had got into his fingers, or perhaps it was that the wind itself had whispered too loudly in the night and they both had heard it.

She accepted her burden grudgingly but then the warmth of the man's legs and something familiar about the smell of him settled her into her stride and soon they were riding easily. Up on the track they passed a tumbled-down building made of incongruous breezeblocks, its hard concrete floor cracked and poking out wires. He looked down at the road they were riding on and realised that its surface could only have been made by humans and machinery. Soon they came to a wire fence round an electricity pylon with a battered and rusting sign that read DANGER. Trailing from the pylon were loose cables which sagged and were distorted, one of them coiled on the ground at its feet. They passed through an opening that had been left unlocked, its padlock firmly shut round a bar in the gate that had swung open. The horse broke into a canter again and kicked up the dust on the road, slipping through the opening on the other side of the wire perimeter. They were glad to leave it behind; this cruel reminder of civilisation. David was breathing hard again and the eyes of the mare beneath him were gleaming; the steel and the concrete were an ignominy, an ugly thorn like the thorn of a cactus in the desert set there to spite them.

David wondered what he was doing here, in a place which the drifting slopes of the pale mountains and the great plain had neglected. Almost immediately the hard road ended and the rude interruption of the power station was behind them. The rock was red and crumbling as they proceeded and although there was a clear track in front of them, the bulldozers and other heavy machinery that had fashioned it had forgotten to finish it. The aimlessness of their wandering into the canyon the night before was forgotten too and horse and rider deemed it unpropitious to remain in the vicinity. Further on they came across a sharp bend in the road on a promontory where there was a sign that had been bent backwards by the force of the wind. It read 'Atuel River'. They tore up the track heading downwards with the red rock crumbling, staggering round a boulder or a lump of the clayey soil as they put distance behind them, loose earth and dust clattering into the air and filling their passages. After an hour or more the horse trotted down a bank to the side of the river where the land was more forgiving and they could drink from the stream. They were still inside the precipitous walls of the canyon but here there was a larger space where the air was sweeter and a few wild flowers poked their heads out of the grass clinging to the banks. David picked a small yellow flower when he had dismounted and held it up to the sunlight – its petals were slightly sticky and soft to the touch. For no particular reason he put it carefully in the pocket of his jacket so that he might keep it there, in the jacket that Pedro had given to him on the farm.

As they climbed back up the bank to rejoin the track the sun that had been partially hidden scouring the dry plains above crept into the creases of the canyon and rounded on its corners. For an instant the smile of his old friend Balthazar greeted him, but it was soon gone, like the retreating figure of the man beside his house. He could see that the boulders perched high above on either side of the canyon were balanced precariously, pushed and propped like marbles put there by giants in a game; though they were still far away at the high end of the reddening slopes their weight looked colossal and truly dangerous. At the head of another turn in the valley, the dark shapes of two huts could be seen poking through the trees.

The wood was straight and tall here, poplars again, waiting like matchsticks to be bowled over. But in amongst them, more compacted and perched on their craggy holds, were other species of tree and bush, algarobbo and myrtle, sagebrush and huge tufts of rosemary. David approached the huts with some caution as he drew near to them. He couldn't be sure who might inhabit them and he mentally prepared a speech with which to counter anyone who might surprise him or chance to be about. He remembered what Balthazar had said to him, about the adventure, and he decided to anticipate anybody's interrogation of him by casually informing them that he was a tourist on holiday and was enjoying the scenery.

There was no sign of movement and no noise as David and the horse approached the entrance to the huts. Their roofs were covered with rolls of asphalt that had been nailed onto them, which their builders had deemed unnecessary to trim to any precise fashion. There was an old steel drum that had been painted bright blue placed underneath the overhanging lip of one of the roofs, presumably put there to catch rainwater. Now that they were close by the huts, David could see that round the back of the second one there was a long low building which, ludicrously, looked like a canteen of sorts. He decided to use his advantage and called out to any occupants that might be inside, clapping his hands loudly as he did so in the manner of someone who might be trying to attract their attention, not trying to avoid it.

He clapped his hands together loudly again and the horse whinnied for good measure. Then he waited a good five minutes in the ensuing silence but nothing happened. Nothing at all. He turned round to look at the horse and found her muzzle right next to him, her lips slobbering with saliva.

It was easy to force the lock on one of the doors; he hit it with a rock and the padlock snapped open. It was exactly the same size and the same make as the padlock hanging on the wire gate at the entrance to the power station, but David hadn't noticed this. He proceeded with caution inside into the interior where the curtains had been left closed. He put his hand up to something to the side of him and succeeded in pulling down a shelf that gashed him on the head and rattled its contents onto the floor. He sensed immediately that he'd been bloodied and began preparing his excuses, his alibi. He wasn't on holiday at all, no; he'd come here looking for refuge after several days' hard riding and could they accommodate him? He'd pay for the damages, of course, and even thought of offering to chip in a little bit more to help them do up the place. They'd understand, of course they would. But there was no-one there, not a soul. It wasn't much of an invitation and David found himself feeling quite disgusted at the people who had left these chalets in such a state.

"Not much of a welcome," he said to the horse as he went back outside.

He was tempted to break the lock of the other hut to see whether it was in any better state, but then decided against doing so as it would leave him with an awful lot of explaining to do. He walked round to the long low building and knocked firmly on the door. It swung open on its hinges as he was walking away from it and he went back and climbed the steps to it again to take a look inside. David could see that it was indeed a canteen. There were rough Formica tables that looked peculiarly out of place in such a wild and remote place as this. What on earth the proprietors were thinking of using these tacky tables and awful plastic chairs David wasn't at all sure. No wonder the place had been abandoned; no-one in their right mind would decide to stop here through choice.

"I bet there's a rotten choice of menu," thought David as he manhandled the row of tin cans behind the counter and held them up for inspection. He went to the back to a small adjacent room and poked a finger in a dry sack of flour, then he kicked another sack as first one, then another potato with tubular sprouts on them rolled across the floor. He flicked a switch on the wall in disgust and to his amazement the light came on. This incident so surprised him that he went back into the dining room and pulled up a pink plastic chair to one of the tables situated beneath the television that was mounted on the wall.

As the television was already plugged in all he had to do was press the button on its side. Ha, he thought to himself, that ought to do it. With a crackle and a fizzle the television screen came into life at full volume. He was so taken aback that it was some moments before he had recovered himself and was able to move to the television set to turn it down by jabbing at the button on the front of it. He turned it down to a volume that was almost inaudible and laughed at his temerity like a nervous schoolboy. He was still laughing at himself as an irate policeman in an over-sized hat was holding up a picture of a man he was anxious to arrest. It was him, in a picture that he recognised as belonging to the driver's license that had been lost along with the rest of the contents of his briefcase. Frantic to know what was being said about him, he ran to the television and jabbed up the volume just as the policeman with the indignant expression on his face had stopped speaking and was turning into the crowd of reporters. His face was replaced by a prolonged shot of the flag of the republic set blaringly to the strains of the national anthem.

In the middle of a hut in the middle of nowhere, the rousing tones of the national anthem were ringing out loudly across the canyon. In a panic David sprang at the television and almost dragged it to the floor, grappling with its weight for a few seconds before managing to right it again and heave it back onto its support like a strongman heaving a granite boulder onto a plinth.

It rang out at him again for a second time when he plugged it back in, before he lunged at it and a chef who was dicing up meat on a cookery program lurched into view. He jabbed frantically again and was able to enjoy the vision of the meat being chopped on the board at a slightly lesser volume.

He left the television purring away and went into the room with the sacks where he had previously seen a pair of kitchen scissors lying. He picked them up and hacked at his hair like a madman in an asylum, watching it come away in tufts that fell to the floor. Satisfied that he had changed his appearance significantly, he set to rummaging through a draw full of cutlery in the canteen to find a sharp knife to shave himself with, but he stopped himself just short with the blade when he remembered that he had a better knife in his haversack. He strode out of the building purposely, passing the innocent horse on the way, then turned on his heel and strode back into it, sack-less and knife-less. In a moment of clarity it had occurred to him that he didn't have a beard in the photo that had been held up on the television screen. David scratched his jaw; it had been some considerable time since he'd had a shave and both moustache and beard were coming along nicely. It was only then that he realised that he'd just cut his hair to a more approximate length to that of the photo on his driver's license than it had probably resembled moments previously.

He put a hand to his hat and was immeasurably grateful to find it still sitting there; how he hoped that some creature that was definitely of the four-legged variety had made away with the other one and eaten it.

CHAPTER TWENTY

The horse looked at him suspiciously when David finally summoned up the courage to brave the outside world two hours later. It shifted its weight from one foot to another as David reeled with the enormity of the consequences of his actions. His intuitions told him that he could trust Rosa and the others on the farm not to give him away, but how long they would be able to keep his passing through there quiet he didn't know for certain. There was Ramiro, after all. Balthazar was hidden away from prying eyes in his valley and the group of musicians had done so much for him that although they'd obviously realised he was on the run, they seemed to be on his side. The men with the grey jackets had been positively friendly towards him, at one point; but the hotel in San Luis was a luxury that might prove to be too altogether too expensive.

He looked up towards the teetering boulders and thought hard about what his plan was. After some considerable machinations on the subject he came to the conclusion that he didn't have one. The best plan was to do nothing at all, for the moment. He would eat as well as he could, rest the horse and sleep on the problem. That was the best plan of all. To do nothing.

On a white horse across a great plain a horseman was galloping through the snow as it fell, covering their tracks behind them and muffling the trickle of the stream alongside as it slowly froze over. His superior had been against the idea, but the young man had insisted on it and whilst the main party rode out to meet the officials who had come out from Buenos Aires, the lone horseman went on ahead in search of the stranger.

There was a nip in the air and the poplars were sawing backwards and forwards with the breeze. For an awful moment it seemed to David that they were waving at anyone who might have overlooked this fissure in the land as if to remind them of its existence, and then he pushed the thought out of his mind. He looked up at the steep walls of the canyon achingly and realised that if he was found there he would be cornered.

David led the horse out of sight behind the cabin whose door he had broken open and wrapped its reins round an outstretched branch. He sat on the wooden step to the cabin facing the scree slope before him and peered at its red earth through the trees where the light waved in and out between them and the murmur of the river disappeared. There he sat for a very long time before the light had dimmed in his eyes and the whinny of the horse made him rub them.

David flicked his head up at the sky and saw that in the still clear air as the light of the sun shut down on the earth the light of the cosmos was whispering its riches. Directly overhead infinitesimal candles were being lit whose trails shone a path through a dark corridor in the sky; it curved and it twisted like the giant root of a tree that was scattered into a million particles of light. The sky opened up vertiginously above him as the gravity of his solitude and the silence of the place held him deep into the dark earth. 'Come away with me' whispered the horse and he stood up stiffly to untie her.

He closed the door to the hut carefully without a sound and they tiptoed down to the river where the mare drank with the stars on its back and the leather of its flanks shining under them. They walked up the echoing canyon like sleepwalkers to where the water had slowed to a trickle, like mercury spilling onto the sand greenly and slowly. As the sun shut down its light completely upon the land the candles of the stars were flickering in their moorings. As David led the horse back up the road with their steps ringing out boldly under the dry night he lifted his hand above him. Fingertips reached out towards the tunnel he had seen in the sky where stars and the galaxies that spun them were intricately weaving their web out to space. He could feel the chill of the wind across his fingertips and the ice of a wall whose face was too cold to climb.

They walked together step by step while their faces froze in the water in the potholes in the road and their reflections disappeared underneath them. David thought of his daughter, his wife, the lover he had taken and everything that had been was, burning in the slow candle of his mind as the million particles of its phosphorescence glowed and were hushed. In what memory was his presence remembered, and in what eye?

Carefully they picked their way through the boulders that were slumped on a bend in the road. One held the next behind it up the hill, and that one held the next one and so on. Huge as planets that had come crashing to ground, the red of their iron rich cores was slowly seeping away. One, immense as houses, had jumped through space and crashed across the road into the stream in the valley bottom, where a trickle of water dammed up behind it and was forced to inch its way around; but the water was persistent and would not be detained forever. The wind sighed in the scrub and the strange tree that peppered the opposite bank, just out of reach of the fallen boulder.

They turned back then, for no reason, and David led the horse to the cabin. No vehicle would be able to pass on the road where the fallen rocks of the cliff were resting, held in suspense where a tiny trickle of water, green and silver had inched its way round them and was quietly gathering momentum.

He slept uneasily in the narrow bed that night with the curtains open at the window, at any moment expecting to hear the rumble of the world collapsing in on him. But night held its breath and wearily and under protest, David was dragged towards sleep. Outside the horse nibbled at the grass around her ankles, but her ear was open and cocked to the night, ready to dance away with the wind.

Morning came and claimed them but David was drowsy with fatigue and the enchantment of the night. Several times he stared into the bleached sunlight of morning before he realised where he was and heard the sound of the horse munching outside. The thin sheets on the bed were for decoration only - his bedroll had dropped onto the floor and the blood was trapped in his boots where his feet had swollen inside them. Shivering and famished he shook off the last splinters of sleep where day scratched at the windowpane, though night still steadfastly clung to him. Outside the horse chattered through her teeth and as she shook her flanks David could see the darting light of thousands of tiny arrows turn to moisture in the air and rise.

"He must be heading over the pass towards Chile," said the police captain, "We've had reports of a sighting in San Luis from some, (he was referring to the press who had beaten them to it) sources."

"Very well," said the Chief of Police, "He's probably somewhere in San Juan right now, if he's not already over the border," he added with a slight trace of menace.

"No, no, I'm sure he's still somewhere in the country," responded the subordinate who had detected the veiled threat in his superior's voice. "Yes, that's correct," he continued, "We already have a car waiting at the head of the pass at the border control. Two snipers. No uniform. Yes, sir. Right away. Immediately."

He put the phone down and marched outside to address his men. The sergeant saluted him briskly with his white-gloved hand stiff like a visor. The rest of the men repeated the motion a split-second later, their white hands rising like the crest of a wave. The captain nodded to the sergeant.

"Right!" shouted the sergeant, "You know what we're up against and you know how little time we probably have. This is a matter of national security," his bottom lip quivered as he said the words, "It's our duty to stop this man. We must and we will!"

The gloved hands snapped back to their sides one after the other with an infinitesimal separation of time between them. The sluggish green water had filled up to capacity behind the slumbering rock and the crest of its wave was breaking.

"What the hell was that?" shouted David to the horse as it reared on its hind legs and strained at the reins. It came clattering to earth just as the aftershock of the huge boulder that had fallen sent tremors underneath them spreading through the land.

The men were formed brightly on parade in front of the Minister. The Chief of Police who had joined him from the city and the regional Chief of Police stood one slightly behind the other, both of them slightly in deference to the Minister, his cream slacks pressed neatly and the creases in them starched. It had got quite cold in spite of the sun that was shining but the sky blue of the Minister's shirt was uncovered in an air of relaxed elegance. The telescopic rifle of the man beside him stood at a perfect angle of ninety degrees by his side and the bayonets on the rifles of the men before them were gleaming.

"Right men," said the Minister as he walked down the row addressing them, "We all know the task ahead of us."

He turned abruptly in front of the row, and as he did so the two men to the side of him coiled in a whiplash, the most subordinate of the three snapping into place just in time.

"We will be bringing up the rear, but our task is the most important, for we must spread a net with holes so small and of such a width that no fish can slip through it."

He paused, pleased at the poetry of his metaphor, the memory of his mistress's fishnet stockings in his mind. Then he stopped like a ship that had run suddenly aground.

"Captain!" he shouted with such ferocity that the bayonets of the men moved involuntarily. He nodded at the Chief of Police beside him who in turn nodded at the other policeman.

"Yes, sir!" bellowed back the official. The telescopic gun at the leg of the police chief twitched. His subordinate continued,

"Advance scouts have gone out to the border with San Luis and are moving to the south and to the west as we speak. A car is waiting to accompany the foreigner at the border control where we have set up a road block in the mountains. One especially trained mounted policeman has gone on ahead and should be in San Juan within the day."

"And I," interrupted the Minister, "Will be directing proceedings from above in the helicopter, from where I should get a better view of things."

He swept a hand through his hair and thought of his collection of framed photographs. He was actor and director, a consummate performer.

The blades of the helicopter were whirring as the men saluted and he ducked inside the aircraft. He bid them farewell and strapped himself into the seat beside the two unsmiling men in black suits and sunglasses who had been waiting there all the while, leaving the Chief of Police to carry on in his absence.

"Right men," said the police official as the helicopter wafted into the sky and he raised his gun in salute. He was pleased to be back in control where he should be, and if his language wasn't quite so poetic and his dress sense quite so flamboyant as those of the departing Minister, it was perhaps because the nature of his affairs was all the more routine. He turned gruffly towards the battalion,

"We've got to catch this bastard before he can do any more damage. Shoot on sight," he lowered his rifle, "Just make sure it's not one of our own," he added, not without a trace of irony. He nodded curtly to the official beside him, who took his turn to address the men,

"Groups of six. You've already got your paths mapped out for you. Sergeant, you're in charge of deploying the men. Any news, you relay back through your leader,"

"To me," intervened the senior officer who was testing the sight of his rifle on the desert that was stretching infinitely away from them. "What of your horseman?" he added, dropping his rifle.

"I expect to be hearing from him at any minute," said the regional police chief who had sanctioned Ramiro's leaving.

David untied the mare when she had settled nervously to the ground. The land still trembled under them and the impact of the dislodged boulder had shaken the foundations of the cabins. He tried to close the door to the cabin whose padlock he had smashed open but it swung open on its hinges in obstinate refusal. He was about to saddle up but then had an afterthought. He ducked inside the cabin again and smoothed out the sheets on the bed. He put the pencils and other implements in the tins that had fallen from the shelf and stacked its broken remains neatly in a corner. Then he led the horse to the canteen where he left her waiting outside. He stacked all the plastic chairs neatly in rows again and shuffled them to the side. He unplugged the television then went to the storeroom and turned the split sack of potatoes around to face the wall. He strode across the floor of the canteen heedless of the noise of his boots, then he stopped and plugged the television back in again; but not before he had jabbed at its controls and made sure it was set on a different channel.

He shut the door firmly behind him, and, with the three empty tins of beans he had eaten safely stashed away in his haversack, he mounted the mare and they raced up the road. They slowed down when they reached the group of fallen boulders, David involuntarily glancing past his left shoulder at the precarious slopes as the sun pricked his eyes. There were clouds of dust hanging in the air where the recently plummeting rock had ripped through the road and left its indent there, before it had continued headlong down the riverbank and smashed the silence of the stream. He glanced nervously upwards and crossed his chest, mumbling to himself as he did so.

Ramiro had already crossed into San Juan, urged on by the fire that was burning in him. He outrode the pain of the fatigue in his limbs and fed himself on the emptiness that was hourly growing inside him. He had preferred to keep the solitude of the journey to himself, the company of his horse to that of other men.

David and the mare turned north where the track they were on crept out of the fissure in the land. Ahead of them shining in the distance was the solitary cone of the highest mountain on the continent, Aconcagua. David remembered what Balthazar had said to him about the south and the colder places where snow and ice might blind a person and freeze bones as if they were paper. "Damned bloody report," he said to himself, if only he'd kept it in his head instead of writing it all down. He kept the shimmering wall that was now just visible to his left and rode out onto the raised plain where one province would inevitably meet another.

They stopped in the midday sun when the wind sweeping down from the distant mountains had entered the man's bones and the cruel sun had parched them, its heat in his face but his fingers numb. There they found a small gully where water was dripping from the mouth of the black rock and David ventured inside it. It was narrow, so he had to dismount and lead the mare strung out behind him as they picked their way up it in Indian file. What little vegetation there was was prickly here and David had to make his way around cactus and other scrub that picked at his clothes. After an hour or so of walking the mare found herself a dark pool to drink from where the thin transparency of butterflies wavered above its surface. He left the animal there and pulled himself up over the lip of a rock to where an even darker and more secluded pool was emptying its contents beneath it. He lapped up a handful of the water but it was bitter with the taste of minerals that bled from the ores in the rock. David filled his canister and set it down beside him.

Suddenly revived he set down his haversack also, and, free of the saddle, clambered up a bank to where larger cactuses than the ones they had scraped through stood proudly on its crest. Behind him was a wall of crumbling rock that prevented any thoughts of a climb to the top to see what there was. On this particular sparse and craggy hillside the sun seemed to linger; fruits were bursting on the thumbs of the cacti and when he looked closely there were the smallest of flowers growing between the stones. He looked down at the horse where it was swishing its tail and saw the shapes of insects that droned above the water. He had read something at school once, about how an insect flew on the edge of extinction every time it got close to the surface tension of water, which was enough to glue its wings permanently to it and drown it. They hovered and skimmed the surface fishing for other creatures even smaller than themselves, and every time they dipped towards the surface they risked their lives.

He took off all his clothes and sat naked on a rock that had been warmed by the sun. He sat cross-legged and let the sun warm his limbs also, feeling the ancient history of the stone peel off layer after layer of himself, letting the cooling breeze play on his face.

He put his boots back on and carried his pile of clothes down to the pool. There he removed them and plunged into the freezing water the colour of midnight; for an instant he was submerged in the water and all the secret of its quiet existence spilled into him. David laughed as he shook himself dry and pulled on the clothes which stuck to him and would not slide over his skin. He picked up the beret and stroked the rough velvet of its surface.

The mare did not seem to want to leave the spot and although the grass she was nuzzling at was dry and bristly amongst the stones, she appeared content to stay. David tugged at her reins but the horse was resisting.

"Come on, girl," he said quietly to her, "We have to be leaving."

They had ridden for only half the day and David was wary that they hadn't travelled far enough away from the cabins, not realising that the next village was only a day or so away, across the border in San Juan. But the breeze whispered soothingly and the tingle of the dark water where it had touched his skin felt pleasant beneath his clothes. He had few supplies left, for he had not dared to take more than he had already eaten from the canteen, but they would be just sufficient for the night even if he had to ride on an empty stomach in the morning. David scraped his hand into the bottom of the horse bag and let the mare lick at the meagre, floury remains.

"We'd better give you a name," he said to her, realising for the first time that he had given her none, nor that he knew what name Balthazar had called her by. He looked back at the rocks and saw the suggestion of Indian faces there, noble and defiant but crumbling with age; it was just his imagination, but perhaps they had been here as well.

"Maitén," he called to her, and then he wondered where the name had come to him from.

He lay down by the edge of the pool the horse had been drinking from, sure that they would be hidden here. As he turned his head once more to cast a glance at the rocks guarding them from behind, he saw what looked like a rabbit with an upright bushy tail jump incredibly from one rock to another, or perhaps it was a squirrel with rabbit ears. Its ears seemed peculiarly well shaped to catch the slightest of noises and the light slanted through them opaquely. It was some forgotten species that had not written itself into any natural history book that he'd ever read. He took out the three empty cans, lined them up and listened to the sounds that came from them where the breeze that was blowing passed like a hand cupped over mouths.

"Maitén," he whispered to the horse again and she came close, nuzzling at a clump of dry grass that he held out to her in his hand.

Day lingered all afternoon while the butterflies shared the quiet of their pool with the travellers, the transparency in their wings grew as the sun picked them out, holding them against its transitory rays as they ceaselessly fluttered and then, in the blink of an eye when David had turned, disappeared.

"Maitén," called David, and she came close to him.

He felt no need to tie her as he scrambled back up the bank where he'd sat previously in the sun. He was curious about the red swollen thumbs sticking out from the cactuses and cautiously touched the barbs sticking out from the plant as he climbed up to them. They were needle-sharp and not worth risking his fingers on, so he took out his knife and cut one of the fruits away from the cactus carefully. The aroma of its flesh was not unpleasant and he bit into the unknown fruit in an explosion of taste, his tongue savouring the sweetness of the pulp on it.

In the late afternoon beneath the sun the dry grasses and shrubs released their pungent fragrances into the air. He looked down at Maitén and she was calm as he sat on the hillside gorged on the fruits that he had cut. The sky bowled slowly to orange on the horizon as underneath its canopy David sat quite still listening to the earth's great discourse; if he remained perfectly quiet and without moving he could hear the land speaking. Huge and rolling in front of him, the sunset drew his eye into the crevices in the land, strange painted shapes whose images floated in his mind. The sentinels on the hillside stood patiently pointing off in the direction the sun was leaving as shadows were cast and the busy world of insects began to hum and chatter beneath the growing night. Day heaved its last glowing breath across the land and all creatures in its presence fell silent.

The clackety-clack of the dimly droning helicopter was slipping through the sky, pulling the darkness about it as it spun away to where night was already waiting.

David spread out his bedroll beside a rock that was close to the pool, having eaten the last of his food from the haversack. But he knew that there, up on the hill where the fingers of the cactuses were dipped in the night, the blood-red fruit that swelled on them would still be growing. He didn't feel any need to tie Maitén to anything and in any case there was little that would have served had he wanted to do so. He dozed off as she shuffled in the dust and the clamour of day was replaced by the passage of night. Voices were calling out in the darkness but David was asleep.

He dreamt of a horseman clattering down a lane but the horse was white and not dark like Maitén. He could see the vague outline of a road sign but could not tell what it said on it. Higher up among rocky peaks the eyes in the face of a rag doll that had been dropped and abandoned looked blankly up at the sky and the sound of a young girl laughing somewhere in a village far below could be heard, but her voice was strangely unfamiliar although the name she was calling was his. Six horsemen drummed across a plain but the man they were pursuing outpaced them; the white horse on which he rode flashed under evening and galloped beyond the thunder that broke off from the mountains.

It had rained in the night when David woke. He was surprised that rain should fall in such a place as this place where dry twigs snapped under feet and their bleached wood turned to powder. But the spots like tears on the ground were unmistakable and when he touched his bedroll it was damp.

He led Maitén out of the steeply curving gully, picking his way back down it with care, though once he stopped to turn back and look at the rocks behind them. Their faces were already hidden by the curve of the slope and the words they had called to him could no longer be heard.

"Maitén," he said to the horse and she lowered her head as if she understood him.

Back out on the flat where the morning strung out its web a mist like silk was slowly slipping before the sun, uncovering its expanses where the eye confined itself to limits again and the vast range of the land became unimaginable. Houses, trees and people were invisible scattered in the immeasurable distance, and any village that might be hidden there would decide alone when it would find them.

"How far to Calingasta?" called out the horseman breathlessly. The farmer who was leading his goats down the lane was taken aback, startled by the intrusion of this rider into his early morning world and the horse that foamed and was panting. The tinkle of the bells as the goats moved chimed slowly but the stranger was impatient and would not hold still for an answer. His accent was not from these parts and the horse looked as if it had been ridden through hell and back.

"You have a long way to go yet," answered the peasant removing his cap, "The mountains are in between and at this time of year they are dangerous. You won't make it today," he said, but the rider cast him a scurrilous glance and the eyes of the man were black and sleepless.

"There's a group of houses at the foot of the mountains. If I were you, I'd rest..." the farmer continued, but the rider was already cantering off down the lane before he could finish. The rider could not hear him and the jingle of the bells among the goats chimed into morning where leaves that still foolishly clung to branches would soon have snow laden on them. Like a white blossom the goats scurried down the lane that was full with the sound of their ringing, where walls rose on either side of them.

The dark speck of Maitén and her passenger inched across the landscape. Sometimes she was visible where her hooves sank in the mud, but at others she was just an inky spot like a spider slipped from its web whose legs have been crushed and rolled into a ball. The smell of the horse was bleeding across the land, slowly and inexorably it drifted into the high swaying stalks of the grasses and made itself one with the earth that was clayey and held it. In a featureless landscape the ripple of high mountains that scraped the sky flat was for miles the only point of reference. Distance was measured not by how far away they were from you, or how close, but how silent you had become; how far the emptiness of it all had become part of you.

David barely stopped to wonder when they had crossed the dry riverbed and passed the sign which read *San Juan*. The great mountain chain that coiled like the back of a silvery eel remained aloof and unreachable off to their left. The solitary cone of the highest mountain set apart from the rest was behind them now but it loomed even higher the farther behind they left it. It cast its swinging shadow like the great forefinger of a giant forever pointing their way ahead.

Ramiro had reached the foot of the mountains whose name was the Sierra Invernada. They were older than the Andes and stood before them; a hard jagged place whose lofty heights had once been higher than their cousins but had since been ground down by time, whose mill forced all things, even rock, through it. At more than 3,000 metres the pass through the Sierra on the way to Calingasta encountered little in the way of company. But a desperate man seeking solitude might find in them a means by which to clothe his silence before stepping down from their hard heights to the fertile valley below. He had taken food at one of the houses and had been forced against his will to let the horse rest there. After so many days of riding it understood the nature of his quest and had grown hard too with the miles that disappeared under it. It, like its rider, thirsted for a final destination in a place where it might see an end.

They were hesitant about entering the village where the white and blue cloth and the gold of the sun upon it stood flapping on the white pole in the plaza. Midday was not long past but the town was asleep and the infants of its school were at home now as the dark mare and her passenger stopped on the edge of the town. But in the fields that had risen and the orchards where plump apples waited suspended beneath the ticking of the clock, there were farmers who had to tend them. Hats bent low, backs turned to the sun, nevertheless they were too numerous for a rider and his horse to step through their territory unnoticed.

Maitén and David stepped briskly down the main avenue, at the end of which in a hard clean plaza made of shining concrete the cool blue of the flag shining in the golden sun slapped on its pole. David rode purposely down the avenue, the clip-clop of Maitén's hooves ricocheting along the length of the abandoned road where not a single vehicle made a noise and the farmers' sweet scythes marked time elsewhere beyond the boundaries. On reaching a store David wrapped the reins expertly round the bar with one coil of his hand. He pushed the door to the village store open where its female owner and a long-time friend were counting up numbers in the empty tills of their eyes.

"Can I help you?" asked the storekeeper addressing him.

David had tugged the front of the beret down over his face and pointed to a large lump of ham that looked as if it had been there a century.

"Half," he said without any preliminaries, looking at the ham.

"Half a kilo?" asked the middle-aged woman.

"Half the ham," answered David matter-of-factly.

He turned his back on the women, not intentionally out of

322

rudeness, and scoured the shelves for other things of use. These he obtained mostly by pointing at them and when the bill had been written on the crisp white paper of a bag and the numbers had whirred and clicked in their eyes, David counted out the notes and coins and laid them on the counter before the women. He was quick to notice the silver coin that had somehow got mixed up with the pile. He retrieved it and bit it and quickly replaced it with a peso coin.

"Thank-you," said the storekeeper and David was swiftly outside.

"Horseman," said the older, grey-haired companion whose services were free of charge.

"Yes," said her friend, "You can smell it on them. Gruff as buggers they are, all the time in the world on their hands and no time at all for courtesies."

David swung into the saddle with one slick movement and clip-clopped on past the plaza down the avenue that led out of town. There were very few people in the streets and those few whom were there were not surprised to see a red-skinned horseman and his darker horse go riding by.

'Calingasta 20kms' said the sign. With a daring preposterously bolstered by pragmatism, David stopped at a public fountain and refilled both his canteen and the empty bottle whose sweeter contents he had emptied earlier. No-one lifted an eye to him, but an old man who had been carefully set out and left to ripen in the sun tugged at his own worn beret and flushed with the memory of when he was younger too, and all the plains and all the mountains had trembled as he rode by.

They stopped by an orchard on the outskirts of town whose fruits had drunk in too much sun in the open, south-facing field. Withered and maggot-ridden their carcasses were being eaten where they crashed to the ground. Maitén nosed the apples but was not impressed. A little further on David noticed a dirt road turning off and a red-bricked building that said 'hotel' set some way back, although as they drew near, its colossal incongruity in a place like this struck him. The villagers were so unused to tourists that even he hadn't been recognised. The fact that such a large recreational building was standing in a place like this was absurd in the extreme – the door was standing wide open and a musty air of tranquillity emanated from its interior.

No-one who was anyone gave them a second glance as they trotted up to the hotel and David dismounted and entered cautiously. He walked to the furnished counter fashioned expertly out of deep red-coloured wood. An old-fashioned silver-coloured bell was mounted firmly there and the wooden shelves partitioned into little boxes behind it were empty, save for one forlorn yellowish envelope in one of the boxes. An old but immaculately preserved lamp stood in a permanent state of innocuous idleness on a shelf running below the desk. David raised his hand hovering above the bell but took it away again.

"Hello?" David called out feebly with his beret firmly pulled down. He walked timidly off to his left where the darkness of a long room recumbent with furniture invited his curiosity, there he peered through the open door into the lounge but saw that the curtains were drawn and no-one had taken up residence. There were fine white tablecloths laid out on the heavy tables but there was no-one present to eat off them. He went back out into the corridor and put one foot on the creaking stairs before retracting it and repositioning himself in front of the counter. Impulse got the better of him and hesitantly, conscious of the grime on his hand that might tarnish the bell, tapped it ever so lightly with his finger. No bespoke-suited bellboy appeared to carry his luggage. No hotel manager with an air of contempt was there to frown at him. He walked back outside to where he had left Maitén waiting and cautiously led her round the side of the building, ready to barter over the price of the artfully produced ham he would offer them should he chance to meet anyone and they ask him what he was doing there. But there was no-one. He opened the door to a large, airy barn and led the horse inside it where he found that the hotel management, both considerate and absent in the extreme, had thoughtfully provided for any occasion with an abundance of hay for their customers' mounts.

David whispered in Maitén's ear and closed the door behind him, taking care to close the latch that had been so generously left open before him. He brushed his shoulders vigorously with his hands and, not without a certain trepidation, walked back into the hotel lobby. A hand reached out for the bell again but an innate sense of diplomacy that was struggling to the surface in him suggested that it wasn't the proper thing to do, so, after one brief peak into the peaceful lounge he creaked his way up the stairs to inform them that they had forgotten to lock the entrance to the hotel. Anybody could simply walk in unannounced if they weren't careful.

"Hello," he called out timidly at the top of the stairs with the ham in his hand, but no reply was forthcoming. He opened the door to a splendid room where the bed was already made and the sheets were immaculate. There was hot running water that steamed out of the showerhead into a deep enamel bath that rested on ornate feet, but most intriguingly of all, someone had left a 'Do not disturb' sign looped round the door handle on the inside. This he graciously took and slipped over the externally facing part of the doorknob before he closed the door to. What interested David most of all though, after he had showered and then soaked his feet in the tub, was an old framed map of the country which allowed him to see exactly where he was, as indicated by a precisely placed red dot on it.

CHAPTER TWENTY-ONE

Downstairs in the cool of the lounge David found a covered platter full of bread rolls and, directly underneath the shelf he found it on in a covered rectangular dish there were small oblongs of butter wrapped in silver foil. These he proceeded to strip of their paper, one after the other, 'til several bread rolls and various oblongs of butter had been consumed. He did feel guilty that he was consuming the hotel's fare without first having formerly checked in, but a fine sense of propriety in the man encouraged him to do what any other honourable person in his position would have done. He took out the silver coin he had bitten, polished it on his trousers and deposited it into the rectangular dish from whence he had taken the butter.

However, he couldn't help but feel nervous and there was an old, (probably black and white) television set mounted on a cabinet at the end of the room. David noted with relief that it was unplugged. He tiptoed out to the lobby, but not before he had deposited two large oranges into the depths of his jacket and considered leaving another coin in payment for them. But then he remembered from past experiences that it was never a wise decision to throw too much money about in a hotel; especially if one didn't want to attract the wrong kind of service. He waited patiently to be attended but, and this is what most galled him, the hotel management didn't seem to care whether he was there or not.

Now that he had paid for the food he allowed himself to feel critical of the establishment. They had a fine hotel here, but David was guessing that the heavy, finely crafted furniture hadn't been constructed under *their* supervision. Indeed, there was dust on the arms of the chairs when he investigated further and the curtains could certainly do with laundering. Furthermore, one of the arms of the chair he was presently seated in was loose and in need of repair.

"Disgusting," David said to himself, "What a way to run a hotel. The least they could do is be here to see to the guests."

He strode into the lobby again and waited for some assistance. He waited and waited. He had things to do and he was growing impatient.

"I demand to see the manager!" said David ringing the bell.

Its magical clang echoed in the musty air of the interior but its slowly dimming noise was the only thing that stirred.

His eye caught the yellow of the envelope again, sitting alone in one of the partitioned boxes. He cast a quick look behind him and walked round to the other side of the desk to retrieve it, holding it up by one corner and allowing its contents to slip to one side. Then he held it by an opposite corner and repeated the process in reverse. He lifted it to his nose and smelt it. There was a faint air of a faded perfume on it, rosy and feminine in an antique sort of way. He slit the envelope open carefully with his knife and unfolded the note that had been inside it. It read simply: "Not here today."

David hastily inserted the note back inside the envelope, looking around him as he did so and threw it and its contents onto the floor in disgust. He retrieved it, dusted it down and deposited it through the hole in the antique wooden mailbox that was positioned at one end of the counter.

"Well that's my vote," he said to himself as he marched back upstairs to the room. The framed map that was hung on the wall continued to intrigue him and he lifted it gently off its hook to get a better look at it. It was heavy because of the glass in its frame and he set it down on the bed to balance it. As he was doing so, a hinge at the back of the frame gave way and the glass that was covering the map slid out and fell flat on the bed in front of him. The map slithered out after it and curled up at the edges as David was left holding the empty frame in his hands. Carefully he set down the frame and smoothed out the map on the sheet of glass. The red dot that had been marked on it proved extremely helpful and, with the map insistently curling up into a cylinder, David helped it on its way and rolled the whole thing tighter. This he deposited in the open haversack he had left by the bed, then he proceeded to fit the glass back into its frame, closed the hinge that held it there and lifted the frame and its glass back onto its hook on the wall. He pulled it slightly to the left on its wire and succeeded in balancing it where it had been hanging sharply to the right before. One thing was for sure; he was in the middle of nowhere and there was no-one here to tell him otherwise.

Well, the owners of the hotel certainly weren't going to get any business like this. David wondered what on earth the management was doing in charge of the hotel when they obviously had no real interest in maintaining it in the first place. They ought to leave the establishment in more capable hands, then they could go off and enjoy their leisure without having the whole place falling into neglect.

It's not much fun being in a hotel when you're the only one, and David had decided to check out immediately. He went back to the lounge and retrieved the silver coin from under the lid of the butter dish; he was appalled at the service and had also decided that he was in no mood for tipping.

"Well, if that's their idea of a hotel," he said to himself when he was in the saddle again, "Then I'm the town mayor."

He spat at the earth as Maitén and he went clip-clopping down the red dirt road. When they had left the town and the last orchards far behind they detoured to stop at a river so that Maitén could drink. A few poorly clad children were playing upstream and David noticed that none of them had shoes on. Maitén had caught a whiff of something in the air and was unsettled. The children were playing at fishing with a pole and they ambled down to see the strangers who had appeared out of nowhere. There were two little boys, one of whom was a toddler and had to be carried over the large stones that bordered the river, and a girl of about seven or eight; presumably their sister. Her clothes were in rags and on her face she wore the vacant expression of a child who was severely undernourished.

Her large doe-like eyes were unmoving and she looked at David and the horse as if they were ghosts who had picked their way over the stones like shadows. She stretched her empty hand out towards them without saying a word and it hung limply when nothing was put into it. Maitén snorted but the girl showed no sign of being frightened.

"What do you want?" said David looking into the hollows of her eyes.

"Give me," said the girl without smiling. She continued to hold her hand outstretched in front of her and David reached round to take the sack from his back. He broke off a piece of the ham and beckoned for the girl to come closer, but she remained standing where she was with her hand still outstretched. The older of the two boys held his baby brother firmly and stared wildly at the rider, half-hiding behind his older sister's legs.

David geed Maitén a little closer and when his stooping figure came into reach the girl snatched the meat from his hand. David fished into his pockets where the weight of the fruit was and held out the two oranges for the two boys. The older of the two dropped them onto the rocks as David tossed them to him.

"Who are you?" David asked the girl softly.

"Who are *you*?" replied the child as she picked up her brother and ran away laughing, retreating into the brush by the top of the riverbank with her giggling companions. As he turned to look at their disappearing forms David could make out the roof of a shelter behind the brush that was so poorly devised and made of such shoddy materials that he had earlier mistaken it for part of the land. Surely they must live there, he thought to himself, but it was impossible that they did so.

The little boy's nose had been running but they were none of them wrapped up for the cold. It swept down now from a great icy place that had mysteriously and invisibly camped each time closer to the travellers without them being aware of it. The glittering peaks were still some way off, but the river flowed from the foot of them where the wind shook like a dry serpent down the water-course and rattled in the stones that were lodged there. The meeting with the children had unsettled Maitén and she lifted her head at intervals to catch the breeze in her mane. She had scented something far off that was growing nearer; almost undetectable at first like a far-flung snowstorm that was just a hint of ice in her nostril; but when she breathed in its menace was deeper. David, too, had been unsettled by the appearance of the children; the eyes of the girl called to him from within the depths of a dream.

The road to Calingasta was back where they had come from, where they had entered the rocky course of the water further down stream. But when he pulled her Maitén resisted turning and her nostrils were

329

lifted towards the highest peaks. She flung her head down towards the water and the motion of something passed over her limbs.

"Where to, girl?" David whispered to her. She raised her head as the figures of the poorly clad children appeared once more through the brush at the top of the bank; the empty expressions haunting their faces. David geed Maitén up with his knees and they moved off up river. He turned round to look for the children once more but they had disappeared; the empty hollows of their eyes and their rags camouflaged by the thin trees. Horse and rider picked their way over the stones carefully, and in every rounded shape of every stone they passed, David saw the rounded eyes of the girl; he saw a rag doll that had been dropped and abandoned in the wind.

A white horse was riding hard over a summit. In a desolate place where chills shook the sides of the walls each breath was torn from the lungs of the rider. His coat flapped about the flanks of the stallion and the only heat there was was squeezed into its eyes. The Sierra Invernada is a cruel place, where a lone telephone box that has been dropped from space dials numbers too meaningless to exist. Its glass sides freeze up and frost over even when flowers in the valley below have heralded in the spring. There is no season but winter there and any traveller fool enough to wander where the wind is the only king might wish themselves elsewhere; they might hear ghosts walk upon the mountains.

"Ramiro? Where are you?"

"Yes, sir. Calinga..."

But the words of the horseman were cut off abruptly by the howls that screamed and blew down the telephone line.

Maitén was leading David away from the village. She had been nervous all along the course of the river, ever since the appearance of the children, and she picked her steps with her head low to the stones as she tried to find a way through. The wind had chattered in the scrawny trees that afternoon but by evening it had become a fierce gale blowing; now they were travelling into the teeth of the storm. David struggled to wrap a thick towel from the hotel round him under his jacket. It was better than nothing and he was left wondering what scrap of cloth, what scrap for improvisation the children on the riverbank might use to keep themselves warm. He didn't expect that they had any, or that the roof of their precarious home would stand up to many onslaughts like this without failing.

Since the hidden shelter of the mestizo children on the riverbank David and Maitén had passed no other sign of human presence. Of course, he'd never intended to stay a night in the nice warm bed at the hotel; it was only chance that had led him inside in the first place, that and a sense of curiosity. Perhaps it was the need to be near people again. The curious thought struck him that the front door of the hotel might be torn open by the gale and left knocking against its frame without anybody realising.

There was nowhere to take refuge that he could see, so when Maitén crossed a place in the river where the water was shallow and rocks had been put there as stepping stones, the evidence of some human hand was comforting. The storm was picking up down the flat of the riverbed and Maitén took them higher up on the opposite bank, out of the reach of the fingers of the storm where the flank of the slumbering hillsides offered more protection. She was climbing steadily and breathing hard, all the time travelling upwards.

"Where to, girl?" said David, but she had a resolution of her own and not even the storm would stop her. Then it began to snow, whipped flakes that were lashing their faces and stinging their eyes. The whiteness was being flung behind them, sucked into a void where the long-reaching finger of a brooding giant had pressed down on the surface of the land, the hurricane that spun there drawing everything to it. A rider was coming over the mountains and while one horse went upwards, another was drawn down from its heights.

"What is it, girl, what can you see?" asked David as the path that Maitén was taking grew steeper and steeper. Through his half-closed eyes he could make out a crouched shape that was looming large on the opposite hill. The air was growing rarer and the words sticking in David's throat were being plucked from him by the force of the storm.

He was suffocating and the eyes of the little girl were watching over him as the horse pushed on ever closer beneath their black brooding shapes on the hill. She was silent and terrible and the only words that came from her were the roar of the howling wind and its screams round the rocks. The looming mass up above them was showing the white of its skull as the snow began to stick there. One word. Then another.

"Help me," called David, "Help me!"

But Maitén was pushing upwards relentlessly and the sound of David's voice was being drowned out. Two holes appeared in the darkness and into their great caves the horse was moving. Horse and rider finally disappeared underneath them and then, with the wind sailing over the huge outcrop of stone, the snow like lightening whipped over their heads. Suddenly they were standing at the entrance to two huge caves and Maitén was panting hard.

"What is it, girl? Where are we?" he wanted to say, but the storm had robbed him of his voice and the unmoving eyes of the child from the valley were pressed blackly into his.

They took refuge in the back of the caves where the darkness of centuries swam in their depths. David pressed himself close against the mare's flanks as his frozen hands fumbled with the canister and the water he sipped burned in his throat. He wanted to ask her were they were, but somehow he already knew. They were in the place where centuries had slipped over the mountains and God had once looked out over the valleys; they were in the place where the words of children had been muffled as if they were tiny vanquished insects. They had been born and grew suffering into adults; their children were born and grew suffering too. And all the while on the plain the others came. They brought with them great destruction, death by a slow disease that was still eating at the people.

Ramiro came thundering down the mountain just as the worst of the storm had tried to trap him on its heights. He'd heard terrible, strange noises that had tugged at his ears; the stallion had heard something too and was chasing it. It pushed on relentlessly underneath its rider and when the man faltered it caught him. Too many sleepless hours were on him and too many miles. The anger that consumed him was leaving him and his heart, pumping furiously, spilled the blood away from his veins. He'd felt the claws of death upon him, pulling at his coat and sticking to him with its tongue raking over him; the wind howling stiffly as bones. He could not shake it off; he could not shake it off and when the wind howled, her face came back at him pressed too closely to his heart.

The fire that burned like two candles in his eyes had frozen over, but in his memory images flickered idly and could not be put to rest. They stirred beneath the crust of ice that was forming, even into the frozen stone that sank there and sent out its ripples black like scars; even unto his heart. The smile playing round her lips mocked him, coyly innocent, and when the foreigner had looked at them, he'd known, yes he'd known that he'd lost the girl. She was his now. He knew, yes he knew, that he'd lost the girl.

The people on that distant farm had once welcomed him, but he'd done away with that memory too and pushed it like a closed fist unfeeling into his pocket. He was riding away from all of them, but somewhere deeper he knew that he was leaving her behind; his memory did not trust him and it wanted its revenge. So sweet the snow falls, ripping up roads and cracking them. So sweet the snow falls, covering looks and smiles. So deep the snow falls, freezing over miles.

The hard ragged rider who came clattering into town would not let the people rest; some said that he was possessed and that his horse would die under him. But the horse was as strong as its rider and would not give up its quarry. They found a house and took lodging there from a man too afraid to turn them away. He said he'd seen the storm riding after them and heard the mountains break over their heads.

In the caves the storm ravaged round David and Maitén. Pressed into the back of its skull out of its dark recesses she heard a horse whinny across the falling snow.

A white horse was restless beside its rider who stood feeding it, its nostrils flared with hail and ice and it stamped as it tried to shake them from itself.

A man's eyes peered out from caves where another horse was still panting.

"What is it, girl, what is it?" David said to Maitén, but one look at the mare told him all he needed to know and they weathered the storm tightly.

The blizzard blew all night and long into the morning. Perched high above in the great caves David had thought he'd heard voices and several times he'd woken from his fitful sleep with words in his mouth that weren't his own. The horse had lain down beside him but her head, too, was turned to where the voices seemed to call from outside the shelter of the caves. The land fell away from them steeply where a horse and her rider had staggered upwards and all about the broken silence of the world snowflakes stuck one by one and amassed a weight and volume of their own. David was shivering in his bedroll but the cold that flashed over the caves had frozen on other summits, upon the jagged teeth of heights where a horseman had gone riding by.

In the sapphire blue of the morning when the storm had travelled over and the wind had shipped the clouds out to sea, David and Maitén woke from their stupor. Half awake with sleep, man and animal finally stood up in the caves. The day was as blue as the limitless land over which it sailed and was unsteady on its feet in the altitude. The land fell away and everything beneath them was new born. As David's eyes cleared with the morning he thought he saw the tiny droning speck of an insect whirring away from him, far out on the horizon. He searched for it again but it had disappeared like the chattering storm.

An old woman was sitting spinning at a wheel. It was her husband who had shown the man into the house the previous night when the storm was at its height. She could smell the scent of the sweat still on the horse as she sat thinning out the wool into a single strand between her fingers.

"Where did you say you've come from?" the old woman asked Ramiro. He was sullen from his journey and resented her intrusions into his privacy.

"Córdoba," he answered gruffly.

"That's a long way to travel," she replied.

Ramiro did not answer her but stared into the corners of the room. The woman continued to spin her wool with the clackety-clack of her spinning wheel cutting through the silence.

"Pass me another one, would you?" she asked him and he picked up the white-grey wool from the table and handed it to her. Her nimble fingers twisted it round the bobbin and although the clear light of day shone through the window no light shone into her eyes. The woman sensed the urgency in the man as she sat there patiently spinning and twisting her wool. Her bony fingers, precise as needles, teased out the mass to a single finely spun strand. The snow had piled up in the village, blown into swelling drifts that prevented no traffic into it or out and she could sense that the man was impatient to be leaving.

"A girl, is it?" she asked him.

Ramiro glowered as if the storm was still in him.

"Official business," he contested her brusquely.

He could not say what it was that had brought him to this remote village wedged into its valley where the weight of the high Andes was laden above. He had taken a course due west from his village in Cordóba without thinking about the mountain ranges he would encounter on the way, but now that he was here, he felt an uneasy sense of having arrived although he could not be certain that he was in the right place. He'd brushed the horse down in the peasant's stable and he could still feel the urgency in its limbs. Now the weight of snow piled up deeply in the village and on its roads as the long journey caught up with him and memory after memory slowed him down.

The spinning wheel turned and in the fascinated light that rained in through the window the woman teased out her strands. Quick fingers, never idle where her mind was untangling a riddle. She could hear the sound of his heart beating underneath the muffle of his coat. Her husband brought them food when she had filled one bobbin but the younger man picked at it aimlessly.

"Eat," she said to him, "You have come far and who knows how far you still have to go."

He bit into the bread and the slab of cold meat was tasteless, the crumbling goats' cheese like powder in his fingers. He washed it down with a cold sip of cider.

"It doesn't look like you'll get out of here for a while," the woman's husband suggested cheerily, but although the day was glad where the back of the storm had been broken and daylight had flooded in to relieve them, their guest stood brooding.

"Official business, you say?" said his host who was drawing the curtains back further, cancelling out what had been so real the evening before with one deft movement of his hand.

"Police," said Ramiro with a false sense of pride, "There's a foreigner on the loose and he's been involved in something nasty back in the capital, in Buenos Aires," he added to make them understand. It wasn't that Rosa had been with someone else, it was who she'd been involved with that mattered. Or so he lied to himself.

"I've been sent ahead to track down his whereabouts," he continued, warming to the task and sparing himself the worst, "I'm sure he's here somewhere in these parts and the horse," he looked round sheepishly at the pair, "Has got the wind of him as well."

It was the most that he had spoken to anyone during his journey, but the more he talked, the more he got the feeling that he was holding something back. The more he heard himself speaking the more he retreated into himself.

"I'm not at liberty to inform you fully of his crimes," he added halting himself, feeling the weight slip from his shoulders, "But I can tell you that what he has done is against the laws of this country and he must be caught. Do you have a phone?" He asked.

"Hello, yes, Ramiro speaking. Yes, in the mountains. I got cut off, a blizzard. No, I haven't seen him yet, but something happened in one of the villages I passed through. I'm certain it must have been him – there'd been some kind of festival there and he seems to have been involved. What? Yes, sir, of course it could have been somebody else, but I have a feeling that he's," here he paused for a moment, "Arrogant enough to try such a trick."

The line went dead for a moment. The Chief of Police was on the other end. There was a pause in which the suspicions of one man were confirmed by the silences of the other and then Ramiro was given instructions.

"Right away, sir. I've taken lodging with some locals while I wait for the snow to clear. Yes, sir. No, of course they don't. I quite understand."

He put down the receiver and smiled grimly at his hosts. He was himself again, and now wore an air of authority as he straightened himself up in the room.

"I don't expect to be staying here long," he addressed his hosts, "But while I am here I would be obliged if you would keep this matter to yourselves. There's no knowing what allies he's managed to make or what contacts he might have. He's a dangerous man," he added in a threatening tone, "And there's no point in giving away my whereabouts to him unnecessarily."

He strode to the edge of the table where the woman was still spinning, and stopped short of placing his hand on her arm. He bent his head down towards her quietly but the woman feigned to notice him and no words came from his mouth.

"That'll be all, for now," he said, regaining his composure, "Ah, but there is one other thing, if you would," he smiled as cleanly as he could to the owner whose cheerfulness had been checked in its stride, "Perhaps you can show me where I can find the local constabulary?"

The owner put his cap and scarf on and led the officer down the road through the deep drifts that had collected towards the direction of the local police station. But by the window the spinning wheel turned clickety-clack, the light that shone through it making long fingers white.

Fragile and alone in the caves, save for the company of Maitén, David was worried. He'd walked several times out onto the edge of the natural balcony where the lip of rock cradled him dangerously above the void. As if a sleepwalker or a tightrope walker testing his equilibrium, he made his way out to the jutting rock then walked back inside. He was afraid to let the light of the day cast its spell on him and skulked around in the corners of the cave retracing his steps.

What had appeared to be two separate caves when they had stood before them during the storm had proved to be one roomy chamber with a narrow passage through some fallen rocks connecting one space with another. Outside on the shelf there were yellow stalks of cobs of corn that had been blackened by frost and by age whose contents had been eaten earlier. Amazingly, it seemed to David, somebody else must have been up here and had at one time eaten their food in this place. He felt safer exploring the territory of the caves from the inside and squeezed himself through the passage where, on closer inspection, it appeared that at one time it must have been much wider. As he stepped into the second space, which was much larger than the first, his eye was drawn to a large, smooth-looking rock situated at the edge of the main entrance.

As he brought himself close he was astonished to find that the rock was as smooth as if it had been polished and had quite a deep hole in its centre. The smoothness of the cool rock invited him to slide his hand over the side into the elbow-deep cavity. He let his fingers feel the grey stone and they felt warmth in it where the flat of his hand had felt cool on its surface before; he pulled his hand up sliding it over the rock enjoying the sensation but then stopped abruptly. His hand was resting in a shape exactly like the shape of a hand that was worn into the rock. He felt something there for an instant before he removed his own hand quickly.

When he looked closely at the place where his hand had come to rest on the edge of the cavity, his eyes told him that the shape of a hand had been carved into pure rock where hand upon hand had mashed corn there. Staggered, David walked outside to retrieve a stalk from the pile that had been tossed there. It all fitted, but the enormity of the discovery was too much to take in. He could hardly trust his own eyes, but the feel of the rock was on his fingers and he held one of the small eaten cobs in his hand. He sat down on the shelf and let his feet dangle into space. The sun was glinting on an object beside him and when he picked it up and held it close for scrutiny he found that he was holding a small and exquisitely formed arrowhead.

Maitén was standing with her head outside the cave they had slept in. David turned round to hold the arrowhead up to her but she was looking far, far away off across the valley.

"Look girl, look where we are," said David in tones that barely contained his excitement, but the horse was looking elsewhere, letting the pure air breathe in her nostrils. David put the arrowhead into the pocket of his trousers for safekeeping. Now that he was out in the sun, David felt ready to explore his surroundings and the curious sense of foreboding that he had felt earlier in the caves had been replaced by a feeling of sudden elation. He stood up on the lip of the rock and walked precariously along its edge with the whole space of the mountain swinging beneath him. He put his arms round Maitén's neck when he reached her but she was aloof and kept herself for the most part inside the shadow of the cave.

The quietness disturbed her and where she looked not a living thing moved. Out across the valley in the snow that was deep as arms all was quiet; no town hurried about its business for there was none, no shepherd pulled his flock across the straggling mountains and no bell was heard. But deep in a stable a white horse was listening, where its master had gone through the town on foot. It listened for where the footsteps of another creature had become motionless, where it flicked its head and the wind pulled its mane and its owner called it but it stood still and alert in its body, ready to run at an instant.

David left Maitén and clambered up behind the caves to where the roof shone white and glistening. Their tops were frozen over so that he had to prevent himself from slipping.

"Maitén!" he called out to her, "Maitén!" into the sounding valley, but the horse was attuned to something else beyond the ear of her rider, where a creature fiercer than herself was listening. It neighed within its stables behind the wooden doors that closed it in. The woman spinning at her wheel heard it also; she felt the long thin thread that her fingers were holding though no light reached into her eyes or their corners. And on her forehead the pale of the snow that she had once seen as a girl was vanishing, where the shadows cast down from the mountain blocked it out and seeped into her, whispering.

The echo of David's voice came back to him from the deep mouth of snow out of the cave of the valley where loneliness had made a passenger of him in diminishing tones and chanted his name. He shouted out twice but after the echo only silence followed. He climbed back down to the caves where they had sheltered and led Maitén warily out onto the ledge. Her footsteps were unsteady and she flinched when the buckle of the saddle was fastened underneath her. With David leading her slowly, she picked her hooves up high between the stones that had fallen. She stood shivering, turned sideways, when David lifted himself onto her. She slipped almost at the first turn when David had tried to urge her back down the slope from where they had come, her forelegs together, sliding through the scree and snow before she managed to pull up.

"Whoa, steady, girl," David called when they had come to a stop. She dipped her head downwards, then downwards again as if a noose were being teased over her neck. She moved off only when David dug his knees into her sides and his bobbing weight threatened to bring them both crashing down. She went more carefully then, picking her steps with caution as the weight of David's body pushed her downwards. Then suddenly she slipped again as they rounded a steep corner, her knees folding under her, rocks and the mass of her disappearing beneath David. One leg was pinned excruciatingly by her flank, forced hard against the sharp stones. Then almost at once it was free and the weight of her was sliding off him. She whinnied and tried to stand up with the stones sliding dangerously under her; for a second she righted herself and then she rolled over as the entire hillside moved into motion.

"Maitén!" called David, "Maitén!" He stood panting hard as the part of the hillside that had given way and which had almost carried both of them over the edge disappeared downwards. It tugged at smaller stones that followed after it where David lay close to the ground and felt it slide beneath him. When the world finally stopped spinning David stood up gingerly, desperately searching the valley above which, minutes earlier, he'd walked suspended on its ledge.

"Maitén!" he called again and her name came back to him diminishing out of the great valley of snow. Half sliding and half stepping where the purchase on the slope had disappeared, he felt his way down to an outcrop where heavy boulders bordered a precipice. He skidded the last of the way and came to a stop behind the largest of the rocks, panting and drained with the effort.

"Maitén!!" called David, but as he peered over the edge the minuteness of the stones that showed through the snow beneath told him that nothing could have survived the fall. Below him was a small dark shadow spreading like a bruise on the snowfield, like the stain of some dark berry that had been flattened. Sickened and leaning with both hands against the stone, David drew in his breath in quick gasps. His rucksack was on his back but his bedroll had been strapped to the back of the saddle – he swore at himself for putting thoughts of his own survival before that of the horse. A great pain welled up in him and he shook his raised fist at the sky.

"You bastards!" he shouted, and all the surrounding hillside shook with his words, while hands that had threshed corn slid over rock like the centuries passing, smoothly wearing the stone down. Their brown arms, dark as the mare, had slipped one after another into that hole, into the great throat of the snow.

He groped his way back up the steep incline as if in a trance, crying and cursing the mountains where they were laughing at him, the sound of their weight rushing still in his ears though not a single stone moved now. In the sapphire blue of the late morning David was alone. He moved off to his left fearful and fretful and mumbling to himself. His eyes fixed on the slope; watchful of its fissures he stepped down unseeing where the land was less steep, wary as of an invisible serpent that had pulled everything down with it into its hole.

When he reached a safer place where the snow had piled deep he let out the breath he'd been carrying inside him. There was only the dark spreading bruise on the snow. With eyes stinging with the snow he tried to penetrate its glowing whiteness. But its flat hand had spread over the land levelling all, where in the dark crevices of his memory David still searched for Maitén. The area off to his side looked deeper and more treacherous still. There was a hollow where the land curved into a basin and then, sloping down, disappeared off the edge of the world. He kept far away from it, even climbing out of his way up to his left so that hands could feel out the permanency of the rock where it jutted black and icy above the weight of snow perched there. Like a dreamer stepping out of a nightmare, David picked his way blindly down into the valley.

CHAPTER TWENTY-TWO

Ramiro had returned from the village police station with the senior officer and three of his men. Together they had commandeered the only tractor in town and used its plough to clear a path as best they could through to where another road met their track. The local official had tried to insist that at least two of his men accompany him down to the border with Mendoza, where it would be easier for him because of the inter-state highway. Reports suggested that their valley had caught the brunt of the storm, and he would be glad of some assistance in finding his way out. Ramiro declined and was determined to set out alone.

He paid the couple that had lodged him for the night and urged on them the necessity of keeping both his passing through the town and his affairs quiet. The old man held his wife round her shoulders as the policeman put down the phone. He walked out of the stable leading his white stallion and it was the last that they ever heard of him.

Not many travellers from other provinces passed through the town of Calingasta, and the snow that was heaped on the houses and had drifted against their doors kept most of its people inside and the story of the young policeman's passing to a rumour. But after he had left and the people were once again about their business, when the snow had melted with the sun shining on it, the story of a romance dropped quietly from lips like the drip of ice.

Ramiro was convinced that the foreigner must be making for the border crossing behind Aconcagua into Chile. He marvelled secretly at the foolishness of the man to attempt the dangerous crossing alone in the middle of winter; or else the man was brave and very, very daring. But the man's arrogance knew no bounds. There he must perish, or else be free. Ramiro dug his knees sharply into the sides of the stallion and when the horse slipped and was slowed by the snow he cursed it.

The Minister had watched the snow come down muffling the blades of the helicopter when it was falling too thick to fly in and the signals of the radio had faded. They'd covered the road to the high pass of Agua Negra there and back many times. It was the most direct escape route out of the village in Córdoba where they'd had definite confirmation of a sighting and at nearly 5,000 metres it was almost inconceivable that the fugitive would attempt a crossing of the pass alone. Somebody had to be harbouring him. It was a difficult game; spreading the rumour and keeping it as quiet as possible at the same time. The more he'd read the report that had been inside the briefcase, (and he had the original in his hands) the more he was convinced that first perceptions of the man had been mistaken. The manner in which the report suggested that the disinformation would be spread seemed to him the work of an agile mind; keeping reports of the virus localised and letting the news filter down through the country without parading it loudly was an intelligent strategy. He instructed the heads of the police force and their captains to ask unobtrusively about the whereabouts of the man and meanwhile did his best to ensure that coverage in Buenos Aires was kept to a minimum. It was no good blowing a trumpet and blurting out the story to all and sundry on national television, otherwise the foreigner would be alerted to the chase and might slip through their net.

He eased into the cushioned leather of the helicopter seat whilst he finished reading the report. He felt that he had learned much about the man – the document was certainly the work of an intelligent mind; one it would be dangerous to underestimate. Reading between the lines of the text, he had begun to understand its author. He let his hand rest on the black leather of the seat and, reclining fully into its luxurious interior, stared with concentration in front of him. He could see the scene unfolding in his mind. The pass through the north of San Juan was one of the highest in the country, it was extremely dangerous, but it was also the quickest and straightest line the fugitive could take. They had men already waiting for him there. He, the Minister, would be there to call the curtain on him at the end.

David's mouth was bleeding from the cold and the icy river made his teeth chatter. It was too cold to drink where the snaking water detached the snow from its banks. The horrible thought that Maitén, or what was left of her, was being sucked dry in death and pulled towards the river made him feel sick. In amongst all that snow, all that frozen rubble, her carcass would eventually collapse with the landslide into the river. He could not find a crossing over it, so, stumbling and frost-bitten, he kept to the far side all day, making his way back in the direction of where the girl with the haunted eyes had tried to warn him. When finally he got there, bruised beyond recognition, he saw the place of their meeting where the brush grew at the top of the opposite bank. He stared into its mystery but he could not be sure if any children were playing there; or whether they laughed at him through the obscure bushes or in their houses.

He felt alien, separated by the width of the river, and snow had fallen like an eternity. Half in a dream he remembered a horse that had carried him into the mountains, but no horse was with him and he had left her behind. Ice broke off and was carried away by the river, the tiny speck on the other side growing smaller and smaller with the figure of the child. Unconscious, David lay freezing on the stones.

The white horse was out of the valley and its rider urged it faster along the road, though the horse had slowed where a scent still lingered in its nostrils flowing across the plain. Ramiro spun the horse round again but it was tarrying.

"Come on, boy!" Ramiro cried and the hard clatter of its hooves left their imprints where snow was beaten harder.

The metallic clack of the helicopter's blades cut through the silence high above the valley. Visibility was good now and the crisp peaks were magnificent and within their reach, shining on the tinted lenses of the man in the expensive coat, growing as the helicopter approached them.

"Have you got the camera?" he called to his bodyguard, and the man handed him the expensive piece of machinery. The majesty of the highest wall in the Andean chain was captured with the purring click of a button on a camera that had been imported. The minister flashed his teeth as the red sun stained one moment in time for history.

"Quite something, aren't they?" he said to the man seated at his side. For thousands and thousands of miles their sharp silhouette cut up the spine of the continent of South America, dividing those countries that faced the Pacific from those that faced the Atlantic. Some of those countries were poorer than others, but all of them had at one time been invaded. Brave fisherman set sail in tiny boats when sails had flickered off shore and their craft been beaten back.

"Nothing to report. Over and out."

They had flown in as far as they could; the Minister was assured by the dot he had seen on the map and the helicopter was turning back. The men who had reached the post and waited could be relied on to do their jobs.

His body was throbbing like one mass of pain. There was a thick smell of smoke mingling with the smell of fish within the confines of the darkened room. He looked up, his head pounding, and saw a man standing over him - he had the same eyes as the little girl. The man turned and said something to a shadow in the doorway. She came and stood next to her father, one of her brothers at her legs. Then the girl came forward tentatively and looked at him. As his eyes grew accustomed to the light in the room he could see an infant suckling at a brown breast, wrapped up in the skirts of its mother.

"We found you on the other side of the river," said the man simply.

David peered into the gloom; a mother and father and two young boys. And the girl.

"What's your horse's name?" she asked holding her father's hand.

"I have no horse," David answered feebly.

The girl looked from David to her father, but the man said nothing. He went to tend the fire that was burning in one corner of the room between some bricks, where a metal grill charred black had two fish balanced on it. The man jabbed the fish with a stick and the flesh split open. He broke off a piece with his hand and brought it over to David on a loosely woven grass mat, setting it down before him where he was laying.

"Eat," the man said to him as he broke up the rest of the fish and put it in piles onto similar mats. He handed one of the larger piles to his wife who fed with her fingers while still suckling the infant, pausing at moments to stuff morsels of the white meat into her mouth. The man and the two other children did the same.

"Wait," said David trying to search for his haversack and finding his head spinning. His hand felt it close by him and reached inside. He drew out a hardened chunk of bread and offered it to the head of the family, which the man accepted and took a bite of, chewing it slowly. He broke the rest of the chunk into crumbling pieces and shared them out, urging David to eat as he did so. David lifted the grass mat close to his face and pressed the hot fish to his mouth with stubborn fingers, almost choking.

"I've, I've seen you before," struggled David to the tussle-haired girl when he had finished eating. She put her hand to her mouth, laughing, and skipped out of the room.

"You have come far," said the dark-haired man, though it was partly phrased as a question. David nodded to him and felt the weight of his journey on him, too much to bear. He stared into the black corner of the room at the ashes of the fire. The man understood his suffering; in his dark, hollowed eyes the precariousness of an existence that dimly followed one day after the other was smouldering. The children were laughing outside but in the stuffy interior of the room the only noise that could be heard was the suckling baby.

David spent two nights in the company of the family, most of the time feeling himself unable to move. Once the girl and the elder of the two brothers brought in an armful of apples each, giggling as they came in. Their father chastised them for stealing them, though when his wife spoke harsh words to him he fell silent. The little girl tossed one to David and when he dropped it on the floor, the children fell about laughing.

When David was strong enough and about to leave he remembered something. He reached inside the bottom of his haversack where a hard bundle was knotted inside a handkerchief. He undid the knot and into the hand of the little girl's father he thrust three silver coins. The man's mouth opened with the roundness of the shapes but the little girl's eyes were glittering.

On the inter-state road David flagged down a lorry that was heading north. He asked the driver and was signalled to climb up on the back.

There was plenty of room behind in the truck that was covered with a tarpaulin and he slept for long periods of the journey, only waking up fully when the vehicle came to a standstill at a railway crossing and a long slow cargo train shook them as it passed by. The stars were clear and bright in the night sky and there were weird shapes on the line of the horizon; some of them looked like sculptures but they were too huge to have been carved by any human hand. As these curious statues were being left behind David saw a sign moving away from him. It read 'Ichigualasto.'

The driver's mate stopped once to take a pee and David screwed his eyes up tightly, pretending to be asleep. The man slapped the side of the trailer and tossed his cigarette away.

"No, man, he must still be asleep. Poor dumb peasant staggering round like that on that stretch of freezing road. He can't have a coin to his name."

David opened his eyes when the grunting engine had started up again, watching the fleeting orange spark of another cigarette that had been flicked through the driver's window whiz past him. He thought he'd caught the smell of onions wafting through the crackling night air, but then he dismissed it. It must be a memory of his time in the truck on the long descent of the mountain with Balthazar, when they had travelled lumped against the sacks of onions and potatoes the guards were transporting. He wondered what his old friend would be up to now, tucked away in his valley like a rabbit in a hole. He wanted to tell him that he was sorry about Maitén, but he'd taken the horse further than he should have done and the apology seemed empty.

"You must have seen him after the concert!" The Police Chief demanded, walking round to the back of the chair where the old man with the long thin hair was seated. He hovered over the shoulder of the man so that his presence, unseen, was felt all the more.

"So, you're trying to tell me that this man who brought you and your group so much money simply appeared then disappeared again? And I'm expected to believe that?"

"Yes, sir, that's the way it is. He just went his own way and didn't tell me where he was going. I, that is we, the members of the group, believed he was having some kind of romantic problems, if you know what I mean, Sir."

Just then the phone in the village bar rang. It was the regional Chief of Police, who was commanding the forces directly under the supervision of the Minister. They had covered San Luis with a fine-tooth comb and were now fanning out across San Juan, to the south and to the north.

"Yes, sir. They've been concentrating on the main pass through San Juan... Ramiro? Yes, it's about him I'd like to speak to you... Well, there was some kind of *personal* involvement, certainly. I'm not sure I understand how far his attachment to the girl... What? Oh, undoubtedly. He rode out of the station like a man possessed. I should certainly say so. No, not at all, sir, I'm glad I can be of service. Oh, there was one other thing, about Ramiro. Yes. He's on his way back from the border in Mendoza. He's absolutely certain the foreigner's doubled back on his tracks. Yes, I quite agree, sir. A confused heart doesn't make for a clear mind..."

The Chief of Police of Buenos Aires put down the receiver and walked round to face Balthazar again. It was just possible that the old man was telling the truth but he mustn't let him know it.

"Tell me your story again," he said to the musician, and Balthazar duly complied. Of course he missed out the part about the performance itself; nobody would have believed him and in any case, the community on the other side of the mountain had no reason to corroborate his story. There was one other small detail that he neglected, but then a hat is a hat by any name.

The truck halted with a bump at a gas station. The driver and his mate were chatting to a man in uniform who was showing them a map and pointing to it under the neon light. The driver stretched and yawned amicably while his mate took up the conversation with the official.

"A foreigner, you say?" The two men looked at each other then back at the officer. Then suddenly the three of them were striding towards the back of the truck. The driver's mate slowed when he reached the edge of the tarpaulin then he undid the catch on the tailgate quietly.

"Well I'll be...!"

The policeman turned to face the driver.

"It could have been anywhere, I tell you. We stopped several times on the highway. It's a long journey, and sometimes nature must take its course."

The policeman looked at him accusingly.

"There was one time," added the driver's mate, "When we pulled up to let the train past."

The three of them huddled over the map again under the buzzing light. The officer dashed into the room that served as a bar adjacent to the gas station and the two men could hear him speaking to someone on the telephone. When he came out he saluted them briefly and leapt onto his motorcycle; he was gone with a flash of dust and his siren blaring over the hundreds of miles of desert. Minutes later the truck started up again and the sacks of potatoes and onions they were taking way up north rolled in the back.

David was pressed flat against the cold whitewashed wall of the outside lavatory where he'd stood shivering for the last ten minutes. Someone who'd come outside from the bar was whistling a tune to himself over and over again and the rustle of pages being turned could be heard. The man let loose a particularly loud fart, closed his newspaper and pulled the chain. He could hear the man fastening the buckle on his belt and for one awful moment it reminded David of the noise of the cell closing.

"Damn belt, must have shrunk in the washing machine," the man cursed out loud, "How many times have I told her to take my belt out before she puts my trousers in the machine?"

There was perspiration on David's forehead even though the chill of the air was freezing his fingers to the wall where his hands were held motionless. He'd counted up to a hundred so many times he'd forgotten what number he'd reached. Counting had saved him, only in the nick of time had he decided something didn't feel right and jumped. At last the man was going back inside and he could move from his hiding position.

He relieved himself against the side of the outbuilding and let out a sigh.

"You, you filthy dog! What do you think you're doing? Can't you see there's a perfectly good lavatory right next to you?!"

David came out from the side of the building with his hands up in the air.

"What's the matter with you? You some kind of crazy, or what?"

David turned to face his accuser and saw a fat man with a cigar hanging out of his mouth. He dropped his hands immediately and thrust them into his pockets.

"I could do with a place to wash them," David said sheepishly.

"Well why the hell don't you come into the bar and spend your money like the rest of them?" said the owner. The man led the way muttering into the bar and David followed him nervously.

"Hey, Pepe, what's the matter? Didn't the asado go down too well?" A raucous guffaw went round the bar and the fat man kicked away a stool that was blocking his entrance to the counter. David stood in the middle while cards were slapped onto a table.

"What do you want?" said the owner of the bar.

David looked round him and saw that most of the people in the room were absorbed by the card game.

"Do I have to ask you again?" said the man chewing on his cigar.

"I could do with a place to wash myself," said David feebly.

"That I already know, and from the smell of you, you'd better make it a good one," said the fat man who was tiring of his customer. He poked the ash on the end of his cigar into a large glass ashtray.

"Well?!" demanded the man as a woman strolled over.

"Don't worry about him," announced the woman, "He's always like this, aren't you, Pepe?"

"Pleased to meet you," she said and once he could see her properly she was younger than he'd originally thought her to be.

"Are you two going to stand there making love while I have to stand here all night like a dummy?" The man was fuming.

"He'll have a beer and a steak sandwich, won't you?" said the long-haired woman moving closer.

"Oh, so you two already know each other, do you?" asked the man whose patience was straining, like the night, at the end of a very long leash, "Well ask him if he can improve his toilet manners."

"Bea'," said the woman extending her hand towards David while the owner rattled his pots and pans in the kitchen.

"Dav*id*," said David who had pushed his hands into his pockets again, acutely aware of himself now that he was once more amongst people.

"Hmm, you certainly are a strange one, aren't you?" said the woman taking back the hand she had offered, "I like your hat, anyway."

David felt nervously for the beret and pulled it down tight with a single tug on his head. The woman raised one eyebrow in a strangely familiar gesture and took a sip at the beer she was holding.

"Do you know *Balthazar*?" asked David mysteriously, his gaze intently on her. The woman put down her beer.

"No, I can't say as I do. But then again, it would depend on who was asking for him," answered the woman equally mysteriously.

The owner of the bar set David's beer and his steak sandwich down on the counter with a clatter. David looked at the woman.

"Well, are you going to eat it or not?" asked the fat man who had watched all this with interest and wanted to see what the stranger would do next, "The damn thing's going to go cold any minute and you're not having me slave away in that kitchen just so you two can…"

"Thanks, Pepe," said Bea, "That's just fine."

The man went off grumbling into the kitchen again and rummaged through his pots.

"Where exactly am I now?" David asked her.

"What do you mean?" asked Bea suddenly cautious.

"I mean, I've got a map but I don't know *how* to get to where I want to go," said David lowering his voice. Bea's expression changed radically and she addressed him with confidence again.

"Eat up," said Bea, "I'll take you to see your *Balthazar*."

Astonished at the good turn in his fortunes, and smiling inwardly to himself at the prospect of meeting up with his friend again in such an unexpected fashion, David quickly downed his food. Bea was already putting her leather jacket on and was turning towards the door as David made to follow her.

"Wait a minute!" called the owner from the doorway of the kitchen, "Who the hell's paying for all this lot?"

"He is," said Bea, "Aren't you?"

"Er, yes," said David who had eaten his food rather too quickly.

He reached into his sack and tossed a coin made of silver at the owner.

"Damned animals!" exclaimed the man squinting at the coin, "This generation, there's no knowing what they're getting up to."

"Come on," said Bea, "I know where you want to go. Get on."

She kick-started her motorbike and David hopped on behind her.

"We've got a long way to go and it's going to be a bit of a rough journey," said Bea as they were pulling out of the forecourt, "I hope you're used to long rides."

"Yes," said David confidently, remembering the long days after leaving the valley, "But how I'm going to explain the loss of the horse to Balthazar, I don't know. Have you known him long?" asked David, who had become fearful of upsetting his friend.

"Well, I've always known him by another name," said Bea, "But I know he's got many. I don't know about the horse, though."

"Maitén," said David sadly through the wind that was sailing through them.

"What?" said Bea who was concentrating on the road ahead and could not hear everything the man said. They came from many parts but this one was intriguing. She'd liked the look of him from the moment he'd walked in behind Pepe; he looked travelled, weather-beaten. Kind of tough like a man on the run, but there was kindness in his face. The hat was a dead giveaway, especially when he'd signalled to her with it. So the guy had got a map, had he? She hadn't realised the boss had sanctioned maps of the place. This guy must be pretty important if he'd been given a map, when even she hadn't seen one. The horse business must be some personal issue between them, better not ask too many questions, she knew the rules. She twisted her hand on the throttle and put the machine through its paces as they eased onto a stretch of open road where the moonlight was clear on its back beneath the night sky.

"Hold on tight," she said, and he clasped his hands firmly round her midriff where the leather of her jacket was soft.

There was no doubt about it; he'd been born under a lucky star. In the truck coming down from the mountains after that weird experience in the concert hall, the feeling that Balthazar was on his side had grown on him. He, Constantino and Dimitri were part of a 'band' that was obviously larger than they'd been prepared to admit. The girl he was holding so tightly was proof of that. The old fox was not so old as he looked; David had noticed that in him, and many of the things he had said made him think in a way that he had never done before. There was something in the kindness of the man, the way he had sheltered him, given him food and even money, which had made David feel worthy. Or not, as the case may be. Constantino had helped with the disguise when he was bareheaded and about to blow his cover, and perhaps theirs' as well. What skill there had been in the ways of his old friend to divert his questions away from it on the farm.

David, as he called himself, certainly had the smell of the country on him. He rode a motorbike like a horseman as well. But his accent, and the way he spoke were a different matter altogether. Bea always trusted her instincts, and David was trusting to his.

"Yes, sir, that's right, on the train. The drivers of the lorry are sure he must have jumped out of the back when they stopped at the railway crossing. We've sent out a message to the authorities and the Minister is airborne and on his way to the station at Jachal right this minute. Yes, sir, one lieutenant Gomez. He's with me now. Yes. He came in by motorcycle and had been travelling for quite some time. Yes, sir, I'll see to it personally. Over and out."

It is a long way from the dry, rocky uplands of San Juan to the greener and more fertile slopes of Catamarca. Bea and David travelled through the rest of the night as the motorcycle gradually climbed upwards through the hills. He was pressed against the smooth leather of her jacket and the firmness of her body and her long back held the motorcycle straight on the road. He had half drifted off and his chin was resting on her shoulder when she spoke to him.

"You want to get off?" said Bea.

She had stopped the machine and the engine was purring. Her long soft hair brushed against David's face as he struggled to wake up and straighten himself.

"We can, if you want," she said, then she added, "Perhaps you're tired."

She dismounted and pulled a long thin cigarette from her jacket pocket that she lit as she rested against the machine. A strange odour permeated the air.

"Want some?" she said to David who had been enjoying the caress of her hair in his dream-like state. He sat resting on the motorcycle with his feet to one side on the ground.

"I don't smoke," said David, "And I'm not tired," he added, looking into her eyes, "You're very beautiful," he said to her.

She leaned forwards towards him and, placing her hands on his shoulders, kissed him fully on the lips, letting the smoke of her cigarette fill his mouth.

Bea wasn't used to a man being so direct with her; usually they were more timid. But this one was different, and when he had said that he thought her beautiful he'd looked so deeply into her eyes and said it with such sincerity that she knew it was pointless to resist the attraction. It would simply be prolonging the inevitable. David felt her face brush against his, then she pulled him to the ground and they were kissing each other. She unzipped him and took him then and there, and as David looked skywards the stars seemed to glow brighter in the firmament. Beside them, the chrome of the motorcycle shone like silver under the moonlight.

Afterwards when they were back on the motorbike and the wind-full sky had broken into clouds, David fastened his arms even tighter round her and felt the ground rise under them. They were into mountainous country now and miles away the red burning lights of a first town could be seen, burning, gently burning lit up against a black sky as the purr of the motorcycle slipped into dawn. Bea stopped the engine and looked at the town down in the valley.

"What's that place, over there?" David asked her. It was colder now and he pressed himself closer still against her firm body.

"Oh, you don't want to go *there*," said Bea who was transfixed by the vision of the valley in front of them. The soft tresses of her hair blew in the gusts that rocked against them as David kissed her on the cheek. "We're heading straight for Catamarca. Where, I cannot tell you, as I'm sure you understand."

David looked at the great divide in the two high mountains before them and understood in the immensity of this great country what she meant.

"We're going to have to do some refuelling, though," she added, "And that means a stop somewhere down there."

A chasm split the land where two steep backs arched on either side like the backs of dolphins swimming through motionless dark waters. Off to their right, in the east, dawn had started creeping in.

"I'm easy," said David as he rested against her again with eyes dreaming under the sky. He held the weight of one breast in his hand like the full-grown moon and Bea kicked the motorcycle into life. The eerie town shone with the light that had begun to infiltrate it as its people turned over and carried on sleeping.

In the onion capital of Jachal a black insect was glued above the spotlight that poured over the station as it sent people running. Men who had been roused from their beds were systematically checking each compartment of the train.

Ramiro found himself riding down a frost-hardened road where pools of water glimmered under starlight. Above him the vortex of the stars spun thickly into the Milky Way and cast their light over the limbs of the stallion as its footsteps retraced a route through an echoing canyon.

A man was dreaming in a far-away city. He dreamt he had returned to a village where the trucks had left them. When they returned to their houses they found the rest of the village empty and the shops all boarded up. They ate what food remained in their larders until this ran out also, but to their good fortune on the following morning the trucks returned to collect them from the abandoned village. Obviously, there was no room for them to take all their possessions and it was easier and more convenient to put all the men in one truck and all the women and young children in another. It was the last they ever saw of each other.

When daylight finally staggered into town Bea refuelled at a gas station much like the one David had met her at. A few cold customers filed out and one put his hat on. Either they were very early risers or had passed the night taking refuge from it, playing cards or drinking away its loneliness. The man who had just left the bar looked at Bea intently, but she looked him up and down in one cool glance with such assurance that he turned away. She left the air of the strange-smelling cigarette wafting in front of them as she kick-started the machine with ferocity and they buzzed out of town. On each side the great walls rose up into immense peaks, steep and foreboding now that they were near them, like the crests of two eagles pinned to shoulders.

"Something tells me I've been somewhere near here before," said David. The anticipation of his meeting with the son of Count

Rodinoski was warming him and he took solace from it. Bea's hair flicked against his slowly warming skin, where the magic of the night and the miles they had covered were still sleeping. She passed one hand back round her waist and David took the cigarette from her and inhaled. He saw a man with large eyes step out in front of them into the road, pulled into it by a large dog that was straining at its leash where it snarled.

"And you!" said Bea saluting him, "You want to watch where you're going," she maintained the salute as her arching body twisted into David's. He blew the smoke out through his nose and smiled with satisfaction at the welcome he had reserved for his friend.

They passed out of the unknown province with colours flying as the red of the motorcycle glowed beneath the black hanging walls that were turned purple by the dawn. The throb of the finely tuned engine disappeared as it hung in the space between them for miles. As slick as a phoenix rising, the dawn bursting, purple and indigo the mountains left them and they broke free humming into swinging valleys where the green of a new land unfolded.

"It's not that far now," said Bea, "And you can meet the Man."

It all made sense to David now, even the journey in the back of the truck with the other musicians. By midday the engine of the motorcycle was cooling against the waspish sun that beat against it. David could still hear its hum far stretching through lands they'd come where rocks were shattered and verdant groves sprung up unexpectedly. They'd been steadily climbing all the while and David tasted the rarefied air he had breathed in before but had once forgotten. How he would even try to explain the loss of Maitén to Balthazar he did not know, but the loss of the horse was loss enough for himself and the words were heavy inside him.

"She would have loved it here," said David.

"Who would?" asked Bea.

"Maitén," said David sadly.

The man spoke in riddles and Bea was not sure whether she'd possessed him like she always had with the others. But no man, not even this one, was a match for their cause. They crept up a furred hillside where the spines of the cactuses were as high as small houses and the road grew narrower and steeper, 'til finally they passed through a passage in the rock where no tree grew and boulders had been picked clean on the skyline.

"Look," Bea said, and a straight road peeled off under the canopy of a hanging sky. They had climbed considerably but ahead of them a vast bowl, the largest of its kind in South America, rolled outwards towards the precipitous mountains that bounded it on all sides.

"I have to stop here for a moment," she said when they were passing through a tiny village where small houses were immaculately whitewashed against the midday sun. The bell in the church was ringing and round the sounding walls the great enclosed plain rang also. She emerged with a bundle of leaves and a bottle of water and there was a lump that looked like charcoal in her hand. She pushed a handful of the leaves into her mouth and bit off a piece of the coal, which she chewed on slowly as she handed the packet to David.

"I'm not hungry," he said, "But thanks."

He returned the bundle of leaves to her as they were speeding away on the motorbike and the sun broke through the crust of the oxygen-starved air. It was as if they were balancing on a line strung out over deserts where the mouths of volcanoes opened all around them. The road stretched long and straight into the distance where the blue sky grew immensely. Feeding off the mountains were small oases where clusters of green, verdant and emerald were tightly packed. Suddenly on a hidden corner after hours of travelling Bea swooped the motorcycle up a ravine where the green bushes camouflaged the hum of their machine.

"Wait here," she said as she walked off with tremendous stamina. After some minutes during which the quiet tick of the motorcycle subsided, Bea returned.

"The Man will see you now," she said as David dismounted and followed her up a sinewy path through the vegetation and up towards the treetops.

It was a small, enclosed place, and David wondered at its existence within the enormous capacity of the bowl they had travelled through. He wondered also at what his friend was doing here so far away from his valley. A door was kicked gently open and on the threshold of a single room in a wooden construction hidden among the trees, Bea showed David in, his eyes picking out a multitude of eyes watching him in the spinning silence.

"Who the hell are you?" said a tall man rising.

"I've come to meet Balthazar. Who are you?" asked David.

He heard the heels of the man's boots walking towards him across the wooden floor.

"I'm The Man," said the man.

CHAPTER TWENTY-THREE

It was some time before David recovered his composure. As his eyes grew accustomed to the half-light of the room, he could make out the stature of the man who had addressed him. He was tall and bearded and wearing a hat not unlike his own. His voice was quiet with the weight of authority leaning on it. Bea shifted nervously to one side and went to sit down with the rest of the group.

"I've come to meet Balthazar," repeated David who had come too far in search of his friend to let the matter lie.

"Yes," said Bea, "And there's the matter of the horse."

Casting round for stones to throw, David asked after the other members of the band.

"Is Dimitri here?" he asked.

Another, blonde-haired man got up and spoke from the corner.

"I am Dimitri," he said, coming forward into the light at the centre of the room.

"No you're not," said David, and he sat down.

The group were sat in a circle with a multitude of eyes focused tightly on him. The tall man sat down in the centre of the room facing David, then he turned towards Bea. She looked back blankly but knew that she would have some explaining to do.

"There seems to have been a misunderstanding," said the man taking charge of the situation, "Dimitri does not know you and there is no Balthazar here."

The words were spinning in the room and the din of the abandoned motorcycle was humming in David's head.

One by one the pairs of eyes assessed him and no more words were spoken. Then Bea and the tall man got up and left the room together. David tried to search for Dimitri but in the shadows cast on the ill-lit gathering everyone looked the same. Presently Bea and the man walked back into the room.

"I think I know who you are," said the tall man holding up a newspaper.

On its front page was a picture of David, the same one he'd seen on television that had been taken from his driver's license. The likeness was less familiar now and underneath his beard even the expression on his face seemed to have changed, though there was still something in the eyes that gave him away. The tall man studied the picture and walked across to David where he held it alongside him.

"I'm going to have to ask you some questions," said the man.

David removed his hat and nodded, still seated cross-legged.

"Where have you come from?" he was asked.

"I've been in many places," said David, "Some of them poorer than others, but originally I come from the States."

"What is your purpose here?" The Man continued.

"I'm not sure any more," said David honestly.

His inquisitor was persistent; he had no time for the man's games.

"Be more specific. What was the original and intended purpose of your visit to this country?"

"Well," said David, prepared to accept the cost, "You could say it was a kind of industrial espionage. It was never intended that way, to hurt the people directly, you understand," he added hastily, "But it *was* designed to hurt the economy, though I didn't know it at the time."

"How?"

"I was to prepare the way for imported European beef."

"Here, in Argentina?" the man asked incredulously.

"Yes."

"Mmm. Who are your contacts in this country?"

"There was a director in Buenos Aires," responded David, "He was the only one with access to the information. But I began to suspect his motives and I left him behind. I spent a night in the cells and then made a run for it on my own when I was let out. I didn't like the deal anymore, I felt like they were setting me up for something."

"Who was?"

"The police, and probably the people who sent me here," he said.

There was a long pause in which David felt all eyes in the room on him. He'd told them the truth and there was no going back on it.

"How long have you been in hiding?" asked The Man at length after a pause. David looked down.

"It's hard to say," he said ruefully, looking at the floor as his past life flashed before him, "It feels like years."

"And you have no allegiance to the men who sent you?" asked his interrogator. David shook his head; he thought of Rosa, Balthazar and the others who had all helped him in their own way.

"Loyalty can't be bought with money," said David, "Though I used to think it could; and, I believe, so did the men who sent me."

The Man stretched himself to his full height and placed his hand on David's shoulder.

"Do you recognise the flag of Argentina, the true flag whose colours cannot be bleached by the sun or diluted by rain, the *blanco y celeste?*"

"Yes," said David, "When I came out of the desert it was the first thing I saw."

There was a round of applause, then the man turned to discuss something with two other men who had stepped out of the shadows.

"Welcome," said the tall man presently, greeting him formally with a starchy embrace.

"Bea, take him for debriefing. He's tired... You've come to the right place, Mr. Salsa," said The Man.

Bea led David out of the room along a passageway and then down through a trapdoor into a cellar. An unshaded light bulb shone bleakly and there were two cast iron beds and some newspapers scattered about the floor. On a wall behind two of the beds was a huge flag of Argentina that had been tacked to it with nails. On the other wall there was a framed picture of someone he half-recognised standing next to a horse where he looked out over a ridge with three peasant children standing close by.

"Come and lie down," said Bea sitting on the edge of one of the beds, "You've had a long journey. We both have."

She leaned forward and kissed him, helping him remove his heavy jacket and then his trousers. Pulling him close to her they intertwined in each other's arms and fell soundly asleep.

A bird was singing outside above the trapdoor when David awoke. He left Bea sleeping and went to stand underneath it close to the exit. He could hear the bird ruffle its feathers and there was a chink through the planks where sunlight shone in; particles of dust were filtering through the air. Then another bird came to join it and they sat cooing in the sun before they both flew away. Bea had her eyes open and was looking at David when he turned round.

"You'll have to stay here for a while until they've decided what to do with you," she said.

"I suppose I've got no option," said David as he went back to join her in bed. They made love again passionately before Bea dressed herself briskly and walked to the stairs where she pushed the trapdoor open, putting her finger to her lips as she left David alone in the cellar. He walked over to the framed picture and was struck by the familiarity; he was dressed almost identically and from another angle it might have been him when he was younger, if his life had taken him on another course. Quite soon Bea's face reappeared above the stairs. She signalled for David to join her and two other members of the group whose faces David dimly recognised were waiting when he emerged. One of them, the woman, addressed David directly.

"They've got a plan," she said and David was escorted back to the room where he'd been originally introduced to the group. Their leader was standing motionless in its centre.

"You will be taken across to El Rodeo," he said addressing David with his hands pressed together, "It's safer there and our comrade," he looked at Bea, "Will introduce you to people who are in a position to help you. I myself will follow later when we are sure that they're not on your tracks," he added.

One of the group opened the door and the meeting was concluded. It was the blonde-haired man who called himself Dimitri.

"God be with you, friend," he said and Bea led David out of the room.

They walked back down the gully and Bea wheeled the red motorbike out of the cover of the bushes where they had left it. The engine was kicked into life again and David sat pressed against Bea with his arms even tighter round her waist, the memory of their lovemaking still in their bodies. The glassy sun of winter shone hard and on the highest peaks in the distance the air shimmered as in front of them the vast bowl stretched out to meet the horizon. It was two hours before they reached a dense green valley that was bounded on three sides by steep hills. Bea stopped the bike at a small house where chickens ran freely on the drive and without knocking on the door or calling to the occupants inside, she wheeled the machine to the side of the building, leaving it half-covered by some bushes that were growing there.

They walked down the hill on foot and came to a footbridge made of two heavy trunks lashed together where the river beneath it ran fast, breaking white where it was cut through by rocks. David looked at Bea closely, but she didn't seem afraid and was already walking across the bridge to the other side. David took hold of the fragile handrail, not daring to look down and joined Bea on the other side. They walked a short distance down a cobble-stoned lane and came to the door of a thatched, low-roofed building. Bea picked up a heavy padlock that was attached to the door by a chain. A notice had been nailed to the door alongside.

"What does it say?" asked David.

Bea turned round to David and shook her head,

"The building's closed," she said, "By order."

She let the padlock fall and swing heavily into the door where it crashed into it.

"Come on, David, we'll have to try somewhere else," she said.

As they were walking back up the lane a small dark-skinned man stepped out of a doorway.

"Rodriguez," said Bea, "Where is everyone?"

The man looked up and down the street quickly and urged them inside. He bolted the door behind him when they had entered the house and went to the window to close the blind.

"They've shut down the meeting room," said the man, "Things are getting worse."

"Yes, I know," said Bea.

Something flashed on the other side of the narrow street like a mirror catching the sunlight. Rodriguez put a finger through the blind and squinted through it.

"Open the door," he said to Bea with a flick of his hand. The heavy bolt was pulled back from its slot and almost immediately two other people, a man and a woman, stepped inside. Bea locked the door again behind them and looked at her companions.

"When?" she asked, urgently.

"Last night," answered the woman whose fine nose and high cheekbones seemed to David of Arabic descent.

"Two men from the civil guard came, at about ten o'clock," she added.

Her large almond-shaped eyes were darkened over and she didn't look at Bea directly when she addressed her. It struck David that the demure habit of the woman perhaps owed more to her upbringing than to her character; perhaps it owed something to her treatment too. Rodriguez looked at David and made as if to ask him a question.

"He's with me," said Bea before the man could say anything, "And The Man may be coming."

The two people who had recently arrived looked at each other and then the man, who had remained silent up until then, spoke.

"That would be unwise right now, in my opinion. We don't know who it was that tipped the civil guard off. The best plan is to keep to ourselves for the moment until we've worked out who it is."

Rodriguez looked at the man and nodded.

"Okay," said the husband of the dark-skinned woman, "Come with me."

Rodriguez put his finger through the blind and squinted through it again.

"Now," said the small dark-skinned man and Bea unbolted the door. She pushed David after the couple and didn't even stop to bid farewell to the man left standing alone by the window.

"Where's your motorbike?" asked the owner of the house they had crossed into when they were all safely inside.

"We left it up the hill," said Bea, "It's at the side of Paco's house."

"Good. I need you to take this back with you," said the man, handing her an envelope, "Make sure he gets it, it's important."

"I will," said Bea, unzipping her jacket and putting the envelope inside.

"Best to go back by the old way," said the man who had given her the letter.

"Yes," said Bea, "I'd already thought of that. It'll take a couple of hours longer but they may be out on the roads already."

She kissed the man and the woman on the cheeks and they stepped forward to do the same to David.

"God be with you," said the almond-eyed woman and her husband showed Bea and David through a back door where a long narrow garden stretched down to a wire fence.

"Turn right, keep to the bank and then cross where the stones are so that you can cut up through the lemon trees opposite Paco's," said the man, "Quickly, go now."

And with that David was running after Bea through the dry stalks of grass and the vegetable patch. She held down the wire for David to pass over and then stretched her leg over it herself. As they were coming up through the terraces where the lemon trees were, out of breath, David asked about the people they'd met.

"It's better you don't know," Bea said to him, "Better for them."

She wheeled the motorbike back down the drive, scraping the paint of the fuel tank on the bushes as she retrieved it. They freewheeled down the hill with the engine silent then turned left where a small path disappeared into the woods. Not until the slope of the hill had carried them as far as it would take them did Bea kick-start the engine again; its low growl thundered along the track that had widened like that of a cat leaving. The track was broad enough for a mule or a horse but not for anything wider. Bea handled the motorbike skilfully and picked her way round the stones in low gear as they travelled upstream, soon passing a house with orchards that was hidden amongst the dense vegetation on the opposite side of the river. Finally they were away from the village and a high, conical shaped peak swung into view above them.

"It's a bit of a rough crossing," said Bea, "But we'll make it."

They came to a strange place where grey beards hung down from trees that were tightly bunched together and Bea brought the bike to a stop. David was feeling light-headed. They went to drink water from the side of the river and David scooped some over his face. He reached round to take the water canister from his pack but couldn't find it. The trees were unlike any others he had ever seen and David rested a hand against one of their trunks; its bark was old and peeling, powdery in his fingers.

"Is it true what they say about you?" Bea asked David when she had rejoined him.

"What's that?" asked David, removing his hand from the tree and inadvertently letting a strip of its bark fall away as he did so.

"That the ideas in the report were your own?"

Bea was looking at him with her hands on her hips. At certain times he'd noticed a hard look on her face and he tried to guess her possible response to his answer before he spoke.

"They weren't entirely my own," said David looking up at the mountain that seemed to block their way, "But," he continued as he swung round trying to calculate her response, "You could say that the means by which they were to be disseminated was more or less my own work. More, rather than less, to be truthful."

"Good," said Bea, "We need somebody like you who understands propaganda. The most direct route isn't always the best one."

David looked at Bea's beautiful arching body where her long straight back sloped to her waist.

"Do you think we'll get over that thing?" David asked her with his head turned upstream once again.

"Oh, that? Sure, I wouldn't give it a second thought," replied Bea.

David sat a little further back on the seat this time, and his arms weren't quite so tight round her waist as before. The beards of the trees hung loose on the branches, growing as time thickened on them 'til it spun out their ends. Their bark, like paper, dropped in rolls to the floor.

The engine snarled and they crept along the head of the valley. Soon they started to pick their way through cactuses where the trees had been left behind and the land had become bare and stony. As the memory of the light that had shone through the trees faded, the hillside grew steeper and the engine laboured. They were zigzagging up a track where the line of the hills became visible like a row of teeth, bared and devoid of all vegetation.

It was some time later when they peered out at the bowl in the land where they had entered, where on the horizon the jagged peaks of impenetrable walls cut through skies that were too immense for imagining. As night fastened itself in behind them where they had come from they cut through the pass and were carried down into the hush of the valley that had descended. Feeling the weight of the machine slide under them like the hills, they finally reached the road that led back to the meeting place they had set out from that morning.

There was no Balthazar here. He would not be coming. Bea stopped the engine now that they were back on solid ground and the single streaming road that led north and south pressed itself flat into a silver rope whose ends disappeared into the distance. Across in the west the steel hand of juddering summits heaved and shivered where they fractured and no creature that had ventured onto them was safe.

David could still feel the hills where they rolled underneath him, where the weight of the heavy machinery that Bea manipulated so slickly pressed them and was present. The road flashed ahead of them like the ribbon of the river he had come to with Balthazar. With Maitén they had trodden on the plain as if one hoof or an imprint had stirred the swirling water and spread out all before them. He was riding south then and he was riding south again now; none of it seemed to make any sense. The roaring broken whisper of the skyline over Chile hissed where the wind blew over it; it glowed purple and foreboding as the bruise in the snow grew thicker and the silence settled.

"I can't go with you," said David.

"I don't understand," said Bea.

"Neither do I," he replied, "But I have to leave."

David looked over his shoulder and knew that he had to turn north.

They reached the ravine where the hut was sheltered as the purple hand of day dyed the ink of midnight. The clocks had stopped ticking and hours dropped from the thickening trees and on the slopes of mountains. In huge paleness of frozen slopes all heartbeats had frozen too. Time cut off the words in the mouths of its creatures and on the fresh snow let their wounds bleed.

The purring engine had stopped and Bea leant into David where he felt his heart racing beneath the pulse of stars. He couldn't live up to all that was expected of him. Time had stopped but was moving onwards too, inexorably painting over patterns where his mind was leading, choosing footsteps in which to set his footsteps. Funny, how circumstances play their tricks. Funny how small we are, he thought to himself.

"What are you going to tell him?" Bea said, suddenly afraid of losing him.

"Nothing," said David. "I'll tell him who I really am. That should be enough."

Bea held herself close to him that night. As she slept he drew the hair in strands over her forehead, he felt the paleness of her skin that after daytime sheds its colour. Her hand held his tighter when he felt it disappearing in it; his finger stirring on the surface of her skin as if the moon had the power to break through water. And in her dark eyes he saw the eyes of many people.

The line of hills on which I walk is infinite. One after another they curve upwards, the spine of a woman sleeping - I can feel her soft contours ahead of me but always they are just out of reach. The day glows and it is full of promise, driving hope into me even when I most fight against it. Andalgalá, the town below is a distant jewel taken from a ring I'd once borrowed but have tossed aside. Up here the air breathes, blue like the first morning created.

The cactuses press themselves against me with their white needles, some of them so sharp they pass through the leather of my boots and lacerate the soles. I am balanced on a ridge where the land disappears on both sides and at times I have to detour round the thick green trunks of cactus that point out across the valley with thorns that rip the air. When I look out now on the early morning the hum of the motorcycle is just a dot in the air that hangs suspended.

How so many living things can grow in such a dry place is a mystery, but the vegetation is so thick I have to squeeze through gaps in the thorn bushes and take care not to cut my hands on the serrated edges of the leaves. The way ahead is impenetrable so I contour down to a gully where rocks crack and slip under my boots and are sent downwards. There is a pungent smell next to the opening of a small cave hidden under the overhanging rock. I bend my head into the darkness and the stench of cat is about the place. Quickly, for I am unprepared if it should attack, I swing up to the top of the rock and force my way up through another part of the gully.

Breathing hard I am balanced on the knifepoint of the ridge again. It is only a metre wide at best and when I look down I can see small stones still slipping where I have clambered over them. I crouch down and take a swig from my canister and as I look out I see nothing that is moving in the vast bowl of the land. Day is hard and the treacherous white slopes to the west lean backwards as if bending away from the sun. I put my hand to the ground behind me to steady myself and feel the warmth in its the stones. No-one has come this way before, I am the first.

I am following the thin line of the ridge as it twists and disappears upwards, fragile and ascending. There is something blurring my vision on the crest of the hill as I approach it; huge cactuses at least five or six metres high. When I reach them their flesh seems as dense as stone, the green of them as solid as if they were ancient trees in a forest. I duck below an overhanging limb and at once I am into a clearing. In its centre, lying like the raised tomb of a giant, a flat rectangular rock about four or five metres long rests where it is propped on smaller rocks that support it. On its surface there are a few berries, crushed red staining the rock. My breath is drawn out into the valley.

From here it is possible to see everything on the valley floor; a trail of water flickering far away where a line of minute but upright poplars accompanies it. To the south it is just possible to see the gap in the mountains where the road that comes from outside penetrates this world. They would have been able to see anything from here; I am wary of their presence and the solid fingers of their ghosts make me feel suddenly claustrophobic. I pass my hand along part of the rock where it lies recumbent and the blue air hangs over the valley as if they had breathed it. I say a prayer and leave the clearing.

The ground slopes down before it slopes up again, still following the line of a ridge that is strung out like a thin rope a person might hold onto. It is even narrower than before and I have the sensation that I am balancing from one spiny hump to the next, the craggy rock face falling away in red earth and dust as sweat stings my eyes. I turn and almost lose my footing when three or four goats come scrambling up the earth where it cascades steeply away, the tinkle of their bells ringing in my ears reminding me of my own mortality. In an instant they have disappeared; tightrope walkers becoming invisible.

There is where I'll head. Up above on the bulging hillside that moves away again there is a small solitary tree that grows there, grown against the forces of gravity that defy its existence. The sun is forcing its way through the cracks in the land.

The tree looks as if it is leaning forwards but it is still a considerable height above me as I put both hands firmly on the rock for fear of falling. The thin bridge swinging up to the summit and the anchor of the tree seems made of air; too much to inch my way towards. I am pinned to the ground even when it is not ascending, as much animal as human now, taking my life in every handhold where the spinning air on either side constantly falls away. I find myself standing upright, piecemeal, as if testing my height when the overhang the tree protrudes from is almost within my grasp. Panting and elated, drunk on the air, I grab a branch and steady myself. In a small space beneath the tree there is a stone seat positioned with a view over the valley where the mountains in the distance seem to have swung in closer. I move on the seat of my trousers towards it and find that it is propped in place by three or four smaller stones, the bigger, flatter surface of the seat balancing on them. No accident of nature could have positioned it thus.

I am sitting on the stone with my boots firmly dug into the earth in front of me to stop me from falling. How high am I here? Ten thousand feet? Down below me are the humps over whose backs I've climbed which float there, buoyed in the thin air where a haze shimmers over the smallest of things. You are smiling at me and I know you are close; so close that I can almost feel your touch. I hear you laughing, welling up inside me and I do not know why I am crying, tears fall from my face as if they were someone else's.

I feel elated and rush back down the hill swinging a branch that I have snapped from the tree to clear my path. My feet glide into footsteps as I chant and I dance through the tilt of gravity; though where the song has come from I do not know for it is not in my own language, nor is it Spanish. I sidestep every stone and thorn as if I had been up and down this path a thousand times. I am singing master of these hills, cutting through the vegetation even though I am able to squeeze through the tiniest gaps between it and my clothes do not get snagged. There is silk on my back and the thorns of the cactuses cannot harm me.

Then out of the corner of my right eye a dark shape is rushing towards the ravine drawing all blackness towards it. The song goes from me and my head is turned in movement as my eyes are glued to the flight of the creature past me. My eye is fixed at a point but there is no bird hovering in the air there; no beat of wings. I am looking into it but it is not there; it is void and it is real, no part of this world but a part of me, drawing all light from my eye. When I try to reach out to it it no longer exists. I look again but it has vanished, though I feel its presence, growing inside me.

Frightened, I pick my way down carefully now and keep the stick lowered in my hand. When I reach the clearing where the slab of rock is I draw in my breath feeling them here, once where they walked. Perhaps they are still present and I cannot see them; perhaps I am dreaming. The cacti are thick round the circle pointing unmoving across the valley. I touch one and, taking care where the spines are protruding, feel the flesh of its trunk. The hard sap that is hidden there is alive, running beneath the surface where it is rooted in the ground. Once they must have silently watched the invaders crawling over the valley floor, and listened where horses and canons were dragged after them. But they were threatened from the north as well as from the south, where a bigger civilisation crept down from the high places of Peru and devoured whole villages. The Incas stopped just on the other side of these mountains, while the people here held their breath and the Spanish marched towards nine gold plates hidden in the ground. In San Luis they dug them up not noticing their resemblance to the planets and the corpses of the Incas from the north began to pile up on the ground.

There is a bus that will take me out of town up into the Puna. If I stay on it long enough I should reach the province of Salta. Bea has arranged to meet me in a village there, but I have told her that I cannot stay on the run forever. She understands, but is reluctant to let me go.

371

She says that I could become part of their cause but I cannot see the point in it and feel I have nothing to offer. I think she does not know who I really am. I know that she will be waiting at the village for me to change my mind. But my mind is made up. I will take the bus and sleep on it as much as I can, and when I wake up after the villages and passengers have been left behind, I will be in the north.

"What is your position now?" asked the Minister.

"We're moving over the border into La Rioja, Sir. I did not want to tell you at the time but I had a hunch all along that the foreigner would choose a more indirect route. He must have realised that we would put men at the border and quite frankly the press aren't helping matters."

"Yes, he can speak the language, he must have read the papers. I myself am taking the helicopter to rendezvous with the rest of the forces in the provincial capital. What is your plan now?"

"Well, Minister," said the Chief of Police, "There's been report of a disturbance up in Catamarca. We can't rule out anything at this stage and my guess is he could have been involved. He's a dangerous man, Minister, any chance he gets he'll use to provoke trouble before he leaves the country."

"Ah, so you think he's leaving then?"

"I have no doubt," said Chief Carrasco sighting a man loading parcels on the station platform, "That we'll catch up with him. Trust me, Sir."

"You can bet your life on it," replied the Minister picking his dentures with a toothpick. The phone line went dead while across deserts and over hillsides an army was swarming into the north. Reinforcements had been called up directly from the city and the commander who had set out from Córdoba had joined forces with the local military where a battalion awaited the Minister's word.

The people stood back in shock when a young policeman leapt from the train compartment on his horse. Its hooves clattered onto the concrete of the platform and the sacks it had dislodged fell sending fruit spinning over it. He had been in touch with his commander and was anxious to meet him in the city; he would not wait for the army to set out with him. His mind was concentrated on the task and all the mountains that fled behind him blurred into one. It was snowing in the capital of the province now and the white horse pranced through snow leaving its hoof prints on the road. The girl could go to hell and he would take her there. It was the man he was after, he would wear him like a coat when he had slit him open. The passers-by lifted their heads to see the horseman cantering down the street, from beneath their hats where snow collected on their brims and in their eyes he seemed a ghost to them amongst the traffic. There had been rumours in the city and many had seen the movement of men. The drivers on the road drove carefully; ready to let any vehicle that might come rolling heavily on its tracks past.

CHAPTER TWENTY-FOUR

The bus was pulling its way up into the Puna. Sleepy villages where sheep straddled the road and impeded its progress passed out of sight as if they were only alive in the memory, or in the imagination of its inhabitants. A light swung from the porch of a house with a veranda and a woman got on where others had got off before her. She was loaded with parcels and the driver cursed as he stamped his feet on the hard ground outside and loaded the packages into the belly of the bus. He ripped the ticket she pushed into his hand and flung the butt of his cigarette into the trailing darkness. The woman was dark-skinned and was wearing a broad hat as she moved down the aisle of the bus holding onto the backs of the seats to steady herself. She stopped and sat on a seat just behind David, although the bus was practically empty and only a young teenage couple cavorted on the back seat and a couple of old men argued over something in the front.

"I'm telling you, Miguel," said one of the men, "It was in 1976 if it happened at all. I remember it clearly."

"No," said his companion with affected disinterest, "It was the following year and they couldn't get through because of the winter."

"Winter? Why, you're crazy. It was in the summer."

And so they went on. The middle-aged woman who had just got on pointed down the bus towards the old men who were still arguing, addressing David as if she had known him all her life and leaning over the back of the seat to speak to him,

"Just listen to those two," she was saying, "They don't even know what year it is," she laughed at her joke.

"Want one?" she asked David offering him a sweet.

He declined politely and the woman who had got on carrying so many parcels and packages sat back in her seat. The silence rushed into the darkness and even though the old men carried on bickering at the front of the bus, their noise was like the chatter of insects or a neon light that had been left on too long where the bus steeled itself between the walls of the mountains.

It pulled its passengers through the remotest places; all along their flanks the Andes grew and were solid where abandoned buildings with holes in them let the stars inside. David tugged his hat over his face and slipped into a dream. He dreamt of a continent floating in the sea like an island, attached by a slender thread like an umbilical chord to a solid mass of land above it. It seemed to him to be a child sleeping, curled up with its knees pressed to its chest; every time it stirred or tried to move in its sleep the thread that held it threatened to sever and cut it adrift on an infinite ocean. And the great mass of land above it and to which it was attached was implacable. It hung over the infant, brooding.

David turned in his sleep and his face was pressed into the cold glass of the window. Starlight sucked the warmth out of the day on the backs of the mountains and the sun had retreated on David's skin also where day was replaced with the frost of night. He saw a million faces whose skin was white and pallid although the sun beat down on them daily, their mouths opening and darkness spilling out of them. On a sparse hill tombstones were toppled by the wind or by neglect or by forgetting so that only one or two still stood upright. He peered closely at one and on its greying surface he divined a name. He pushed himself closer towards it and his fingers fitted into the grooves on it. '*David Salsa: born 1964, died....*'

"What? What? Are you alright, mister?" said the middle-aged woman in the wide-brimmed hat who was sitting in the seat behind him. David opened his eyes fully in the darkness but the faces would not retreat before him. He removed his fingers from the glass where they had stuck to it and felt the cold of the windowpane on his cheek. It left him like a second skin parting in the water.

"I'm fine," said David looking into the unblinking darkness, "I'm fine," he repeated. The land stretched before them and he suddenly became aware of his own tiny presence inside the bus travelling across the landscape that was in turn part of another landscape. The image of the sleeping child attached to its parent came back to him wrestling on the end of its chord.

"Up here dreams can be strange," said the woman in the wide-brimmed hat. Her voice came from behind him and he had not turned to face her although she continued to talk to him. She was chewing on something and pushed her hand through the gap in the double seat to offer him something wrapped in a sticky paper. David took it and unwrapped the sweet before putting it into his mouth.

"It's the altitude," continued the woman, "For those who are not born here it can be difficult to get used to."

The plasticy taste of strawberry fizzed on his tongue and David let the remnants of his dream slip from his consciousness in their own time as the harsh lights of the bus's interior woke him fully.

"I was dreaming," he said to the shadow of the woman behind him. She said nothing but continued to chew at a steady, unhurried rate as if she had the measure of the journey and knew how many sweets she had to last her until she had reached her destination. A road sign whizzed by but it was the only thing remotely present in the vast darkness; the village to which it was addressed had disappeared out of sight, or perhaps it had slipped out of existence altogether.

The bus gathered momentum as it passed over the brow of the hill it had been struggling up and creaked down the other side. It careered dangerously towards the u-bend at the bottom of the hill and jolted its passengers as it dipped into the watershed that was dug there.

"Do you think the driver's still awake?" asked David panic-stricken, fearing the prophetic nature of his dream.

"Oh yes," she answered back in the midst of her chewing, "He knows this road in his sleep."

At the very last moment the strong hands of the driver wrenched the steering wheel and the weight of the bus and its passengers was catapulted round the corner and up the next incline. They could feel the weight of the hill racing towards them, rushing underneath, even though gravity pulled them back down. In David's mind a pair of condors he had once seen slip into a blue sky in San Luis slid underneath him.

Twelve hours after he had got on the bus in Andalgalá, David disembarked in the province of Salta. He had turned round to say goodbye to the woman whose constant chewing had accompanied him throughout the night, but when he had done so he found her missing, presumably carried away by the noise that flurried around them now.

The bus back up into the mountains to the village of Cachi where he was supposed to meet with Bea was crowded. He'd had no problem in purchasing a ticket, but the man selling them at the counter in the station must have had his mind elsewhere, for when David got on the bus he found it full to spilling. Small children were sitting on the laps of grandparents and bundles and parcels protruded at every angle. David forced a way down the aisle, past those who were bound for the village with him and those whose goodbyes to their relatives continued in the passageway. The engine grumbled into life and even as the bus was beginning to move hands were still being held onto while bodies reluctantly moved towards the door.

David placed his hands on the backs of two seats on either side of him, and though the hair of one passenger rested over the grip of one of his hands where she had tossed her head to make a comment to an acquaintance, she didn't seem to notice. Uncomfortable with the hair that fell softly over his hand and not daring to change his grip for fear of disturbing the woman, David stood up uneasily in the aisle as the bus swayed on its way out of the town. He ducked as two traffic policemen waved the bus through a set of lights, meeting the woman whose hair cascaded over his hand face to face as he stood up again. She smiled at him and turned back to her companion, continuing chatting.

As the bus left the limits of the town behind and began to climb higher and higher into the mountains, so the conversations of the passengers on the bus grew louder and louder until it seemed that the whole population aboard it was in competition. Parcels jostled parcels on the racks above, a tin can went hissing underneath the seats as it rolled backwards and then came back hissing the same way it had come.

David saw money change hands as two notes were handed backwards over a head, but for what transaction the money was intended escaped him. A grandmother laden with a small infant and a bag was having a conversation with another grandmother seated four rows in front of her, and every time the second woman turned her head to address the former, she pressed her parcel into the ribs of the man seated next to her.

By midday they had reached the highest point in their crossing and piping hot pastries were being sought at a roadside café as if they were nuggets of gold. David stretched his limbs and climbed a bare patch of hillside adjacent to the little caravan in order to get a better view of the snow-capped peaks across the valley. Scrawny cactuses straddled the hill and David was out of breath from having climbed it. There was a sign at its foot that read "3,400 Metres", as if they had been intending to build a village there but had neglected to do so; substituting the height at which any settlement might be constructed for the name of the same which as yet remained imaginary.

"Are you going to Cachi?" asked a man whose headrest David had been helping to keep steady as they jolted along. He'd bought a ticket for Cachi, the name on the bus said Cachi. The question struck David as ridiculous and given that the only inhabited place they'd passed on the whole of their morning's journey was a tumbled down house where two identical brothers had jumped down onto the red soil, it was preposterous that any other place for miles around could exist. David smiled at the man and answered him politely that he was indeed going there, and upon doing so the man related the news to his travelling companion. David looked at the windswept hillsides and wondered if any village by such a name existed at all, but then he surmised that the busload of passengers and their voluminous belongings would have to be deposited somewhere and that it was hardly likely that they'd be left here to starve. Especially not after the freewheeling café had departed the scene.

As the bus descended a steep ravine the cactuses grew in greater abundance. Like sentinels they pointed the way to the village.

When he got off David passed through an archway into the cobblestone square that had been decorated ready for the festival that evening. It was empty and had been swept briskly clean early that morning. In case David had any misconceptions concerning the village he had arrived at, a banner proudly proclaiming its name in bold red letters on a white background informed him where he was. Bea had said to meet her by the tree in the centre of the village square on the night of the festival and David had reluctantly agreed to it even though he thought it might compromise her safety. He didn't want her cherishing any lingering romantic aspirations concerning him; it wasn't that he found her unattractive, in fact he found her extremely so. It was just that the idea of being martyred for something he wasn't had become an increasingly unattractive proposition to him.

He climbed a hill and found himself lodging near a municipal campground that had an outdoor swimming pool, (which was full with clean water) and pitches for tents that were immaculately mown and fed by a sprinkler system. All of them were numbered with white markers spaced at regular intervals. There was not a soul there, and although the sprinkler system continued to feed the lush green grass of this manicured oasis with a tick-tick swishing and spraying, it marked time to no-one and no-one was there to attend it. Of course, it was just possible that the busload of passengers he had travelled into the village with had come equipped with tents and sleeping bags to brave the chill of the winter night. But they hadn't looked like campers to David and he doubted whether any of the villagers he had seen were. On the same piece of land was a building divided into rooms with all its doors open.

He was tired after standing up so long on the bus so he slept on a bed with its bright blue and orange woven blanket over him, his feet pointing to the open door and the marvellous views of the tiered lawns of the municipal camping ground. The evening would put in its appearance without need of his assistance and he didn't doubt that Bea would somehow reach him in the heart of the village underneath the swaying branches of the algarobbo tree.

Like a town in reverse, as the idle afternoon dissipated into evening its first inhabitants began to occupy it ready for the party that followed. The television crew had sauntered out from their hotel and were leisurely setting up their camera in a corner of the village square. The shopkeepers had opened their doors and peeled back their blinds ready to commence business. By the time David had woken, the bus that had deposited him in the village had retraced its arduous journey past the mobile café back down to the provincial capital. There the driver had sat patiently in the bus station as another full load of passengers and their attendant hangers-on had packed his bus to bursting point once again and been ferried to the same village it had visited at midday. Now the driver parked his bus to one side and cleaned it before placing a hand-written sign on the windscreen. Any passengers who had been unfortunate in not being able to find suitable accommodation in the village would be welcome to sleep sitting upright in their seats at a discount price only mildly superior to the cost of a return fare from the capital. A bathroom service was provided and in the morning they could take a tour back to the town they had come from. The driver removed his tie, changed his shirt and slipped a fine wool pullover over his shoulders that he knotted at the front. He winked an eye and raised his hand in greeting to the owner of the mobile café as it came trundling into town for the festivities. The bus driver went to get a coffee, which the owner of the caravan duly paid him for, although the price of the coffee might have seemed unseasonably expensive to anyone who had chanced to view the encounter.

Members of the establishment were there too, not excepting officers from both the local and other military police forces, principal amongst them being the Chief of Police of Buenos Aires who had travelled on ahead of his colleagues for the festival. He'd had a tip from a man he'd met on the way up through Catamarca that the event would be worth attending, and though not exactly a friend, he was sure that the man's advice was worth acting on. By sheer good fortune they'd passed the girl on the motorcycle on the road into the village and had been happy to offer her lodging at the hotel where he and two of his best men were located. She'd certainly be present at the festivities, and no doubt she'd be quite an attraction.

The prospect of meeting Bea again had become increasingly inviting to David after he'd woken from his sleep and found himself alone in the hollowing darkness. There was only the swish and spray of the sprinkler system for company, which they seemed to leave on day and night, keeping the grass immaculately green. He polished his boots with a piece of rag he found before setting out into the cooler night air, and though not in possession of the finest set of clothes, the noise he made with his boots on the cobblestones suggested otherwise. Jauntily he tipped his cap at an angle and thought back to their first meeting at the service station. She'd seen something in him that he'd been trying to play down ever since, and now he was trying to find it again.

On the way down the hill people passed him coming up. Some of

them were wearing masks and there was a man with a feathered
headdress with brightly coloured plumes. A Tannoy system had been set
up in the corners of the square, from where the incessant chimes of
cumbia and salsa were drifting up to him. It is true that there had been
an unwitnessed battle for territory taking place between the
representatives of the television channel and the people contracted to
provide the music via the Tannoy system. But the party atmosphere of
the festivities was not to be spoilt and in any case it was easy to turn
up the volume and drown out the television company's complaints.
They each had their own corners they could fight from.

The music was swaying as David submerged himself in the party
atmosphere that had descended on the village. He felt a spring in his
step as the revellers sashayed round him, some of the girls rocking their
hips in time to the music as the night air clung to them and became
their invisible partner. One of them spilled a plastic cup of beer that her
fiancé took off her and deposited on the pavement away from her. Not
one to spurn a piece of good fortune, David retrieved the large plastic
cup and drank from it.

Though David didn't know it, Bea was already waiting for him
beneath the branches of the tree in the centre of the pretty square. The
Chief of Police, a man with the utmost respect for land ownership, had
conveniently positioned himself in the remaining corner vacated to
him by the television company and the committee contracted to
provide the music. From his vantage point on top of a wall behind a
bougainvillaea bush which was in splendid bloom, he had an excellent
view of the proceedings in the square and, in particular, of its heart. He
had Bea perfectly in his sights. But, in exception to all but a minority
of the other revellers, (the boyfriend of the young woman from whose
cup David was at this present moment drinking being one of them) she
was not wearing a look of careless abandonment.

The party was in full swing now. The presenter from the television
channel, buoyed by the general bonhomie and the dancing of the
beautiful girls near him, eased himself onto the dance floor with his
microphone in his hand. He was rather formally dressed for the
occasion but this did not prevent one or two young couples from
showing off their dancing skills around him as the cameraman tracked
their steps. It had begun to rain and the patter of quickly thickening

drops pattered onto the cobblestones. A young man and his partner whose short-skirted rear had been the principle focus of the camera dipped out of view as they slipped on the cobblestones and dragged each other down. Instantly the cameraman found his focus again and the camera lurched towards the face of the presenter as he straightened himself.

There was a commotion in the centre of the square as the couple struggled to get to their feet. The Chief of Police was temporarily unsighted as his narrow field of vision was drawn to the fracas; Bea thought about making a run for it but the black-suited friends of the Police Chief who had entertained her since escorting her into town stood firmly in the corners. The head of the committee in charge of the Tannoy system had an attack of professional jealousy and turned up the volume to a deafening thud. All the while the rain came down harder.

There had been too many people on the improvised dance floor for David to see past the crowds to its centre. He could see the tops of the tree waving in the steadily increasing rain but he could not see whether Bea was waiting for him at its base. Muffled by the rain and pounding in an intermittent flow, the music was drowning out the words of the television presenter as he attempted to explain the proceedings to his audience.

He was mouthing gaping sweet nothings and for an instant the camera caught the look of fear on Bea's face for the viewers who were watching in the comfort of their homes. Bodies pulsed to the thud of the rain-drenched music, a twitchy trigger finger convulsed and for one horrible moment a television presenter's unfashionable dress sense was almost wiped out live on T.V. The question that had been slow to formulate in the Police Chief's mind had almost found an abrupt response. With the instinct of a coiled cat, feeling someone watching him and making sure they had the very best of his smile, he turned round and Chief Carrasco presented his face to the nation.

Precisely at this moment David got a glimpse of someone who looked like Bea through the gap in the crowd and started walking towards her. People were drenched to the skin and their skirts and jeans stuck tightly. The rain dripped off David's beret and in the mist that was forming in front of his eyes he couldn't be certain whether it was Bea who had been standing there by the tree or not.

Suddenly someone shone a powerful light onto the dance floor from above and the tree rocked about lashed by the wind, so much so that it shone and swayed round the girl he was walking towards but who seemed at the same time to be disappearing in front of him. There was a fearsome noise like a storm falling directly on them and everyone looked up to see the eerie face of the Minister lit up in the electric light of the cockpit, the clack of the helicopter convulsing with the boom of the stereo system. The banner with the village's name on it was ripped free from its moorings and flapped into the sky like a terrible bird. A shot rang out and tore a hole through the monster and a bullet ricocheted off the helicopter landing gear. A black bird flew away swiftly as a white one sagged limply to the ground.

A scream rang out as paper cups and decorations swirled in the air and the stampede of people trampled those who had skidded to the floor. The thumping noise of the music was like a heartbeat and David was running away, jostled by the crowds, away from the girl who had been waiting for him, the stench of fear mingling with the rain.

Chief Carrasco wiped the sweat from his forehead and searched in vain for the woman he'd been observing under the tree. As David was caught in the stampede up the hill he caught sight of the man with the feathered headdress he'd seen earlier walking against the flow. He and a group of companions seemed oblivious to all the fuss and were walking calmly towards the square.

It had been abandoned except for members of the television crew and a few people jealously guarding the sound system. The rain was drumming incessantly on the empty square and the television presenter who had so nearly become part of primetime television was plastering his locks to one side where the rain interfered with his hairstyle. In all the excitement somebody had forgotten to switch off the camera and when the fancy dress party arrived the presenter saw his opportunity. Daring to step out from underneath the cover he beckoned to the cameraman to interview what was undoubtedly the most exotic group at the festival.

They had positioned themselves round the tree at the centre and were chanting something even as rain ran into their mouths and they moved in circles round the base of the tree, their arms outstretched and opening up towards the tree's branches at intervals, the rain falling down even harder as they danced. The man with the microphone stood like a guilty schoolboy at the edge. The dance continued regardless, unaltered to any extent whatsoever. Unable to establish eye contact with the man in the costume even more elaborate than his, the presenter was left miming the dance as viewers watched in astonishment. The troupe were making a spectacle of themselves and there was little alternative but to film them.

Suddenly the dancers stopped and the man in the swaying head-dress walked over to the television presenter to catch him by surprise. He addressed him directly but did not look into the camera, closing his fist and then opening it in an extended gesture as his arm swept across the square curving inwards towards the tree. Then he spun round and the sweep of his arm took in the gigantic sleeping peaks of the mountains.

"Mother Earth gives to us, but she also takes away," was all he said and the startled presenter watched as the man in the head-dress and his group of brightly painted followers walked away from the square without further commentary. Fortunately for the audience who'd been unable to attend the spectacle in person the presenter's look of astonishment was recompense enough, even if his smile had started to fade as long ago as the sunset.

David was panting hard when he reached the sanctuary of the room. He did his best to make his recent stay there as invisible as possible, even stuffing the bit of rag he'd used to clean his boots into his haversack. He'd passed a large group of armed policemen on his way back up the hill and he couldn't take any chances; that stray bullet had startled him just as much as it had the other spectators. He closed the door carefully behind him then turned round, went back and opened it again. He'd already learnt his lesson at the hotel in San Juan and immaculate as the empty hostel was, he wasn't about to question the professionalism of its porters.

The Chief of Police and his accomplices were frantically combing the streets for Bea. He was soaked to the skin and by now a river of water was gushing down the hill. He couldn't be sure whether the Minister had seen him, but it was unlikely that the stray bullet fired from his rifle would help further his political aspirations. Fortunately, and for this he thanked God, the love of his country and the healthy benefits of altitude, the Minister's attempts to contact him on his cell phone had been severely frustrated due to the bad weather. The Chief of Police had heard the Minister's voice when he'd picked up his phone, but his communication back to him had been cut off by the static in the storm and the line had gone dead. Acting quickly on instinct, he took his beloved rifle from his arm and dumped it in a trashcan halfway up the hill, making sure his two accomplices were ahead of him when he did so. He could always say he'd been parted from the weapon in the frenzy and that *he* had been as surprised as anyone at the appearance of the Minister's helicopter, which was perfectly true. Damned separatists, you couldn't trust anyone these days.

David had taken an unpaved side road away from the multitudes milling about in the rain in their confusion. There were not a few stragglers the worse for wear owing to the festivities and David didn't want to get caught up in any random arrests or drunkenness. He couldn't be sure the girl he had seen was Bea as the tree whipped round violently in the storm; even if she were somewhere here in the village taking refuge from the weather, how could he be sure he would find her or that she would want to be found after the incident in the square? David knew where he was going and he had to get there fast. As he cut in down a side street he saw the mobile café mysteriously reappeared but washed off its blocks and nose-dived down an earthen embankment. Stuck to one of its windows was a sticker advertising a flame-grilled whopper with a flag alongside it that was not the flag of this country.

'Let them burn in hell,' thought David.

A river was running beneath his feet and streams of rubbish and debris left over from the festival were being washed down an embankment, directly at the foot of which lay the poorest houses in the village. There were lights on in the bus that was to have served as an overnight hotel and the driver was desperately trying to start the engine. It was full to capacity with most of the seats already taken and David was lucky to obtain one of the last seats available. Finally, after what seemed like an age and with many of the passengers undecided as to whether they were checking in for the night or being transported back to the provincial capital, the driver started up the vehicle. The rain was guzzling down and the way back up the steep incline would be a test of both his skill and nerve. Notwithstanding, most of the guests understood the professionalism needed of him and had acquiesced in paying the larger fee advertised on the windscreen, which was running with stained ink. It was true it was slightly more than the return fare to and from the capital but most were happy to pay it.

As the bus started into life some of the passengers woke up and not a few remonstrated with the driver, claiming that they had been misinformed as to the services provided in the advertisement. The driver pointed to the back of the bus where the latrine was and suggested that any of them who had been sufficiently foresighted to have brought their cameras might care to take advantage of the wonderful panoramas there would shortly be on offer. True to his word, precisely two hours later as the bus reached the summit where the unfortunate transport café used to be, the passengers got a glorious view of the menacing storm over Cachi La Nevada as bolts of pure electricity lit up the empty stage and sent them all dancing. David put up his hand to shield his eyes and got an x-ray of his hand into the bargain.

Stranded in the village for the night, the Chief of Police made a weak salute against the glare as the Minister's helicopter made an uncomfortable landing. It was long after the party had finished but he was the first on hand to help the Minister down from his helicopter, the first to cast aspersions on the nobility of the individuals in the crowd and the first to offer his condolences. Chief Carrasco had retrieved a battered umbrella from the same trashcan he'd deposited his rifle in and with it he vainly attempted to fend off the downpour. Ducking his head under the still-swirling blades the Minister mistakenly took this as a sign that the man had finally acquiesced to his power. He did, however, notice that the rifle was missing from Chief Carrasco's side.

"Seen anything?" he asked when they were clear of the blades and had taken shelter under the tarpaulin where the members of the television crew stood huddled and shivering.

"I heard the shot, if that's what you mean," answered the policeman guardedly, "But at the time I was in surveillance of a suspect and couldn't say from which direction it came."

The Minister grimaced inwardly and decided it was better to ignore the Police Chief's role in the matter for the moment. That would be revised when they were back in some drier and more civilised place, where savages were much easier to control.

In spite of the fact that the electrical storm was threatening to fry them all, the cameraman had had the presence of mind to plug in his camera again. The roles that the Minister and the Chief of Police acted out in front of it could be analysed in greater depth at their leisure by the viewers. Fortunately for him, the television presenter had had one shot too much and had conveniently decided to sit out any further filming.

"Any leads?" asked the Minister to his subordinate while the cameraman continued working. Chief Carrasco thought for a moment of the girl they had apprehended on the motorcycle and then shook his head. It was better to smile brightly and keep his mouth shut while the Minister did all the talking.

With the interview concluded but the cameraman too tired to switch off the camera, Chief Carrasco instinctively swung the apparatus in his hand up over his right shoulder and succeeded in spearing the material. This upset the fragile balance of things so much that just as the Minister was stepping out, his business concluded, the bulging promise of the tarpaulin was suddenly deflated. Someone let an umbrella drop; a cameraman stopped filming. A Minister who'd had one flight of fancy too much dripped sourly.

"There's something not right about this," he muttered through clenched teeth and strode off towards the helicopter. Narrowly missing him, a bolt of lightening lit up the stage and almost preserved his exit for posterity. With the pilot decreeing conditions too dangerous to fly in or to attempt a take-off, a saturated minister sat steaming in an evacuated cockpit. The Chief of Police had tiptoed to his limousine like a ballet dancer. Apparatus had been dismantled and was nowhere to be seen.

"There to the left you can see the shadow of the great Shivering Mountain, so-called because at times of seismic activity the different layers move within it and it seems to shiver," announced the tour-guide to his passengers, revelling in the greater freedom afforded him by his new job description. He had half a mind to make a go of this thing when he got back to the capital and had thought it over properly. There were those too amongst the tourists who had had their own lights come on and were planning to adapt the black plastic bin liners they used to protect their parcels as ponchos for any who might be willing to purchase them. Black clouds were swirling ominously over juddering peaks and now and again electricity flashed out of them.

"It's not a question of what I can do for you," said the man whose face seemed vaguely familiar to David when he was back in the capital and trying to negotiate a lift to the border, "You must understand," said the small, dark man slowly, "That to make the crossing of the high places you must be sufficiently prepared."

It was the middle of the night and the crack of lightening split through pounding thunder to the north where David watched. The incessant rain had created churning mud and David was anxious to get out of town before travel became totally impossible. He was tired and impatient with the man he was trying to agree a price with. To his frustration and despite repeated attempts on David's part to lead the conversation back to the issue, the man seemed more preoccupied with what David perceived as his worthiness, as he understood it, to accompany him on the journey. Surely, the guide had got it wrong and it would be he who would be accompanying *him*, not the other way round. But the man would not be rushed into making a decision and the more David tried to downplay his preoccupations the more the man dwelled on them.

At last David stopped talking and listened to what the guide had to say to him and, after agreeing to put himself under the man's orders, the man accepted to escort him to the border. To David's great frustration, a price had still not been agreed on. It was not so much a concern on David's part that the man might later take advantage of the ambiguity of the situation; so much as David was concerned that he might unwittingly undercut the fee for the guide's services.

"What about the money?" asked David as he followed the man out of the bus station. The old man threw his arms in the air and made a gesture like so many leaves being scattered in the air.

"That's not important," said the guide as he looked deep into David's face, "You will pay me a price that you think is fit once we have crossed the mountains, and if you try to cheat me you will pay for it."

They were both soaking by now but the rain glistened on the skin of the Indian and he did not seem to mind it.

The rain glistened too on the back of a horse that was cantering over a hill. In its eyes the lightening flickered as it tore through the night that had become one continuing blackness since it had started out on its journey. Its rider had disobeyed the express command of his superior and hidden the animal in the back of a covered truck that was heading north. The vehicles had rolled out of the city too slowly on their axels for the impatient rider and the noise they made as they left their tracks in the covering of snow that dusted the city had startled its inhabitants. Then the snow had turned to rain and the horseman had set out alone when the single-file procession was commanded to wait by the droning helicopter that buzzed backwards and forwards above them.

David and his guide could see the floods gushing down the valley they had left behind as they reached a higher place in the hills. The Indian lifted his hand in an outstretched gesture and cast it across the valley as if he were sowing.

"This is for the poor and the infants who must live their lives blindly in ignorance if they are not helped to better," intoned the Indian with the rain running in rivulets through his lips.

"This is for those who have too much and have become too blind to see what they have," he continued as their horses stood motionless.

"And this is for all the people of the earth who have forgotten that all things, themselves included, come from the same place. So that they awaken that memory in themselves where it was born and never again forget it."

Ramiro had craved solitude and a desire to settle the matter on his own terms from the outset. He'd been inexplicably angry when he'd been forced to regroup with the rest of them where the Minister had been waiting, but he'd found comfort when he set out alone again. Where before he had urged the horse on when it had seemed on the point of collapse, now it was the animal that rode faster. The bolts of lightening on the far side of the mountains had only made it run stronger, as if it were trying to outpace the storm.

David was troubled by the raging skies that lit up and were ripped by an eye that blinked open in them and then shut closed. And after every intrusion in the ink black sky the silence was deafening. He lifted one hand from the reins and could feel the bones and the sinews in it where it had been holding them in the icy rain. His companion had said nothing since they had stopped on the rise above the town of Salta and they looked back down at the terrible swirling water. The silence was becoming oppressive in David's mind with the weight of the water and for each long mile they covered the absence of words became more unbearable. Abruptly the Indian stopped and turned to him. He stretched his arm towards David and put a closed fist to his heart.

"Do you hear the thunder?" he asked David as the water teemed down their bodies. He opened his fist as a terrifying volley that was too close for comfort shattered the mountains and cannoned off them. In this strange upland world the mountains seemed fragile as glass.

"Yes," said David.

"A heart is deeper and more terrifying," the Indian said as the eye of the storm passed directly overhead, "It has the power for both hate as well as love."

The white stallion whinnied as it caught the scent of scorched earth and grass in its nostrils. Its rider tried to pull it along an easier course but it was taking him where it wanted to up a more dangerous route. As the earth shook with the tremors that spread down from the black hill to its left the horse tugged towards it with its hooves churning up the ground. Its rider had outridden the need to be away from other men and the rage he had felt when forced to regroup with the slowly moving vehicles had disappeared under him with the miles. The memory of the girl was a slowly burning fuse in him but that had been snuffed out also and only a question remained where emptiness had filled him. His hands slipped on the wet leather of the reins as the stallion bent its back to the incline; there were many things he did not know and growing amongst them was the as yet unconscious need to see the face of the man he was hunting.

"There is one who comes seeking you," said the Indian hours later when he and David had crossed the barren plateau and had stopped on the edge of a descent, "You must understand the need to forgive him."

David had felt it through all the solemn miles of their journey. He had felt it too at times with Maitén when the horse had lifted her head to the wind and been distant from him. In the caves and as they travelled across the desert leading to them where a river had announced their crossing into another province, indivisible from the other except for its marker, David had had an uneasy sensation. The Indian had merely given voice to the fear that had been growing steadily inside him. His guide turned away from him now.

"If you have not forgiven yourself you will not find peace with this man."

Ramiro knew what the horse knew. He knew that the foreigner was headed for the border where a road split through a canyon whose walls were streaked with seven colours. The name of the place came whispering to him although up here on the plateau not a soul stirred. Purmamarca the place was called, though he had never heard of it before and he did not know what to expect when he got there. Let the heavy dull tanks crush the grass where they pressed into it; he would be there before any of them and catch up with the man. His belly was empty and he wondered whether it was the fatigue of the journey that had caused him to imagine the name of the place, but he had heard it as clearly in his mind as if someone had spoken it to him. The girl was like a painting to him now, one that was fading with age where a light that had been too intense had shone on it for too long. Ramiro had first noticed the man he was chasing when the foreigner had come in late one day with Pedro, but his mind was playing tricks on him and the face of the man had become invisible.

He was exhausted as he began his descent from the plateau with the water draining round the horse's legs. The storm had passed overhead and disappeared out of sight, but it would be raining somewhere else now causing swollen rivers to flood. And when it had left it would continue on to another place, flooding the people who lived there.

The Indian's words were echoing in David's mind. Along with the streams that washed down the steep hillside they were descending, David could hear the noise of his daughter laughing. He let the noise of the water and the young girl's laughter run ahead of him so that he could hear what had been said to him. When the hooves of their horses stopped churning mud and finally found a harder dirt road the Indian turned and stopped. Way down in the valley there was a single light burning. The Indian tapped his chest with his fingers and pointed to where the light was coming from, then tapped David's chest three times. David dismounted as the Indian had done.

"You will make your own way now, I can help you no longer."

He remounted and rode off down the slope leading the other horse behind him before David had chance to pay him or say goodbye, disappearing into the darkness so that only the vanishing sound of the hooves on the road could be heard. David was alone and wondering whether the man had really accompanied him on his journey or whether he had travelled across the great plateau alone. He heard the sound of water gushing loudly from a spout up the road on his left and walked towards it. As he reached the top of the slope the clouds parted and he could make out the reddish wall of a canyon whose strata was of many colours. There was a cluster of houses made of mud bricks and an outside lantern shone on one of the walls underneath a porch. He took off his beret and shook the rain from it where it had collected as he walked towards the house, which had a bench running underneath the window beside the doorway. Wearily and with some caution David knocked on the door. After a few moments a woman wearing slippers came to open it. She went back inside where there was a commotion in the room and after a few more moments her husband appeared with her at the doorway dressed in his night gear.

"You look as if you need something to eat," said the man before David had a chance to say anything and he went to fetch a plate for the stranger. They left David with the food and a glass of water and they went back inside, leaving him to eat outside alone. In the distance drawn ever closer by the noise of the water, David could hear the sound of hooves approaching.

For a moment he wondered whether it was the Indian returning, but he could only detect the sound of one horse and not two. As the half-moon that had been in hiding during the night of the storm put on its silk it shone on the seven colours that were engraved in the rock. It shone on the head of a white horse that was panting up the hill and on the face of a rider who rode in a trance. Fear gripped David's heart and he heard the thunder that rumbled when a mountain had shook at him in mockery.

There was a face sitting beneath the lamp and it was the face of the man he had been hunting. Ramiro came up and drew close to the foreigner. He dismounted slowly from the snorting horse and his feet moved towards him, his legs heavy with the miles where they had passed under him. The man pushed his back against the wall of the house, the sound of his breathing rasping beneath the noise of the water that was still gushing onto the road where he had passed it. He breathed in deeply and tried to speak, but no words came out.

Ramiro came up to him with his last ounce of will as his boots sank into the mud running from the ditch.

"You!" he exploded.

David could not answer him.

With his heart thumping he heard the sound of his daughter laughing above the sound of the water as he closed his eyes on it forever.

"Why?!" exclaimed Ramiro, and then, shouting, "Why?!"

He took his pistol from its holster and held it shaking in his hand, pointing it at the man. David shook his head slowly as he opened his eyes to see the man a last time, but not a word came from him. Ramiro lifted the pistol and raised his eyes with all his strength to meet David's. The gun was pointing at his chest where Ramiro tried to hold it steady.

A canon of water volleyed into the night.

He had closed his eyes at the last moment and was smiling at the face of his daughter as she played in front of him.

"I forgive you," he said. And he was reconciled.

Ramiro felt the gun tremble in his hand. He staggered on his feet as he suffered the smile on the face of his accuser. He dropped his eyes to the ground and tossed the pistol away violently over the embankment. With super-human effort he urged himself back into the saddle of his horse as it bore him away back down the hill without him once looking backwards.

I have been walking now for several days. The clouds continue to menace in the sky above but I feel protected. My face is sore from the wind; I know that the wind that blows across the Puna can hurt as well as it can soothe. I heard you laughing the other day, when the noise of the water where your mother broke her leg vanished like the single beat of time falling; all I could hear was the sound of your laughter. There was a man there but he is gone now. That was yesterday, or the day before that, and ever since I left the place where the mountain is dyed like the tapestry of a scar whose crimson colours bleed into it, I have felt at peace.

They cannot hurt you now. I was frightened that they might take you away from me, but now I know that you are always just ahead of me leading me on towards the border. I can see you playing, hiding there where the bushes that have grown green with the rain give off their perfumes – sometimes you are ahead of me but sometimes you are walking beside me. I would like to speak to you but I know that you understand me even when we are silent. Please tell your mother I am sorry. It was I who let her go. Perhaps you are travelling somewhere even though it is I that am walking towards you. Sometimes I stand still and the world is moving around me, but tomorrow or the day after or the day after that I will be free, even if I stay where I am and do not take one step further. At least I know now that I do not have to look for you any longer and that you will always be here with me. There are always other paths we can take, even when we think there is just one path ahead. I never doubted you for one instant; it was I that doubted myself.

The sky is often blue overhead these days and sometimes I can see the lazy white streams left behind by the aeroplanes that have crossed in it on the way to their different places. How tiny they seem to be above - I wonder if they know how big the land down below them here is. I wonder if they can see the place that I am walking towards because I know that it is just up ahead of me somewhere. Probably though they are not curious enough for them to look out of their windows and are already ahead of themselves at their destinations in the cities.

How slowly time seems to travel round the planes, it slips over their bodies and wings as if it were breathing them into it, while I am breathing down here below. When I have crossed the border over the high places into Bolivia I will imagine myself part of you and watch the blue yawning miles rush under me as I travel to meet you.

On a farm in Candelaria in Córdoba Rosa looked into the sky. She thought of the dark young man who had left the village and had not been seen since. She thought of the daughter she was carrying and the man who was her father who would never know he was.